Feel f

TRAGIC

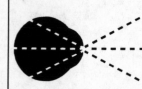 This Large Print Book carries the
Seal of Approval of N.A.V.H.

TRAGIC

ROBERT K. TANENBAUM

THORNDIKE PRESS
A part of Gale, Cengage Learning

MOORESVILLE PUBLIC LIBRARY
220 WEST HARRISON STREET
MOORESVILLE, INDIANA 46158

GALE
CENGAGE Learning·

Detroit • New York • San Francisco • New Haven, Conn • Waterville, Maine • London

GALE
CENGAGE Learning®

Copyright © 2013 by Robert K. Tanenbaum.
Thorndike Press, a part of Gale, Cengage Learning.

ALL RIGHTS RESERVED
This book is a work of fiction. Any references to historical events, real people, or real locales are used fictitiously. Other names, characters, places, and events are products of the author's imagination, and any resemblance to actual events or locales or persons, living or dead, is entirely coincidental.

Thorndike Press® Large Print Thriller.
The text of this Large Print edition is unabridged.
Other aspects of the book may vary from the original edition.
Set in 16 pt. Plantin.

LIBRARY OF CONGRESS CATALOGING-IN-PUBLICATION DATA

Tanenbaum, Robert K.
    Tragic / by Robert K. Tanenbaum. — Large print edition.
        pages ; cm. — (Thorndike Press large print thriller)
    ISBN 978-1-4104-6159-9 (hardcover) — ISBN 1-4104-6159-9 (hardcover)
    1. Karp, Butch (Fictitious character)—Fiction. 2. Ciampi, Marlene (Fictitious character)—Fiction. 3. Stevedores—Fiction. 4. Labor unions—Corrupt practices—Fiction. 5. Large type books. I. Title.
    PS3570.A52T73 2013b
    813'.54—dc23   2013018897

Published in 2013 by arrangement with Gallery Books, a division of Simon & Schuster, Inc.

MOORESVILLE PUBLIC LIBRARY
220 WEST HARRISON STREET
MOORESVILLE, INDIANA 46158

Printed in Mexico
1 2 3 4 5 6 7 17 16 15 14 13

To those blessings in my life:
Patti, Rachael, Roger, Billy,
and my brother, Bill;
and
To the loving Memory of
Reina Tanenbaum
My sister, truly an angel

ACKNOWLEDGMENTS

To my legendary mentors, District Attorney Frank S. Hogan and Henry Robbins, both of whom were larger in life than in their well-deserved and hard-earned legends, everlasting gratitude and respect; to my special friends and brilliant tutors at the Manhattan DAO, Bob Lehner, Mel Glass, and John Keenan, three of the best who ever served and whose passion for justice was unequaled and uncompromising, my heartfelt appreciation, respect, and gratitude; to Professor Robert Cole and Professor Jesse Choper, who at Boalt Hall challenged, stimulated, and focused the passions of my mind to problem-solve and to do justice; to Steve Jackson, an extraordinarily talented and gifted scrivener whose genius flows throughout the manuscript and whose contribution to it cannot be overstated, a dear friend for whom I have the utmost respect; to Louise Burke, my publisher, whose enthusiastic support, savvy, and encyclopedic smarts qualify her as my first pick in a game of three on three in the Avenue P park in Brooklyn; to Wendy Walker, my talented, highly skilled, and insightful editor, many thanks for all that you do; to Mitchell Ivers and Natasha Simons, the inimitable twosome whose adult supervision, oversight, and rapid responses are invaluable and profoundly appreciated; to my agents, Mike Hamilburg and Bob Diforio, who in exemplary fashion have always represented my best interests; to Coach Paul Ryan, who personified "American Exceptionalism" and mentored me in its finest virtues; to my esteemed special friend and confidant Richard A. Sprague, who has always challenged, debated, and inspired me in the pursuit of fulfilling the reality of "American Exceptionalism," and to Rene Herrerias, who believed in me early on and in so doing changed my life, truly a divine intervention.

PROLOGUE

Roger Karp grimaced as he stretched one of his long legs into the aisle next to his seat. He rubbed his knee until the ache — a frequent reminder of an injury sustained as a star college basketball player many years earlier — subsided and he could turn his attention back to the stage in front of him.

His wife, Marlene Ciampi, looked at his leg and then his face. She frowned as she whispered, "You okay, Butch?"

"Yeah, just a little stiff," he replied quietly with a smile. "These seats seem to get harder every year."

Marlene smiled back. "I was just thinking the same thing and hoping it had nothing to do with age."

They were sitting six rows up from the stage, just off-center, at the Delacorte Theater, an open-air amphitheater in the middle of Central Park. Situated on the southwest corner of the Great Lawn, with

Turtle Pond and Belvedere Castle as a backdrop, the Delacorte could not have been a lovelier spot to watch a play on a warm late summer evening, even if the tiered rows of wooden seats were not designed for comfort. A sliver of a moon rose behind the castle and a slight breeze stirred the leaves of the trees that surrounded the amphitheater and the shadows beneath — a perfect setting for that season's Shakespeare in the Park offering of *Macbeth.*

Karp and Marlene were with their twin teenaged sons, Zak and Giancarlo, who'd been dispatched that morning to stand in line for the free tickets that were handed out starting at 1:00 p.m. for the evening performance. That had allowed Butch, as he was known to family and friends, and Marlene to arrive just before showtime by taking a yellow cab to the 79th Street entrance of the park and then follow the footpath to the theater. The boys would be rewarded for their efforts after the play with a stop at the Carnegie Deli on Seventh Avenue and 55th Street, a dozen or so blocks north of Times Square, where they could do battle with legendary hot pastrami and corned beef sandwiches, chili cheese fries, and New York's finest cherry cheesecake.

Attending each season's Shakespeare production, including the post-play stop at the deli, had been a family tradition since the days when Marlene was pregnant with their first child, Lucy. She was absent that night, back home in New Mexico with her fiancé, Ned Blanchett. However, Karp was pleased that his sons were still willing to indulge their parents by "sitting through some old play where they don't even speak real English," as Zak, the more macho and impatient of the two, groused when reminded of the date. Fortunately, *Macbeth* had a fair amount of witchcraft, ghosts, murder, and intrigue to hold their attention.

Act 2, scene 1 was just winding to a close. The Scottish Lord Macbeth stood alone in the dark hallway of his castle trying to summon the courage, and cold-bloodedness, to murder King Duncan as he slept and seize the throne at the urging of his power-hungry wife, Lady Macbeth.

The Shakespeare in the Park productions were always first-rate, and Karp enjoyed the Bard's frequent theme of man's battle between his good and evil natures and, of course, how justice eventually prevailed. He'd come by his love of theater, as well as of movies, thanks to his mother, an English

11

teacher, but had also learned to see evil as a real entity, not some theoretical sophistry to be debated in church. When Karp's mother died of cancer at an early age he learned to fight evil vigorously. In fact, the crusade against evil was the driving motivation behind his actions as the District Attorney of New York County.

Onstage, a hologram of a dagger floated — a bit of technical wizardry — above the actor playing Macbeth, who tried to grasp it while it remained just out of reach. Karp knew from discussions with his mother that the ghost knife eluding Macbeth was a metaphor for his troubled conscience as the deadly moment of truth approached.

Is this a dagger which I see before me,
the handle toward my hand?
Come, let me clutch thee.
I have thee not, and yet I see thee still.
Art thou not, fatal vision, sensible
To feeling as to sight? Or art thou but
a dagger of the mind, a false creation,
proceeding from the heat-oppressed brain?

In his seat, Karp repeated the words "heat-oppressed brain" to himself. He'd used that very description in his summation at a murder trial he'd just concluded to

12

explain the motive behind the prosecution's star witnesses' testimony against the defendant. That and Macbeth's lament in act 2, scene 2 that he'd "murdered sleep" when neither he nor his wife could find peace due to the guilt that weighed on them.

"So why did they take the stand and testify without any sort of deal being offered or attempting to lessen their own guilt?" Karp had asked the jury as he faced the defendant. "Because, ladies and gentlemen, what they did — the part they played in the conspiracy to commit murder — was evil, but for them it came at a high price to their consciences. To paraphrase William Shakespeare, they could not escape their 'heat-oppressed brains.' They couldn't enjoy life, or forget, or close their eyes at night and rest. As Mr. Shakespeare wrote, they had 'murdered sleep' as surely as they and the defendant murdered the victim. But evil comes in shades of gray."

In some ways, Karp felt a certain degree of sympathy for Macbeth. The man wasn't a murderer by nature; he'd been courageous and faithful defeating a traitor in defense of Duncan. But his ambition had driven him to commit a crime that initially accomplished his goal, and in the end spelled his doom.

Onstage, the actor grabbed again at the knife, but it danced just out of reach. *There's still time to walk away,* Karp thought as he had when he was a boy and wished that Macbeth could make a different choice leading to a happier ending. But onstage, even as Macbeth worried about getting caught, he chastised himself for being a man of words and not actions.

Mine eyes are made the fools o' the other
    senses,
Or else worth all the rest. I see thee still,
And on thy blade and dudgeon gouts of
    blood,
Which was not so before. . . .
Hear not my steps, which way they walk,
    for fear
Thy very stones prate of my whereabouts,
And take the present horror from the time,
Which now suits with it. Whiles I threat, he
    lives;
Words to the heat of deeds too cold breath
    gives.

Karp reflected on how, in some ways, the themes inherent in *Macbeth* were mirrored in the trial. The corruptive influence of power. The shades of evil. The eroding power of conscience on guilty secrets. And the consequences of sin.

It even broke down into acts and scenes, he thought. The conspiracy, the murder, the investigation, the swift-paced plotting of confrontations, violent reactions, and bouts of conscience that led inexorably to the dramatic climactic moment in a New York City courtroom, and its inevitable epilogue.

A bell rang offstage. *Lady Macbeth letting her hubby know that the chamberlains, who she's set up to take the rap for Duncan's murder, are asleep and it's time to do the deed,* Karp thought as the actor suddenly straightened and resolved to go forward with the plan.

I go, and it is done: the bell invites me.
Hear it not, Duncan, for it is a knell
that summons thee to heaven, or to hell.

With that, the actor turned and stalked off the stage toward where the audience knew King Duncan slept. *Too late,* Karp thought. *It is too late for everyone involved.* The scene came to an end and the stage went dark so that the stagehands could change the set for the next scene.

All of the players acted out their roles on the courtroom stage, too, he thought. *It all began with act 1, scene 1 . . . three young men sit-*

15

ting in a car on a cold winter's night, nine months ago, contemplating a horrific deed.

1

"Pra klyast," the young man in the backseat of the Delta 88 Oldsmobile said in Russian. "Is fucking cold, man!" He leaned forward and tapped the driver, another young man, on the back of his head. "Turn the car on and get heat!"

"It's a waste of gas and we're already low, unless you want to throw in some money," the driver, a freckle-faced redhead named Bill "Gnat" Miller, said. "And keep your frickin' hands to yourself."

"Relax, *sooka,*" Alexei Bebnev sneered from the backseat. Twenty-seven years old and slightly over six feet tall, he liked to think of himself as a ladies' man. But his light blues eyes were set too far apart in his round-as-a-basketball face, an unfortunate feature accented by a wide flat nose above a scraggly mustache and crooked, tobacco-stained teeth. Bebnev looked at another young man sitting in the front passenger seat. "Hey, Frankie, I thought you say your friend was cool?"

"Gnat's cool, he's cool," Franklin "Frankie" DiMarzo assured him.

"What's *sooka* mean?" Gnat asked, scowling as he looked over his shoulder at his antagonist.

"Means 'bitch,' man," Bebnev said. "You my bitch." He laughed and made a kissing expression with his lips.

"Fuck you, Bebnev, I'm out of here," Gnat snarled and reached for the key in the ignition. "This guy's a nutcase. It ain't worth it!"

DiMarzo reached over and grabbed his arm. "Chill, Gnat, we're gonna get paid, and that's going to make your old lady happy," he said before turning around to plead with the Russian. "Give him a break. We've never done anything like this. He's just a little nervous, that's all."

Alexei Bebnev laughed derisively again and took a drag on a cigarette before blowing a cloud of smoke at the back of Miller's head.

"And don't throw your fucking butts on the floor of my car again," Miller complained.

Bebnev flipped him off but rolled the window down just enough to flick the butt out at the curb before rolling the window up again. He held up a snub-nosed .38 revolver. "Is easy. I stick this in the asshole's face and 'BANG BANG,' asshole is dead! All you have to do is drive car and keep watch."

"Put that thing down before someone sees you or you shoot one of us," Miller said before spitting a stream of brown tobacco juice into a beer bottle.

"Is nasty habit," Bebnev pointed out with a look of disgust.

"My girlfriend don't want me smoking around the baby, so I chew." Miller shrugged. "Besides, I'd rather eat cat food than smoke whatever it is you got there. What the hell is that shit?"

"Belomorkanal cigarette," Bebnev replied as he shook another from the pack and lit it. "Good strong Russian smoke, not pussy shit like American cigarette."

The three young men fell silent. They were parked next to the curb in front of the Hudson Day School in a well-to-do neighborhood of New Rochelle, keeping an eye on a large split-level house down a hill and across the street from where they were parked, waiting for the occupants to come home.

Although it was only six o'clock, it was

19

already dark outside and the neighborhood was glowing with Christmas decorations. But there were no lights on in the house, just a porch lamp and a fir tree on the front lawn adorned with twinkling blue Christmas lights. So they waited, sipping on beers to keep their courage up, lost in their own thoughts.

Miller had been called "Gnat" since elementary school due to his small size and inability to sit still for any length of time. It didn't bother him. What did was the fact that he was a twenty-two-year-old, out-of-work housepainter with a six-month-old infant and a teenaged girlfriend, Nicoli Lopez, who was constantly reminding him that she was tired of living off food stamps in the basement of her parents' house in Brooklyn. He hoped that the money he'd been promised for this job would allow him to find them an apartment of their own and prove he was man enough to support her and their child. He'd buy them both something nice for Christmas and life would take a turn for the better.

Sitting in the car, he was preoccupied that his Delta 88 stood out like a sore thumb in the neighborhood. He was nervously aware that not a single car that had passed them since they got there was older than a couple of years, while his old car's green paint job was faded and in some places covered with gray primer. He wished he was home with his girlfriend, even if her father had referred to him as a "no-good bum" from the moment he walked in the door.

Next to him, Frankie DiMarzo was contemplating heaven and hell, and what it would do to his parents if he got put in prison for murder. The DiMarzo family was staunchly Roman Catholic. His mother kept a small shrine to St. Jude in her living room and went to Mass at least five times a week, most of the time to pray for Frankie's soul. Even his four sisters, all of them older, went to Mass at least weekly and, as his father liked to point out, had never been in trouble with the police.

Frankie, a good-looking young man with dark hair and Mediterranean features, was the black sheep of the family and had strayed frequently. In the past, he'd go to confession, do some penance, and all would be forgiven. But it was hard seeing how each new run-in with the law aged his mom and dad.

And that was back when it was all penny-ante bullshit, he thought. No matter what the priests said about God's unconditional forgiveness, he wasn't so sure that murder could be easily absolved. He shook his head.

DiMarzo had grown up in Red Hook, a neighborhood on the northwest side of Brooklyn on the Hudson Narrows and about as rough as it got. He was a tough kid, only twenty-three years old, and lived by the code of the streets: he didn't rat on nobody, and he didn't take shit off of nobody either. But he had a soft spot for his momma, and knew that a murder rap would probably kill her, and that his old man would disown him. It troubled him greatly and, like Gnat, his best friend since they'd met in a juvenile prison in upstate New York about eight years earlier, he too wished he was somewhere else. But he was tired of never having any cash in his pockets and of having no prospects for anything better than part-time construction work when the weather got nice. At least not until Bebnev had come to him with a job that would earn him and Gnat seven thousand bucks each.

DiMarzo had met Bebnev a few months earlier at a pool hall down in the Oceanside Brooklyn neighborhood of Brighton Beach, otherwise known as Little Odessa because of its large Russian immigrant population. The young Russian talked a big game about the women he'd had and often hinted that he was a hit man for the Russian mob that controlled the area. DiMarzo thought he was all talk until his new friend pulled out a small newspaper clipping about two old men who'd been shot dead in their apartment by an unknown assailant. Bebnev hadn't said anything, just wiggled his eyebrows and grinned with his crooked brown teeth as he pulled his jacket to the side to reveal a revolver stuffed in the waistband.

When Bebnev had come to him a week earlier with his offer the Russian had made it clear that he was going to shoot someone and was being paid well to do it. He hadn't said much about where the instructions or money was coming from, just that a "friend" named Marat Lvov had set him up to meet two men, "Joey and Jackie," in Hell's Kitchen, who hired him to kill some union boss. Bebnev had said he wasn't told directly who ordered the hit, but had overheard the other men tell Lvov that "Charlie wants it done ASAP."

DiMarzo had balked until the Russian convinced him that all he had to do was find someone to drive and then act as a lookout. "Don't worry, my friend," Bebnev had assured him. "I do dirty work. You make easy money."

So DiMarzo had let himself be talked into

the plot. But sitting in the freezing cold in an old sedan waiting for a man to show up at his New Rochelle home so that Bebnev could shoot him was harder than it originally sounded. He figured there were going to be a lot of sleepless nights putting this one out of his mind.

In the backseat, Alexei Bebnev fingered the gun he'd put back in the pocket of the long black leather coat he was wearing. Unlike the other two, he was not troubled by a conscience. He'd been raised in an orphanage on the outskirts of Moscow — an odd, distant child, who'd been unwanted by any prospective parents and eventually ran away to the streets, where he made his living as a small-time criminal. He'd come into some real money when he attempted to rob an old Jewish watchmaker in his apartment and ended up killing the man, but not before his victim told him where he'd stashed a small fortune in gold coins. It was enough for Bebnev to buy his way out of Russia to the United States, where he'd believed he would soon be living the sweet life. Life, it turned out, was not that easy. He became a dishwasher at a Russian restaurant in Brooklyn and dreamed of having money and respect as a hit man for the Russian mob.

Trying to prove himself, Bebnev accepted

four hundred dollars to kill two nobodies who got behind in their gambling debts to Lvov, a small-time loan shark and bookie with connections to the Malchek *bratka,* or "brotherhood," the Russian mob equivalent of a gang. Bebnev had hoped that his cold-blooded efficiency would get him noticed by the bigger mob bosses and help him climb the organized-crime ladder.

It looked like this might be his big break. Lvov contacted him at the restaurant and said a friend of his in Manhattan had a big job that would pay good money, and more importantly get him noticed by "important" people. Lvov said he'd met this guy Joey some years ago down at the Brooklyn docks where Lvov ran small gambling operations and that the job had something to do with problems in the North American Brotherhood of Stevedores union that ran the docks on New York City's west side.

Bebnev met with Lvov, Joey, and Jackie at a bar in Hell's Kitchen. He'd walked up behind the men, who were sitting at a booth, just in time to hear Joey tell Lvov that "Charlie wants this done ASAP."

They didn't mention "Charlie" again, and Bebnev didn't care. Joey, who did all the talking, offered Bebnev $30,000 to "eliminate" a man named Vince Carlotta. Excited by the money and the big-time nature of the hit, Bebnev agreed to take the job.

It was supposed to look like a home invasion robbery that got out of hand. But as the day approached, he started to get cold feet and decided to bring DiMarzo in on it "if you can find someone with a car." He told DiMarzo that he and the driver would split $14,000 while Bebnev would keep the lion's share for pulling the trigger.

"I've got to piss," Miller said and opened his door. He got out of the car and walked over to a hedge that bordered the school grounds and relieved himself on a patch of snow left over from a storm a week earlier. Spitting one last time into the beer bottle, he tossed it into the bush. If they had to take off fast, he didn't want its noxious contents spilling on the front seat.

Miller had just turned to walk back to the car when headlights suddenly appeared from behind his car moving in their direction. He crouched by the hedge as a large SUV passed the Delta 88 and continued on down the hill until it turned into the driveway of the house they'd been watching. A man and woman exited the car, with the woman opening a rear door and removing an infant. Then the family entered the house.

Jumping back in the car, Miller turned to DiMarzo, who was studying a photograph that had been torn from the *Dock: The Official Magazine of the North American Brotherhood of Stevedores* in the light given off by a streetlamp. The photograph showed four middle-aged men, one of them with a circle drawn around his face and some writing. He knew that Bebnev's contact had given him the photograph and that the Russian had turned it over to DiMarzo as the "lookout."

"That's the guy," DiMarzo said, looking up before placing the photograph back into his coat pocket. "That's Carlotta."

"Let's go," Bebnev replied. He put his hand back in his coat pocket to feel the comfort of the revolver and took another puff on his cigarette.

Miller turned the key in the ignition and the old V-8 roared to life. He pulled up to the curb in front of the house but left the engine running. He thought about saying something to put a stop to what was about to happen, but then he pictured his girlfriend's perpetually disappointed face and heard her father's voice. *You're a bum.* He scowled. He didn't know Vince Carlotta. All those guys with the dockworkers' unions were crooks, and this guy just got on the wrong side of some other crooks. What did he care if the guy died?

DiMarzo was experiencing a similar crisis of conscience. *You'll go to hell. And if you're caught, Mom will die.* . . . But the thoughts fled his mind when Bebnev snarled from the backseat.

"It's time," the Russian said tersely. "Come on, Frankie. *Sooka,* keep the car running."

"Just do it," Miller replied, his voice rising from the tension.

Bebnev jumped out of the car, flicking the still-smoking cigarette butt to the side of the road as he walked up across the front lawn and rang the bell. The Russian tensed as the door opened, but instead of the man he'd been sent to kill, the pretty woman he'd seen get out of the car stood there with the infant in her arms.

She looked confused but then smiled. "Yes, can I help you?" she asked with a slight accent.

Bebnev looked from the woman's face to the infant, and then released his hold on the gun in his pocket. "Uh, we are looking for Mr. Carlotta," he said meekly.

"He's washing up," the woman said. "I'm Antonia Carlotta. Can I tell him who's calling?"

Before Bebnev could answer, the man from the photograph walked up and stepped in front of his wife. He frowned slightly. "What can I do for you?"

Bebnev fidgeted. He pulled his empty hand from his pocket and extended it. "*Da*, yes, we are from San Francisco where we work on docks. We hope to find work here," he said. "We were told you might help."

Carlotta shook Bebnev's hand but his brow furrowed. "How did you know where I lived?" he asked.

Bebnev licked his lips. "We arrived late today and went to docks. Man there tell us New Rochelle. Then we ask neighbors. Sorry for intrusion, but we need work."

Carlotta nodded. "Well, you're enterprising and that's good," he said. "Show up tomorrow at the union headquarters, and I'll get you on the rolls. There may be a few openings for good workers."

Bebnev grinned. "Thank you. We are good workers," he said and then turned to DiMarzo, who was standing with his mouth open watching the exchange in confusion. "We leave this nice family alone. Tomorrow we find work."

"Uh, yeah, sure," DiMarzo said before nodding at the Carlottas. "Thank you."

"Not a problem," Vince Carlotta said as

he looked past them at the old sedan parked in front of his SUV. "Drive safe."

As they walked back across the lawn and got in the car, DiMarzo turned to glare at Bebnev. "Why didn't you do it? He was right there!"

Bebnev scowled. "No one pay me to kill woman and baby," he growled. "I am professional, not baby-killer."

"Professional my ass," Miller sneered as he pulled away from the curb. "You chickened out!"

"Fuck you, Gnat," Bebnev yelled. "Next time, I shoot the fucker!"

"Yeah, yeah, big talker," Miller scoffed. "Who's the *sooka* now, huh, Bebnev?"

2

Charlie Vitteli slammed his big meaty palm down on the tabletop, causing four sets of silverware, four plates and beer mugs, as well as the two men sitting with him, to jump. "What the fuck does it take to get something done around here?" he snarled.

They were gathered around a back corner table at Marlon's, a pub popular with Manhattan's longshoremen, located in Hell's Kitchen near the west side of the New York City waterfront. No other patrons had been seated near them, a concession to Vitteli's importance as the president of the North American Brotherhood of Stevedores, or NABS.

Vitteli kept his voice low, but there was no mistaking the intensity and anger that boiled just beneath the surface. He was an imposing man, barrel-chested, and his cinder block of a head seemed to sit directly upon his broad shoulders. With his mashed nose, pewter-gray crew cut, and facial scars, he looked like a middle-aged prizefighter. But the marks weren't earned in the ring; he got them on the streets, most from his days as a "union organizer" thirty years earlier.

He glared at the other two men as if challenging them to answer his question. Of them, only Joey Barros could hold his gaze. Barros, tall and gaunt to the point of cadaverous, had started on the docks with Vitteli when he was young, and both men had come up through the ranks based largely on their willingness to bust heads to protect the union's party line. The difference between them was that as they'd aged, Vitteli was more likely to use his brains to achieve his ends, whereas Barros was happier doing his persuading with bats, brass knuckles, and a wicked straight razor. He was not afraid of Vitteli, who trusted him like no other.

The third man at the table was Jack "Jackie" Corcione. Vitteli didn't trust him like he did Barros, though in some ways he was more valuable. Corcione was the son of Leo Corcione, the union's founder and president for forty-five years until his death almost two years earlier. The old man had hoped that his only child would succeed him, but Jackie didn't have the nerve or leadership skills to lead a rough-and-tumble union. Leo had recognized the weakness and instead packed his boy off to Harvard, where he'd earned an MBA and then his law degree. He was then brought back into the fold as the union's legal counsel and chief financial officer.

Vitteli kept Corcione in his inner circle for two reasons. There wasn't anything about the union's legal and financial operations, including those that were "under the radar," that Jackie didn't know inside and out. The other reason was that, for all his toughness, Vitteli had a soft spot in his black heart for Leo Corcione. He owed the union's founder everything. He'd been a thug and a dockworker, but he'd made a name for himself during the dockworker strikes in the seventies, and the old man had rewarded him by bringing him into management.

And now I'm dressing in silk suits and living the good life, he thought whenever Barros warned him that Jackie was a weak link in his armor. *I owe it to the old man not to let Joey go after his kid. Not unless it becomes necessary.*

While the old man was alive, Vitteli hadn't worried about Jackie because of what he knew about him, including that he had expensive tastes he paid for by embezzling union funds albeit on a small scale. But more important was the fact that Jackie Corcione was gay.

"A raging queer," Barros had said with a smirk when he brought him the news. "With a taste for Dom Pérignon, Brooks Brothers, and pretty Columbia University frat boys."

Vitteli had used the information to his advantage years ago, when the old man was still alive, by sitting Jackie down in his office one day and telling him what he knew. "It don't bother me what side of the bun you butter," he said, "or that you're padding your bank account from the union's benefits account. But it would kill your dad." He stopped and grinned. "If he doesn't kill you first."

Jackie blanched. "Please don't tell him," he'd begged. "I'll stop stealing. I won't see guys."

"Not to worry, Jackie boy. I look out for you." Vitteli had smiled. "You look out for me."

After the old man died, it didn't matter that Vitteli could no longer hold homosexuality over Jackie's head. Jackie was in so deep, stealing to support his habits, that the members would have torn him apart —

along with Vitteli and Barros — if they learned what they'd all been doing with the union's pension funds.

"Goddamn it, I thought this was a done deal," Vitteli swore, now looking only at Barros.

"Lvov told me it was taken care of," Barros answered flatly. "Apparently, his guy went to the house but Vince's wife and kid were there, so he backed off."

"I don't give a shit about his bitch or brat," Vitteli hissed, leaning forward and speaking lower so the others had to move closer to hear him. "This guy, whoever in the fuck he is, should have done all three and that would be that." He pointed a thick finger at each of them. "Every day that Vince Carlotta lives is a day closer to all of our asses being in hot water. Maybe this alleged hit man ain't the right guy."

"We met with the guy. He's not on the dean's list at Columbia," Barros said. "But he's done this before — that's what Lvov said anyways. Remember, we didn't want to use our 'partners,' the Malchek gang, on something this . . . sensitive, and the membership would tear us to pieces if they knew we were dealing with the Russian mob in Brooklyn."

"And maybe it wasn't such a bad call on

his part," Jackie Corcione chimed in. "It's one thing for something to happen to Vince, especially if it looks like a home robbery. Makes the news for a little bit but then goes away. But add Antonia and her baby, and this goes national. The press goes ape shit, and there's all kinds of pressure on the cops to get to the bottom of it."

Vitteli stared at Corcione for a few seconds before he suddenly erupted with laughter and clapped the surprised younger man on the shoulder. "The press is going to go 'ape shit,' eh? I love it when you try to talk like a tough guy. But stick to your Hah-vard faggot bullshit; you're much more valuable to me as a bookkeeper than a gangster. I got Joey for that."

Corcione blushed as Barros laughed. "Yeah, Jackie's gonna make a deal you can't refuse," Barros said with a smirk. "A regular godfairy."

Pushing back from the table, Vitteli grinned at Jackie's discomfiture. The young man was a pansy, useful but no backbone. "Hey, don't worry about it, Jackie, we're only yanking your chain," he said as he pulled a silver cigar case from the pocket of the suit coat hanging from the back of his chair. He removed one of the expensive Cubans from inside and clipped the end.

Then he flipped open an old Zippo lighter with his left hand and puffed furiously on the cigar until a red ember appeared on the end. It was illegal to smoke in any bar in New York City, but no one in the waterfront area was going to tell Charlie Vitteli he couldn't light up.

Old man Corcione had been no saint but a street savvy, tough son of a bitch. He had to be, in the years when he was fighting to keep his independent fledgling union from being absorbed by the bigger, more well-known International Longshoremen's Association, as well as from the Italian mob. He'd been a man who made sure that interlopers were met fist for fist and bat for bat until both had backed off. As such, he was a man who recognized Vitteli's talent for strategic violence and his intense loyalty to the union and had rewarded him with his trust.

Leo had two favorites. The other was Vince Carlotta, a handsome, charismatic man who'd also come up through the ranks. Although not afraid to fight, and fight well when pushed into a corner, Carlotta had always been the one to negotiate and compromise, especially if it benefited the membership. He had no family and had started working on the docks as a teenager, but Leo saw something special in him and treated him like a son. His protégé had returned the love and respect.

Carlotta and Vitteli had often locked horns over the union, which was a confederation of small dockworker locals scattered across the northeast, as far west as the Great Lakes and up into Canada. Vitteli insisted that without clear direction from the top, and no tolerance for dissent, the union would weaken, as would their influence over its membership. Carlotta was the rank and file's champion, who argued that the old days of ensuring loyalty among the members through intimidation no longer held sway. He contended that allegiance and cohesion would come by working for better wages and insurance benefits, as well as by improving working conditions and safety.

Although Leo Corcione continued to treat Vitteli with respect, listening to his arguments and sometimes even agreeing with him, thereby overruling Carlotta, most of the time the old man sided with Vince. Never really sure of himself despite his bluster, Vitteli grew jealous and paranoid when he started noticing that Carlotta and the old man were spending a lot of time locked away in private talks, even going out to dinner by themselves, according to his spies.

Then came the day when Barros walked into Vitteli's office at union headquarters with alarming news. He said his sources had told him that Leo was preparing to step down as president and name a successor.

"Rumor has it that he's going to choose Vince," Barros claimed, arching an eyebrow as he watched for his boss's reaction. Then Barros suggested that maybe the old man needed to have "an accident" before he named Carlotta as his heir apparent, which the members would have taken as gospel.

At first, Vitteli recoiled at the thought. But the more he thought about playing second fiddle to Carlotta, the better Barros's argument sounded. "I don't need to remind you that if Carlotta is president," Barros said, "he's going to find out about our little retirement fund."

Vitteli had all but decided to let Barros devise a plan to get rid of the old man in a manner that wouldn't arouse suspicions when fate intervened. Vitteli and Carlotta had been in Leo's office arguing over a complaint from several union crane operators that a half-dozen new cranes were unstable under certain conditions and could topple. Carlotta was insisting on an independent inspector, while Vitteli, who'd taken a kickback for pushing through the crane manufacturer's bid, said it was unnecessary and could even put the union in financial straits if "for some trumped up reason" it appeared that management had been derelict in looking out for worker safety.

They had both resorted to shouting when suddenly Leo clutched his chest, gave a gasp, and collapsed to the floor. Carlotta had administered CPR until the ambulance arrived, but the old man never regained consciousness and didn't pull through.

Although Vitteli had to sweat it out for a few days, there was nothing in Leo's will or any other paperwork naming Carlotta as his heir apparent. So it was brought to the general membership for a vote.

Vitteli had recognized early on that he was unlikely to prevail in a fair fight. He'd get the vote of some of the old-timers who'd been in the trenches with him and still looked fondly on the "old ways of doing things." But they were outnumbered by younger members, most of whom would throw in with Carlotta. He'd be able to buy a certain number of votes, but in the end it had taken what Barros euphemistically called "voting irregularities" to seal the deal.

Carlotta had looked stunned when the "final vote" was announced and Vitteli declared the winner. But he'd graciously conceded defeat and promised Vitteli he'd support his presidency. "At least until the next election," he said with a slight smile, reaching out his hand to shake Vitteli's.

Then fate, and bad engineering, again intervened. Just as the operators predicted, one of the new cranes had fallen while unloading a cargo ship when a sudden gust of wind whipped down the Hudson River at the wrong moment. Two men had been killed and four others seriously injured.

Carlotta had been incensed, though he took some of the blame upon himself because the old man's death had distracted him from the crane issue. "Now we have two widows and kids without fathers, and four other families without breadwinners because we failed them," he lamented. He insisted that the union hire an independent engineering firm to look at the cranes.

Vitteli had at first resisted. "Pay the benefits and let's move on," he ordered Jackie Corcione. But his rival had threatened to take his demand for an independent inspection to the members, so he gave in. Then he directed Barros to do whatever it took to bribe, blackmail, or, as it turned out, both to persuade the engineer who headed the study to come out with a favorable report. "The accident," the married engineer, who

41

had a penchant for young prostitutes, had written, "was not due to faulty engineering, but freak weather conditions and operator error."

There'd been rumbling when the report came out and threats of walking out on the job by the crane operators. But Vitteli — through Barros — came down hard on the balky crane operators, threatening to find replacements for what was one of the highest-paid positions on the dock. They all stayed at their jobs.

When Vitteli announced the engineer's report, Carlotta looked at him hard, but he kept his mouth shut, at least for a little while.

A week after the report was issued, Vitteli got a call from an informant he had with the U.S. Department of Labor's office in Washington, D.C., that dealt with union issues. According to the caller, Carlotta and his hotshot lawyer, a young turk named Mahlon Gorman, had traveled to the capital that week to complain about the so-called voting irregularities and wanted advice on how to go about contesting the results.

The informant told Vitteli not to worry just yet. The Labor Department wouldn't get involved because under the Landrum-

Griffin Act such grievances had to be brought before the union first. Only when that remedy was exhausted would the department even consider stepping in. It was akin to telling chickens that they had to complain to the fox about his presence in the henhouse before talking to the farmer, but it was the law.

The day after Vitteli got the telephone call, Carlotta's lawyer filed a formal grievance at union headquarters, demanding a hearing. Among the grievances, which Vitteli knew to be true, were that ballots had been sent to the far-flung locals without Carlotta's name printed on them; there were also claims of good old-fashioned ballot stuffing. But Vitteli wasn't as worried about what an investigation of the election results would reveal as what it might also uncover about what Barros called their retirement fund, a multimillion-dollar slush fund created by siphoning off union monies, as well as recent negotiations with the Malchek gang regarding use of the docks for their "import-export" business. If Carlotta eventually prevailed with the election, he was sure to look into Vitteli's financial practices and the Malcheks, who'd already "invested" a lot of money in the retirement fund and wouldn't be too happy about the deal collapsing.

There was only one thing to do. Eliminate the danger.

Barros had thought that Jackie would balk at the plan to kill Carlotta when Vitteli first talked to his henchman about it. "He ain't got the balls for blood," he'd scoffed.

However, Vitteli knew that Jackie Corcione feared prison and knew he wouldn't last a month in that setting. He was right. After Vitteli spelled out what a victory by Carlotta would mean, Jackie decided to go along with the plan.

Puffing on the stogie, Vitteli looked at the two men around the table. "So when's it supposed to happen now?" he asked around the edges of the cigar.

Barros shrugged. "Lvov was going to talk to the guy tonight," he said. "Maybe he should do it away from the house."

Vitteli blew a cloud of smoke up toward the ceiling, his dark eyes following the forms that swirled and dissipated like gray ghosts, before nodding. "I got an idea. Listen up," he said as the other men drew closer. "This yahoo Russian hit man knows who he's looking for, right? I mean, he's not going to shoot Jackie here by mistake?"

Barros laughed. "We'd have to pay him extra," he said. "Nah, he's got that photo of the four of us from the convention in Atlantic City, the one where you circled Vince's head. And now he's seen him face-to-face, too. What are you getting at?"

Vitteli smiled. "A dead man and the perfect alibi."

Two hours and several more beers apiece later, the men swaggered out of Marlon's laughing loudly, except for Jackie, who looked pensive and hung behind the others. He quickly hailed a taxi and was gone, while Vitteli and Barros, along with Vitteli's bodyguard, Sal Amaya, continued around the corner to find Vitteli's black Cadillac.

"Started off nice today but, man, it's frickin' cold out now. Always fair and foul, eh?" Barros said, pulling his coat tighter as they approached three forlorn figures huddled around a fire they had going in a fifty-five-gallon drum at the entrance of an alley. "Well, what have we got here?"

As they drew closer, the three men realized that the creatures were women dressed in many layers of tattered clothing and threadbare coats. The women saw them, too, and two of them detached themselves from the fire and walked toward them, holding out their rag-covered hands.

"Good evening, gents, spare a dollar or two so three old women can get a bite to eat?" said one of the women as she brushed strands of frizzy gray hair away from her dirt-encrusted face.

"Beat it, you old hag," Barros snarled. "You'd just spend it on a bottle of booze."

"I'd tell you to go to hell," the woman spat back. She waved at a large black woman, walking behind her. "But my friend says you'll be there soon enough."

As Vitteli and the gray-haired woman exchanged glares, the third woman, pale-skinned, said nothing but stood squinting at him. Then she pointed a finger at him.

"Well, what do you know? If it ain't Charlie Vitteli," she said and did a little curtsy. "It took a moment for my brain to clear, but all hail the king of the docks!" Her skinny lips pulled back in a grin, but the effect was horrifying, as she had only a few teeth left in her mouth. "Oh, and high executioner, I might add."

Before Vitteli could respond, the black woman suddenly shouted, " 'Tis time! 'Tis time!" She threw something on the fire that caused the flames to leap and hiss but then went back to mumbling to the flames and no one else.

The gray-haired woman who'd asked for money cackled and nodded toward her friend at the fire. "She's from Jamaica and thinks she's a witch. She's casting a charm of powerful trouble."

"Eye of newt, toe of frog . . . that sort of thing," added the pale-skinned woman who'd addressed him as the king of the docks. "Nothing to worry your pretty head about, Charlie."

Vitteli scowled. "Do I know you?" he asked.

"Know me?" the woman asked. "No more than you would know the cockroaches on the sidewalks or the rats in the alley. But you should, you should. My name's Anne Devulder. That ring a bell, King Vitteli?"

"No, never heard of you," Vitteli answered. "Now get the hell out of my way. . . ."

"So kind he is, so just," Devulder replied unflinching and unmoving. "Maybe it's my first name that threw you. I'm Sean Devulder's widow."

Vitteli's eyes narrowed. Sean Devulder was one of the crane operators who'd died. He nodded. "Good union man, Sean Devulder," he said. "I'm sorry for your loss."

Anne Devulder rolled her eyes. "Yeah, Sean was a good union man through and through, for all the good it did him," she said. "My old man told me what was going to happen, and then it did. He told you,

47

too, but you ignored him and now he's dead."

"You didn't turn down the life insurance check," Barros growled.

Devulder ignored him and stepped closer to Vitteli to look up into his eyes. "Me and Sean had two kids," she said. "I wasn't in a position to be turning down nothing. Forty thousand dollars you paid — to raise two kids and make some sort of home for them and me."

"Yeah? And why aren't you home with your kids now?" Barros sneered.

The woman glanced down at the sidewalk and when she looked back up, tears were streaming down her face. "The state took them away," she replied softly. "When Sean died, I turned to drink. We had a lot of bills and most of the money went to that. That was two years ago. I couldn't get a job that paid anything so we lost our home and lived on the streets until the state took my kids from me, too. But they're better off in a foster home than with me."

Vitteli reached into his pocket and pulled out a wad of bills. He peeled off a twenty and held it out to her. "Get something to eat on me," he said.

Devulder looked at the bill as if it was a snake. She stepped back and pointed again at his face. "The Devulders are done taking your blood money, Charlie Vitteli," she said. "Curse you and this two-legged dog who does your dirty work. You're king of the docks for now. But someday all you'll be king of is a prison cell."

Vitteli felt a chill ripple down his spine as Anne Devulder turned away from him to walk back to the fire. He was too stunned to move when the gray-haired woman rushed forward and snatched the bill from his hand.

"I'll take that," she said. "Think of it as payment for the fortune-telling." With that, the woman scurried off to join the other two.

As though in a trance, Vitteli stood looking at the three women and at the dancing shadows on the alley wall behind them, cast there by the red and yellow flames. He didn't move until Amaya tugged on his coat sleeve.

"Come on, boss, let's go," Amaya said. "The bitches are loony tunes."

Vitteli shook his head as if trying to wake up. Then he laughed. "Jesus H. Christ," he swore. "She had me going there for a moment. Shit, only in New York, eh?"

"Yeah, boss," Barros said with a laugh. "Only in New York."

3

Vince Carlotta looked at himself in the mirror that hung on the wall of his study. He didn't know what he was looking for, perhaps some outward sign of the malaise that had been dogging him for the past week or so. But what he saw were the same striking gray-green eyes set in a handsome, tanned face framed by a full head of wavy brown hair; he felt good physically, too, and worked out regularly to stay fit and trim.

According to the mirror, he was the picture of health — a good thing, as he needed to keep up with his young wife and infant son. Whatever ailed him couldn't be seen. *You're just tired,* he told himself. *Between the election fraud, fighting with Vitteli, the old man's death, and being the middle-aged father of an infant son and husband to an amorous young wife, you're exhausted. And it's affecting your mood.*

Antonia entered the room and smiled.

50

"The peacock is preening," she teased. She spoke with a saucy hint of an Italian accent, which went well with her doe-like brown eyes, translucent skin, and Cupid's bow lips. She had been a runway model from Naples working in New York when she and several friends had gone "slumming" in Hell's Kitchen. He'd been with a table of male friends, and soon the two groups were commingled and he found himself talking to Antonia, hoping the night would never end.

A shy, confirmed bachelor, he'd never been any good at picking up girls at bars or even asking for their phone numbers, so he was surprised and delighted when this beautiful young woman, twenty years his junior, asked for his. The courtship had been fast and furious. She was a delightful mix of sass, class, sex, and intelligence, and he was as befuddled as all their friends that she seemed so completely enamored with him. It took him months to work up the nerve to ask her to marry him and her a second to think about it before saying yes.

Upon marrying, she immediately gave up her modeling career and started working on getting pregnant. Even then it took them a year, though not from a lack of trying. Finally, Vicente Paulito Carlotta Jr. was born, almost two years after their nuptials.

Vince had never thought much about having kids. His own experiences as an orphan bouncing from one relative's house to the next, none of whom wanted an extra mouth to feed, had not been happy ones. He'd gone along with getting Antonia pregnant because that was what she wanted. And yet, once Vincent was born he learned a whole new kind of love.

"I wouldn't want to embarrass you by looking like a slob in public," Vince now replied to his wife.

Antonia laughed and walked over to stand in front of him. She reached up to straighten his tie. "Little chance of that, my Prince Charming who all the women want," she said lightly but then frowned. "I wish you didn't have to go."

Vince reached up and took her hands in his. "I wish I didn't have to either," he said. "But it's important. Charlie called and said he wants to bury the hatchet. . . ."

"He wants to bury it in your back," she retorted.

"Probably, but I still need to hear what he wants to say," Vince said. "He knows he's going to lose if the Labor Department looks at the election results. He might be trying to save face, and maybe prison time, by offering to step down from the presidency."

"I think he would rather die than lose to you," Antonia said. "I don't trust him; he has *cuore nero.*"

"A black heart," Vince translated. "I think you're giving him too much credit; I don't think he has a heart. But he does have an ego, and if he thinks he's going to lose, he'll want to work out some sort of deal. He's really not the confident guy he likes to project; he gets by on a lot of bravado."

"But why meet at Marlon's? And why at night?"

Vince shrugged. "Charlie's still one of those old-school guys who likes to work things out over beer and cigars." He let go of her hands, leaned down, and kissed her. "Don't worry, my love," he said. "Nothing's going to happen. Marlon's will have a crowd. Randy will be there and he's nobody anybody wants to fu— sorry, to mess with. Besides, Vitteli's too smart to throw his life away over who gets to be union president."

Antonia stuck out her lower lip. "I still don't like it. Joey Barros scares me."

"Joey's bark is worse than his bite, and that dog doesn't even bark unless his master tells him to," Vince replied. "I expect Charlie will have him muzzled."

Vince walked over to his big wooden desk. As he picked up his car keys and wallet, he noticed a pad of yellow sticky notes next to the telephone. *FPB 8196.* He thought for a moment, pulled the top sheet from the pad, and put it in his wallet.

"What's that?" his wife asked.

"Nothing," Vince replied as he slipped the wallet into his coat pocket.

"Don't tell me 'nothing' when I see you thinking about something," she replied.

"It's the license plate number of those jokers who came to the door the other night," he said.

"Did they ever come to the union office to sign up?"

Vince shook his head. "No. At least not that I know of; but they could have tried to get on down at the docks and I just haven't seen the paperwork yet."

Antonia squinted at him suspiciously. "Then why do you need the license number?"

"It's just a precaution," he said. "I heard there were a few break-ins in the neighborhood recently. I was going to give it to the police. Don't worry, the cops have really stepped up patrols, so I'm sure whoever was behind the burglaries is long gone. But maybe the license number will help."

Antonia studied his face for a minute. "You are a terrible liar, Vicente Paulito Carlotta, and you shouldn't even try," she accused him. "But I trust you know what you're doing. Just be careful, my darling."

"I will," he said, kissing her again. "Don't wait up."

Antonia pouted again, only playfully this time. "You know I can't go to sleep until I feel your warm naked body next to mine," she purred.

Vince looked up and crossed himself. *Dear Jesus, please let this meeting be short so that I can find myself in bed next to the naked body of this beautiful young woman, grazie,* he prayed.

A minute later, he was out the door, where his driver, Randy McMahon, met him in a Lincoln sedan. Leaving New Rochelle, they headed southwest on the Hutchinson River Parkway, connected to the Henry Hudson Parkway and drove down the West Side into Manhattan. As they traveled, Carlotta thought again about the license plate number in his wallet and the three men who'd come to his house.

That night after he watched the old sedan with its three odd passengers roll away, he frowned and closed the door, locking it and throwing the heavy deadbolt. Only then had he relaxed his grip on the .380 semiautomatic he had in his pants pocket.

The next day he told his attorney, Mahlon Gorman, about the visit when they were discussing filing a formal complaint with the Labor Department now that the union management, as expected, had decided his elections violations complaint was without merit. "I don't know what they were up to but they sure as hell weren't dockworkers," Vince said.

"How do you know that?" Gorman asked.

"I shook the one guy's hand, and it was as soft as yours," Vince explained. "If he's a dockworker, I'm Elvis."

"You couldn't handle 'Love Me Tender,'" Gorman said with a laugh. "What did these fine fellows look like?"

Vince shrugged. "The guy who did all the talking had blue eyes, kind of a wide face, a mustache, and a shaved head. He spoke with a pretty heavy accent, Russian or something like that. Late twenties, thirty maybe. The other guy who got out of the car looked Eyetie or maybe Greek — one of us Med types, anyway. I didn't get a good look at the driver; he parked at the curb and kept his head turned. But he had red hair, seemed young."

Gorman, a tough young Jewish kid from the Bronx, thought about it for a minute. "Think it was some of Vitteli's boys?" he asked at last.

"I don't know," Vince replied, wagging his hand. "Maybe. Maybe sending a message. You know like, 'I know where you live and so do my thugs.' Something subtle like that."

They both laughed. Charlie Vitteli was about as subtle as a bull elephant in must. "It's probably nothing," Vince continued. "Just three guys trying to get a break finding work by pretending they're longshoremen from Frisco."

"And maybe it's something," Gorman countered. "A cornered animal is always more dangerous and Charlie knows he's cornered. We're going to be able to prove to the Labor Department that he bought that election, which will force them to take action. He's looking at prison time, stiff fines, and he'll get booted from the union. He's not going to let that happen without a fight. I wish you'd let me get some security to watch your back. At least until Charlie's put away. These three clowns who came to your door make me nervous."

Vince shook his head. "I'm fine with your guys watching out for Antonia and Little Vince," he said. "But I'm not going to let Charlie Vitteli have the satisfaction of seeing me with bodyguards. Besides, I got all the protection I need." He pulled the .380 from his drawer and placed it on the desk.

"Jesus, where'd you get that thing?" Gorman swore. "May I remind you, you are not Elliot fucking Ness, nor are you untouchable. I know you're a tough guy and all, but if you feel the need to carry a gun, you definitely need security."

"It's only insurance," Vince replied. "And I'm being careful. No frickin' bodyguards."

Turning at Eighth Avenue onto 34th Street toward Hell's Kitchen, Vince glanced at the heavy overcoat lying on the seat next to him. He could see the bulge of the "insurance" in a side pocket and knew his wife would have freaked out if she knew he felt it necessary to carry a gun to his meeting with Charlie Vitteli. He'd meant what he said to Antonia about Charlie not risking his neck over the union presidency. But he'd lied about Barros's bark being worse than his bite. He'd seen the cold-blooded thug carve a man's face into slivers in the blink of an eye with the long straight razor he carried. The man could definitely bite, and his master was cornered and dangerous.

The conversation with Gorman had been several days earlier, and Vince had all but forgotten about the three visitors. Then Charlie called and asked if he'd meet with him at Marlon's. "I think it's time we put this thing behind us," his rival said. "I'm willing to make some important concessions and moves, if you will, in exchange for some concessions from you. But let's talk about it over beer, like the old man would have wanted."

McMahon parked around the corner from Marlon's and they got out to walk. As they approached an alley around the corner from the pub, they came upon three women warming themselves around a fire they'd started in a fifty-five-gallon drum. Two broke away from the third, a large black woman who seemed otherwise preoccupied with the flames, and approached with their hands out. They were filthy, wretched creatures, and Vince felt sorry for them, reaching into his pants pocket and pulling out all the cash he had.

"Here's thirty bucks," he said. "I wish I had more. I know it's cold out." He took a second look at one of the women and his face fell. "I haven't seen you since the funeral, but aren't you Anne Devulder, Sean's wife?"

Anne Devulder smiled. "Hello, Mr. Carlotta. Yes, we met at Sean's service. I'm surprised you recognized me; I've changed a bit."

"I'm so sorry about Sean," Vince said. "It

should have never happened. I'm trying to see that it doesn't happen again to someone else."

The woman smiled sadly and nodded. "I know you are, Mr. Carlotta," she said. "Sean always said you were a good man."

"That's high praise coming from him," Vince said. He pointed in the direction he'd been walking. "I have a meeting I have to get to, but please stop by the union offices tomorrow. It looks like you could use some help, and maybe there's something I can do."

A sad look passed over Anne Devulder's face. Suddenly she clutched his arm. "Don't go to this meeting," she said. "Charlie Vitteli's in there and I have a bad feeling about it. Turn around and drive home to your beautiful wife and son. It's not too late."

Vince clasped the woman's hand, gave it a squeeze, and gently pried it from his coat. "I'm afraid I have to go," he said softly. "Thank you for your concern, and believe me, I'd rather go home, but I need to do this . . . for guys like Sean."

Anne Devulder nodded and stepped back from him. "God bless you, Vince Carlotta," she said. Then she and the other woman turned and shuffled back to the oil drum where the third woman was shaking her hands above the flames.

As he turned away, Vince shivered. For a moment he considered taking the woman's advice and going home to Antonia and Vicente. *Let Charlie have the presidency,* he thought. *Walk away, get another job, maybe with the International Longshoremen's Association, or better yet, get away from the docks entirely, start a new life.* But then he thought about Anne Devulder and how she'd been widowed because the union had not done its job to keep her husband safe. Somebody needed to be a voice for the guys on the docks, and that wasn't going to be Charlie Vitteli.

Vince Carlotta sighed and pulled his overcoat around him, felt for the weight of the semiautomatic against his side. "Time to go hear what the bastard and his dogs have to say," he said to McMahon and strode off for the front door of Marlon's.

The meeting with Vitteli started off on a bad note. Vince had walked into Marlon's ignoring Vitteli's ever-present bodyguard, Sal Amaya, heading directly back to Vitteli's table. No sooner had they sat down around a table in the back and ordered beers than Charlie started to berate him for "causing dissension in the ranks."

Vince countered that speaking out against

61

corruption in union management was not only right, but necessary. "You're a crook, Charlie," he said. "You bought the election, and I'm going to prove it."

"Watch who you threaten, Carlotta," Joey Barros interjected.

"Muzzle your dog," Vince said to Charlie.

Barros jumped to his feet, his hand sliding inside the leather coat he wore. Vince also stood, his hand reaching inside of his own coat, which he'd yet to take off, for the .380.

Charlie noticed Vince's movements and his eyes narrowed. But then he laughed. "Sit down, Joey, damn it," he ordered. "We're trying to do this like civilized men, not a bunch of wild animals at each other's throats." He looked up at Carlotta. "Come on, Vince, have a seat. I apologize. I didn't ask you to come here to rehash the past. I want us to figure out how to move into the future without ripping the union apart and anybody getting hurt in the process."

Vince glanced at him but remained standing with his focus on Barros, who slowly sat back down, keeping his eyes on the table to hide his dark thoughts. "You better listen, Carlotta," Barros mumbled.

"Or what, Joey? Or you'll send three jokers to my house? To my house, goddamn you, where my wife and kid are? How about

I visit your house, Charlie, and let your wife know about your mistresses? Or you, Joey, maybe I should send some of my boys to your house? Maybe your wife and kids could use a good scare, huh?"

"I don't know what you're talking about," he replied.

"These guys show up at my house in New Rochelle and say they want jobs working on the dock, but they got hands like accountants'," Vince retorted.

"Look, Vince, I got no idea what those yahoos were up to, but they weren't my guys," Charlie replied. "I'll have Joey check it out. Let's be fair here. With the old man gone, the International is looking to make a move over here, and the mob is always trying to get a toehold on our docks. They know you've been the guy on the front line keeping them in their place. They're not your friends, but you want to blame me for everything."

"I'll deal with them when I need to," Vince retorted. "You're the one who bought the election. You're the problem right now."

Vitteli hung his head as if he'd reached some monumental decision. "Look," he said. "We got this meeting off on the wrong foot, and I'm sorry for that. But like I told you on the phone, I think I may have a compromise that will work for all parties. So come on, sit down and let's break some bread and talk like we used to when we were young. We didn't always agree then, either, but we always worked it out for the good of the union."

When Vince hesitated, Jackie Corcione spoke up. "Come on, Vince," he pleaded. "I've heard Charlie's compromise, and I think you'll like it. You know Dad loved both of you, and I think it would break his heart to have you guys at each other's throats."

Vince looked at Jackie. He wanted to tell him about the conversations he'd had with the old man in the weeks before his death, when he was talking about stepping down and anointing Vince as his replacement. Leo Corcione had warned him to watch out for Charlie.

"I had high hopes for him." The old man shook his head slowly. "I knew he was wild and resorted to force too quickly. But he also loved the union and did a lot of good things. I thought maybe with my influence, and to be honest, yours, we could temper his worst instincts and bring out the good ones." The old man paused and then sighed. "But Charlie is ambitious and likes power; it overrides and corrupts everything else about him. He wants this job, but not for the right reasons. He doesn't want to look out for the little guy; he wants to look out for Charlie Vitteli."

Leo warned him that "when I'm gone," Vitteli would try to seize the reins of union leadership. "And he'll do it by whatever means necessary." The old man also told him to watch out for Barros. "He's dangerous, though without Charlie he's just a rabid dog without direction."

Surprisingly, Leo also told him not to trust his own son, Jackie. "I love the boy," he said with tears in his eyes. "And yes, I know he's queer, even though he thinks it's a big secret. Doesn't bother me. But what does bother me is he's weak and has already let Charlie manipulate him into being another one of his dogs. If I didn't love him so much, I'd fire him. So I'm hoping that when you're president, you can bring him back into the fold. Make a good man out of him; I seemed to have failed."

These conversations had obviously been private, and then the old man died before he could name Vince as his successor. Instead, the presidency had gone up for a general vote allowing Charlie Vitteli plenty of time to manipulate and buy his way into power. There was no sense bringing up the old man's wishes now. So Vince nodded and took a seat.

"Okay, Charlie, spit it out. What's this compromise?" he asked.

Vitteli looked at him and moved closer so that he could speak lower. "I ain't saying you're right about the election results," he began. "I ain't saying you're wrong. But that's behind us. I think we both know that getting the Labor Department involved won't be good for anybody — not the union, not me, not you."

"So what are you proposing?" Vince asked. He was tired and the black mood he'd been experiencing hovered near the edges of his thoughts.

"Just this," Charlie said. "I'm going to announce that, for the good of the union, and so everything is on the up-and-up, there will be another election."

"When?"

"April."

"You going to cheat and buy that one, too?" Vince scoffed. "You just trying to buy time here?"

"Nah, nothing like that," Charlie replied. "In fact, I'm going to throw the election. I'll start having some 'medical issues,' make some noises in some circles that maybe I'm not the right guy for the job after all."

Vince thought about it for a moment. "So what do you want in return?"

Charlie smiled. "You drop the Labor Department complaint, and we hear no more about that shit. It's in the past. Also, you name me vice president and my boys here work for me, except Jackie, who you will, of course, keep as chief financial officer."

Vince shook his head. "Sorry, can't do it. Everything else is good, but you and your lapdogs have to go. I need to be able to trust my right-hand man, and I don't trust you farther than I can throw you. Jackie, you stay, but you'll be reporting to Mahlon Gorman, who will be the new union attorney, not that crook Syd Kowalski. We'll work out some sort of golden parachute for the rest of you so money won't be an issue. But I don't want you around me anymore, Charlie, that ship has sailed, and I'd rather have a scorpion in my bed than Joey."

For a moment rage played across Charlie Vitteli's face like a storm across a sea, but then he smiled and nodded. "Sorry you feel that way," he said. "But to be honest, I wouldn't have kept you around, either. As long as the financials of my 'early retirement' work out, and the Labor Department matter is dropped, I'm good with it. May be time to enjoy my golden years with the old lady and our brats."

The rest of the evening went about as well as it could. Charlie was in fine form talking about the early days. "We busted some heads together, huh, Vince," he said. "Before you went all academic on me. And hey, remember the 'management meeting' in Atlantic City? We had a good time then, and if I remember right, there was a cute little dancer who had an eye for you. I got a photo of the four of us put in the latest edition of the *Dock.*"

Vince laughed and told a few stories of his own while the cigars and whiskey made the rounds. At one point he excused himself and called Gorman to tell him how the evening was going. He couldn't wait, however, to get home and let Antonia in on what had happened. He imagined holding her tight and telling her that everything was going to be fine.

"I need to get moving," he said at last, feeling the effects of the last shot of whiskey.

"So do I," Charlie agreed. "You parked around the corner. We'll walk with you."

Vince waved Randy McMahon over and sent him to get the car warmed up. "I'll be right there."

"You go with him," Vitteli told his bodyguard, Sal Amaya.

Amaya, a huge man who'd had a brief career as an NFL lineman, frowned. "You sure, boss?"

"Yeah, I want to have a few last words with Vince," Vitteli said and laughed. "I swear you can be a mother hen sometimes, Sal."

"That's what you pay me for."

"Yeah? Well I also pay you to listen to what the fuck I tell you to do, so get going," he said, frowning.

As the four remaining men left the pub and rounded the corner to the side street, Vince noticed that the three women were no longer gathered around the oil drum, which stood black and cold at the alley entrance. They'd just about reached it when Vince spotted the old Delta 88 parked across the street. A man was sitting at the wheel.

"Hey, that's the —" he started to say when two men wearing ski masks stepped out of the alley entrance.

"Give me fucking wallets," one of the men said in a heavily accented voice as he pointed his gun at Vince.

In that instant, Vince recognized the voice. He could see the eyes beneath the mask; they were blue and widely spaced. He also knew that this was no ordinary robbery as his hand dove into his coat pocket and found the .380.

The young robber was slow to recognize the danger. Vince had the gun out of his pocket and had started to move it forward to aim and fire, but then he felt a hand grip his forearm, stopping him. He glanced over and saw Charlie, his face a mask of hate. Vitteli held tight to Carlotta's arm, trying to wrestle the gun from him.

"You son of a bitch," Vince swore.

"Do it," Charlie shouted at the gunman.

Vince looked back just as the first round caught him in the chest, knocking him to the sidewalk as his own gun clattered to the ground. He sat up and tried to reach the .380 but the next shot caught him in the head, killing him instantly.

The masked gunman and his associate stood still for a moment as if trying to figure out what to do next.

"Our wallets, you idiot," Charlie hissed.

"What? Oh, *da,*" the gunman said. "Give me your wallets and your watches!"

As the others took their wallets out and removed their watches, the second masked man stepped forward to get the loot.

"Now get the fuck out of here," Charlie said, aware that people were starting to come out of Marlon's down the street, having heard the shots.

The two men ran across the street and jumped into the Delta 88, which peeled away from the curb and tore around a corner, away from the crowd.

Charlie knelt next to Vince Carlotta, placing his hands on the dead man's chest as if to administer CPR. "Help!" he yelled. "Somebody call 911. My friend's been shot!"

Jackie Corcione, who had been staring at Vince and the growing pool of blood around his body, suddenly jerked as if he'd been awakened. He ran toward the crowd that was approaching. "Help! Somebody shot Vince Carlotta, call an ambulance!"

An ambulance showed up a few minutes later, the paramedics taking over from where Charlie Vitteli had been pushing on his dead rival's chest. One of the rescuers looked up at where Charlie stood, his hands dripping with blood, and shook his head. "He's gone," the paramedic said.

Charlie slumped against the wall and took out his silk monogrammed handkerchief to try to clean the blood off his hands as Joey and Jackie gathered around as if to comfort him. A flash went off and then another. The press had arrived. "It will look good for the papers, but goddamn it, the shit doesn't want to come off," he complained, just as he glanced over Barros's shoulder in the direction of the alley and stepped back as if he'd seen a ghost. Standing just inside the shadows were the homeless women who'd been around the oil drum several nights before.

Anne Devulder was staring right at him, damnation in her eyes. The second woman cackled and pointed at him as the third, the large black woman, mouthed the words, " 'Tis time! 'Tis time!"

Wild-eyed, Charlie turned to Barros. "Those bitches are back!" He ducked to hide behind his man.

Corcione and Barros both turned to look in the direction indicated, but then turned back around with confused looks on their faces.

"What bitches?" Barros asked.

"There's nobody there, Charlie," Corcione added.

Charlie straightened and peered around Barros. It was true, there was no one standing in the shadows of the alley. "They vanished!" he swore. "They were there but now they're gone . . . like a breath in the wind."

Barros's mouth twisted. "Jesus, boss, you're giving me the willies," he said.

"There's no one there, and Vince Carlotta's not going to give us any more problems. Here, give me that." He reached down and took the bloody handkerchief from Charlie, then walked over and threw it in the oil drum. "It will be gone the next time some bum lights a fire," he said. "Now, let's get you home."

Charlie nodded. "Yeah," he said. "Must have just been my imagination. The mind can play funny tricks on you. But let's go back to Marlon's first. I need another drink."

4

"Hey, Butch, who . . . crap son of a bitch . . . am I?" the little news vendor with the pointed and perpetually dripping nose and thick, smudged glasses said to the tall man in the navy blue suit standing in front of his newsstand. He puffed out his chest, and threw back his head pugnaciously.

"Here goes, here goes, take a guess," he said, pulling his old down coat patched with duct tape around him as he hopped from foot to foot. "You ready? 'You don't understand. I coulda had class. I coulda been a . . . balls tits oh boy whoop . . . contender. I coulda been somebody, instead of a bum, which is what I am, let's face it.' "

"Um, let's see . . . a very poor Marlon Brando as Terry in *On the Waterfront,*" Roger "Butch" Karp replied with a laugh. "And please, don't ever do that again; you'll ruin one of my all-time favorite movies for me. That was even below your standards, such as they are, as a trivia question. However, I take it your 'impersonation' was motivated by last night's events and meant to make a point."

As they spoke, the morning crowd swept past on the sidewalk in front of the Criminal Courts Building on 100 Centre Street in downtown Manhattan where Karp worked as the district attorney of New York County. The newsstand was owned by "Dirty Warren" Bennett, who now smiled mischievously and hooked a thumb over his shoulder at the front pages of the *New York Times* and the *New York Post* tacked to sides of his newsstand.

"Read 'em and . . . fuck piss . . . weep," stuttered the little man, who suffered from Tourette's syndrome, which, besides giving him facial tics and sudden muscle twitches, caused him to spout profanity.

Karp scanned the headlines: UNION BOSS CARLOTTA KILLED ON WATERFRONT; SUSPECTS FLEE, read the *Times*. MASKED BANDIT BLASTS CARLOTTA, the *Post* boldly advertised.

Karp nodded. He'd known what the headlines would be — or at least had a good idea — after he got a telephone call at one in the morning from Clay Fulton, the head of the NYPD detective squad who worked

75

for his office.

"Thought you'd want to know," his old friend had said. "Somebody shot and killed Vince Carlotta outside of Marlon's. Looks like a robbery. I'm on my way over to the crime scene now. The press is going to be all over this, and I want to get there before the rumors start flying."

Karp had swung his legs out of bed and turned on the nightstand light. It was no secret that Vince Carlotta's supporters had been raising a stink about the last union election. The popular union boss had also been in the papers recently threatening to reopen the union investigation into a fatal accident involving dock cranes. The conspiracy theorists were bound to be out in droves. "I'll get dressed and join you," Karp said.

"Stay put. I think we're okay," Fulton replied. "Ray Guma heard about it from his Italian mob connections on the docks almost before we did. He called off the ADA who was catching cases on the homicide bureau night chart and is taking it himself. I want to talk to the detectives on the scene, maybe sniff around a little bit. But the initial report I got was pretty cut-and-dried. Carlotta got jumped and tried to pull a gun.

76

Bingo, bango, he took one to the chest and one to the head. Gunman ran away. I'll let you know if it looks like more than that; Ray and I will see you in the morning and get you up to speed."

Karp thought about it for a moment. Special Assistant District Attorney Ray Guma was one of his oldest friends. They'd both come onto the DAO at the same time, fresh out of law school and as different as the law schools they'd attended. Karp at Cal-Berkeley and Guma at NYU. Karp was tall, long-limbed, with gold-flecked gray eyes; a highly recruited college basketball player who still worked at staying fit. Guma was built like an ape with a gargoyle's face; he'd gone to Fordham on a baseball scholarship and played for a year in the minor leagues for the Yankee organization.

Karp was a straight arrow, the son of a Brooklyn businessman and an English teacher. A dedicated family man, he'd always preferred an evening in with his wife and kids to going out on the town with the boys.

Guma grew up in the rough section of Bath Beach in Brooklyn, one of six children of an Italian plumber and his stay-at-home wife. Through his extended family, Guma had connections to the Mafia, though he'd put plenty of mobsters away. Also, there was an understanding that "those" members of the family kept their business affairs out of Manhattan. Most of the time Karp had known Guma, his friend had used a hard-drinking, cigar-chomping, womanizing front to hide a heart of gold. He would lay his life on the line, and had, for his friends.

What they had in common — besides their Brooklyn roots and an obsession with Yankee baseball — was their love for the law and the work they did with the New York DAO. Under the guidance of the legendary District Attorney Francis Garrahy, they'd both discovered early in their friendship a mutual admiration for the beauty of the justice system when applied fairly and objectively.

However, even in the courtroom their differences in demeanors stood out. Karp was the methodical, persuasive tactician who wielded dramatic moments — such as when a touch of righteous indignation was called for — like a fencer with a rapier. Guma, with his hot Mediterranean blood, was more emotional in his delivery, also skillful and smart but more likely to use emotion as a cudgel. They were both formidable in court, striking terror in the hearts of the defense bar because they knew they'd be in for a dogfight and there'd be no plea bargain and after conviction the maximum sentence would be imposed.

Sitting on the edge of his bed, Karp knew that Guma could handle anything at the scene and didn't need "the boss" hovering over his shoulder. So he hung up with Fulton and started to turn off the light when the woman beneath the sheets next to him turned over.

"Who's dead?" his wife, Marlene Ciampi, asked.

Turning to look at her, Karp smiled. He was amazed at how she could look so good awakened from a dead sleep. Even though she had one glass eye — a casualty of a letter bomb intended for him many years before — she was still a beautiful woman with short dark curly hair that framed her olive-hued face. The petite body beneath the sheets was still lithe and desirable, though he noted the pink puckered wound where she'd been shot that past summer, a new reminder that the woman he'd married when they were both young assistant district attorneys was pretty as a rose, but also tough as thorns.

"What makes you think that anyone's dead?"

"Well, even if I hadn't been able to hear Fulton clearly, which I could — I swear the man's getting deaf he talks so loud — I could tell by your demeanor and the fact that you were ready to hop out of bed with me and rush off to play with your cop friends. That usually means some sort of murder and mayhem is afoot."

Karp laughed. "Excellent detective work, Ms. Ciampi."

"Thank you. Now give. Who bought the farm?"

"Vince Carlotta," Karp said.

Marlene's playful countenance turned instantly to a frown. "That's horrible," she said. "He seemed like a good guy, at least from what I've read. Remember we met him at that Hell's Kitchen Boys' Club fundraiser? Him and his wife. A good-looking couple, sort of a spring–fall romance; she was lovely and he clearly adored her. I think they recently had a baby."

"Yeah, I remember them," Karp replied. "I've actually run into him a few times over the years. Dockworkers' union guy, tough as nails, but he was also fair and reasonable. The word 'integrity' comes to mind when I think about him, unlike his counterpart, Charlie Vitteli, who's a walking felony if I could just prove it."

"Think Vitteli had something to do with it?" Marlene asked.

Karp considered her comment. His wife did not ask idle questions about murder. She'd once been the head of the DAO's sex crime bureau, and had quit there to start a VIP Security Firm. Most recently, she'd hung up her shingle as a defense attorney/private investigator, working mostly cases in which she felt the justice system was messing up.

"I wouldn't put it past him," Karp replied. "But apparently Carlotta got caught up in an armed robbery outside of Marlon's. I'll know more after Clay fills me in when I get to the office. I'll be heading in early."

"Well then, you better turn off that light and come over here and hold your wife," Marlene said. "This has given me a chill."

"You don't have to ask me twice," he replied, and did as told.

"Hey, Karp! Did ya . . . whoop nuts tits oh boy . . . hear what I asked or not?" Dirty Warren demanded, squinting up at him.

"Uh, sorry, Warren, I got sidetracked," Karp said, pulling himself away from the memory of how the night ended before Marlene let him go back to sleep.

"Uh-huh, you had kind of a funny look

on . . . whoop oh boy . . . your face," Dirty Warren replied. "I said that I . . . whoop . . . had a good trivia question for you."

"Boy, you're a glutton for punishment, but go ahead," Karp said. The two friends had been playing a game of movie trivia for years; Warren had yet to win a single point, but it didn't stop him from trying.

"Yeah, yeah, I'll get you . . . bastard asswipe . . . one of these days," Dirty Warren joked. "So . . . in the cab scene with Marlon Brando and Rod Steiger from which I just did an Oscar-worthy rendition of Marlon's most famous . . . whoop oh boy . . . lines, why are the blinds pulled?"

Karp pursed his lips. "Good one," he said. "Not many people even notice that you can't see out of the windows of the cab. Even fewer know that it's because producer Sam Spiegel forgot to pay for rear-projection equipment, hence nothing playing outside the cab's windows."

"Damn it, Karp, it's not fair," Dirty Warren exclaimed as he hopped up and down. "How can one man's head be so . . . whoop whoop boobs . . . full of worthless trivia?"

"Uh, thanks for the compliment, I think," Karp said. "But I've got to go. Duty awaits."

"Sure, sure," Dirty Warren said. "But just one more." He pulled a piece of crumpled notepaper from the pocket of his dirty jeans. "Okay, okay . . . shit whoop oh boy . . . so there were two inspirations for *On the Waterfront,*" he said, reading from the note. "One was the series of articles written for the *New York Sun* about all the killings, corruption, and extortion on the waterfront in Hell's Kitchen. Can you tell me *who* wrote those articles?"

"Malcolm Johnson. He won the Pulitzer Prize . . . back when it meant something to be a journalist," Karp said.

"Now, now, your feelings for the Fourth Estate are . . . whoop crap oh boy whoop . . . showing and that's my business." Dirty Warren grinned. "But okay, you got that one. Now, what was the other inspiration for the story?"

Karp looked sideways at his friend. "Again, the question is below your usual degree of difficulty and comes with a hidden meaning. The other inspiration was the 1948 murder of a popular union boss. It reinforced what Johnson's stories had said and sort of woke New York up to what was happening down at the docks. It was the beginning of the end for the worst of it, though no one doubts that there's a lot that still goes on under the radar. But I get your point. This is about the murder, isn't it? You know something?"

Dirty Warren looked around as though he feared being overheard. "Word on the street is that this shooting ain't all it's cracked up to be in the press."

Karp looked carefully at his friend. At first brush, Dirty Warren was just a simple news vendor with an odd affliction, but the man had a lot of contacts among the street people and more than once the information he'd given Karp had proven invaluable. "Anything specific?" he asked.

"Not yet . . . oh boy, ohhhhhh boy . . . just rumors that maybe it was a setup," Dirty Warren answered as he handed Karp copies of the two newspapers. "I'll let you know if I . . . piss shit . . . do."

"Okay, thanks, you know I always appreciate it," Karp said, giving his friend a five and then turning to walk around the corner of the building to the secure Leonard Street entrance reserved for judges and the district attorney. Inside, a private elevator deposited him in a small anteroom on the eighth floor outside his inner chambers, a way for him to bypass the reception area.

Fulton and Guma were already waiting for him. The detective was standing at the bookshelf that occupied an entire wall of the office, while Guma kicked back in a big

84

overstuffed leather chair off to one side of Karp's desk with an unlit cigar dangling from his mouth.

"Good morning, gentlemen," Karp greeted them. "Clay, you're looking good for someone I assume was up all night." The big black detective still looked like the college football star he'd once been other than the slightly receding, and graying, hairline on his melon-sized head.

"Thanks, boss," Fulton replied. "And you got that straight."

Turning to his other friend, Karp said, "Guma, well, you don't look much worse than normal."

All three men laughed but it wasn't that long ago that such a remark wasn't such a joke. The once-muscular and spry Guma had been reduced by cancer to a white-haired shell of a man with an old man's body and lines of pain permanently etched into his face. However, his mind and, at least according to his own accounts, libido were in fine shape.

"Very funny," Guma said. "I didn't see you up at two a.m. taking statements from Vitteli and Co. I had to go home and take a hot shower with Mrs. Milquetost just to get the smell off. Charlie was bad enough with the big fake alligator tears. But that Barros character is bad news; he didn't even pretend to be upset."

Trying not to let the image of Guma and his receptionist in a shower together disturb his train of thought too much, Karp settled in behind his desk and got out a yellow legal pad so he could take notes. "So what do we got?"

Fulton tilted his head to the side and twisted his mouth before answering. "First glance, looks like a pretty straight-up robbery. Two bad guys on foot and another in a getaway car. Carlotta apparently went for his gun and one of the guys blasted him. They took off with wallets and watches."

"Any witnesses?"

"Yeah," Fulton said. "Vitteli, Barros, and Jackie Corcione, the union attorney and son of the founder, were all there. Apparently there'd been some sort of meeting to patch things up between them regarding the election. They were walking to their cars when it went down."

"How convenient," Karp said. "I guess we know what their alibis will be."

"Yeah, pretty airtight," Fulton replied, rolling his eyes. "Anyway, they were just getting ready to move the body when I got there. I talked to the officers and detectives on scene. Goom handled the witness statements and we've been all over the reports. I agree with my main man here, something stinks, but we got nothing right now to prove it."

"Anybody else see anything?" Karp asked.

"Carlotta's driver, a guy named Randy McMahon," Fulton said. "He'd been sent to get the car and was just driving back when he saw it go down. But it was dark, and he didn't know what he was looking at. Saw flashes from the gun and two guys running across the street to the getaway car."

"He get a license plate number?"

"No. Just a description: older model, four-door American sedan. Gray primer on the trunk."

Karp made a few notes on his pad, then looked at Guma. "What did you do after you left the scene?"

"I went to talk to some of my people who know what's going on down at the docks," he replied.

"And?"

"And it's no secret there was no love lost between Carlotta and Vitteli, especially after Leo Corcione died," Guma replied. "There was a power struggle, and the union had an election a year ago to decide it. Got pretty ugly. Lot of charges flying around, particularly from Carlotta's side after Vitteli won."

"Any rumors about the shooting from your gangster friends?"

Guma smiled and shrugged. "There's always plenty of rumors. Mob guys like to gossip more than little old ladies. But it's too early to say what's real and not, even for wiseguys with ears to the streets. However, no one I talked to was buying the 'robbery' charade. Also, I found this interesting; the Italians are a little nervous about one of the Russian gangs nosing around the docks. But no one knows if there's a connection to this."

Karp looked at Fulton. "What about you, Clay?"

"I went out to New Rochelle with the detective assigned to talk to the widow."

"How's she doing?"

"Not well," Fulton replied. "I guess she collapsed when she was told by a captain with the New Rochelle Police Department. The paramedics had her drugged up when we got there, but she was pretty much in shock and crying nonstop. Tough thing to see; she obviously loved him. She kept saying that she begged her husband not to go to the meeting and claims that Vitteli is behind it. She couldn't provide anything to go on. But it could be worth talking to her again when she's had a chance to pull herself together."

"I take it Vitteli and his guys all told the same story?"

"Practically word for word, which is suspicious enough," Guma replied. "Two males jumped out of an alley, at least one of them with a gun, and demanded their wallets. Carlotta apparently was packing a .380 and tried to draw down on the gunman but got beat to the punch and took one in the chest and another to the head. He was gone by the time the paramedics arrived. I don't know if you've had a chance to look at the papers yet, but there's a photo of Charlie Vitteli slumped against the wall with blood on his hands. He says he tried to give Carlotta CPR."

"I'll bet," Karp replied sarcastically. "Somehow I think a photograph of him with blood on his hands may be apropos when all is said and done."

"Maybe," Fulton said. "But Vitteli's a crafty son of a bitch. You can bet that if he's involved, there isn't going to be a lot pointing directly at him."

"Probably not," Karp agreed. "But what about Vitteli's men? Maybe there's a weak link."

"I'll stay on the boys over at homicide," Fulton said. "Maybe call Vitteli's guys in one at a time for a few questions. Might get somebody to slip up."

"I'll bet somebody already has," Karp said. "We just need to figure out who."

5

"Hey, *detka,* come here, baby," Alexei Bebnev shouted drunkenly as he grabbed at the waitress, who slapped his hand away from her hip and deftly moved past the table where he sat with Frank DiMarzo. A wave of anger passed over his face as the woman disappeared into the crowd at the bar, but then the Russian laughed as he glanced at his companion. "I don't want that *telka* anyway; she's a fat bitch. Plenty of fish in sea, right, my friend?"

DiMarzo smiled though he disliked the Russian and wished he was elsewhere. It had been a week since the murder of Vince Carlotta and the guilt weighed on him. All he had to do was close his eyes and he'd see the look on the doomed man's face when Charlie Vitteli grabbed his arm and the first bullet slammed home. *"You son of a bitch!"* The words echoed in his mind and caused his gut to clench as though they'd been directed at him and not Vitteli. He heard them again as he watched the evening news coverage of Carlotta's funeral and saw the man's grieving widow holding his infant son.

Only at the moment of the shooting did DiMarzo realize that Vitteli was behind the plot. He'd of course recognized him as well as the other four men from the photograph that had been ripped out of the magazine and assumed that Joey Barros, pictured in the magazine and present at the murder, was the "Joey" who Bebnev met, with Marat Lvov, to set up the assassination. And Bebnev's account of the comment he overheard that "Charlie wants this done ASAP" could have only meant Vitteli.

The photograph was now safely tucked away inside the Bible on a bookshelf in his childhood room at his parents' modest brick row house in Red Hook. He wasn't sure why he was reluctant to get rid of it — after all, it might be evidence to connect him to the crime — but something told him the photo could be important later, so he stashed it.

He just wanted to be done with it all, but things kept dragging out. Three days after the murder, Bebnev had paid him eight thousand to split with Gnat Miller. When he complained that they were owed another six thousand, the Russian said he needed to collect the rest from Lvov, which was why they were now sitting in a noisy club in the Little Odessa area of Brighton Beach, Brooklyn.

At first, DiMarzo wondered why Bebnev insisted that he accompany him to the club. The Russian made it sound like he just wanted to party before handing over the money. But looking around, DiMarzo figured that his partner in crime wanted backup.

DiMarzo was a tough kid from a bad neighborhood, but the crowd in the club was made up of some of the roughest-looking men he'd ever seen in one place. Many of the rugged Slavic faces bore scars and disfigured noses; the predominant language was Russian spoken in loud, coarse shouts over the repetitive pounding of Euro/techno/Russian music, and he knew that many of the dark tattoos he could see on various arms and necks represented Russian Mafia affiliations. Everybody, including the women — some of whom looked as tough as the men — seemed to be dressed in black leather.

Making DiMarzo even more nervous, Bebnev apparently felt so emboldened by his presence and several beers that his boasts about pulling off "the job" kept growing in volume. He also made a show of pulling out a fat roll of bills to pay for their drinks, tipping the waitress lavishly. DiMarzo noticed that some of the clientele were paying attention.

"You see look on asshole's face," Bebnev shouted over the music. He laughed as he made his fingers into a gun. "It was like, 'Oh shit, man, now I'm going to die.' And 'bang, bang,' I make it happen, fucking damn straight, man."

"Not so loud," DiMarzo said. "You're talking too much."

"Fuck that, *sooka,*" the Russian replied, slurring his words. "These are my people. And no one fucks with Alexei Bebnev."

At that moment, a fat, bald man entered the pool hall followed by a couple of big, thuggish-looking men dressed all in black and wearing sunglasses. The fat man looked around the bar until his eyes settled on Bebnev.

"There's the money now," Bebnev told DiMarzo. He waved at the fat man and yelled. "Marat! *Zdraast vooee che!* Come sit!"

Lvov saw the wave and headed for the table, followed by his goons. He did not look happy.

"Who is this?" the fat man asked, nodding at DiMarzo.

"Just a friend," Bebnev replied. "He sometimes is great assistant, if you follow me."

Lvov looked DiMarzo over with small, piggish eyes set in mounds of pink flesh and said, "Then he will not mind leaving us."

"Not at all," DiMarzo said, getting up before Bebnev had a chance to say anything. He headed for the door, and without looking back walked across the street to wait beneath the elevated Q train tracks.

A few minutes later, the fat man emerged, followed by his entourage. He spotted DiMarzo and studied him for a few moments before saying something to one of his men, who also gave DiMarzo a hard look. He had made his mind up to run if they decided to cross the street toward him, but instead the trio walked up to a dark sedan parked illegally in front of the bar, got in, and drove away.

When they were gone, Bebnev emerged from the bar. He, too, saw DiMarzo and sauntered over.

As the young Russian walked up, DiMarzo noticed that Bebnev had a fresh bruise surrounding one eye that was well on its way to swelling shut. "What happened to you?" DiMarzo asked.

"A misunderstanding," Bebnev said. "Sort of like initiation. Me and Lvov are like brothers now."

Some brothers, DiMarzo thought. *More like the fat guy didn't like Bebnev's big mouth.* But he didn't say anything. He just wanted his money and to get the hell out of Little Odessa. "He pay you?"

Bebnev nodded, pulled an envelope from the inner pocket of his leather coat, and offered it to DiMarzo. "Here is four thousand."

"Four? You owe me and Gnat six," DiMarzo complained.

"That was before this," Bebnev said, pointing to his eye. "I take all risks, you do shit. Take it or leave it."

DiMarzo snatched the envelope from Bebnev's hand. "We're done, asshole," he spat. "Don't call and don't come around."

"Fine, little *pedik,*" Bebnev snarled. "I don't hang with homos. I have new friends."

"Yeah, I can see that," DiMarzo replied. He turned to leave but stopped when he saw a large man who'd just come out of the bar standing across the street staring at them.

Even from that distance, he could see that the man had a long, jagged scar running from the top of his big bald head, across his nose, and down to the jawline on the other side. Although it was winter and cold outside, he was wearing a T-shirt that seemed to barely contain his muscular chest and arms, which were covered with dark tattoos. The man took a drag on a cigarette and tossed it down in the gutter without taking his eyes off DiMarzo and Bebnev.

"I think I'd avoid that bar for a while," DiMarzo said to Bebnev, nodding toward the man.

Bebnev looked in the direction indicated and DiMarzo saw him swallow hard. But he managed a weak smile. "I'm not afraid of him," he said. "But I have other things to do."

With that, Bebnev scurried off down Brighton Beach Boulevard in the direction of Coney Island. DiMarzo watched him go, and when he turned to look back across the street, the large man was gone. He shuddered and trotted up the stairs to the train station above. *If I never see Bebnev and Little Odessa again, it will be too soon,* he thought as he pulled out his cell phone and called his friend Gnat Miller.

6

Marlene paused outside the East Village Women's Shelter to wait for three raggedy, middle-aged women to move from her path into the building. Noting the tattered layers of clothing, she marveled that such people survived the brutal winter months in New York City, where sunlight rarely made its way down through and between buildings to warm the streets. She knew there were never enough beds in shelters to house Gotham's street people, nor, for that matter, enough space on steam grates or protected nooks around buildings to shelter them from the elements.

On closer inspection, these three seemed livelier than most, more like hard-luck gypsies than down-and-out street people as they huddled together while carrying on an animated conversation. One was a large black woman who'd stuffed her copious dreadlocks beneath a colorful scarf and rolled her eyes and muttered; the other two were white, at least beneath the grime that coated their faces, one thick and the other perilously thin. But they didn't seem to belong to the streets like other homeless people, at least to Marlene; it was more like they were acting out parts in a play.

Nor did they seem to belong at this shelter. The former deli on Avenue C and 6th Street wasn't a way station for the homeless, but a refuge for women from many walks of life trying to escape violent domestic situations.

The shelter had been started by Mattie Duran, a stocky, combative woman with long dark hair, a swarthy complexion, and an even blacker personality. She'd executed her stepfather, in his sleep, the man who raped her since childhood, and she'd served time in prison, which had done little to improve her social skills or outlook on life. Fifteen years earlier, she'd shown up in New York City with a trunk full of cash obtained under mysterious, probably violent, circumstances. She used the money to open the shelter as a place of refuge for women and children in immediate danger from the men in their lives.

After opening, Duran refused all funding from national, state, and local governmental resources. She wasn't going to let them have that kind of control over how she ran her shelter. Instead, after her own money ran out, she relied on private donations to stay open.

Marlene started volunteering at the shelter not long after it accepted its first client. She was in a dark period of her life as well, pushing the boundaries of the law as well as her marriage when dealing with men who abused women. She'd even killed a few — always in self-defense, though she'd certainly put herself in positions where the violence had been inevitable. That little fact had earned her Duran's grudging acceptance if not her friendship. Nor had Duran turned down the substantial funds that Marlene donated, which had earned a gruff "thank you," but little else.

Mattie had disappeared several years earlier. No one knew if it was because the mercurial woman, who had never been able to quiet the ghosts of her own disturbed past, had decided to try a different path to peace. Or perhaps one of the many enemies she'd made over the years had finally caught her in a moment of carelessness and silenced the ghosts forever.

Marlene had devoted quite a bit of time and money to trying to locate Duran but had come up with nothing. However, she continued to donate money and volunteer at the shelter and knew the type of clientele it served, most of whom didn't carry themselves with the same confidence and aplomb as the three women she was speaking to now.

"When do you want to meet again?" Marlene heard one of them ask the others.

"In thunder, lightning, or rain?" the black woman added in a thick Jamaican accent.

Suddenly, the woman who'd spoken first noticed Marlene and poked the other white woman, who had her back to her, in the shoulder and nodded. "Here she is now, Anne," she said. "Go on, tell her what you know."

Marlene smiled as Anne turned and saw her. A fleeting storm of emotions — fear, uncertainty, anger — played across the woman's face. "Tell me what, Anne?" Marlene asked.

"Are you Marlene Ciampi, the wife of the district attorney?" Anne responded.

Marlene's expression turned serious. Plenty of people asked her that question, but rarely just out of curiosity. "I am," she replied. "Why do you want to know?"

The woman's face contorted as if mirroring some internal debate, but then she shook her head. "Nothing, it's nothing," she said. "Sorry to bother you."

The woman turned back toward her friends. But Marlene reached out and touched her arm. "Really? Nothing?" she asked. "Your friends seem to think you have something important to tell me, something to do with my husband."

Though she didn't turn back around to face Marlene, the woman's shoulders sank and she sighed. "Not so much your husband as Charlie Vitteli and Vince Carlotta," she said.

Marlene's radar suddenly went on full alert. Her husband had told her about Dirty Warren's remarks that the murder was a "setup," as well as Butch's own suspicions that Charlie Vitteli was somehow involved. In the weeks that had passed since the murder, there'd been plenty of rumors phoned into the police and DAO, but so far no leads had panned out, nor had any credible witnesses stepped forward. This woman might be just another street person who tended to mix fantasy with reality, but Marlene had been around long enough to know that sometimes the information that tipped the scales of justice came from the most unusual places. "What about them?" she asked.

The woman turned and looked at her for

a long moment and seemed about to speak, but then her hand went to her mouth. "I don't want to get involved," she said. "Nothing good ever comes of it."

"If you're afraid, my husband can arrange for your protection," Marlene said. "And I'll help, too. What's your last name, Anne?"

The woman backed away from Marlene as if Marlene were holding a poisonous snake. "No one could protect my Sean; no one could protect Mr. Carlotta," she said. "And you can't protect me. No one gives a shit about me."

Marlene took a step toward the woman as she tried to think of what to say to assuage the woman's fears. But the other two edged between her and Anne.

"Scared she is," the other white woman warned.

"Too much trouble," added the black woman.

"I understand that, but if you know something that could help solve a murder . . ." Marlene tried to continue, sensing that this woman might be aware of something important.

At that moment the steel door of the shelter opened and an enormous man the size of her husband and Clay Fulton put together emerged and walked up to the women. Mark DiGregorio provided the daytime security for the women's shelter. No violent boyfriends, husbands, stalkers, or other miscreants ever made it past his vigilant eyes or prodigious girth; those who tried once never tried again.

"Good morning, Marlene, are these ladies bothering you?" he asked, eyeing the three women suspiciously. "They've been asking for you all morning but don't seem to have any real business with the shelter."

"No business with you, mon," the black woman said, scowling up at him. She then looked at her friends. "With this woman, yes. But not today, says Anne, so let's go, my weird sisters."

"Wait," Marlene said. "Tell me where I can find you."

The other white woman cackled. "On the heath, of course." And with that, the three hurried down the sidewalk toward Houston Street.

As she watched them go, Marlene shook her head. "Weird sisters is right. Guess it takes all sorts, eh, Mark?"

DiGregorio grinned. "My family, including my parents, my sister, and me, spent a lot of time as missionaries in Jamaica teaching English and the gospel. All that juju gives me the creeps. Let's just say I heard a

104

lot of strange stories about witches and shit like that, and sometimes there's more to this old world than we can see."

Marlene nodded. "I agree, and I think there's more to those three than meets the eye, too. If you ever find out anything about them, or they come looking for me again, give me a call."

"You got it, sister," DiGregorio replied with a laugh as he hurried up the stairs to open the door for her.

Walking into the shelter, Marlene made her way to the office of the shelter's new director, Bobbi Sue Hirschbein. "Good morning, Bobbi Sue," she said after she'd knocked and been invited in. "Got anything you'd like me to do first?"

A tall, austere woman who tied her long gray hair back into a bun that made her face more severe than necessary, Hirschbein had been the assistant director when Duran disappeared. She'd had her own horrific experiences with domestic violence; her alcoholic ex-husband after years of beatings and emotional abuse had shot her and left her for dead before committing suicide. She could be tough when it came to championing the shelter's mission and fierce in her defense of women who needed help. But, unlike Duran, she had not let one man's cruelty change her kind and gentle nature, nor cause her to blame all men for the actions of some.

Marlene always suspected that Duran recognized that she needed someone to balance her grim outlook with a more positive perspective when she appointed Hirschbein to the position. After Mattie disappeared and it was clear she wasn't coming back anytime soon, the shelter's board of directors, which included Marlene, had promoted Bobbi Sue and never regretted the decision.

"Good morning, Marlene," Hirschbein replied, her sudden smile making her look ten years younger. "Yes, if you don't mind. A seventeen-year-old with an infant came in a few nights ago. She told us her boyfriend hit her — she's got a pretty good black eye and a split lip; said that it was the first time and that he's been acting out of character. She thinks he's in some sort of trouble and took it out on her. But after that she clammed up and won't give us his name or press charges."

"What's her name?" Marlene asked.

"Nicoli Lopez," Hirschbein replied. "Says she lives in the Bronx now, and she's originally from Brooklyn but her father won't let her come home."

"Want me to talk to her?"

"Yeah, if you would. Maybe you can get her to open up. I'll send someone to bring her to the room."

A few minutes later, Marlene was sitting in what the staff called "the Room," or "the Room of Tears," a small, but comfortable place that looked more like a young woman's bedroom than where battered women were asked to describe why they'd come to the shelter. The room had once been not much different than an interview room at a police station with its plain, unadorned walls and institutional furniture. But it had softened under Hirschbein's direction with some of Marlene's money. Landscapes and still-life paintings dominated the wall art; light was provided by windows and lamps rather than harsh fluorescents; and the furniture consisted of overstuffed chairs and a fainting couch with a small coffee table in front of it.

Marlene had settled on the couch when there was a knock; a frightened-looking Hispanic teenager entered. Noting the girl's swollen lip and a purple bruise around her eye, Marlene felt the old anger surge in her again. Few things in the world raised her ire like men beating on women. She smiled as much to calm herself as to reassure the teen.

"Hi, have a seat," Marlene said warmly. "Are you Nicoli?"

The young woman nodded but didn't speak as she sat down in the chair across from Marlene.

"Nice to meet you. I'm Marlene Ciampi. I'm an attorney and private investigator, and I volunteer here at the shelter, where I try to help determine how to keep you safe and, if necessary, deal with the person who did this to you. I understand you have an infant."

The girl looked up and smiled slightly. "Yes. Billy Junior. He's six months."

"Such a nice age," Marlene said. "I'd give anything to go back and relive those days with my own kids."

"How many do you have?"

"Three. A girl . . . or I should say, a young woman now; she's going to be married next fall . . . and twin boys in high school."

"Wow, you don't look that old," Nicoli responded.

Marlene laughed. "Well, thank you. But I think I'm supposed to be helping you, not fishing for compliments." Noting that the teenager seemed to be relaxing, she forged ahead. "I'm sorry about what happened to you, and I know it's difficult to talk about, but I understand that your boyfriend hit you. If that's true, then we need to make sure that behavior doesn't continue and that you and your baby are safe, whether you and your boyfriend remain together as a couple or not."

Nicoli's smile disappeared and she lowered her eyes. "He didn't mean to," she mumbled.

Marlene frowned. "That's a pretty good black eye to get from somebody who didn't mean to. Maybe there were extenuating circumstances, but that didn't give him the right to hurt you."

The girl remained quiet and a tear fell from her cheek onto the table. She sighed. "What I meant is that it wasn't like him to hit me," she said. "Bill's usually really nice and puts up with a lot, especially from my dad before we moved out. He's never hit me before."

"There's a first time for everything, honey," Marlene said. "The important thing is to make sure there's not a repeat performance. If he needs to get counseling, maybe we can do something about that."

Nicoli looked at Marlene again through teary eyes. "He never used to even yell at me until . . ." Again, the teen stopped talking and looked away.

"Until what?" Marlene asked.

Nicoli shrugged. "I don't really know," she said. "He got involved in something. I could tell he was nervous, or scared about it, but he said it was going to pay a lot of money and then we could get our own apartment. Things were going to be good for us."

"So what happened?"

"About three or four weeks ago, sometime before Christmas anyway, I started noticing changes in him," Nicoli said. "I'd wake up at night, and he wouldn't be in bed. He'd be standing over by the window, staring outside. A couple of times, I'm pretty sure he was crying. But when I asked him what was wrong, he'd tell me to mind my own business."

"You think maybe he committed a crime?"

The girl's lips twisted. Then she nodded. "I think he did something with his friend, Frankie DiMarzo," she said. "Frankie's no good. They met in juvie and Frankie is always trying to get him to do stuff they shouldn't. My Gnat's no angel —"

"Gnat?" Marlene interrupted.

"It's Bill's nickname," Nicoli explained. "Anyway, this wasn't their usual bullshit crime, like selling pot or a grab-and-run at a liquor store. I heard him talking to Frankie on the phone after whatever it was they did and he was pretty upset. He said, 'That Russian fucker didn't tell us this was big-time. Now it's all over the papers. I want my money and then I want to forget about it.' "

Marlene frowned. "All over the papers? Any idea what he was talking about?"

"No. A couple of days before that he went somewhere in his car with Frankie. He didn't get home till late, and the car smelled like cigarettes."

"He doesn't smoke?"

"Uh-uh," Nicoli said. "Neither does Frankie. Gnat used to, but he quit because of the baby. Now he just chews tobacco. It's disgusting, but he says it calms him down."

"So you think it was something he did that night that has him on edge?"

The girl thought about it for a moment, then shook her head. "No. He was nervous and wasn't sleeping good after that, but he went out again with Frankie, and whoever smokes the cigarettes, again a few nights later. That's when he changed. The call to Frankie about the Russian guy was after that."

"He say anything more on the phone to Frankie?"

"No. He turned and saw me standing in the doorway. He told Frankie he had to go. He was pissed off that I was listening."

"Is that when he hit you?"

"No . . . at least not right away. I asked him again what was up, and he said nothing and told me to quit sneaking around," Nicoli replied. "That night he got up again and was crying, so I asked him again. He got mad and things got out of hand from there. He called me some names, and I told him I was taking Billy Junior and going back to my folks. He tried to stop me from leaving, so I pushed him. That's when he hit me."

Nicoli stopped talking and her chin fell to her chest as her shoulders shook and a sob escaped. "I'm so worried about him," she said at last. "He's a good guy, he really is. He tries so hard. I just think he's in something over his head."

"Sounds like it," Marlene replied. "But what? Maybe I could talk to him sometime and if he needs help . . ."

"That's what I told him after he hit me . . . that he needs help."

"And what did he say?"

"That no one could help him now."

7

Jackie Corcione looked at himself in the mirror and didn't like what he saw. But it wasn't the beginnings of a receding hairline or the still-faint lines etched around the corners of his mouth and eyes that troubled him. The small pot belly and the random gray hairs he couldn't seem to keep dyed weren't the big concern. Nor were the dark circles under his eyes from lack of sleep, though they were a consequence.

It was the accusations he saw in those eyes that disturbed him. *Murderer. Betrayer. Coward.* Or the last words of Vince Carlotta, *"You son of a bitch!"*

Jackie leaned closer to the mirror to see the man behind those eyes, the one making the accusations. But there was no one.

Judas. The voice inside his head almost screamed the name at him, and he stepped back from his reflection. He took a deep breath and then let it out slowly. Vince Carlotta had never done anything to him. Quite the contrary, he'd always treated Jackie like a kid brother. He was always the one with a kind word or praise when his own father mostly registered disappointment.

Although he'd never told Vince that he was gay, he was pretty sure that Carlotta knew his secret and had not judged him. Never called him a faggot or queer or pansy like Vitteli and Barros. Never threatened to tell his father. *And yet look who you're in bed with,* he thought.

Greed had done him in and set him on this course he seemed unable to alter. He liked nice things, nice clothing, and nice, good-looking friends who fawned over him as long as he was paying the bills. He liked going to trendy clubs and throwing money around. He liked taking those friends and lovers to Broadway shows and the latest, hottest restaurants in Manhattan. He lived in a 3,500-square-foot loft atop a former warehouse overlooking the Hudson River in gentrified Hell's Kitchen, and took frequent vacations to the Hamptons and Martha's Vineyard and Key West. He gladly played the part of a young, successful gay man in New York City. But it took money, lots of money, more than he made.

So he'd started stealing from the union.

At first it was just a little bit, just pocket money. Then it was more and more, though it never seemed enough to keep up with his needs. He told himself that he deserved it and that it made up for his father's lack of faith in him. And as chief financial officer and legal counsel, it was easy to hide the transgressions. He thought he could get away with it forever.

Then one day several years before Leo's death, Vitteli walked into Jackie's office at the union headquarters, followed by Barros, who closed the door behind them. "I know you're cooking the books," Vitteli stated flatly. "Joey's been asking around, and there's no way your salary covers your little habits."

Jackie felt a ball of cold fear settle in his stomach and radiate out into the rest of his body, but he tried to lie his way out of it. "My dad gives me money on the side," he explained. "Sort of an allowance."

Vitteli guffawed while Barros smirked. "Shit, Jackie, you're a terrible liar," Vitteli said. "You started sweating before I said a word. But tell you what I'm going to do. I'm going to talk to your dad about this 'allowance,' and maybe some of your other habits. We'll see what he says."

"No, please," Jackie had begged. "I'll stop

stealing, I promise. I'll change my lifestyle, I mean it."

The other two men laughed. Then Vitteli put his knuckles on Jackie's desk and leaned forward. "I don't give a shit about your little butt buddies," he sneered. "That's your business as long as you play ball. You've been cooking the books and now I want you to cook them for me. But not this penny-ante bullshit you been getting away with; we're going to go whole hog and you're going to figure out how to do it."

Although it wasn't really necessary, Vitteli had also made it clear that Barros didn't like him. "And Joey is the one guy you don't want showing up in your bedroom some night if you get my drift."

So Jackie had figured out a way to siphon money from the union pension accounts, which was then invested in a lending company that "loaned" the money to a false corporation that listed cronies hired by Vitteli as its owners and corporate officers. That money was then invested in stocks, other companies, and ventures, some of them quite risky but with big upsides.

A quick review of the union financials showed a small but steady return on the investment, but the truth was that the enormous profits generated went into the pock-

116

ets of Vitteli, Barros, and himself.

Still, it was a house of cards, and any number of bad-luck or bad-timing scenarios could send it crashing, losing the pension funds and bankrupting the union. However, Vitteli, Barros, and Jackie would be protected by many layers of obfuscation while the blow to the membership would be explained as a downturn in the economy or investments that had turned sour.

The plan had worked to perfection for several years. In that time, Jackie had made sure that he was the only one who truly understood the ins and outs of the scheme. He was no idiot and wasn't going to leave to chance that Vitteli would consider him to be an asset and not sic Barros on him.

As long as the uneasy alliance lasted, and the status quo was maintained, there was little danger of discovery. However, his father's death had thrown a wrench in the works: he would have to be replaced in an election. And Vitteli was sure that if Carlotta won the election, he'd bring in auditors.

"Bastard doesn't trust me," Vitteli had said to Jackie the day after it was announced that there would be an election for the next union president. "Can't say I blame him. And if he does, they're going to find our

117

little business venture. Then my ass, Joey's ass, and your ass are all going to end up in the joint. Now me and Joey, we'll be okay; we can watch each other's backs and take care of ourselves. But imagine what life is going to be like for your cute little rear end. You'll be some big hairy hillbilly's girlfriend from the day you walk in and hear the gates clang shut behind you. And he won't be gentle."

Terrified by the thought of prison, Jackie had come up with a way to rig the election. He'd also contacted an old Harvard fraternity brother who was working for the Labor Department and asked him to keep an eye out for any complaints from Vince Carlotta or his lawyer, Mahlon Gorman. As a union lawyer, he was well aware of the Landrum-Griffin Act's "exhaustion of union administrative remedies" rule that required any complaints be dealt with first at the union level. To be sure, Carlotta's complaint would be dismissed by union management, but it would only buy them time. He'd still have them over a barrel, and eventually he would have prevailed.

Vince wished it could have been as easy as Charlie and Barros leaving the union, and himself stepping down as union chief legal counsel to work under Gorman. But

Carlotta would have discovered the financial manipulation and he wouldn't have hesitated to go to the district attorney to press charges. That's what Vitteli said when he announced that Vince had to die.

Jackie had recoiled at the suggestion. But reminded again by Vitteli of what his life would be like in prison — "if the membership doesn't kill you first for fucking with their pensions" — he'd agreed. "It's him or us." And so he helped lure Vince into the trap.

Now, a month later, his hands shook and his eyes were often bloodshot, with dark circles. He didn't even want to think of what his father would have thought of him at that moment. *Murderer. Betrayer.* His eyes locked on the stranger in the mirror. *You son of a bitch.*

"Judas," he said aloud. He was suddenly reminded of an article he'd seen in the *Times* announcing the lineup for the summer's Shakespeare in the Park productions. *Macbeth* had been the headliner. It was a play with which he was very familiar, having played the part of Banquo in high school, and a particular quote from the main character sprang to mind: *I am in blood stepped in so far that should I wade no more, returning were as tedious as go o'er.*

Jackie forced himself to stand up straight and look his mirror image in the eyes. *There's no going back,* he thought. *You're just going to have to learn to live with the guilt. It's that or prison.* He shuddered. *And that's not even a choice.*

Leaving the bathroom, Jackie walked out of the bedroom suite and into the living room, where his current boyfriend, Greg Lusk, sat reading the *Times.* Lusk was a big, rugged guy who rode a Harley-Davidson and liked to watch sports on television. He played college football and might have made the pros except for tearing his ACL during his senior college season. When they'd met at Therapy, a gay bar on 52nd Street in Hell's Kitchen, he'd joked that he dated the lead cheerleader but was in love with the quarterback.

Lusk was different than other lovers he'd had in the past. He was a successful entrepreneur who made a good living and didn't look for handouts from Jackie. He was something of a homebody, and while he could dance like Patrick Swayze and looked great in a tux, he preferred a good book and dinner at home to the club and restaurant scene.

Looking up when Jackie entered the room, he smiled and said, "Hey, good-looking, you off to your meeting with the boss and his pal?"

Jackie barely managed to smile back. "Yeah," he said without enthusiasm. "I shouldn't be too late."

Greg frowned. "You okay?" he asked. "You've been looking like you got the weight of the world on your shoulders, and I'm getting worried. You want me to go with you?"

"No, I wouldn't subject you to those guys. I'm fine," Jackie replied. "Just tired. You be here when I get back?"

Greg grinned and nodded. "Until you tell me different, Jackie," he said, "I'm here to stay."

Jackie shook his head. "You're too good to be true. I don't deserve you."

Greg walked over and gave him a hug. "You're too hard on yourself, sweetheart," he said. "You're a good man. Now you be safe out there."

Jackie patted Greg on the shoulder. "I will," he said and left the apartment before he broke down and started crying.

A taxi waited for him at the curb and took him to a warehouse on the Hudson waterfront that Vitteli sometimes used to meet at when he didn't want to be seen. He was waiting with Barros when Jackie arrived, their breath coming out in clouds of condensation inside the unheated building.

"Ah, here's the prodigal son now." Vitteli grinned. "How's Jackie today?"

Ignoring the stare from Barros, Jackie shrugged. "I'm okay," he said. "Just a little tired."

Vitteli nodded. "Good, good," he said. "You know, Jackie, I wish things could have been different with Vince. But it had to be done, or all of us would have been neighbors at Sing Sing."

"We might still be," Jackie pointed out.

"Not if everybody keeps his damned mouth shut," Barros growled, but left it at that after a look from Vitteli.

An uncomfortable silence fell, but only for a moment before Sal Amaya poked his head in the door and said that their guest was arriving. A minute later, a fat, bald man entered the warehouse, followed by two large bodyguards.

"Marat Lvov," Vitteli said with a smile, extending his hand. "Thank you for coming."

"Always a pleasure, my old friend," Lvov replied as they shook hands. He looked around and shivered. "Perhaps there is a warmer place to have this conversation."

"I apologize, but I'd rather no one saw us together, and I won't keep you long," Vitteli said.

"Yes, of course. You said there was something urgent?"

"Maybe," Vitteli said. "It's come to my attention that the man you hired for our little project has been overheard boasting in a bar over on your side of the East River. One of my associates over there heard him and while he wasn't giving any details, you know how these things go. Too many shots of vodka and he lets something slip."

Lvov scowled. "If there's a problem, I will take care of it."

Vitteli shook his head. "I want your guy to take care of his pals, if you know what I mean. Then Joey will deal with your problem after they've had a little talk."

Lvov thought about it for a moment and then shrugged. "I don't give shit about him. He is nothing."

"Good, then you'll let me know how to find this fucker after he's put his two pals in the ground."

"His name is Alexei Bebnev. I will get back to you with how to locate him. He moves around a lot." Lvov held out his hands. "My apologies. It was not part of plan to have so many involved."

Vitteli looked hard at the Russian for a moment. "No, it wasn't. You told me it would be one guy, a guy who knew how to

123

keep his mouth shut. I gave you fifty thou to get it done. You go cheap on me, get some numbskull?"

Lvov's fat face darkened. "Of course not," he said, scowling as he looked at his bodyguards, which seemed to give him nerve. "Do not be angry with me. You know who my friends are in Little Odessa."

"Fuck your friends, we have friends, too," Barros said, keeping his eyes on the bodyguards. "Get us what we need."

Lvov glared at Barros but then smiled. "Look at us," he said to Vitteli, "fighting like a couple of dollar whores over a customer. I will be happy to get you information; then we can share a friendly drink someday when it is all over, no?"

Vitteli looked like he was going to say something, but then smiled back. "You're right. We'll take care of this mouthy bastard and his friends and drink a toast again like old friends."

A few minutes later, after Lvov and his bodyguards had left the warehouse, Jackie turned to his fellow conspirators. "When does it end?"

"What's that, Jackie?" Vitteli asked. "Did you say something?"

"I said, when will the killing end? First it was Vince. If he actually was the first,"

Jackie said, looking at Barros. "But Vince for sure, and now these guys?"

"What do you care about 'these guys,' Jackie?" Vitteli said, gesturing the sign for quotes around "these guys." "They're punks. They'll put a gun to your head for a few thousand bucks and pull the trigger. The world will be better off without them."

"It's still murder."

"Uh-oh, someone developed a conscience," Barros sneered.

"They're loose ends, Jackie," Vitteli said. "Something happens and one of them gets popped for some small-time beef and suddenly they want to talk and make deals. The mouthy Russian is one thing. Joey will take care of him. I don't know what the other two punks have been told — not much, probably, but still, I don't want to take any chances."

Jackie's head dropped. *I am in blood stepped in so far that should I wade no more, returning were as tedious as go o'er.* "Yeah, we don't really have a choice," he said at last. "Even if we wanted to, there's no undoing the past."

8

The disembodied voice of Karp's receptionist, Darla Milquetost, suddenly crackled
over the intercom sitting on his desk. "Mr.
Karp, Mr. Gorman called to say he's running a couple of minutes late, but he's
downstairs and will be right up."

"Thank you, Darla, send him in when he
arrives," Karp replied into the intercom and
then sat back as he looked across his big
mahogany desk. Guma was sitting in his
cushy club chair; Fulton was standing at
the window behind Guma looking east,
watching the foot traffic eight floors below
in the park that separated Chinatown from
the Criminal Courts Building.

As the lead men for his office in the Carlotta murder case, Karp had asked Guma
and Fulton to the meeting with Mahlon
Gorman, who'd identified himself as the
victim's attorney when he called the day before. "It wasn't an armed robbery," he'd

126

said at the time. "It was an assassination, and Charlie Vitteli was behind it."

"Do you have any proof of that?" Karp had asked without saying anything about his own suspicions.

"Not yet," Mahlon said. "But maybe I can add to what you know and talk a little about motive. But I'd rather do it in person if you can spare the time."

Karp had agreed, and an hour before the meeting, he'd asked Guma and Fulton to come to his office so they could go over the case before Gorman arrived, including the rumors on the streets about Vitteli's involvement.

"It's not hard to believe," Fulton said as he stepped back from the window. "Vitteli's dirty and everybody knows it. The problem is that nobody's got any hard proof, but everybody knows somebody who knows something."

"Typical," Karp said with a shake of the head. "If Vitteli's behind this, we'll have to find the killers and then pyramid the case from the bottom up."

"Could be tough if he brought in somebody from the outside," Fulton said.

"That's the way the old-time Mafia would have done it," Guma agreed. "Fly a couple of guys over from Sicily, and then after the job gets done, send them home on the next plane."

The truth was, there were few real leads. Vitteli, Barros, and Corcione were all sticking to their story that two unknown masked gunmen had jumped out of the alley and demanded their wallets; Carlotta tried to pull a gun but the other guy was quicker. Carlotta's driver had been sent ahead to get the car and only arrived back in time to see the getaway car drive off — a late-model sedan with gray primer and New York plates. A waiter had witnessed what appeared to be a minor altercation inside Marlon's, but the men had appeared to patch things up by the time they left.

"Or that's their story, anyway," Fulton said. "We don't have any good descriptions of the shooter or his buddies. No solid links to Vitteli, either, other than we know they didn't like each other. Rumors are flying on the streets, but I don't have to tell you that conspiracy theories are a dime a dozen in Gotham."

"What about the widow? Antonia Carlotta?" Karp asked.

"She's convinced that Vitteli's behind it," Fulton replied. "She says that her husband thought Vitteli stole the election for union president and that Vitteli asked for the meeting to discuss stepping down. But she doesn't have anything to prove it was a setup."

"Anything new from Dirty Warren?" Guma asked.

Karp shook his head. "Not much. He says that according to the grapevine, there was another witness to the shooting who can finger Vitteli. He's got feelers out, but so far this alleged witness isn't coming forward."

A knock on the door stopped the conversation. Darla Milquetost opened the door and then gestured for the visitor to walk through.

As he stood to greet him, Karp was surprised when he saw Mahlon Gorman. He'd been expecting an older man, not the boyish-looking attorney who strode up to shake his hand.

"Mr. Karp, a pleasure to meet you. I'm a longtime admirer," Gorman said.

"Thank you," Karp replied and then introduced the others. "The gentleman in front of the desk is Special Assistant District Attorney Ray Guma, who's been involved in the case from the beginning, and the big guy over by the bookshelf is Detective Sergeant Clay Fulton of the NYPD, currently assigned to my office. He also went to the scene that night and has been the liaison between the NYPD homicide division and this office regarding Mr. Carlotta's murder."

The introductions over, Karp pointed to the seat next to Guma and invited Gorman to sit down. "We're all ears," he said, flipping to a new page on his yellow legal pad.

Gorman nodded. "Thanks, I appreciate your time. As I said on the phone, this so-called robbery was a ruse. There's a reason that Vince Carlotta was singled out and shot, and that reason is Charlie Vitteli. As I said, I can't prove that yet, and you're better equipped to do it anyway, so let me just begin with a little history."

With that, Gorman launched into how the North American Brotherhood of Stevedores was formed by Leo Corcione as an alternative to the International Longshoremen's Association for local unions who either didn't like the tactics or the impersonal size of the best known of the dockworker unions. As the size of NABS grew, so did interest in absorbing it from the International, as well as attempts by the mob to control it. Tough and smart, Corcione had fought to keep his union free, "sometimes in court, but, when occasion called for it, with bats and fists, too.

"And starting some twenty years ago,

wherever the old man made a stand, Vince would be there at his side, and in fairness, so would Vitteli," Gorman added.

Although both of the younger men were dedicated to the union, they were different as wine and whiskey. "Vince was always about the workers and identified with them first, never forgetting his roots. Charlie liked the power the union represented. He also liked the trappings of power, too — the nice cars, the silk shirts, the big house, the expensive vacations. But where they were really different, at least to me and I've known them both for about ten years, was that Vince was comfortable in his own skin. If Leo had never put him in management, he would have been fine working on the docks. But Charlie, he's always looking over his shoulder, wondering who's talking behind his back. Oh, he comes off as the tough, confident guy, but he's paranoid as hell and needs to feel important. I think that's part of what eventually led to all of this."

"How do you mean?" Karp asked.

"I think he knew that Leo was going to name Vince as his heir apparent," Gorman said. "And I don't think he could handle the thought of playing number two to Vince. When the old man died first, events played right into his hands. It meant an election, but Charlie wasn't going to win it — the men, most of them anyway, identify with Vince — so he cheated and we caught him."

Gorman explained how he and Carlotta had taken their complaint to the U.S. Department of Labor only to be rebuffed. "Applicable federal law says we had to exhaust all of our remedies through the union management first, which meant we had to tip our hand to Vitteli. Of course, Vitteli and his guys rejected the complaint, so we were preparing to go back to the Labor Department, and if that didn't work, we were going to seek redress in federal court here in the Southern District."

"So you think Vitteli had Carlotta killed because you uncovered election fraud?" Guma asked.

"That's part of it," Gorman replied. "But as I said, Charlie liked power and everything that went with it. He and his cronies live a pretty high lifestyle that's hard to justify with their salaries, which are good but not that good. But it would be hard to prove — Leo's son, Jackie, is in Vitteli's back pocket and he's the CFO — unless we could get our own auditors in there, and that wasn't going to happen unless Vitteli was out and Vince was in. That's why Charlie had to win that election."

"So Vitteli wins but you guys figure out he cheated," Fulton said.

"Right," Gorman agreed. "We think he had a guy at the Labor Department filling him in on what we were up to, and of course we had to file that formal complaint with the union. So while he didn't have all of our cards on the table, he knew he was in trouble. That's why I believe he called Vince and wanted to meet so that they could 'work things out,' his words."

"Did Vince believe him?"

"No. In fact, he was pretty sure that Vitteli sent some guys out to his house to try to intimidate him a few days earlier."

"Really? I hadn't heard about this," Fulton interjected.

"Yeah, three guys showed up at the house acting like they were looking for work," Gorman said. "Vince wasn't convinced. He took down their license plate number on a notepad and showed it to me."

Karp leaned forward. "Do you have the note?"

Gorman shook his head. "No. Vince was pretty ticked off about those guys coming to his house. He was going to confront Vitteli about it."

"There were three guys at the scene," Fulton pointed out.

"I've thought about that," Gorman said. "And I wish I'd asked Vince more about them. I know he said one of them spoke with an accent, Russian or something like that. But I should have asked him for a description."

"Was Vince worried?" Guma asked.

Gorman thought about it for a moment and then shrugged. "Maybe for his wife and son," he said. "But he was a tough guy, and confident — always sure he could handle whatever came his way. I knew he was carrying a gun that night. But then he called and said Vitteli had agreed to step down; it seemed like it was all going to work out."

"How do you know that?" Karp asked.

"I was in Washington, D.C., talking to a law firm about our problem with the Labor Department and Vince called from the bar. He said Vitteli knew his goose was cooked and was going to announce that for 'medical reasons' he was going to step down and there'd be another election," Gorman said. "He wanted some concessions; essentially that Vince would drop the Labor Department stuff and work out the 'financials,' which probably meant walking away from any theft charges and arranging for a golden parachute. Vitteli wanted to stay on in a reduced role, along with his pal Joey Bar-

134

ros. . . . You know Joey Barros, don't you? A real piece of work and dangerous . . . But anyway, Vince said they had to go. He was going to let Jackie Corcione stay on, mostly because of his loyalty to Leo, but I was going to take over as lead counsel for the union, and Jackie would have been on a tight leash with me."

"But Vitteli had supposedly accepted these conditions?" Karp asked.

"That's what Vince said. Of course, now I think it was all just to get him off guard."

"I guess we shouldn't be surprised that Vitteli hasn't said a thing about stepping down in the press," Guma said, "though he's certainly been quoted enough talking about what a great guy Vince was. He called him 'my brother,' if I remember right."

" 'To show an unfelt sorrow is an office which the false man does easy,' " Karp replied as he tapped his pencil on the legal pad.

The others looked confused. "What?" said Guma.

"Nothing . . . just a quote from *Macbeth,*" Karp said. He looked at Gorman. "Thanks for coming in and talking about all of this. Frankly, we've had our own suspicions about Vitteli's role. Is there anything else?"

Gorman shook his head. "No. Sorry, I

wish there was. But if I hear anything I'll let you know. I just wanted to make sure you were aware of the players and what they had to lose. Vince was a good man. I hope justice will prevail."

"So do we," Karp said. "Rest assured we'll do everything we can to see that it does."

Several hours later, Karp was still thinking about the conversation with Gorman when he arrived home at his loft on Crosby Street. However, his senses were momentarily overwhelmed by the smell of roasted garlic and herbs emanating from the kitchen, where Marlene stood with her back to him at the stove.

"The famous Ciampi marinara?" he asked as he walked up behind and wrapped his arms around her. "What's the occasion?"

Marlene laughed and turned, reaching up to place her hands around the back of his neck and pulling him down for a kiss. "No occasion in particular," she said. "But it's Friday night, the boys are off to a friend's for an overnighter, and I know how amorous Italian cooking with a glass or two of red wine makes you."

Karp feigned a yawn and shook his head. "Geez, that all sounds great, but I'm wiped," he said. "I think I'll just have a bowl of cereal and turn in early . . . OW!"

"Oh, pardon me," Marlene replied, having just squeezed his cheek, "I didn't mean to pinch your cheek. Now, would you repeat what you just said, please?"

Laughing as he rubbed his face, Karp bent down to kiss her again before saying, "Boy, that smells great and watching you cook turns me on." His hands started to roam.

Marlene giggled and pushed him away. "That's better, lover boy. But enough. Go wash up. Dinner is ready, and then if you're good, you can resume your attentions."

A few minutes later, the couple was seated on the couch in the loft, which was essentially a large open space housing the kitchen, dining area, and living room, where they sat, with three bedrooms down the hall. "So how did your day go?" Marlene asked as she sipped Chianti.

"Mmmph flurgle lafa," Karp replied with a mouthful of meatball. He swallowed and smiled. "Actually had an interesting conversation with an attorney named Mahlon Gorman, who represented Vince Carlotta. He thinks Charlie Vitteli was behind the murder."

"That's no surprise," Marlene said. "He have any proof?"

"Not really, just some compelling reasons," Karp said. He started to tell her about the conversation, but when he reached the part about the three young men who'd shown up at the Carlotta residence before the murder, Marlene frowned and spoke.

"One of them spoke with a Russian accent?" she asked.

"Apparently," Karp replied. "Why?"

"It's probably nothing, but I had an interesting conversation today, too, that involved three young men, one of them a Russian," she said and told him about Nicoli Lopez.

Karp thought about it as he stuffed a forkful of spaghetti in his mouth. "Think that's a bit of a coincidence?" he asked.

"Yes," his wife replied. "But how many times over the past twenty-plus years have coincidence and fate played into this family's life and our careers? You willing to overlook coincidence now?"

Karp looked at her and smiled. "Not at all," he said. "I was just making a comment. I can see the gears turning in that pretty head of yours. What do you have in mind?"

"I have a couple of ideas," Marlene said.

"Care to enlighten me?"

"Well, one will be to call your cousin Ivgeny and see if he's heard anything in the underground Russian community about this," she said.

Karp nodded. It was a subject they didn't talk about much, but Ivgeny Karchovski was not only his cousin — their grandfathers had been brothers — and a former colonel in the Soviet Army, he was also the head of a Russian organized crime family in Brooklyn. Ivgeny had helped him in the past, including assisting in preventing a terrorist attack, but both men knew that they had to stay at arm's distance given their respective careers.

"Fine, let's throw a Russian gangster into the pot and see what trouble comes of that," he replied.

"I'm glad you approve," Marlene said with a laugh.

"I didn't say I did," Karp replied.

"You didn't say you didn't, either," she retorted.

"Isn't that a double negative?" Karp replied. "Are you trying to confuse me?"

"The wine may be confusing you, but I'm not," Marlene said lightheartedly. She was quiet for a moment and then added, "Seriously, and if you also don't object, I think I'm going to go have a chat with Antonia Carlotta."

Karp frowned. "I was going to have Clay talk to her. What would be your standing in the case?"

"Private investigator working for Nicoli Lopez. Maybe if I can find out something about her boyfriend, you might get a break in the case," Marlene said. "And maybe a woman's touch is called for here. I'd like to take a shot at it, anyway."

Karp thought about it for a moment and then nodded. "As long as you call Clay in if this turns out to be more than a coincidence."

Marlene smiled and leaned over to kiss him. "Thanks. Now are you finished with dinner?"

Karp arched an eyebrow. "I believe I am. So I take it you'd like some help washing the dishes?"

Marlene rose from her chair and held out her hand. "The dishes can wait. But I got an itch that needs to be scratched."

9

Marat Lvov woke up shaking from a bad dream in which three grinning hags peered down at him as he bobbed in a cauldron of hot water. His own sweat felt warm and sticky on his back and his head pounded from the liter of vodka he'd consumed the night before.

As though to orient himself in the dark, he reached out with his fat hand to touch the nude body of the woman sleeping in the bed next to him. Actually, "woman" was a stretch. She was a child, fourteen years old, maybe younger, though hard to say about some of the fresh meat off the boat from the former Soviet Union, where records were poorly kept and life was cheap.

One of his many businesses was trafficking in underaged girls lured to America with promises of jobs as nannies or domestic servants only to be sold into sexual slavery. He got a kick out of advertising his merchandise — albeit in thinly disguised code — on the back pages of one of New York's famous alternative weekly newspapers. And he routinely singled out one of the younger, more attractive girls to "sample" for himself, keeping them drugged and virtual prisoners in his impressive home in South Brooklyn.

When he tired of a girl, he'd sell her off as used goods and choose another from the next shipment. Of course, his elderly Russian Jewish neighbors thought he was just a businessman, one of the *Novyi Russkiy,* or "New Russians," known for their conspicuous-consumption lifestyles. That, too, amused him.

Life was good, but the dream of the three hags had frightened him badly. As he touched the girl, he was surprised by how cold she felt. She'd been plenty warm earlier that night as she whimpered, squirmed, and cried out in pain beneath his grunting. He shook her slightly but still she didn't stir. Willing his pounding heart to calm down, he listened for the sound of her breathing and heard nothing but the ticking of the clock next to his nightstand. His voice trembling, he softly called out to her.

"She can't hear you."

It took Lvov a few moments to recognize the deep, cold voice of Joey Barros, whose tall, dark figure he could just make out in a corner of the room. His visitor leaned over and pulled the chain on a reading lamp behind his favorite chair. The light did little to illuminate the room but he could see the skeletal facial features of the man well enough.

"You!" Lvov half whispered, half screamed the moment before his bladder voided, adding more damp warmth to the bed beneath him.

"Yes," Barros said quietly before nodding at the girl next to Lvov. "Wasn't she a little young?"

Trembling, Lvov turned his head slightly to look at the girl. He tried to scream again but his voice was so high-pitched that it came out as a strangled whistle, a frightened tea kettle boiling over as he scooted as far away from her as he could get. He realized in that moment that he had not been lying in his own night sweat but in the warm blood that had poured from the gaping wound in her throat. Her beautiful blue eyes were open but also blank and unmoving as they stared sightlessly at the ceiling. But more horrifying was the smile that curled her lips ever so slightly.

Surprisingly fast for such a fat man, Lvov's hand flew to the red button flashing on the nightstand next to him. It would summon his bodyguards to dispatch the intruder. He would then fire them, if he was merciful enough not to have them garroted, for allowing Barros to make it into his bedroom.

Barros's expression turned to one of amusement. "There's no one there," he said. "I believe they're out back having a smoke and no one's watching the chicken coop."

Lvov's eyes widened as he realized he'd been betrayed. But he wasn't done yet. He rolled over and flung open the drawer of the nightstand, grasping for the Russian-made Makarov pistol he kept there.

"You looking for this?" Barros asked, holding the handgun up with a pencil stuck in the barrel. He dropped his hand and the gun fell toward the floor.

As the Makarov dropped, Barros moved toward Lvov. A straight-edge razor appeared in his hand as if by magic and gleamed wickedly as he held it up.

"*NYET*, PLEASE, NO!" Lvov screamed as he tried to scoot away from the approaching blade, but his progress was stopped by the body of the dead girl. "I did what you asked. Bebnev will kill the others tomorrow. Then you can kill him and have no more problems!"

"Only one," Barros growled.

"I'll pay you anything!"

"You don't have enough."

"Girls, drugs . . . you'd be a happy rich man," Lvov pleaded.

"Not my thing," Barros replied. "I'm happily married, and I don't do drugs."

"Anything!" Lvov squealed.

"You don't have anything I want," Barros said as he held out the blade and leaned over as though he intended to shave his cowering victim.

Desperately trying to sink into the mattress, the Russian gangster sobbed and held out his hands to ward off his attacker. He was surprised that such a thin man could be so strong as Barros grabbed his face with one hand and swung the blade with the other. There was a burning sensation across his throat and the feel of warm liquid running over his skin; then he was choking as blood drained into his severed windpipe.

"Shhhhhhh," Barros said, placing a finger to his lips as if to comfort a child awakened by a nightmare. He straightened up and stood looking down as the fat man clasped his hands to his throat in a futile effort to stop the hemorrhaging. The hands fell away, the body tried to draw a few last gurgling breaths, and then it was over except for the twitching.

When Lvov was still, Barros wiped the blade of his razor on the silk sheet and reflected on how much pleasure killing the man had given him. He didn't often have the time or privacy to watch one of his victims slowly die, but that night he was in no hurry, nor was he afraid of getting caught. Vitteli had made a call to the head of the Malchek gang in Little Odessa for a favor: he'd asked that Lvov's guards take a cigarette break after the fat man went to sleep and leave the back door open.

Barros would have preferred not to kill the girl. He was the father of two nice young women, both of them away now at college, and this girl had done nothing wrong. She was just in the wrong bed at the wrong time.

She'd been awake, nude and lying on her back uncovered when he crept into the room and silently stalked up to her side of the bed. Her eyes were bright and shining in the moonlight that came in through the window but she'd shown no fear, despite her young age, at his appearance like a ghoul in the night.

Then he noticed the fresh bruises on her face and the trickle of blood that ran from a corner of her mouth. *It will be a pleasure to kill that pig for you,* he thought as he held up his razor and showed it to the girl.

"Shhhhhhhh," he whispered and pointed in the direction of the fat man snoring next to her. She'd nodded and he knew she would not scream.

For a moment he'd considered letting her live, but he hadn't stayed out of prison this long by leaving witnesses. She seemed to know what he was thinking and surprised him by tilting her head back to give him better access to her throat. She whimpered once when the razor bit into her creamy white skin but then turned her gaze to the ceiling and died quietly.

When the girl was still, Barros circled the bed to the nightstand and opened the drawer where the bodyguards told him Lvov kept a gun. He removed the Makarov using a pencil lying on the top of the stand and quietly closed the drawer. Then he waited patiently. It was going to be fun to toy with Lvov and watch the terror grow as the fat pig realized that death was near at hand.

Vitteli had agreed with his argument that Lvov needed to go. Bebnev would kill the other two and then Barros would kill him afterward. But first Lvov, the only direct link between them and the plot to kill Vince Carlotta. He had to die.

As a man who hated loose ends, Barros had also suggested that Jackie Corcione needed to "have an accident. Maybe throw himself off the Brooklyn Bridge . . . just another queer who decides to off himself rather than be a faggot." But Vitteli nixed it.

"He's Leo's kid, and I'm not ready to go there yet," Vitteli said.

"I should take care of that loose end now," Barros growled. "It was a mistake to let him stay around this long."

Vitteli cocked his head at the criticism. "You questioning me, Joey?" he said. "After all these years? And everything I've done for you?"

Barros literally bit his tongue. "I'm just saying that Jackie's a danger," he backtracked. "I say we get what we need out of him, and then he takes a fall."

"Maybe, but I'll decide when," Vitteli said. "Or are you the boss now?"

Barros had looked the other way. "No, you're the boss."

For now, Barros thought, as he picked Lvov's cell phone up, made sure it was off, and put it in his pocket. He would leave it with Bebnev's body tomorrow, and it would look like a tit-for-tat gang killing. *But who knows? Charlie's getting a little timid. Maybe he needs to retire.*

Leaving the house through the back door, Barros waved to the bodyguards standing in the shadow of a tree, smoking their cigarettes. They waved back, but he was already gone.

10

"Good morning, Bobbi Sue," Marlene said, poking her head into Hirschbein's office at the East Village Women's Shelter. She smiled as she saw the clutter of books and papers lying about on every piece of furniture and hanging precariously from the bookshelf as though it might grow into an avalanche at any moment and bury the director. "My offer still stands if you ever want my help organizing."

Laughing, Hirschbein shook her head. "Oh, goodness, no. I operate best amidst chaos. I'd never be able to find anything if someone cleaned up after me. What brings you in today?"

"Mind if I ask Nicoli Lopez to meet me in the Room?"

Hirschbein regarded Marlene with an arched eyebrow. They'd known each other for a long time, and she knew when her friend was on the scent of something important, something that was likely to be dangerous. "Anything I should know about?"

"No, at least not at the moment, but I promise to fill you in when I can," Marlene said.

"Okay then, ask reception to see if they can locate her," Hirschbein said. "It's almost noon and I think she was registered for our morning parenting class for new mothers, so she should be in the building. Oh, and nice to see you, too, Marlene."

A few minutes later, Marlene sat in the Room of Tears waiting for Nicoli and wondering if this was the best course of action. She was taking a chance that the girl would turn around and tell her boyfriend that the wife of the New York County district attorney was looking at him as a possible murder suspect; it was clear Nicoli still loved Gnat Miller, and he was her child's father. If she warned Miller, he might run as well as alarm the others, which could greatly reduce the chances of the case ever being solved. But Marlene felt that she needed to take a chance that Nicoli would understand what was at stake.

There was a knock at the door and Nicoli entered. She smiled when she saw Marlene, but then frowned when she saw the older woman's serious expression.

Marlene sat her down on the couch next to her and quickly explained the situation, leaving out the names of Vitteli, Barros, and Corcione. "Three young guys show up one evening at Vince Carlotta's house in New Rochelle acting like they're looking for work. One of them stays in the car; the other two come to the door, one of them speaks with a Russian accent. Vince Carlotta doesn't believe their story; he even writes the license plate number down. A few days later, Vince is murdered; one guy stays in the car, the other two are in an alley, and one of them shoots Vince."

Marlene let it sink in before continuing. "Now, on the other hand, you think Gnat's involved with two other guys, one of them a Russian, in something criminal, something bigger than he's done in the past. He's got no job, but suddenly he comes into a lot of money, enough to rent an apartment."

Nicoli's face looked like she might be sick and she shook her head violently. "He'd never do something like that," she argued. "He was a little wild when he was a kid and got in scrapes with the law, but it was little bullshit stuff. Nothing violent. What you just said, it's just a coincidence."

Marlene reached over and placed her

hand on the girl's arm. "It might be. But there's this, too; the night you said Gnat went out with Frankie and came back with the car smelling like smoke, that's the same night the three guys showed up at the Carlotta house. And the next time he went back out with those guys was the night Vince Carlotta was murdered."

Nicoli's face crumpled and she began to cry. "He didn't do nothin'. He's a good man and a good father. He just needed a break."

"Look, again, it may not be anything; like you said, just a coincidence," Marlene replied gently. "But Nicoli, we . . . I . . . need to check it out. Maybe I find out he's not involved and you can rest easy. But if it turns out he was there, he needs to answer for it. The victim's widow and baby deserve justice. But it's not just for them or the rest of us who can't let murderers get away with their crimes; it's also for Gnat . . . his peace of mind and his soul, if you will."

Tears welled in Nicoli's eyes as she turned away from Marlene. "No, please . . ."

"Listen to me, Nicoli. You've seen what a guilty conscience can do to a man, especially if he's a basically good man like you describe Gnat to be. Maybe he got caught up in something more than he bargained for or that he didn't expect or want, but it's eating at him now like a cancer. You've seen how it's changed him — the sleeplessness, the crying, the paranoia and anger . . . hitting you. It's not going to get better. In fact, it's going to get progressively worse until maybe he's a danger to himself, or someone else. Maybe he loses it again with you, only worse, or maybe it's with Billy Junior, or even a complete stranger. Whatever he did, he's falling apart as a result, and it's partly up to you how far he disintegrates."

"He's Catholic; he could go to a priest," Nicoli said desperately. "Or see a shrink or somethin'."

"That might help, and I emphasize the word 'might' from personal experience," Marlene replied. "It might help his conscience to confess to somebody. However, confessions only go so far when dealing with something like murder if you don't do something to atone for it. But even if this didn't bother him at all and he was sleeping like a baby every night, not a care in the world, he's still not free of it. Like I told you, a number of people involved in this case believe that the three suspects were paid a lot of money to kill Carlotta and make it look like a robbery. Anybody willing to do that is eventually also going to want to tie up any loose ends, if they're smart."

"What are you saying?" Nicoli cried, her eyes widening in fear.

"That if he was part of this, Gnat could be in danger," Marlene said. "Maybe the guys who paid to have Carlotta killed decide there's too many people who know about it. Or maybe it's one of the guys he was working with who starts worrying about one of his pals informing on him. There's a saying in prisons that the only man you can trust with your secrets is the one who is dead and buried."

Marlene knew she was turning up the drama dials, but it worked. Nicoli quit fighting it. "What do you want me to do?" she asked, her voice barely above a whisper.

"The first thing I need to do is determine if Gnat is even involved," Marlene said. "If he's not, we move on, and figure out what *is* troubling him. But finding out is step one, and I have some ideas on how to do that. What I'd like you to do is hire me as your attorney so that I have attorney-client standing to represent your interests while I'm investigating this."

"I don't have any money," Nicoli said.

"You don't need any, at least not for my services," Marlene said. "I'm doing this for you and your child, as well as another woman and hers. And I do hope I'm wrong about Gnat."

"I do, too," Nicoli said sadly, then looked up hopefully. "What if all he did was drive?"

Marlene hesitated. She hated to dash all of the girl's hopes, but she didn't want to lie to her, either. "Maybe it would help at sentencing, especially if he cooperates with the police and the district attorney," she said. "But I have to be honest with you: if he participated he's still just as guilty of murder, in the eyes of the law, as the guy who pulled the trigger. A judge may take into account extenuating circumstances, or cooperation, but however you look at it, if he's guilty, he'll be going to prison for a long time."

Nicoli hung her head and started to cry again. "Then my baby won't have a father," she sobbed.

Marlene reached for a tissue from the box on the coffee table and offered it to Nicoli. "It will be up to you to determine what sort of relationship to have with Gnat for you and your child if he goes to prison. In any event, it won't be easy, and I'm so sorry this happened to you."

Nicoli took the tissue and blew her nose as she continued to cry. "All right," she said at last. "You can be my lawyer. What else?"

"If the time comes, I may need you to help

locate him and this friend of his, Frankie, so that he can be brought in safely," Marlene said. "Otherwise, I just need you to sit tight and please, don't say anything to Gnat. It would just make it worse for him, and you, in the end."

Nicoli sighed. "I won't tell him. If he did this, he needs to pay for it. Otherwise the guilt would destroy him more than going to prison. Just promise me one thing."

"What's that?"

"Let me know if he gets arrested," Nicoli replied. "He'll be scared, and I'll want to go see him when I can."

Watching the poor girl try to be brave, Marlene felt tears spring to her own eyes. She smiled and patted Nicoli's arm. "I'll let you know as soon as I do."

11

Word of Lvov's murder traveled fast in Little Odessa. Before the Russian-language daily *Novoye Russkoye Slovo* newspaper could hit the stands with its front-page story about the gruesome double homicide at the home of "the respected businessman from St. Petersburg," the patrons of teahouses, nightclubs, and butcher and fur shops along Brighton Beach Avenue already knew.

Rumors were rampant. It was a mob hit, maybe the start of a territorial war. Or Lvov's lavish spending habits had caught up with him and somebody came looking for their money. But as the debates grew over borscht and blini, no one knew the truth.

Alexei Bebnev assumed Lvov had run afoul of one of the rival gangs, and his first reaction was one of extreme disappointment. The fat man had found him at the Rasputin nightclub on Avenue X the previous evening and had not only apologized for punching him in the eye, but had given him a new assignment: kill Frank DiMarzo and Gnat Miller.

"They're not *Russkiy* and can't be trusted like you and me," Lvov had said when offering him the six-thousand-dollar contract. "Our mutual friend wants them silenced forever."

Bebnev had not blinked an eye. He and DiMarzo weren't friends anymore, and he'd never liked that *sooka* Gnat Miller. "It will be a pleasure to work for you," he said with what he thought was a professionally casual nod of the head.

"There's one other thing," Lvov said. "Our friend wants to meet you again to pay you personally when the job is done. He likes your work, my brother."

My brother. Bebnev had liked the sound of that and gladly threw down the multiple shots of good vodka that Lvov insisted on buying for them both. It meant he was in, part of the *bratka,* the brotherhood of Russian mobsters.

Then the rug got pulled out from under him when he heard the news of Lvov's murder. He could hardly believe his bad luck, but then his cell phone rang. He nearly dropped it when he looked at the caller ID and saw the name Marat Lvov. Then hope began to grow; perhaps the rumors weren't true and Lvov was still alive.

"Hello?" he managed hesitantly.

"Lvov is no longer with us, or didn't you hear the news?" a familiar voice answered.

"Who is this?"

"We met once before," the voice said. "I'm calling to let you know that the project mentioned to you by Lvov is still necessary. Do you understand me?"

"*Da,* yes," Bebnev answered, encouraged, recognizing the voice as belonging to "Joey." "*Bez bazara.* No problem." Then a thought crossed his mind. "But how will I get paid?"

"Do you remember where we first met?"

"Yes."

"After you've done the job, meet me there at the alley, nine o'clock, and we can settle our bill," the man said. "If you do the job."

"Good," Bebnev replied. "I am told you admire my work." He waited for an answer but the phone was already dead. *Doesn't matter,* he thought, *everything is working out. Who needs Lvov?*

Late that afternoon, he took a bus to the Red Hook neighborhood and walked to the house where Frankie DiMarzo lived with his parents. He whistled an old Russian children's song, one he'd picked up long ago in the orphanage, as he climbed up onto the porch of the home and knocked. He looked at his watch, the watch he'd taken from one of his "victims" the night he shot Vince Carlotta. Four o'clock. Plenty of time to kill two pussies and meet with his new boss, Joey, in Hell's Kitchen at nine.

Frankie opened the door and scowled when he saw who was standing there. "I told you we're through, get the . . ." he said before shutting up when Bebnev shoved a gun in his face.

"What do you say now, tough guy?" Bebnev said, forcing Frankie to step back so that he could enter the house and close the door behind him.

"Frankie?" an elderly woman's voice called from upstairs. "Who is at the door?"

DiMarzo looked at Bebnev, who leveled the gun at his forehead. "Just a friend, Ma," he said. "He'll leave in a few minutes."

Bebnev smiled and nodded as he motioned for DiMarzo to walk into the living room.

"What the fuck do you want?" DiMarzo said quietly.

"I want you to call Gnat and tell him to come over," Bebnev said.

"Why?" DiMarzo said suspiciously.

"Because we're going to go for ride together."

"Fuck that. You're going to shoot us."

"Maybe, maybe not," Bebnev said. "Or maybe I shoot you and then go shoot nice old lady upstairs."

"Leave my mom alone, you son of a bitch," DiMarzo said. He started to move toward Bebnev but stopped when the Russian pulled back the hammer.

"Sit down and call," Bebnev said, pointing to the couch. "And do not tell him I am here or I shoot your mother in the stomach and make you watch her suffer."

Glaring at Bebnev, DiMarzo called Miller. "Hey, Gnat, can you come over?" he said. "I got something we need to talk about." He hung up the phone. "He'll be here in a few minutes."

They sat silently for a minute before DiMarzo shook his head. "Why you doing this, Alexei?"

Bebnev grinned and waved his gun at his former friend. "Someone is worried you and pansy friend Gnat have big mouths."

"Me and Gnat?" DiMarzo said incredulously. "You're the one who was popping off at the bar. I ain't no snitch."

"You are not Russian and can't be trusted," Bebnev said. "No one at the bar knew what I was talking about or cared; they were all *Russkiy* and my brothers."

"And after you kill us, you think these guys that are paying you are going to let you live?"

Bebnev frowned at the question but then shrugged. "You don't understand. I am professional killer. These guys admire my work."

DiMarzo scoffed. "They're using you, just like they used all of us."

"You are not important," Bebnev replied angrily. "Now shut up."

They again fell silent as ten, and then twenty minutes passed. "Where is Gnat, the little *sooka*," Bebnev snarled at last. "If you somehow warned him, your mother is going to die, and maybe I will do some things to your sisters."

Before DiMarzo could answer, there was a knock on the front door. "Answer," Bebnev said, getting up, "but remember, I am behind you and your mother is upstairs."

When DiMarzo opened the door, Miller was standing on the porch. "I'm sorry, Gnat," Frank said and opened the door farther to reveal the gunman standing behind him. "I guess we're going for a ride."

"I ain't going nowhere with him," Miller replied and started to back away.

"Please, Gnat," DiMarzo said. "He's going to shoot my mom if we don't do what

163

he says."

"That's right, pussy," Bebnev said, grinning. He put the gun in the pocket of his coat but kept it trained on the other two men. "Let's go."

For a moment, Miller looked like he might still take his chances and run. But he saw the pleading look in DiMarzo's eyes and nodded. "What the fuck, I don't even care anymore."

As they started to leave, DiMarzo called out. "I'm going out for a little while, Ma," he yelled and then choked up as he added, "I love you. Tell Pops I love him, too."

"Okay, Frankie," the old woman yelled back. "Have a nice time with your friends."

When they got to Gnat's car, Bebnev ordered the other two into the front seats while he got in the back. He took his gun back out of his pocket and placed it against Miller's neck. "Drive," he said.

"Where?"

"Fountain Avenue and Flatlands."

"The landfill?"

"That is good guess," Bebnev answered.

DiMarzo and Miller fell silent. Gnat turned on Fountain Avenue, a major north-south arterial through Brooklyn with the south end where they were heading comprised of toxic landfills and odorous swamps. More germane to the situation they found themselves in, it was infamous as a dumping ground for bodies by various mobs over the years including Murder Incorporated in the 1930s, the Gambino family in the 1970s and '80s, and, more recently, the "immigrant" mobs led by the Russians.

The sky was growing increasingly dark and snowflakes were falling when they pulled up to a fenced-in landfill. A sign on the gate declared that the landfill was permanently closed and warned trespassers of toxic dangers.

"Lock is broken," Bebnev said to DiMarzo. "Get out and open. Do not try to run or first I shoot Gnat and then I go back to your home and shoot your ma and pops. And I rape your sisters before I kill them, too."

"Fuck you, Bebnev," DiMarzo said. "Someday you're going to pay for this."

"Maybe," Bebnev said, then laughed. "But you first."

DiMarzo got out of the car and opened the gate. After he got back in, Bebnev directed Miller to drive to a secluded spot surrounded by mounds of half-buried refuse, scraggly trees, and swampy grasslands. "Far enough," he said. "Get out."

As the two friends marched ahead of Bebnev, DiMarzo turned to Miller. "I'm sorry I got you into this, Gnat," he said.

Gnat smiled. "It's okay, Frankie," he said. "I got myself into this; nobody made me do it." He was quiet for a moment, then added, "Tell you the truth, I'm kind of glad it's over. It's been like a ton of bricks piled on top of me. I can't sleep. I'm a ball of nerves. I even hit Nicoli for no good reason. I was a real shit to her and I wish I could have told her one more time that I'm sorry."

"Me too," DiMarzo said. "The money wasn't worth it. I hate what this is going to do to my ma and pops. I guess they won't have to worry about their no-good son anymore. I hope they can forget about me."

They reached a small clearing. "Far enough," Bebnev ordered. "Get down on your knees."

With the moment of death at hand, Miller and DiMarzo sank to the ground. "You were a good friend, Frank," Miller said.

"You were, too," DiMarzo replied, his voice husky.

"Hey, you pussies, you want to kiss or something before I shoot you?" Bebnev said with a laugh.

"Burn in hell, you ugly son of a bitch," DiMarzo said. "Jesus forgive me for my sins."

"Jesus forgive me for my sins," Miller repeated after him.

DiMarzo looked up at the snowflakes that fell and wondered if there was any chance he'd get into heaven and see his family again. The sound of vehicles on nearby streets and water traffic on Jamaica Bay seemed unusually loud as he waited for the shot.

Instead, something behind them crackled with a blue flash, which was immediately followed by a yelp and a thud. The air smelled of electrical discharge. "You can get up," said a thick, heavily accented voice behind them.

When they realized the voice did not belong to Bebnev, the two friends turned and saw a very large man standing over the body of their would-be assassin, who lay twitching on the ground. The big man leaned over and yanked the prongs from the Taser he held out of Bebnev's back and then put the weapon in his coat pocket.

DiMarzo recognized their savior as the man with the scarred face he'd seen at the Little Odessa club when Bebnev met with Lvov. "Wow, thanks, man," he exclaimed. "Boy, are we glad you showed —"

"Shut fuck up," the big man interrupted. He pulled a cell phone from his pocket and dialed a number. "Is done," he said into the phone and hung up.

A few moments later, a long dark sedan pulled into the clearing. Another man with a scarred face, wearing an eye patch, but not nearly as large as the first man, got out of the car. He walked up and clapped the big man on the shoulder.

"Well done, Anton, my friend," he said, then toed Bebnev, who was starting to come to. "Get up, scum."

"Thank you for helping us," Miller started to say to the man with the eye patch.

The man returned the thanks with a look of scorn. "I am not here to help you," he said. "I am here to help a friend." He looked down at Bebnev, who sat up and rubbed his temples as if he had a splitting headache. "Do you know who I am?" he asked the Russian.

Bebnev looked up and as his eyes focused, his face turned into a mask of fear. "*Da.* You are Ivgeny Karchovski!"

"That's right," replied the man. "And so you know I will do what I say, correct?"

"Yes, sir," Bebnev replied. He looked down at the ground, unable to hold the other man's eye contact.

"Then you and your not-so-good friends sit still while I discuss your fates with another. Is that understood?" he said looking at all three young men.

"Yes, sir," they all replied.

Satisfied, Karchovski took out a cell phone and made a call. "Hello, my lovely friend. I am sorry to bother you but there was slight change of plans. My associate located Bebnev, who led us to the others before they all left in the red-haired one's car. Apparently the dogs are fighting among themselves and Bebnev was going to silence the other two, permanently."

Karchovski listened for a moment and then nodded. "Yes, they are all unharmed. Fortunately, my associate was able to intervene shortly before I arrived."

Moving behind Gnat's car, he said, "The license plate number? Yes, is New York FPB eight-one-nine-six." He listened a bit more and then, looking at the three younger men, said, "Perhaps I should question these dogs, maybe remove a finger for every lie? Only if they refuse to talk? Sigh, okay, we play by your rules, but you know I like to make examples of such as these. Tell my cousin there will be early Christmas present waiting for him in an Oldsmobile Delta 88 at the landfill at Fountain and Flatlands Avenues in Brooklyn. . . . You're welcome, darling, glad to have been of service."

The Russian gangster then turned back to the three young men. "Stand up and put your hands behind your back. Anton, there are plastic ties in the glove box of my car. Would you get them, please? And would you hand me your knife, please?"

"What are you going to do to us?" Miller asked, trembling as the bigger man whipped out a wicked-looking knife from a boot sheath.

"Do?" Karchovski answered then looked at his man and they both laughed. "I guess I am making citizen's arrest!" He sat down on the hood of his car, and, removing an apple from his long wool coat, convincingly cut a slice with the knife and popped it into his mouth in one smooth motion. "Now, who wants to tell me truth about murder of Vince Carlotta?"

12

Marlene looked down at her cell phone lying next to her on the seat of her truck when Tchaikovsky's *1812 Overture* ringtone began to play. According to caller ID, *PYOTR,* otherwise known as her husband's cousin and mob boss, Ivgeny Karchovski, was on the other end of the line again.

It had been a busy day. After talking to Nicoli Lopez, she'd returned to the Crosby Street loft and placed two phone calls. The first was to ask Ivgeny if there was any word on the streets of Little Odessa that might tie into Vince Carlotta's murder.

"Specifically, I'm looking for anything that might involve a young man, speaks with a Russian, maybe Eastern Bloc accent, possibly seen with two other young men, one with red hair, his name is Bill, or Gnat, Miller; the other has dark hair, looks Italian, goes by Frankie," she said. "Maybe they're flashing a lot of money. Or saying things."

Marlene knew it was a long shot. As Ivgeny quickly pointed out, there were a lot of young men with Russian accents in Little Odessa. But it wasn't completely a shot in the dark. She knew that the Karchovski family controlled some of the East River docks on the Brooklyn side for their "import business," so something could have come up on the dockworkers' grapevine. "Or maybe something from your 'other' business interests — the guys I'm looking for may not have anything to do with the union or the docks — they could just be small-time criminals."

"Well, I'm sure I don't know any of those," Ivgeny said with a laugh. "But tell me, this Russian, you suspect him of the murder?"

"Right now he's just a person of interest. Can you help?"

Ivgeny paused, then said, "It is funny you ask me this as I am reminded of something an associate told me just this morning. But let me talk first to my associate again and see if there is more to story. I will get back to you soon."

Marlene's second call had been to Antonia Carlotta to request an interview at her home in New Rochelle. Believing that she needed to meet the woman face-to-face before explaining that she was working for the girlfriend of a man suspected of killing her husband, she omitted mentioning her client by name.

Instead, Marlene name-dropped. She told Antonia that she was the wife of District Attorney Roger Karp and that she, in her capacity as a private attorney, was investigating a possible link to Vince Carlotta's murder. "I'd like to talk to you about it at your home."

Antonia had hesitated at first, and Marlene had worried that she'd ask questions Marlene preferred to answer in person. But then the young widow agreed to meet at four o'clock. It was now a little after three and Marlene was on her way when Ivgeny called back.

"Do you know of an inconsequential gangster named Marat Lvov?" he asked first off.

"No. Should I?"

"Perhaps," Ivgeny replied. "But like I said, he is little tomatoes —"

"Small potatoes," Marlene corrected him.

"Ah, right, small potatoes," Ivgeny said. "This Lvov is small potatoes, but now he is also dead. His bodyguards apparently failed in their duties and Lvov was murdered last night; he and a teenaged girl were found in bed this morning by his cook. Their throats were slit, very professional job."

"Any suspects?" Marlene asked.

"Not yet, though the rumors fly. But he did some work for the Malchek gang, a very rough group from St. Petersburg, and they have many enemies."

"So how does this relate to Vince Carlotta?" Marlene asked, puzzled.

"I am explaining, but you American women are so impatient, you never want to hear a good Russian storytelling," Ivgeny complained and this time they both laughed. "Anyway, as I told you earlier, your question reminded me of a conversation I had earlier with an associate about Lvov's murder. This associate is good man, though perhaps 'good' is a relative term when you work for gangster, no? Anyways, he served with me in Afghanistan in 1980 and works for me now. He was in a Brighton Beach Boulevard bar a few days after the Carlotta murder and he hears this *durak*, this moron, Alexei Bebnev, bragging about shooting somebody for money. It would not be unusual to hear such boasts in this bar, and often they would be true, except this Bebnev is a nobody who wants to be a *krutoy paren*, a tough guy."

"I'm sorry, I'm still not getting the connection, except that this Bebnev is bragging about shooting someone," Marlene said.

"Ah yes, my impatient friend, and normally my associate would not have paid much attention, either, except that Bebnev was joined by, drum roll, please, Marat Lvov."

"Which means?"

"It could mean nothing, but you ask, so here are my observations. One, Bebnev had friend with him, young guy, not Russian, dark hair, maybe Italian as you described. This friend is told to leave when Lvov shows up but waits across street for Bebnev to join him and give him envelope. They argued and then parted ways. Two, Bebnev is dishwasher but suddenly after murder has big bankroll, spends money like madman. Three, Lvov was scum but he would not have had anything to do with such low-class *kakashka* except to hire him for job no one else wants. Four, Lvov is associate of Malchek gang, who rumor says are trying to establish fingergrip —"

"Toehold?"

"What? Yes, toehold, on New York docks. Rumors also say that Malcheks have friendship with Vitteli."

"Now, that is interesting," Marlene said. "Is there a five?"

"Yes, five is Lvov is murdered in his sleep this morning."

"He's a gangster," Marlene noted. "Gangsters get murdered in their sleep all the time; one of the hazards of the job."

"Thank you for the reminder," Ivgeny replied drily. "But to get past bodyguards, somebody called in favor from Malcheks, then kills Lvov. That takes someone powerful or who has what Malcheks want."

"Or maybe the Malcheks killed him for their own reasons?"

"Yes, but why?"

"I guess one reason would be to silence him because he knows about the Carlotta murder," Marlene said. "But that's just one scenario."

"I did not say it was an open-and-close suitcase," Ivgeny said. "Just my observations."

"Open-and-shut case, the term is 'open-and-shut case,' " Marlene said. "But who's quibbling? You made your point. Can I ask you a favor?"

"Anything for the extraordinarily beautiful wife of my favorite, and very lucky, cousin."

"Charming liar." Marlene laughed. "But if you could find this guy, Bebnev, and maybe keep an eye on him for a bit, both myself and your favorite cousin would appreciate it. If it turns out he's involved in this, we don't want him disappearing before we can talk to him."

"So what are you going to do in meantime?" Ivgeny asked.

"I'm on my way to visit the victim's widow," Marlene replied. "And maybe find a link between this guy Bebnev, Gnat Miller, and Frank DiMarzo and the death of her husband. Call me if anything else comes up."

Hanging up, Marlene then called her husband and updated him on all that had transpired. "You've been a busy girl, the usual topnotch intuition," he said. "My cousin's 'observations' are very interesting. I hadn't heard about the murder of Lvov, in fact never heard of the guy. Let me know if you hear something again, or need Clay's assistance. And Marlene . . ."

"Yes, honey?"

"Be careful out there," he said, knowing admonishing her was useless. "If Lvov was murdered because of this case, that's a warning that the stakes have gone up."

Marlene had agreed to be careful, but then she turned her attention back to what she was going to say to Antonia Carlotta. Since climbing in her truck and heading for the West Side Highway, she'd gone over her spiel twice before crossing the Spuyten Duyvil Bridge leading to Henry Hudson Drive, and a half-dozen more times as she continued north on the Hutchinson River Parkway. Then Ivgeny called, followed by her call to Butch, and suddenly she found herself driving down the street toward the Carlotta residence not at all sure about how this meeting would go.

The sky had been threatening to snow all day and the first few flakes were starting to fall as she got out of the car and walked up to ring the doorbell. The door opened and Marlene remembered how she'd thought Antonia was so beautiful the first time she'd seen her at the fund-raiser. The beauty was still apparent — the fine features, large brown eyes, delicate skin, long graceful neck, and model's body. But the dark circles under her red-rimmed eyes and the unhealthy pallor spoke of sleepless nights and days spent crying.

"I'm Marlene Ciampi, we spoke on the phone."

"Yes, of course," Antonia said. "Please come in."

Marlene walked into the large foyer of the house and saw that it was filled with moving boxes and crates. The walls were bare of

artwork and there were no rugs on the hard-
wood floors.

"You're leaving?" Marlene asked.

"*Si,* yes," Antonia replied. "I am going to
Italy to be with my family for a time. And
the house is too large without Vince in it
anyway. I spend too much of my days and
nights wandering the halls looking for something I've lost but will never find."

"I am sorry," Marlene said. "I've been
married for a long time, and I really have
no idea what I'd do if he was suddenly
gone."

Antonia smiled slightly and inclined her
head. "If you have a child, you go on. If I
didn't, I couldn't tell you where I would
be." She pointed to a room off the foyer.
"But come, let us go to my husband's office
to talk. The baby is taking a nap and voices
tend to echo in an empty house."

The two women walked into what was obviously a man's den, done in dark wood
paneling with heavy leather and wood furniture. Framed photographs of New York
Yankee baseball greats hung on the walls, as
well as several front pages of newspapers
with headlines announcing some union victory or stance. There was a photograph of
Carlotta standing with an older man who
Marlene recognized as Leo Corcione. But

one entire wall was covered with photographs of Antonia and their baby. The heavy cherrywood desk also bore several framed photographs of mother and child.

Antonia saw Marlene noting all the family photographs and blushed. "It's a little embarrassing," she said quietly as a tear rolled down a cheek. "Vince was something of a camera nut when it came to our family. I haven't had the heart to take down these photographs yet."

"It's charming," Marlene replied. "Love has a way of turning tough guys into powder puffs when it comes to their women and children. At least, it does to good men."

"Yes." Antonia sighed. "It does do that. Please, sit down and tell me about this possible, how did you put it, oh yes, 'link' to my husband's murder."

Marlene sat and waited for Antonia to take another seat next to her. "I will, but first I have to confess that I didn't tell you everything when I asked for this meeting," she said. "I hope you'll understand when I do."

Antonia visibly stiffened at Marlene's words but she nodded. "Please explain."

"Well, let me start by saying that I'm not absolutely certain yet, which is why in part I'm here, but I may know at least one of the men involved," Marlene said. "However, I need to tell you that I'm working as an attorney and investigator for the man's girlfriend."

Antonia's eyes grew hard and dark as she stood up. "What makes you think I would want to help you?"

Having anticipated the question, Marlene answered, "Because by helping me, you may be helping solve your husband's murder, and not just the guys hired to pull it off, but whoever may have been behind it. I'm starting with this guy, but he's just a pawn."

Antonia gave Marlene an appraising look and then her eyes softened and she sat back down. "Yes, my feelings exactly. Why settle for a pawn when it's the king you want? So tell me about this girl and her boyfriend."

For the next ten minutes, Marlene explained how she'd come to suspect that Gnat Miller and his friend Frank DiMarzo were involved in the murder of Vince Carlotta, "and some guy who spoke with an accent, possibly Russian."

Antonia's hand flew to her mouth. "Oh, my God!"

"What is it?" Marlene asked.

"Those men who came to the house, the one who did most of the talking — the odd-looking man — he was definitely Russian,"

Antonia said. "I worked quite a bit in Moscow when I was a model."

"Odd-looking?"

"Yes. Very pale blue eyes set wide apart, very round head. Actually, you see this a lot in parts of Russia where women drink too much when they are pregnant."

"Fetal alcohol syndrome."

"Yes, I believe that is true," Antonia said. "Anyway, he did almost all of the talking. He made me feel very uneasy. Vince said his hands were soft; that's how he knew he was not a dockworker like he says."

"Do you think you'd be able to identify him if you saw him again?"

"Oh yes. I'd never forget that face."

"What about the other two men? Did you get a good look at them?"

Antonia pursed her lips, then shook her head. "Only one of the others got out of the car. He was not as tall as the Russian; a little stockier, dark hair, dark eyes, maybe Italiano. But he kept his face down most of the time. I couldn't see the driver of the car, but Vince said he had ginger hair."

"Could you describe the car?"

"Um, yes, big American sedan, older model. It had four doors. I know because the Russian fellow got into the backseat; the other two were in front."

"What kind of condition was it in?"

"Oh, beat-up. Lots of scratches and dents. I think it was green, but hard to tell anymore. There was some gray paint on part of the trunk."

"Anything else about the men or the car?"

"I don't remember . . . oh, my husband wrote down the license plate number."

"Yes, actually I believe that your husband's attorney, Mahlon Gorman, mentioned something about that. I don't suppose you still have the note?"

Antonia shook her head. "Mahlon is a good man, maybe the only one Vince trusted completely. But I haven't seen the note since Vince took it off the pad that night."

Marlene sat forward. "What pad was that?"

Antonia pointed at her husband's desk. "Over there by the telephone, why?"

Rising from her seat, Marlene walked quickly over to the desk. She turned on the desk lamp and looked closely at the pad of sticky notes. "Do you have a pencil handy?"

Antonia, who had followed her over, gave her a puzzled look. "There should be one in the drawer."

Opening the drawer, Marlene located a pencil and then lightly began shading the top page on the sticky-note pad.

"What are you doing . . . oh," Antonia said as the images of several letters followed by several numbers began to emerge.

When she was finished, Marlene looked up. "You're sure this is the pad he used to write down the license number?"

"Yes. I saw him remove the note myself."

"And that was the last thing he wrote on that pad?"

"Yes," Antonia said and pointed at the pad. "That is the license plate number of the car that came to our house with the three men. They were waiting when we got home that night."

"Waiting in the driveway?"

"No, up the street, next to the elementary school. We went out for pizza, and when we reached our street and turned left to come home, they were there . . . waiting," Antonia said. "I saw them in the headlights but not their faces; one was out of the car by the bushes."

"I'd like you to show me where," Marlene said. "But first I need to call Detective Clay Fulton. He works for my husband, and I'd like him to be here."

"What about that?" Antonia said, pointing to the license plate number.

Marlene took a scrap of paper out of her purse and jotted the number down. "I'll leave that for the police." She then opened her cell phone and punched in a number.

"Clay? It's Marlene," she said. "Yeah? Same to you, good-looking. Hey, we may have got a break. I'm at the Carlotta residence in New Rochelle and . . . What? You are? Great, see you in ten." She hung up the phone and looked at Antonia. "He's already on his way. But let's go have a look."

Antonia retrieved a coat and soon they were both walking up the street in a light snowfall, their breath coming out in great clouds of condensation. When they were opposite the elementary school, they crossed the road.

"This is where they parked," Antonia said.

Marlene looked around and then spotted something in the grass between the curb and sidewalk. She walked over as she opened her purse and took out her phone, which she used to take a photograph of the object. Returning the phone to her purse, she pulled out a pen that she stuck in the ground next to the item. Then she retrieved a pair of tweezers, leaned over, and picked the object up. She looked closely at it and then turned to show Antonia.

"We may have our smoking gun," Marlene said.

"I'm sorry, I don't understand," Antonia said.

"Just an expression. I need to look around more before the snow covers everything up. Would you have any envelopes at your house?"

"Would plastic bags do?" Antonia asked.

"No, paper envelopes," Marlene replied.

"I'm sure we do," Antonia said and then walked off across the street toward her house.

Marlene started to search the area but was interrupted again by the *1812 Overture* playing in her coat pocket. "Hello, Ivgeny," she answered lightly, but as she listened her face grew grim.

"Are they okay? Butch is going to want to talk to all three." She pulled the note out of her coat pocket. "Can you see their car's license plate? FPB eight-one-nine-six? Great." She paused and then laughed. "No, please, leave the questioning to Butch. We don't want this coming back to bite us in the butt because some Russian gangster started cutting fingers off of the suspects. Thank you anyway, sweetie, and that will be a nice present; just make sure all the pieces are still attached. I'll talk to you later."

Marlene hung up just as a dark sedan pulled up to the curb.

"Someone here call the police?" Clay Fulton said as he got out of the car.

Tilting her head back to look up at the snowflakes that floated down from the dark gray sky, Marlene took in a deep breath before letting it out. "You know, Clay, I think we're going to have a white Christmas after all," she said, then wiped at a tear that formed on her cheek. "But it's going to be a tough one for Antonia and Nicoli."

13

Karp leaned forward from the backseat of the armored sedan and tapped on the glass between him and his driver. "This is good J.P.," he said. "You can let me out here."

NYPD Officer J. P. Murphy pulled over to the curb and frowned as he looked in the rearview mirror. "You sure about this, Mr. Karp?" he asked. "Clay Fulton will have my ass in a sling if he hears that I let you walk into Battery Park alone at ten o'clock at night, much less during a snowstorm."

Looking outside as the wind whipped snowflakes sideways across Battery Place and into the park on the southern tip of Manhattan, Karp shivered. He wasn't thrilled at the thought of venturing into the elements himself. But he'd received a phone call two hours earlier from Fulton, who was in New Rochelle with Marlene, and he wouldn't have missed this conversation if hell itself was about to freeze over.

The first part of his telephone conversation with the detective was to get an overview of what Marlene had learned during her conversation with Antonia Carlotta and their subsequent findings after Fulton arrived on the scene. The second part was to let Karp know that NYPD detectives were transporting three "persons of interest" in the Carlotta murders to the Criminal Courts Building for questioning.

It seemed that once again, Marlene's intuition and some great detective work had paid off. Responding to directions she'd given Fulton to relay, officers had found William "Gnat" Miller, Frankie DiMarzo, and Alexei Bebnev hog-tied in an old Delta 88 at a South Brooklyn landfill, one in the front seat, one in the back, and a third, Bebnev, in the trunk.

"Apparently Bebnev was planning on dispatching Miller and DiMarzo when some good citizen put a stop to it and left them for us," Fulton said. "We got Bebnev on an immigration hold, and the other two we're bringing in for a chat. Um, apparently there was a note pinned to Bebnev's coat, that said, 'Happy Chanukah, A Secret Admirer.' Care to explain that one?"

"Maybe later," Karp had said, smiling to himself.

"Uh-huh," Fulton replied. "That's what I thought, but Marlene says she needs to talk to you about that, so I'm handing you over."

A moment later, Marlene came on the line. "Hello, Butch," she said. "You're not going to believe what I've been up to!"

"Oh, I've lived with you long enough to pretty much know that anything's possible," he replied, rolling his eyes.

"You got that right, and we'll fill you in on the details when we get back," she said. "But right now I need to tell you that your relative would like to meet with you around ten. He says it's about these 'persons of interest' and you won't be disappointed."

"Did he say where?"

"You'll love this: Castle Clinton in Battery Park."

"Ten o'clock tonight?" Karp winced as he listened to the wind howl outside the loft's living room window.

Marlene chuckled. "Afraid so, my love. But I don't think he'd ask on such short notice if it wasn't important."

"No, you're right," he replied. "I'll be there." He thought about it for a second, then added, "Tell Fulton let's all meet this evening at the office about eleven; I'll call Guma. And I hate to do this, but would you ask Mrs. Carlotta to come with you; we'll get her a ride back home with an officer."

"Clay and I thought you might want her there, and we already asked," Marlene replied. "This storm is starting to pick up, but she's anxious to do whatever she can and has a babysitter coming over."

After congratulating his wife on her efforts, Karp hung up and called Guma to fill him in, except for the part about going to Castle Clinton to meet with Ivgeny Karchovski. "I'll see you at my office tonight at eleven," he repeated. "Do me a favor and set up three lineups, one for each of the stooges, and make sure we have a stenographer ready to go."

"You do choose the most inopportune times to champion the cause of justice," Guma responded. "It's going to be tough to drag myself away from the warm attentions of the affectionate Madam Milquetost, but duty calls. Honey Bear, would you hand me my robe?"

"Goom, that was way too much information." Karp grimaced. But now, watching the snow swirl in the light of the streetlamps, he identified with Guma's complaint.

"How about I at least call the park police and get them to let us through the security gate?" Officer J. P. Murphy said. "That way

191

I can drive you right up to the castle."

Karp thought about who was waiting for him and shook his head. "No, I can use the walk," he said with only a touch of irony. "I'll be okay. There's my escort, I believe."

A very large man in a Russian-style fur hat with earflaps and a fur coat, all of which made him look like a bear, loomed out of the gray and white landscape of the park. He stood ten feet from the car, waiting patiently with a large bundle in his arms.

"I think I should at least come with you," Murphy suggested as he looked warily at the stranger.

"Sorry, J.P., you have to stay put," Karp replied. "National security stuff. Need-to-know basis only. Very hush-hush. Get my drift? This doesn't go any further than me, you, and Detective Fulton, right?"

Murphy arched an eyebrow and looked impressed. "Oh yeah, gotcha, sure, Mr. Karp," he said, obviously relieved that he now had a good excuse not to venture forth in his NYPD-issued winter jacket. "Uh, you'll talk to Fulton?"

"We're meeting as soon as this is over; it won't be a problem. I should be about a half hour."

"Okay," the officer said. "I'll be right here. Call if you need something, and I'll come running, or slipping and sliding."

"Good man," Karp said, smiling as he opened the door of the sedan and stepped out into a sudden blast of frigid air from New York Harbor. He immediately wished he'd worn something more substantial than his long peacoat and a sweater.

However, he didn't have to suffer long. The big man stepped forward and presented him with a fur hat. "Is *ushanka*," he growled, though he was trying to smile at the same time. He then offered Karp a long coat with a fur collar. "Wear this too, please."

Noting the long, ugly scar that bisected the giant's rugged face, Karp placed the hat on his head and immediately understood how some animals withstood winter in the open. He quickly shucked his peacoat and tossed it back in the car before slipping into the new garment.

"Thank you," he said to the big man, who only grunted before turning to lead the way into the park.

As they passed the pier on his right, Karp noticed a dark speedboat tied to a dock. He could see the glow of a cigarette coming from a shadowy figure standing on the dock near the bow and another from someone standing in the stern of the boat. He couldn't be sure, with the poor lighting and blowing snow, but they appeared to be armed with rifles of some sort. *My cousin does not travel lightly,* he thought.

There was further evidence of that fact when he and his escort walked up to the circular sandstone building known as Castle Clinton, where they were waved inside by two more guards, though these were not exhibiting any weapons.

Also known as Fort Clinton, the structure was originally built to guard against British warships in the War of 1812, though no one had ever fired a shot in anger from it, and it was named after former governor and New York City mayor George Clinton. It now served as a museum, gift shop, and ticket office for those wishing to visit Ellis and Liberty Islands.

And apparently a clandestine meeting place for Russian gangsters, Karp thought as he followed his guide down a dark hallway toward a light at the end. His cousin's sometimes alarming access to places otherwise off-limits to everyone else amazed him. *I guess money can buy most everything.*

When they reached the small room, apparently an office of some sort, Karp saw his host standing next to a table, pouring a clear liquid into two glasses. The man was tall, as tall as himself, not heavy like his fur-clad guide but again, more like himself, thick but fit. Indeed, the few people who had ever seen them together often commented that they could have been brothers. They both had the same gold-flecked gray eyes and pewter-colored hair, though Ivgeny wore his in a crew cut. The biggest difference was that the right side of the gangster's face had a shiny, melted look to it, and he wore a patch over his missing right eye; a former colonel in the Soviet Army, he'd been pulled, almost dead, from a burning tank in Afghanistan.

Yet he was still a handsome man with a generous smile that he now turned to Karp as he spotted him coming into the room. "Cousin Butch!" he shouted as he picked up the two glasses. "You look good, like true Slav in your fur!"

Smiling as he watched his cousin walk across the room, Karp thought about how they'd met late in life, in fact only ten or so years earlier, and learned a side of his family history that he hadn't known. His grandfather and Ivgeny's grandfather were brothers growing up Jewish in Poland when Russian Cossacks burned the village to the ground. Karp's grandfather had immigrated to the United States, arriving at Ellis Island where his name had been changed to Karp. Ivgeny's grandfather had made his way into Russia and joined the Red Army when the tsar was overthrown.

Eventually, Ivgeny's father, who himself had been a general in the Soviet Army until purged after World War II, fled to the U.S. at his uncle's invitation. However, while the Karp side of the family had walked the straight-and-narrow path, the Karchovskis had settled in Brooklyn and gone into what Ivgeny euphemistically called "the import-export trade." When the Soviet Union dissolved and Ivgeny retired from the army, he joined his father, whom he hadn't seen since childhood, in Little Odessa and was groomed to take over the family business.

Their "business" mostly revolved around providing transportation and false paperwork for immigrants from the former Soviet Union into the United States, as well as the traditional exchange of black-market products between the U.S. and Russia, whether it was Russian icon paintings or pirated American music. They did not deal in drugs, guns, or prostitution. However, as the other Russian gangs were well aware, they were quite capable of swift, efficient violence to protect their turf and themselves; many of Ivgeny's "associates" were former Soviet special forces who'd served under him, and no mere criminals with guns.

Under normal circumstances, Karp would have probably never had anything to do with his cousin. Not that he didn't like the man; he did, but consorting with known criminals was not appropriate for the district attorney of New York County. However, they'd been thrown together out of mutual necessity, and Marlene had taken a liking to Karp's Russian cousin and uncle and stayed in contact. Privately, he was glad she had, both from a personal perspective and because Ivgeny and his men had more than once stepped in and helped thwart terrorist attacks on the city.

The leopard had not changed his spots much. Ivgeny still retained his natural Russian distrust of authority, particularly law enforcement, but he had put family first. And since their original meeting, Ivgeny had come to a grudging respect for the system and its caretakers. "At least, he says, as it is administered by the current DA," Marlene had once told him.

And here he was yet again, ready to step in and help. *We're going to make an honest man of him yet,* Karp thought as he smiled. "Good evening, Ivgeny. It's good to see you, though you might have chosen better weather if you can arrange that like you seem to be able to arrange everything else."

Ivgeny grinned mischievously and laughed loudly. "My apologies," he said. "My 'influence' is greatly exaggerated and God hardly pays any attention to my requests. But come, let us drink to warm friendships and families on a cold winter night," he said, offering a glass to Karp. "Not unlike Moscow, I might add."

Karp tried to turn down the drink. "I better not," he said. "I'm going to need to be on my toes later."

Ivgeny looked like he'd just been told that breathing air was bad for him. "What? Vodka helps clear the mind of everything but the task at hand," he said. "And is just one little toast with your wayward cousin."

Karp held out his hand for the glass. "I knew that wouldn't work, but it was worth a try."

"Yes, I am a bad influence. *Prost!*" Ivgeny shouted. "And happy Chanukah!"

Trying not to cough as the fiery liquid ate its way from his mouth to his stomach, Karp had to clear his throat several times before being able to croak out, "Cheers and happy Chanukah to you, too!"

Ivgeny tilted his head and grinned. "Sorry.

Is homemade. Old family recipe from Poland. Special top-secret ingredients to give it a little extra kick."

"It does have that," Karp agreed. "But I believe the last of the chill has left my toes."

"Good, good," Ivgeny said. Then his face grew more serious as he took the glass back. Indicating two chairs near a coffee table, he added, "I know you have work to do, so I should not keep you longer than necessary. Let us sit and I will tell you some things you should know."

Thirty minutes later, as Karp pulled on the hat and coat to leave, he smiled and patted his head. "Thanks for everything, including the loaners," he said. "I could probably curl up under one of those trees out there and be perfectly warm. I'll give them back to your man when I get to the car."

"There is no need," Ivgeny replied. "Anton will escort you back, but the clothes are your Chanukah gift."

"That's not necessary," Karp said but was cut off by Ivgeny.

"Please, I understand where some of the reluctance may come from," his cousin said. "Knowing you, I make sure the money that paid for these came from one of my legitimate businesses, and the garments themselves were purchased from a struggling merchant who was thrilled to have the sale. Please, a gift of warmth from your cousin."

"You make it tough," Karp replied. "But all right, I'll wear them when it's cold and be thankful that my cousin thought of me while supporting a local businessman."

Ivgeny and his men had walked with Karp as far as the dock when his cousin stopped and pointed to the dark boat. "This is my ride," he said. "Again, my apologies to have brought you out on such a night. This is like James Bond movie, no? But I could not risk being seen with you, or calling you with the details. Too many peoples are trying to listen to me — your government, my government, my enemies. I am careful, but I can never be sure. I would have preferred to have you and your lovely bride as guests in my home, but I understand the . . . impracticality . . . of such a thing."

Karp shook his hand warmly. "It was worth every shiver," he said. "And yes, someday would be great. I hope it won't be long."

"I hope so, too," Ivgeny said. "Okay, see you later, crocodile."

"It's see you later, alligator," Karp said with a wink.

The Russian gave him a puzzled look. "They are both large reptiles with big teeth."

"Yes, but it rhymes. 'See you later, alligator' rhymes. Then my reply would be, 'In a while, crocodile.' "

"I see, okay, 'Pretty soon, you old monkey.' Is better, yes?"

Karp considered suggesting "baboon" but it wasn't getting any warmer outside. He clapped his cousin on the shoulder. "That's just fine."

Ivgeny grinned and patted him back. "You crazy Americans and your sayings. It's amazing you get anything done."

"Remember me to your father; perhaps we'll celebrate the holiday together."

14

Some of those crazy Americans were waiting for him in his office fifteen minutes later as he walked in from the anteroom after getting off the private elevator. He was brushing the snow off his new coat when Guma, who was slouched in his usual chair sucking on an omnipresent cigar, laughed. "Doctor Zhivago, I presume."

"Very funny, Goom," Karp replied, sweeping the hat from his head.

"I think more like *From Russia with Love,*" Marlene said as she walked up and stood on her tiptoes to kiss him. "I think you look great, and I want to hear all about it later."

"Now that's more like it."

"What? Now I have to start kissing you to get a kind word?" Guma said, looking over at Fulton, who was quietly enjoying the repartee. "Clay, would you stand in for me?"

"No way," Fulton responded. "I've heard some of the language that comes out of that mouth and no way am I kissing Butch."

"All right, all right," Karp said, laughing with the others as he took off his coat and hung it on a rack behind his desk. "Enough of the frivolity, the hour is late, and I'm calling this meeting to order. Where's Mrs. Carlotta?"

"She's in an interview room with one of Clay's female detectives," Marlene said.

"We figured you might want to talk first outside of her presence," Guma explained.

"Yes, good call," Karp replied as he sat. He picked up his pencil and jotted down a couple of notes before looking up at the other three, who were sitting down around the room. "Okay, here's what I got. Just don't ask me where I got it."

It took him five minutes to recount the highlights of what he'd learned from Ivgeny about the gangster's "discussion" with Miller, DiMarzo, and Bebnev. "Your thoughts?"

"Yeah, were they missing any fingers or toes?" Marlene asked.

"What?"

"Never mind, it's an inside joke I'll tell you about later," she said. "So essentially it looks like we're right about Vitteli's involvement, unless there's another 'Charlie' who wanted it done as soon as possible."

"And who coincidentally has a pal named Joey acting as the middleman," Fulton added.

"So will this mystery informant be testifying to any of this?" Guma asked.

"Not a chance," Karp replied. He recalled Ivgeny's description of the three conspirators groveling and crying as they competed to tell their side of the story. "Wouldn't matter; the information was gained on the battlefield of good versus evil in the alleged 'fog' of saving two lives and is for background only."

"Ah, or in my people's parlance, somebody beat the living snot out of these three goombahs until they talked," Guma said. "I'm surprised they're not also sleeping with the fishes."

"I think that was part of the original plan," Karp said. "But, as Clay noted earlier, a 'concerned citizen' put a stop to it. Fortunately, no one beat the snot out of anyone, so at least we don't have to deal with that when they get lawyers. I've no doubt, however, that having the snot beat out of them was the least of their worries, so they talked, though the person asking the questions was coming at it blind, so he may not have heard everything there was to hear, or been told the truth."

Guma stared down at his cigar for a moment, then looked up at the ceiling. "If I got this right, even if this witness and these statements were allowed at trial, we wouldn't have enough to convict Vitteli and his cohorts," he noted. "Miller doesn't know much of anything, except what DiMarzo told him, and DiMarzo only knows what he heard from Bebnev. He didn't meet with anybody himself, except this Lvov character briefly, and Lvov is dead. Otherwise, all DiMarzo knows is that Bebnev told him that he met with Lvov, some guys named Joey and Jackie, and that Bebnev says he also overheard part of a conversation in which the name Charlie was mentioned."

"Yeah," Fulton agreed. "And according to your informant even the shooter, Bebnev, doesn't know much more than what he told DiMarzo. He claims to have met with Lvov and this guy Joey — Joey Barros, we assume — and Jackie, probably Jackie Corcione, both of whom were present when Carlotta got shot, and that they hired him to kill Carlotta. Lvov was the moneyman, but as far as we know, Bebnev had no further contact with Barros, Vitteli, or Corcione."

"That's about the size of it," Karp agreed. "But at least now we know we haven't been barking up the wrong tree. There *were* other possibilities — a mob hit from some gang trying to take over the docks, or revenge, or even a robbery that went bad. Now I think we can rest assured that Vitteli and his boys are factually guilty of Vince Carlotta's murder, and that's step one. Now we work on getting the admissible evidence to prove it beyond any and all doubt."

"To do that it's going to take a lot more pieces to put this puzzle together," Guma replied.

"But we have an idea of what the picture's going to look like," Fulton added. "So where do you want to start now, boss?"

As his two old friends spoke, Karp rose from his chair and turned around to look out the window at the snow-covered streets below. With the flakes of snow flitting like moths into the lights from the streetlamps, he thought the city was at its most beautiful after a late-night storm before traffic and the multitudes hit the street. But it wasn't the beauty of the streets that made him furrow his brow at the conundrum Fulton's question posed. *Where do we start from here?*

Then, far below and across the park just east of the Criminal Courts Building, he saw three apparently homeless people wrapped in rags, tramping through the fresh-fallen snow as they struggled up the sidewalk against the wind. *I guess it's not quite as beautiful when you're out in it without a home to go to or even a warm place to rest for a few hours.*

"We start at the bottom and work our way up," he announced as he turned around and looked at each of the men in their eyes. "We nail these three punks and see who they'll roll over on and what else they might know. We keep plugging in pieces until we have enough to convict the bastards who put them up to it. Ultimately, the three killers go first, then on to the conduits and intermediaries who will lead us to the kingpin."

He looked at Fulton, who was holding a large plastic container on his lap. "I take it that's from New Rochelle."

Fulton stood up and carried it over to a table Karp had set up next to his desk. He opened the flaps of the container and announced, "Merry Christmas!"

"I'm Jewish, but you're the second person tonight who's wished me a season's greeting in connection with the detritus of a murder case."

"Yeah? Well, I have no idea what you just said, but you're going to believe in Santa Claus after Marlene and I describe what's in here," Fulton replied.

Twenty more minutes passed, during which time Marlene and then Fulton described what happened in New Rochelle as well as the contents of the box, beginning with the license plate number of the car. "Which, of course, was registered to William Miller of Brooklyn," Fulton said.

"The same car in which Miller, DiMarzo, and Bebnev were 'found' today," Marlene added.

When Marlene and Fulton were finished describing the contents of the container, Karp put down the pencil he'd been using to take notes and sat back in his chair. "Nice work, you two," he said.

"Want me to get this stuff off to the lab?" Fulton asked, closing the container.

Karp thought about it, then shook his head. "At the last bureau chiefs' meeting someone said that the labs are backed up. I'd like a fast turnaround, but without raising a lot of questions, given the sensitivity of the case. In fact," he said, turning to his wife, "would you mind calling Jack Swanburg and the Baker Street Irregulars and see if they can do a rush job?"

"Would love to," Marlene replied. "I haven't talked to that sweet old man in far too long." She looked at her watch. "It's only half past nine in Colorado; I'll give him a call while you're doing the lineups. Anything else?"

"Well, I hate to ask," Karp said, looking at Marlene, "but I'd like to get Nicoli Lopez over here. I have an idea on how to work this."

Now? Marlene thought, glancing out the window at the night and the still-falling snow.

"It may be my only shot at this," Karp explained.

Marlene studied her husband's face and then nodded. "I'll call Bobbi Sue Hirschbein; she's a live-in director and sleeps at the shelter. I'll let her know I'm on my way. Besides, I promised Nicoli I'd let her know when we brought Gnat in; I think she'll want to come anyway."

"Many thanks, my dear; Clay will have a driver for you. And now, if you'd introduce us to Antonia, you can be on your way," her husband replied.

Marlene led the way into the big meeting room off of the district attorney's personal offices, which, among other things, was used every Monday morning for a bureau chiefs' meeting where major cases would be presented by anxious assistant district attorneys for vetting by the senior staff.

Antonia Carlotta was slumped at one end

of the long table. Her face pale and drawn, she sat up as they entered the room. Marlene made the introductions. "Antonia Carlotta, this is District Attorney Roger Karp, Special Assistant District Attorney Ray Guma, and Detective Clay Fulton you already know."

Karp stepped forward to offer his hand. "My condolences on behalf of all of us," he said. "I met your husband a few times and always came away impressed."

Antonia dipped her head slightly but didn't smile. "He had that effect on many people," she said. "Me most of all."

"I'm also sorry to have kept you waiting," Karp said. "A lot has been happening this evening, as I'm sure you're aware, and it's important that we do things the right way and in the right order."

"Of course." Antonia nodded and hesitated a moment before asking, "I understand you caught the men who did this?"

"I'm sure you understand that I can't discuss the details of the case," Karp replied, looking earnestly into her eyes. "But I will say that we're making progress. As part of that, I'd like you to view what we call a lineup in a few minutes. It may or may not include men you recognize."

"Will they be able to see me?" Antonia

said. She suddenly looked frightened.

"No," Karp replied. "They won't even know you're in the building. You'll be in a different room and looking at them through a one-way mirror. Will you do this? Good."

As they all filed out into the hallway, Marlene turned to Antonia. "I have to go," she said. "But I'm leaving you in good hands. Call me anytime, about anything."

"Thank you," Antonia said, shaking Marlene's hand warmly. "You've given me hope that there will be justice."

With his entourage in tow, Karp led the way down a flight of stairs to the seventh floor and then conducted a short walk along the hallway leading to the "stand-in" room and viewing room. He asked Detective Pete McNeely, assigned to the DAO detective squad, who ran the office lineups, to explain the process to Antonia.

"Sure," McNeely said. "The room on your left is the 'stand-in' room; that's where we'll bring a half-dozen men in at a time for you to see. The room on your right is the viewing room, where you'll be with DA Karp, ADA Guma, and Detective Fulton. If the men have lawyers, they can be present in either room, but the lawyers are prohibited from speaking or in any way disrupting the process. They are there strictly and solely to observe."

Leading the way into the stand-in room, McNeely said, "The men will stand here in a line. They will appear to be looking at you, but as you can see, it just looks like a mirror and what they actually are looking at are their reflections. But if you'll step with me into the viewing room" — the detective led the group into the next room — "you'll see that your side appears to be clear, though somewhat tinted."

"How does that work?" Antonia replied.

"Well, I'm glad you asked that," the detective said, obviously pleased to be "the expert" on the matter. "Here's how: A so-called one-way mirror has a very thin reflective coating applied to one side, about half as much coating as would be on there if you wanted to make the mirror truly opaque. In this case, the 'mirror' surface reflects about half the light that strikes it, and that's what the men in the lineup see. The rest of the light goes through so that someone on this side sees what is going on in that other room. But the real secret is how the two rooms are lit. In the stand-in room, you probably noticed that the lights are very bright and we see in there quite clearly; in the viewing room, it's dark, so very little light passes through to the stand–in room —

too little to see anything. Put another way, I'm sure you've stood outside a dark office building at night and all of the windows look like mirrors. However, if a light is on in an office, you can see inside just fine because the light is escaping. Does that all make sense?"

Antonia smiled. "Yes, much more sense now," she said. "Thank you for explaining."

As the detective blushed and stepped back, Karp said, "Are you ready to proceed?"

"Yes," she replied. "As ready as I'll ever be."

"Okay then, Detective," Karp said to McNeely, "let's get cooking."

Once they entered the viewing room, Karp explained what was going to happen next to Antonia. "Six men will be entering the room. They will look straight ahead and then turn sideways before turning straight ahead again. Each individual will be holding a number. I'll ask you at that point if you recognize any of them. If you do, just tell me the number the man is holding. Are you ready?"

Looking nervous, Antonia nodded, and six men were marched into the stand-in room and told to face front, then sideways, then front again.

"Do you recognize any of these men?" Karp asked.

Scanning the faces, Antonia bit her lip; then she shook her head. "No. I'm sorry."

"That's fine. Mrs. Carlotta, would it be fair to say that you did not get a good look at the driver of the car that came to your house several nights before your husband was murdered?" Karp asked.

"I didn't see him at all. My husband saw the back of his head, but I didn't look."

"I see. So if the man driving the car was in the stand-in room, would you recognize him?"

"No, I would not."

"Thank you," Karp said and pressed an intercom button. "We're ready for the next group."

The six men were led out and six more replaced them and followed the same procedures. "Do you recognize any of these men?" Karp asked.

Antonia's brow furrowed. "I'm not sure."

"Take your time."

"Well, Number Four, he looks like the second man, the one who stood behind the man who did most of the talking," Antonia said. "I think it's him but I am not completely positive; he kept his head down and didn't say much."

"Okay," Karp replied before pressing the intercom button again. "Thank you, the next group please."

"I'm sorry," Antonia said, wiping at her eyes. "I'm not much help."

"You're doing fine. Relax as much as you can," Karp said as the second six were replaced with a third set.

"Number Two," Antonia said immediately before she was even asked.

"Number Two? Please explain."

"Number Two, that's him," she said with contempt. "I will never forget that face. He's the one who did most of the talking. The one with the accent and the strange eyes."

Karp was just about to release the group when Number Two spoke up. *"Vali otsjuda!"* He sneered at the mirror.

Quickly, Karp pressed the intercom button. "Number Two, is there anything you'd like to add to your comment? I have a stenographer right here who will want to get every word."

The man did not respond except to continue sneering. "Okay," Karp said. "That will be all." He turned back to Antonia. "I appreciate you coming in on a night like this. Now, however, it's late, and I'm going to ask Detective Fulton here to get one of his people to drive you home."

Antonia nodded. "Anything I can do," she said. She hesitated a moment and then added, "Don't get me wrong, Mr. Karp. I'm glad you have these men, but they're just the tools someone else used. They're not the real reasons my husband is dead."

"You're absolutely right," Karp replied. "But hopefully they will lead us to the real reason."

15

After a detective was assigned to escort Antonia home, Karp leaned back against the hallway wall. "That went well," he said, rubbing his eyes.

"She didn't pick out Bill Miller, the red-headed guy in the first group," Fulton noted.

"Which makes sense if the driver never got out of the car," Karp pointed out. "As for group two, she was tentative, but she picked Frank DiMarzo out. And she nailed Alexei Bebnev in the third."

"All this proves so far is that Bebnev, and probably DiMarzo, went to Carlotta's house," Guma said.

"In Miller's car," Fulton noted. "We got the license plate number. And her story corroborates the other evidence we gathered, too."

"Right, which probably puts all three of them in New Rochelle," Karp said. "But it doesn't put them in Hell's Kitchen a few nights later."

"And none of those jokers who were with Carlotta — Vitteli, Barros, and Corcione — said anything in their statements to the detectives on the night of the occurrence about the gunman having an accent; plus the perps were wearing masks," Guma said.

"One step at a time, my friend. We have the car now, and maybe somebody will recognize it from the crime scene. Let's talk to Carlotta's driver, Randy McMahon," Karp said. "In the meantime, you're right, Goom; it certainly looks suspicious, but we need to flip one of these three before they all lawyer up."

"So who's going to be first up to the plate?" Guma asked.

Fixing his friend with a sideways glance, Karp made up his mind. "I want to talk to Nicoli Lopez before we try Gnat Miller. So why don't you see where you get with Di-Marzo first, Goom; then we'll try the shooter, Bebnev. He has the most information, but I think he'll be the toughest nut to crack, and we won't be taking any lesser pleas than murder from him. But considering Bebnev was ready to shoot DiMarzo, a little falling out between friends, maybe Frank will be willing to talk about it."

"Where do you want to do this?" Guma asked.

"The lineup room, so I can watch from the other side and get a feel for these guys."

Guma and Fulton walked into the stand-in room, where they were joined by a stenographer. A few minutes later, there was a knock on the door and DiMarzo was shown in by McNeely. Karp noted the deep dark circles under the young man's eyes. *Doesn't look like Frank's getting much sleep,* he thought.

Motioning to a chair across the table from him, Guma sat down and said, "Have a seat, Frank." He looked at the stenographer and nodded. "My name is Ray Guma; I'm an assistant district attorney with the County of New York. We're here tonight with Frank DiMarzo. Mr. DiMarzo, I'd like to ask you some questions about the December fifth shooting death of Vincent Carlotta outside of Marlon's Restaurant in Hell's Kitchen. But first I want to introduce the other people here in the room. The gentleman leaning against the wall in the corner behind me and to my right is NYPD Detective Clay Fulton, assigned to the New York District Attorney's Office. The stenographer is Carole Mason; she works for the DAO and is here to take down every word we say.

Is that clear?"

DiMarzo, who for the most part kept his head down since sitting, except to glance up briefly with each introduction, nodded.

"Mr. DiMarzo, you nodded," Guma said. "But I'm afraid you'll have to speak up so that Ms. Mason can record your affirmation."

"Yes, I understand," DiMarzo said sullenly.

"Good, now I'm going to advise you of your Miranda rights," Guma continued, and did just that. "Do you understand your rights?"

"Yes."

"Okay, but before I start asking questions, I want to repeat again, if you'd like a lawyer present, but can't afford one, you can have one free of charge and confer with him before you and I start talking. Do you understand?"

"Yes, I understand."

"So are you willing to answer my questions at this time without a lawyer present?"

DiMarzo shrugged. "For now."

"Okay, you've consented to answer my questions," Guma said. "So let's get started. As I said, I want to talk to you about the murder of Vince Carlotta —"

"Who?"

Guma stopped talking for a moment and leaned forward to look the young man in the eyes. "Let's not waste our time here playing games. We're investigating the murder of Vince Carlotta, and I'm giving you a chance to talk about it. Maybe you'd like to get it off your chest."

DiMarzo stared at Guma for a few long moments and seemed to be on the verge of saying something, but then his eyes darkened and he shook his head. "I ain't no rat," he said.

Guma sat back in his chair and tossed his pencil onto the yellow legal pad in front of him. "So that's it? Play the tough guy, live by the code of the streets," he scoffed. "You're not going to answer my questions, are you? But what about one of your boys? What about Gnat? We know he was just the driver. Maybe he'll talk?"

"Gnat wouldn't rat on me." DiMarzo scowled.

"No? How about Bebnev then? Wasn't he getting ready to shoot you and leave you in a landfill? You think he's not going to be an informant?"

DiMarzo remained quiet, looking down at his lap. He sniffed a little, but that was the only sound in the room for a full minute, until he shook his head and muttered, "I can't."

Guma snorted. "You can't? Or you won't?" He sat forward, forcing DiMarzo to look up into his eyes. "Who you protecting, Frankie? Who you taking the fall for? Right now, they're in their nice warm beds with full stomachs, and tomorrow morning they'll get up and look out on the new snow and think, 'What a beautiful day to be alive!' But what will you be thinking, Frankie? That you're lucky to be alive with a guilty conscience the size of a Doberman eating at your mind? They couldn't care less about you, unless it's to figure out how to kill you now that Bebnev messed up this afternoon."

The room was quiet again as everyone waited for Frank DiMarzo to choose. But when he did, it wasn't what they hoped to hear. "I didn't do nothin', and I want to leave, and I want a lawyer."

With a sigh, Guma sat back in his chair. *Game over,* Karp thought in the next room. *Nothing from here on out is worth a damn. Well, except for a couple of parting shots to make him think on it.*

"Okay, so we do this the hard way," Guma said. "You're going to cling to that tired old crap about 'the code of the streets.' You ain't no rat. But it doesn't matter; you're going down, Frankie. All three of you."

"I've got nothing more to say to you," Di-Marzo replied.

Guma smiled as he stood up. "That's okay, Frankie, because I don't have anything more to say to you, either. Well, except that you look like hell. Like maybe you aren't sleeping so well. It's not going to get any better, you know, not until you own up and try to make it as right as you can. We'll get you that lawyer now."

After DiMarzo was led out, Guma looked at the mirror as he spoke. "I think I was close but no cigar."

Karp pressed the intercom button. "Had him looking at that curve you threw, but he didn't swing," he said.

"Bebnev next?" Fulton asked.

"Yeah, but I'm not holding my breath," Karp said.

When Alexei Bebnev walked into the room, he looked around the room with scorn. "What do you want?"

"My name is Ray Guma; I'm an assistant district attorney with the County of New York," Guma replied, indicating with his hand that Bebnev should sit down across from him. "We're here tonight with Alexei Bebnev. Mr. Bebnev, I'd like to ask you some questions about the December fifth shooting death of Vincent Carlotta outside of Marlon's Restaurant in Hell's Kitchen and —"

"I have nothing to say to you, *zhopa*," Bebnev snarled as he remained standing. "I know my rights. I want lawyer."

Guma stood and glared at the Russian. "Very well, Mr. Bebnev," he said. "Then I'll just inform you that you are under arrest for the December fifth murder of Vince Carlotta outside of Marlon's Restaurant in Hell's Kitchen. And now I'll advise you of your rights. You have the right to remain silent; anything you say can be used against you. You also have the right to an attorney; if you can't afford an attorney, one will be provided free of charge. Do you understand?"

"*Vali otsjuda!*" Bebnev cursed and spat on the floor.

Guma shook his head. "That's the second time you've spoken some Russian. What's it mean? Or would you like me to get a translator?"

"It means 'fuck off.' I want lawyer now!"

"I take it, then, that you understand your Miranda rights and have invoked your right to remain silent and have a lawyer present," Guma said as a police officer, summoned by Karp, entered the room. "You'll now be taken to the Tombs to be booked, and at your arraignment in court a lawyer will be appointed to represent you. Sleep well, Mr. Bebnev."

After Bebnev was escorted out, the men met in the hallway. "Guess I walked him," Guma said with a smile.

"I don't think he ever came up to the plate," Karp laughed. "It wasn't going to go any other way though, but still I got a good look at what we're going to be dealing with."

"Miller?" Fulton asked.

Standing, Karp replied, "Yeah, but not here. I got a call from Marlene; she's on her way back with the girlfriend, Nicoli Lopez. I want to talk to her in the conference room, and if things go the way I hope, we'll put them together up there before I try to talk to him."

"I hate to miss the rest of the festivities," Fulton said. "But if it's okay with you, I have something I want to do before the snow gets any deeper. If I'm right, I'll tell you about it when I get back."

Karp clapped him on the shoulder. "Okay, international man of mystery, I'll look forward to exchanging debriefings in the morning."

Ten minutes later, Karp was sitting at the conference room table with Guma when

Marlene walked in with a young woman. They stood as his wife made the introductions. Marlene then left to go home.

Karp turned to Lopez, who looked like she was about to cry. "Please have a seat," he said. "Can I get you a water, or a cup of coffee?"

"No, thank you," Lopez replied. Her voice trembled as she asked, "Are you going to arrest me?"

Karp shook his head. "No, I have no knowledge of any wrongdoing on your part. However, I do want to ask you some questions about your boyfriend, Gnat Miller, who I believe is involved in a murder, so if you feel like you need to have a lawyer present, I will get you one free of charge. And you can speak to the lawyer before talking to ADA Guma and me."

"No, that's okay," Lopez replied. "I just wanted to know if I was going to have to go to jail. I have a baby at the East Village Women's Shelter and I would want my mom to go get him. But your wife said I can trust you."

"Well, thank you," Karp said. "And to be clear, I'm not recording this conversation or, at least at this point, taking a statement from you to be used in court. I just wanted to talk to you about your boyfriend."

Lopez's large brown eyes filled with tears. "Is he going to be arrested?"

Karp nodded. "I'm afraid so. But maybe you can help me and help your boyfriend at the same time."

"Ask me anything then," Lopez said.

When she was finished talking, Karp left her with Guma to see if Miller had arrived.

When Gnat Miller entered the room with Karp and Detective Pete McNeely a minute later, Nicoli Lopez flew into her boyfriend's arms. "Guma and I are going to wait outside," Karp told the couple, "and give you two a chance to talk for about ten minutes. Detective McNeely will remain with you."

Signaling for Guma to leave with him, Karp led the way back into his office.

"So what do you think?" Guma asked.

"I think we got a shot," Karp said. "We need this guy to roll over, or we may never make a case."

The two men sat quietly for the next ten minutes, each lost in his own thoughts. Then Karp looked at his watch. "Time's up," he said. "Let's go see what we got."

Karp and Guma were met outside the conference room by the stenographer. He knocked on the door and the three entered. The young couple was standing over by the window looking out with their arms around each other's waists; Nicoli leaned her head against her boyfriend's shoulder. They turned to face Karp and the others.

"Have a seat, Mr. Miller. Nicoli, you can sit next to him if you like," Karp said, waiting for Mason to set up her stenographer's machine. "All right then. My name is Roger Karp; I'm the district attorney for the County of New York. We're here tonight with William Miller. Mr. Miller, I'd like to ask you some questions about the December fifth shooting death of Vincent Carlotta outside of Marlon's Restaurant in Hell's Kitchen. . . ."

Karp introduced the others and went through the litany of advising Miller of his Miranda rights. "Do you understand your rights?"

"Yes."

"And are you willing to speak to me now without a lawyer present?"

Pale and shaking, Miller looked over at his girlfriend, who placed her hand on his arm and nodded. "Yes, I am."

"As I said, Mr. Miller, we're here to talk to you about the murder of Vince Carlotta and what part you, Frank DiMarzo, and Alexei Bebnev played in that," Karp said.

Miller ran his fingers through his unruly red hair and rubbed at his eyes as he rocked in his seat. "Please, no," he whimpered.

"Look, Bill, I can understand getting caught up in something you didn't intend to do," Karp said. "But it's taking its toll. You look terrible. You're not sleeping. You're taking it out on people you love." He looked meaningfully at Nicoli. "And it's tearing you apart, destroying you from the inside out, and there's only one way to stop the process . . . and that's to tell the truth."

The rocking stopped. "I can't," Miller said. "Frankie's my best friend."

Karp straightened up again. "Look, it's up to you. Right now, you've got to do what's right for Bill Miller."

He let that sink in for a moment before continuing, his voice softer. "And there's one more thing. I know you're a new dad, and this is hard, thinking about what it's going to mean to Nicoli and your baby. But Vince Carlotta was a new dad, too. Think about what this has done to his wife and *his* baby, who will grow up without knowing his father. You have to ask yourself, 'Is that something I can live with? Or will I see Vince's kid every time I look into my boy's eyes, asking why I helped kill his dad? Why I wasn't enough of a man to admit it when I got caught?' Is that something you can live with, Bill?"

Miller's hands flew to his face and he sobbed. Nicoli patted his arm. "It's okay, Gnat," she said. "It's going to be okay. He's right, this is destroying you."

Wagging his head back and forth, Miller cried a few minutes more. "Jesus, I'm so fucking tired. I haven't slept a wink since . . ." The young man's voice trailed off.

"Since what, Gnat?" Karp asked.

Miller started to speak, then hesitated. "Can I get some sort of deal if I talk?" he asked hopefully.

Karp frowned. "I'm not making any deals here," he said. "If you're going to give me a statement and answer my questions, you have to do it of your own volition and without the promise of any sort of deal."

Miller licked his lips nervously and swallowed hard. Not without genuine sympathy for a ruined life, Karp laid his last card on the table. "And you know in your heart, Gnat, that this isn't about making a deal. It's about your soul."

For a moment, Miller sat absolutely still and silent. Then he stopped crying and for a moment Karp wondered if he'd lost him, but he didn't need to worry.

"Okay," Miller said at last, drying his tears and laying his hand on top of Nicoli's.

"Where should I start?"

"At the beginning, Gnat, and keep going until you get to the end."

"Well, it started when my friend Frankie DiMarzo . . ."

16

"Well, it started when my friend Frankie DiMarzo called me. He said this guy Alexei Bebnev had a job that would pay a lot of money."

Six months after the witness first said those words to him on a snowy winter's night, Karp stood in the well of a courtroom questioning Gnat Miller. He then turned away from Miller and looked over at the defense table. "Are the two men you just mentioned in the courtroom today?"

"Yes," said Miller, who sat forward on the edge of the witness chair. He wore a gray suit with a white shirt and paisley tie, and spoke with his head down and his mouth to the side of the microphone.

"Could you identify them for the jury, please?"

Looking directly at the defendants, Miller said, "Alexei Bebnev is on the right side of the table; he has short blond hair." He pointed at the young Russian, who just smirked and shook his head.

Miller hesitated as he shifted his gaze to the second defendant, his best friend, who glanced up at him but quickly looked away. "Frankie DiMarzo is on the left, with dark hair."

Addressing the court, Karp said, "Your Honor, let the record reflect that the witness has identified the defendants, Alexei Bebnev and Frank DiMarzo."

New York State Supreme Court Justice Robert See nodded and said. "The record will so note. Mr. Karp, please proceed."

"And how do you know the defendants?"

"I've known Frankie ever since . . ." Miller hesitated; he'd been told to avoid talking about their previous incarceration or crimes. "Since we were kids."

"You're friends?"

"Yeah, or at least we were."

"How about Alexei Bebnev?"

Miller frowned. "I met him through Frankie about seven months ago."

"What was the reason you met him?"

"Frankie said that Bebnev had a job for me and him."

Karp looked back at the witness on the stand. "What was the job the defendant Bebnev had for you and Frankie?"

"It was a job to kill a guy," Miller said.

Given the intense media coverage that the case had generated, it had taken two weeks to swear in twelve "tried-and-true" jurors. During the prosecution's opening statement, Karp had laid out a very concise and brief statement. "This was not a robbery," he'd said. "Not an argument in which tempers suddenly flared. Or for personal revenge. This was a cold-blooded murder planned and executed for money. The three defendants — Bebnev, DiMarzo, and Miller — were paid to murder a man they didn't even know. While Miller, the wheelman, sat in his car across the street, Bebnev and DiMarzo hid in the darkness of a Hell's Kitchen alley waiting for their target, Vince Carlotta. Wearing masks, they pretended to be simple robbers. As Vince Carlotta approached the alley, DiMarzo, the lookout, and Bebnev, the shooter, with his .38 caliber pistol, executed the deceased by firing two shots into his defenseless body, one shot to the chest and then one to the head. . . ."

Anticipating in trial preparation that whatever else the defense might attempt, their primary objective had to be discrediting Gnat Miller and questioning his motives, Karp emphasized that the case revolved around the issue of conscience. "Both those who have it and those who don't."

The most unusual aspect of his opening was explaining why he would not be calling the three men who were walking with Carlotta when the murder took place. When an attorney, particularly a prosecutor, calls a witness to the stand, he essentially vouches for the credibility of that person. Absolutely convinced that Vitteli, in league with Barros and Corcione, had orchestrated the murder, he couldn't put them on the stand knowing that they would lie about their involvement and the circumstances surrounding the murder. "Since this is not a trial about a robbery, we will not be calling the three individuals who were with the deceased at the time he was summarily executed in their presence. In fact, we have turned them over to the defense to call them in their case if they so wish. Simply, they'll do as they see fit."

After Karp's opening statement, the defense counsel exercised their right to delay making a statement until after the prosecution had presented its case in chief. Karp believed that this defense strategy was directly related to the personal motives of Conrad Clooney, the lead defense counsel.

In New York, indigent defendants charged with murder were assigned private counsel, not Legal Aid public defenders. The lawyers were selected from an eligibility list filed with the presiding Supreme Court justice at the time of the arraignment of the accused on the underlying indictment. The lawyers who comprised this pool were primarily the private counsel who practiced in the criminal courts on a regular basis. Occasionally, exceptions were made when the prestigious so-called white-shoe Wall Street firms requested to be included; sometimes to provide pro bono, sometimes for other less noble reasons.

While DiMarzo was appointed two of the regulars from the eligibility list, Bebnev was represented by the firm Peabody, Schmidt, Reich, and Fritz. Conrad Clooney was the firm's senior partner in charge of litigation and opted to represent Bebnev. Shortly after the indictments of the three suspects, he announced he was taking on the case pro bono. He claimed that he was drawn to get involved when his "assessment" of the case was that "the State has overreached without sufficiently considering other viable suspects."

As Clooney's firm was known for complex Securities and Exchange Commission litigation, questions were raised about why he wanted to get involved in a murder case.

However, skeptics believed that Clooney's ambition to be appointed to the federal bench steered him toward the high-profile case. Rumor among the Wall Street white shoes was that he believed he would receive major ink and face time in the print and electronic media that would demonstrate his alleged expertise and enhance his chances.

Six months after Clooney jumped into the fray, Karp wondered if the short but movie star–handsome attorney regretted his choice of battles. It would have been a tough hill to climb even for an experienced criminal defense attorney. While Clooney claimed to have "cut his teeth" as a prosecutor with the U.S. Attorney's Office in Baltimore, a quick check of his record there indicated he'd never tried anything more serious than basic fraud.

In fact, the average caseload of an assistant U.S. attorney was about one-tenth of that of a Manhattan ADA assigned to the Homicide Bureau, who was responsible for between thirty-five and fifty murder cases. Not burdened with a heavy caseload, assistant U.S. attorneys could spend anywhere between six and eight months chasing semicolons and commas while reading grand jury testimony to determine whether or not to recommend an indictment for fraud or other white-collar-related crimes.

Without an opening statement to give him a feel for the strategy of the defense case, Karp had to anticipate any possibility. But that was not an issue, as he believed that success in the courtroom was all about intense and comprehensive preparation, leaving little room for the unexpected.

After Clooney declined to give an opening statement, Karp launched into the prosecution case by calling the technical witnesses who, though playing bit parts, were necessary to set the stage for the main characters. The first was the civil engineer Jack Farrell, who'd gone to the Hell's Kitchen and New Rochelle crime scenes, measured the areas where evidence was found, and reduced his computations to two diagrams, People's 1 and 2 in evidence. Next up was the police photographer who'd arrived at the crime scene the evening of the murder and then gone to New Rochelle at the request of Detective Fulton. The photographs also included a large black-and-white aerial view of the Carlotta house and neighborhood. He testified that he had taken the aerial photo from an NYPD helicopter so that he was able to say that it fairly and accurately represented the scene as he observed it.

The NYPD photographer was followed by a procession of pro forma homicide witnesses: the first police officers on the scene, as well as the paramedics and the assistant medical examiner who dispassionately described the fatal wounds observed during autopsy.

Karp controlled the pace of the testimony, careful to let the witnesses make the points necessary but without boring the jurors. Then he called William "Gnat" Miller to the stand to begin the second day.

As Karp waited for Miller to take his place in the witness box, he looked over the other "players" in the courtroom. The pews in the gallery behind the defense table were lightly populated. Alexei Bebnev, who he knew was in the country illegally and had no family, also apparently had no supporters in the room. The defendant didn't seem to mind, though, as he laughed and joked with Clooney.

On the other hand, Frank DiMarzo appeared to have a large family comprised of an elderly couple, who Karp took to be his mother and father, and a half-dozen younger women ranging in age from their teens to thirties who he guessed were sisters, cousins, or family friends. They'd already been seated that morning when the defendants were brought in. They greeted DiMarzo's appearance with small cries of support and grief. He looked at them briefly but then hung his head. Karp had not seen him look back since sitting down at the defense table, nor did he engage with his two court-appointed lawyers who sat on either side of him.

There was one young blond woman sitting several rows behind the defense table who sat taking notes on a yellow legal pad. Karp had learned from Guma, who'd seen a pretty face and chatted her up, that she was a law intern for longtime union lawyer Syd Kowalski, a crony of Charlie Vitteli.

Elsewhere in the gallery, a dozen or so tough-looking men who Karp thought might be union members sat on the "prosecution side" of the courtroom. Scattered throughout were members of the media, who sat scribbling on notepads or quietly talking and giggling among themselves.

There was also the usual assortment of "court buffs," people who followed interesting or high-profile cases and appeared each day to watch the wheels of justice grind. Some looked like retirees who actually dressed up for the occasion; others were more ragtag street people looking for a place to rest for a few hours with, perhaps, free entertainment. Nothing unusual on this day except for three shabbily dressed women who entered the room just a few moments before Judge See took the bench. Looking lost, they sat down in the back row and put their heads together in hushed conversation, looking up now and again as if worried someone might overhear them.

As William "Gnat" Miller was sworn in, Karp glanced over at Judge See. Built like a one-iron, with a very calming demeanor, the jurist was highly knowledgeable and well trained; in fact, he'd been a brilliant trial lawyer. He commanded respect and diffused emotional court exchanges with his even temperament.

See also liked to move his cases along, and Karp had wasted no time asking Miller to identify his co-conspirators. "A job? What sort of job?"

Taking a deep breath, Gnat let it out as a sigh, then answered. "Bebnev was going to shoot somebody and he needed a lookout, which was Frank, and somebody with a car who could drive, which was me."

"And were you to be paid for participating in this crime?"

Miller nodded. "Yeah, Frankie and I were going to split fourteen thousand."

"And were you in fact paid?"

"Most of it. We each got six thousand. Bebnev cheated us on the rest."

"Did you know who Alexei Bebnev intended to shoot?"

"Not at first. Just some guy in New Rochelle."

"When did you learn the victim's name?"

"When we were parked up the street from his house," Miller said. "Frankie had a magazine photograph Bebnev had given him to make sure it was the right guy. I didn't get a good look at it but there were four guys standing together; one of them had a circle drawn around his face. When they drove up to the house, Frankie looked at the photo and said something like, 'That's the guy. That's Vince Carlotta.' "

"When you say 'they' drove up to the house, who do you mean?"

"The Carlottas," Miller responded, glancing quickly at the defendants before averting his eyes again. "Mr. Carlotta, his wife, and his . . . his baby."

"Did Bebnev intend to shoot Mr. Carlotta at that time?"

"Yeah. That was the plan."

"Please explain?"

"Bebnev had a gun and kept saying how he was going to point it at the guy's face and pull the trigger. He kept saying, 'Bang, bang, asshole is dead.' "

"You said the defendant DiMarzo spotted Mr. Carlotta while you were parked up the street from the Carlotta residence in New Rochelle."

"Yeah."

"Mr. Miller, do you use any tobacco products?"

"Yeah, I chew tobacco."

"And were you chewing tobacco the night you waited outside the Carlotta residence?"

"Yeah."

"What were you doing with the tobacco juice?"

"I was spitting into an empty beer bottle."

"Do you remember what you did with that beer bottle?"

"Yeah, I had to take a leak, so I got out and went over to that bush on the picture there," Gnat said, pointing at the easel. "I took the bottle with me. That's about when the Carlottas drove past, so I just tossed the bottle into the bushes."

"Was Frank DiMarzo using any tobacco products?"

"No. Frankie don't chew."

"What about smoke?"

"Nah, he don't smoke, either. He's kind of a health nut."

"What about Bebnev?"

"Yeah, he smokes like a chimney," Gnat agreed. "Some crappy Russian cigarette. He thinks they're better than American cigarettes but they smell like shit."

"Fuck you, *sooka*," Bebnev muttered, loud enough to be heard by the jurors and the judge, who gave him a blistering look that caused the Russian to drop his head.

"He was smoking while you waited in the car?"

"Yeah."

"What was he doing with the cigarette butts?"

"Mostly tossing them out the window. One time he put one out on my floorboard, which pissed me off. He's a pig."

Bebnev's eyes widened but he said nothing, just looked back up at Gnat with a tight smile on his face.

"What happened after the Carlottas got home?"

"Well, we drove to the front of the house and Frankie and Bebnev got out."

"And what did you do?"

"I waited in the car."

"Then what happened?"

"Nothing."

"Nothing?"

"The lady answered the door. Then the

guy showed up. They talked but nothing happened. Frankie and Bebnev got back in the car and we drove back to the city."

"Did anybody explain why nothing happened?"

"Yeah, Bebnev said he wasn't paid to shoot no lady and a kid. I think he just lost his nerve."

As he spoke, Gnat looked over at Bebnev, whose eyes bugged. He looked like he was going to yell something, but his attorney grabbed his arm and spoke to him quietly. The Russian yanked his arm away from the attorney, his face a mask of rage, but he remained silent.

Karp turned to the judge and asked for permission for Gnat to step down and walk over to the easel. "Mr. Miller, have you ever seen this aerial photograph of the Carlotta residence and neighborhood before?"

"Yes, you've showed it to me before in your office," Miller answered.

"Did I tell you at that time why I was showing it to you?"

"Yes. So that I would know what I was looking at in court. And you wanted to know where I parked that night."

Karp handed Miller a black marker. "Would you please draw a circle to show the jury where you parked when you were waiting for the Carlottas to return that night."

"Right about here, in front of that school," Miller said as he drew the circle.

"Okay, would you write 'C' inside the circle to indicate 'car'?" Karp said. "Now, take the marker and indicate where you parked on the street after the Carlottas arrived."

Gnat did as he was told and then faced Karp, who towered over him and said, "Thank you, you may return to your seat."

When Gnat was seated, Karp asked, "So after the defendant Bebnev got cold feet you drove back to Brooklyn?"

Gnat nodded. "Yeah. I thought it might be over. I was hoping it was over. But then Frankie called a few days later and said it was back on. Only now it was going to go down in Hell's Kitchen outside of a restaurant called Marlon's."

After this reply, Karp looked at his watch and then at the judge. "Your Honor, it's about the lunch hour, and this would be a good place to break," he said.

Judge See glanced at the clock on the wall over the courtroom doors and nodded. "I'm sure we're all ready for a bite," he said to the jurors. "The court clerk will escort you back to the jury room and we'll see you in an hour." He banged the gavel. "Court is in recess."

17

After speaking quickly to Guma, Karp left the courtroom and hurried down to the street to grab a hot dog at the vendor next to Dirty Warren's newsstand. He barely had time to take a bite of the dog garnished with mustard and hot sauerkraut when his eccentric friend poked his head around the corner of the stand.

"Hey, Karp," Dirty Warren yelled. "How's it . . . fuck piss shit . . . going upstairs? I hear you got one of the . . . oh boy whoop . . . perps on the stand."

"Yeah, the getaway driver," Karp acknowledged. "A guy named 'Gnat' Miller. You know him?"

"Nah, I don't hang . . . tits oh boy ohhhh boy . . . out with murderers, well, other than David Grale."

Karp rolled his eyes at the mention of the insane killer vigilante who haunted the subterranean bowels of New York City with his army of Mole People, preying on evildoers like some sort of dark comic book antihero. "How is David these days?"

"I'm going to go . . . whoop whoop . . . see him tonight," Dirty Warren replied. "He got word to me that he may have some important info about your case. Not to change the subject or anything but this guy, Gnat Miller, I guess his . . . whoop whoop . . . conscience got the better of him?"

"Yeah, that's about the size of it," Karp replied. "That and Marlene nailed his butt, no pun intended, and we had him dead to rights."

"Yeah, she's a regular Nancy Drew. Hey, here's one for you: 'Conscience . . . that stuff can drive you nuts!' Whoop oh boy nuts balls."

"I thought I told you to never again imitate Brando doing *On the Waterfront,*" Karp growled, feigning a serious look.

Dirty Warren giggled. "I thought it was appropriate given the circumstances."

"Maybe so, maybe so," Karp replied with a grin. "By the way, you hear anything more about these supposed eyewitnesses to the murder coming forward?"

Dirty Warren acted like Karp had just revealed a state secret. He came out from his newsstand and walked up next to Karp.

"Careful," he said. "The streets got . . . crap my ass . . . ears. Nothing but rumors still. People are scared. Folks are getting their throats . . . oh boy whoop oh boy . . . cut, if you know what I mean."

Karp nodded. "Yeah, I know," he said. "But if you get a chance to talk to any of these people, you tell them that I'll personally guarantee their safety, but I can't do that if I don't know who they are."

"Yeah, yeah, sure," Dirty Warren said. "If I talk to them I . . . boobs titties . . . will."

"All right, my friend, got to run," Karp said, stuffing the last bit of hot dog into his mouth and sipping the remains of his orange soda as he headed back into the Criminal Courts Building.

As he rode the elevator up, Karp wondered if he would ever be able to knock over the last domino in this case, the seemingly elusive Charlie Vitteli. He would have loved to see the photograph Miller had mentioned that DiMarzo used to identify Carlotta and wondered if it would have led him to the end of the game. But a search of DiMarzo's home and Miller's car had not turned it up.

But the game's not over till the fat lady sings, he reminded himself. *And we're a long ways from that.*

When Karp reentered the courtroom he

noticed that among the few spectators already there were the three poorly dressed women he'd seen previously. "Good afternoon, ladies," he said as he walked past.

The women looked at him, their eyes widening with surprise or . . . something he couldn't put his finger on. Then they went back to their conversation.

"When?" one asked the others.

"When the hurly-burly's done," the black woman replied.

"When the battle's lost or won," added the last.

Karp shook his head. *Street people quoting Shakespeare in court,* he thought. *The denizens of this city never cease to amaze me.* He considered whether to toss a line at them, but decided to check in on Miller, who was in the witness room adjacent to the court.

"How you holding up?" Karp asked when he walked in.

"Okay," Miller said and shrugged. "I wish I could talk to Frankie and try to explain why I'm testifying. We've been friends for a long time and been through a lot of good times and bad. He's my kid's godfather. I remember talking to him in our cell at juvie; we swore we'd never turn on each other."

"That was before the two of you helped kill a man for money," Karp pointed out.

"I know, I know, and it was weighing me down like I was buried under a pile of bricks. It's got to be tough on Frankie, too. I know you think he's a scumbag, but he's really not a bad guy deep down inside."

Karp nodded without commenting. He was thinking about that night when Miller first confessed to Marlene at the East Village Women's Shelter and then later to him in his office and talked about the crime's effect on his conscience. The money had been nice, he said, allowing him and Nicoli to get a cheap one-bedroom apartment in the Bronx. She'd been so happy to get out of her parents' house. For a few days he had a glimpse of what life could have been like in the loving arms of his wife and child. But in the quiet of the night guilt crept in like a burglar, stealing sleep and whatever happiness had been bought with blood money.

It had been a relief to confess, he said. A brick lifted with every answer he gave Karp until, at last, he felt he could breathe again. Later, he told Karp that the night he confessed, surrounded by the hell known as the Tombs, he slept like a child. He even came to regard the tall prosecutor as a stern, yet understanding, priest to whom he'd confessed his transgressions.

Later, during one of their many meetings, Miller told him about seeing Nicoli the day after he confessed in the visiting room. "She said, 'You're so fuckin' stupid. We could have made it. You could have got a job; I could have done day care and still looked after Billy Junior. But you let Frankie and that Russian asshole lead you down the path straight to hell.' I told her that I couldn't blame them, that I could have said no. She said, 'That's right and now you got nothin'.' "

The sound sleep Miller had experienced after his confession had eluded him the night after he talked to Nicoli as her words played in his mind like a skipping record. *"You ain't got nothin'."* By morning he knew it was true, he had nothing left and had despaired. So he was surprised when a guard told him the next day that he had a visitor and discovered it was Nicoli.

" 'It's gonna take a long time for me to forgive you, Gnat,' " he recalled for Karp. " 'You've destroyed our life together, but I don't want nobody but you. You may be stupid as a stick, but you're my guy and Billy's father. I want him to know who his daddy is . . . and I want his father to know he's loved.' "

253

Miller said he'd broken down and wept, but then he tried to talk her out of caring what happened to him. Although he didn't mean it, he told her she was being stupid and that he didn't really love her so she might as well move on. "I lied and told her she was just a piece of ass to me."

It didn't work. She just told him to shut up, that she was going to visit him and write to him whether he liked it or not. Although it replaced a brick or two of guilt, in all honesty he was grateful that she had kept her word. He'd been put in administrative segregation to protect him — informants' lives weren't worth spit in the general population and word was, according to one trustee he talked to, a lot of very dangerous people wanted him dead. But she visited him with Billy Junior at least once a week since his incarceration, even after the DA's wife, Marlene, moved Nicoli and their son to a safe location.

Gnat didn't feel that he deserved Nicoli's loyalty, but he knew he needed her support to get through the trial and sentencing. He figured that at some point in the future, she'd meet someone new, someone with possibilities, and then the visits would grow fewer and maybe stop altogether. If he was lucky, she might drop him a line and a photograph from time to time to let him know how she and their son were doing. But for now he'd take what he could get.

Early that morning, she'd been sitting in the gallery trying to be brave as she clutched a tissue and smiled slightly. Her father was even sitting next to her and though his face was impassive, he'd nodded slightly when Gnat looked at him.

As he waited now to take the stand again, Miller told Karp that he wished he could tell his friend DiMarzo how liberating it had been to come clean. He hoped Frankie could see it in his eyes when they looked at each other over the distance between the witness stand and the defense table, but his friend wouldn't look at him.

"Frankie's got to live with himself," Karp said and started to leave. "You have to live with Gnat Miller."

The young man nodded and dropped his head, but then he quickly looked up. "There's one more thing," he said. "Something I got to say now even though I know it doesn't change anything."

"What's that?" Karp asked as he hesitated at the door.

"If you get a chance, would you tell Mrs. Carlotta . . ." Miller said, choking up, ". . . I'm sorry. I'm so sorry. I don't expect her forgiveness, but I am truly sorry."

Without looking back, Karp nodded. "I'll let her know," he said and left.

Karp walked back into the courtroom from the side door leading to the witness room at the same moment that Charlie Vitteli entered from the main door in the company of Syd Kowalski and the blond intern. The prosecutor and the union boss locked eyes. Although it might not have been clear to most of the people in the room, the look they shared was between mortal enemies who know that eventually one must fail and the other triumph.

Vitteli smirked and began to walk forward to find a seat. Then he glanced to the side and suddenly stopped when he saw the three ragged women Karp had spoken to a few minutes earlier. His face turned pale and his eyes bugged while the three women shrank away from him.

Wonder what that's all about? Karp thought, but it was over in a flash. Vitteli set his jaw and marched forward to find a seat as the women resumed their incessant chatter.

Soon the judge returned from lunch, quickly assembled the jury, and directed Miller to retake the stand. "Mr. Karp, you may continue your direct examination of the witness, who I will remind is still under oath," Judge See said.

"Thank you, Your Honor," Karp said, walking out into the well of the courtroom. "Mr. Miller, I'd like to turn now to that evening last December, the night Mr. Carlotta was murdered. Would you please tell the jury your role in the night's events?"

"Uh, yeah, well, Frankie called and said it was back on," Miller began.

"When you refer to Frankie who are you referring to?"

"Frank DiMarzo, the defendant."

"So you just testified that the defendant Frank DiMarzo called you and said it was back on. What was back on?"

"The hit," Miller said. "Bebnev was going to shoot Carlotta and we were supposed to help."

"Okay, go on."

"Well, I picked Frankie up at his folks' place in Red Hook and then we met Bebnev in Little Odessa off Atlantic Avenue. Then we drove through the Battery Tunnel into Manhattan to Hell's Kitchen. We cruised past Marlon's and I let Bebnev and Frankie out near the alley; then I went down the street and pulled a U-turn and parked on the other side, where it was away from the streetlight."

"Did you know what was going to happen?" Karp asked.

"Yeah, I mean, if Bebnev didn't lose his nerve again," Miller said. "They were supposed to wait for Mr. Carlotta to come out of the bar, and then jump out of the alley like it was a robbery, except Bebnev was supposed to shoot Carlotta."

"While you were waiting, could you see the defendants in the alley?"

"Not real well, but a little. Sometimes they'd poke their heads out."

"Could you tell what else they were doing?"

"Just watching and waiting, I guess. Bebnev was smoking. I could see him when he lit up and the glow from his cigarette."

"Then what happened?"

"Well, first these two big guys came out of the bar. Frankie and Bebnev ducked back in the alley, and they walked right past them. Then this group of four guys came around the corner. Maybe the same guys that were in the photograph, I don't know for sure, but one of them was Carlotta."

"Continue, please."

"When the guys got near the alley, Bebnev jumped out and Frankie kind of walked out behind him. They had masks on . . ."

"So how did you know who was who?"

"Well, Bebnev's taller and skinnier. And Frankie didn't have a gun; only Bebnev had a gun, which he had in his hand."

"What did Bebnev do with the gun?"

"He was pointing it at the men. It was kind of hard to see everything that was going on; they were sort of bunched up close together. But the next thing I knew, there was a flash and like a 'pop,' and one of the guys goes down sort of on his back. Then he tried to get up and Bebnev shot him again."

"What were you doing while this was happening?"

Miller furrowed his brow. "To be honest, just kind of sitting there, like I was numb or something."

"So what happened next?"

"It looked like something got said and then the guys from the bar started handing over their wallets and watches. Then Bebnev and Frankie started running across the street, so I started the car, and when they jumped in, I took off."

"Where'd you go?"

"Back to Brooklyn."

"You stop anywhere along the way?"

"Yeah. I took a different way back because Bebnev wanted me to go to the Brooklyn Bridge. When we were on the bridge, Bebnev told me to stop, and then he threw the gun into the East River."

"What happened to the wallets and the watches?"

"Bebnev kept the watches, and we split up the money, a couple hundred bucks."

"How long before you were paid for the murder?"

"A few days, and we only got part of it. A week or so later we got the rest, or at least the rest of what he said we were going to get."

"Tell us how you received the second payment?"

"Frankie said he had to go to a bar in Little Odessa with Bebnev to meet with the guy who arranged the hit. But Frankie had to wait outside while they did their deal. The guy smacked Bebnev in the face and that's why he said he was keeping some of our money. He gave Frankie an envelope with the money."

Karp strolled over toward the gallery and looked at Vitteli as he asked, "So the murder of Vince Carlotta wasn't some robbery that went bad?"

"No, it was a hit," Miller said. "That guy hired Bebnev and Bebnev hired us."

Exchanging another hard look with Vitteli, Karp turned and walked slowly over to the jury box, where he leaned against the rail. "Mr. Miller, were you offered any kind of deal by my office, or any other, for your testimony today?"

Miller looked out into the gallery at his girlfriend. "I agreed to plead guilty to manslaughter in the first degree."

"Was any promise of sentence made?"

"No."

"Do you realize you could receive as much as twenty-five years with a mandatory minimum of eight years, four months before you would be eligible for parole?"

"Yes. I agreed to plead guilty to manslaughter and I could receive the maximum time. The only other thing you told me was that if I told the truth here, you would tell the judge at the time of my sentencing."

"Have you told us the truth, the whole truth, Mr. Miller?"

"Yes, sir."

"No further questions."

18

"You may proceed with cross-examination, Mr. Clooney."

At Judge See's invitation, the defense attorney stood up and strode purposefully across the well until he stood directly in front of Miller, scowling up at the red-headed young man. "Mr. Miller, do you have a criminal record?" he demanded.

"Yeah, I already told you I did when Mr. Karp asked me about it."

"Would you tell us again?"

"I did some time in juvie for burglary. I've also done some small-time stuff as an adult and been in jail, no prisons."

"So you have a long history of committing crimes, isn't that right, Mr. Miller?" Clooney said.

"I guess you could say that."

" 'I guess you could say that,' Mr. Miller?" the attorney mocked as he looked over at the jurors and rolled his eyes. "Do you think that makes you a trustworthy person?"

"What do you mean?"

"I mean, should these fine people," Clooney said, extending his hand toward the jury box, "trust the word of a criminal?"

"Depends."

"Depends? Depends on what?"

"On whether he's telling the truth."

"And how do we know that you, who spent a good deal of your life being a dishonest criminal, are telling the truth?"

"Hey, I'm here because I pled guilty to manslaughter, and I'm looking at twenty-five years in the can, because I was stupid enough to be the wheelman with Bebnev and Frankie as part of a plan to kill Mr. Carlotta," Miller replied, his voice growing angry and defiant. "And, by the way, I watched Bebnev shoot Mr. Carlotta. That's how you know I'm telling the truth."

Karp wasn't surprised by Miller's reaction. Generally witnesses who testify struggle on both direct and cross; it's an environment that they don't want to be part of and certainly are not used to.

"We're just supposed to take your word for it, right?" Clooney said but didn't wait for an answer. "Let's go back to that night you were supposedly in New Rochelle with the defendants. You've explained already that today isn't the first time you've seen that aerial photograph, is it?"

"Correct. As I said before, Mr. Karp showed it to me in his office."

"And he pointed out which house was the Carlotta residence, correct?"

"Well, yeah."

"Did he point out where you were supposed to have parked your car?"

For a moment, Miller looked confused; then he shook his head. "No. He asked me to show him where I parked."

"So he didn't give you any help?"

"Mr. Clooney, I was there and Mr. Karp wasn't," Miller retorted. "He didn't offer any help, and I didn't need any."

Clooney scowled. "I object and ask that answer be stricken."

Judge See, who had his chin resting on his hand as he leaned on an elbow, raised his eyebrows and said, "On what grounds, Mr. Clooney?"

"His answer was not directly responsive to my question," Clooney complained.

"Quite the contrary, Mr. Clooney," Judge See advised. "You asked him if he needed any help, and it's clear how he responded. Your objection is overruled, please proceed."

Glancing nervously back at the amused

media seated in the first two rows of the gallery, Clooney asked, "Well, did Mr. Karp ask you about someone smoking cigarettes in your car?"

"Yeah. I told him Bebnev was smoking."

"And did he suggest that, perhaps, Mr. Bebnev casually tossed these cigarette butts on the ground where they could be found?"

"No. He asked what Bebnev did with the cigarette butts. That's when I told him about the one he crushed out on my floor-board."

"Yes, I remember, you were angry," Clooney replied drolly. He walked over near the witness box with his head down as if deep in thought. "So, Mr. Miller, let me get this straight: you parked up the street near the school, and then drove over to the Carlotta house, where the defendants got out of the car, knocked on the door, and when the Carlottas answered, your friends asked for jobs?"

"That's what Bebnev told Mr. Carlotta."

"So then we're to believe that here's a perfect opportunity to do the job and get paid thousands of dollars, but instead he asked for work on the dock?"

"He just made that up, Mr. Clooney," Miller said matter-of-factly. "He said he

265

didn't want to shoot a woman and her baby."

"You think he chickened out?"

"That's one way to put it."

"But three nights later, he's a cold-blooded killer who walks up to a man and shoots him in the chest and then in the head. Quite the change."

"Yeah, there was no wife, no baby there. You still don't get it, do ya?" Miller said, shaking his head.

"No, I don't, Mr. Miller," Clooney retorted. "But since you've assured us that we can take the word of a career criminal, we have to believe it's true."

Miller didn't bother responding other than to just stare at the attorney and shake his head again.

"Mr. Miller, did the defendants wear masks when they went to the door of the Carlotta residence?"

"No."

"Was the front porch well lit or dark?"

"Uh, there was a porch light and light from inside the house when the door was opened."

"So the Carlottas would have seen their faces easily?"

"Yeah, I mean, I could see them and I was sitting in the car."

"So was the alley well lit, too? Was there a streetlight right there?"

Miller looked at Karp, who sat expressionless. "No, it was pretty dark."

"So why wear masks at the alley but not at the house?"

"Because they were going to kill Mr. Carlotta but were pretending to be robbers. Man, you just don't get it!"

"Objection! I ask that be stricken from the record."

"What part exactly, Mr. Clooney?" Judge See inquired.

"Well, all of it."

Judge See sighed. "Mr. Clooney, be careful of the questions you ask, because you may not like the answers. Your objection is overruled."

Clooney stood staring at the judge for a moment, obviously flustered. This wasn't going the way he'd planned. Trying to get back on solid footing, he returned to the old cross-examination ploy of questioning the crime partner's true motive: the deal.

Clooney returned to his position in front of the witness stand. "Mr. Miller, you testified that you received a plea bargain from the district attorney?"

"Yes."

"And you've pleaded guilty to manslaughter?"

"Yes."

"Have you been sentenced yet?"

"No, not yet."

"That won't happen until after this trial, correct?"

"That's right."

Clooney turned toward the jurors. "Then how, pray tell, are we supposed to know that you will not be given a deal between now and your testimony on that stand," he said, pointing back at Miller, "and your sentencing?"

"Objection, Your Honor," Karp said "The record will reflect that Mr. Miller has pleaded guilty to manslaughter in the first degree and may be facing a sentence of twenty-five years in prison with a mandatory minimum of eight years, four months. Now, if Mr. Clooney is suggesting that I, as the district attorney, would alter that disposition in an attempt to deceive the jury and this court, let him come forward with his evidence . . . NOW!"

Clooney stood with his hands on his hips, looking up at the ceiling as if waiting for divine intervention. Finally, Judge See broke the silence. "Mr. Clooney, do you have any good faith offering substantiating the serious charge of prosecutorial misconduct you intimated?"

At first speechless, Clooney stammered before finally saying, "Well, Your Honor, these things do happen, you know?"

"Is that the best you can do, Mr. Clooney?" the judge responded. He turned to the jury. "Ladies and gentlemen," he said in a very slow, dispassionate voice, "please do not accept as evidence counsels' questions alone. The evidence you consider is the question coupled with the answer. Now, I'm going to ask you to please disregard Mr. Clooney's last question, because I'm going to strike it from the record."

Licking his lips, Clooney grimaced before turning back to the witness stand. "Mr. Miller, are you a criminal?"

"Yes."

"Are you a liar?"

"Sometimes, but not now."

"How are these jurors supposed to know that?"

Miller looked over at the jurors. "I guess they'll have to look at everything and decide."

Clooney did look somewhat surprised by the answer. But he just sneered one last time at the witness and said, "No more questions."

"Care to redirect, Mr. Karp?" Judge See asked after Clooney took his seat.

"Yes, Your Honor," Karp said, rising but remaining behind the table. "Mr. Miller, have you answered all these questions — mine and Mr. Clooney's — truthfully and completely?"

"Yes. As best I could."

"And that includes confessing to taking part in the murder of Vince Carlotta?"

"Yes. I knew we were going to kill the man, and I drove the getaway car."

"What will be the consequence of you telling the truth and confessing to murder, Mr. Miller?"

"I'll be going to prison for a very long time," Miller replied.

"Mr. Miller, do you have a family?"

The young man's head fell and he covered his face with his hands as he nodded.

"I'm sorry, Mr. Miller, but you'll have to answer so that the court reporter can hear you," Karp said not unkindly.

A sob escaped from Miller, but then he wiped at his nose with his sleeve and looked up at Karp. "The only family I got is my girlfriend, Nicoli, and our baby, Billy Junior."

"So the price you'll pay for your confession and testimony is that you'll be going to prison for many years," Karp said. "And the only way you'll get to see your son grow up is if his mother agrees to bring him to see you in the prison visiting room."

"Yes," Miller said, choking on the word. "That's all I'll have."

As the witness started to cry again, Karp gave him a few moments to gather himself. He walked over to the witness chair, picked up a pitcher of water, and poured it into a cup for Miller. He then looked out at the gallery and saw Nicoli with her face buried in her father's chest. The man had his arm around his daughter's shoulders, trying to hold her as her body shook in grief.

Karp walked a few feet closer to the jury box and looked at the witness. "Mr. Miller, why did you confess to this crime and agree to testify at this trial?"

Miller looked up with tears streaming down his face. "Because I did what I said I did. I helped kill a man for money."

"But why not take your chances at trial? Why aren't you sitting at that table with the other two defendants?"

Miller now looked over at Frank Di-Marzo. "Because I couldn't live with it anymore. Mr. Carlotta was a new dad, too, and because of me, his son will grow up without him." He wiped at his eyes. "Just like my son will be growing up without me."

Speaking gently in a quiet courtroom, Karp asked his last question. "Mr. Miller, what motivated you to come forward and testify?"

Miller sat silently just staring at Karp, and then said, "I'm afraid to think about what I've done, because I believe in heaven and hell."

"Thank you, Mr. Miller. Your Honor, I have no further questions."

Judge See glanced at Clooney. "Defense counsel care to recross?"

Without looking up, Clooney waved a hand dismissively. "I've heard enough."

Nodding to the court clerk, the judge said, "Very well, Mr. Miller, you may step down from the witness stand, and Mr. Karp you may —"

The judge was interrupted by a loud scream in the gallery. Everyone in the courtroom instantly turned in that direction. An old woman dressed in black, DiMarzo's mother, stood pointing a bony finger at Miller, who stood transfixed in the witness box. "He lies!" the old woman shrieked. "My Frankie would never do such a thing!"

The elderly man next to her, DiMarzo's father, placed a hand on her arm, as a younger women embraced her. "Please,

Momma, don't make a scene," she said, trying to comfort Mrs. DiMarzo. But the old woman just wailed.

Judge See banged his gavel several times, but when Mrs. DiMarzo continued to cry out, he had court security remove her. The courtroom was shocked into silence, but then a single loud sob ripped the dead air.

All eyes turned to Frank DiMarzo, who sat with his elbows on the defense table and his face in his hands. "I'm sorry, Momma," he cried. "I'm so sorry."

The courtroom drama caught everyone by surprise. Judge See was the first to recover. He peered over at the jurors, several of whom looked to be on the verge of crying as well, and smiled benevolently. "I think this is a good time to take a break. As you are aware, a trial can be a very emotional event. Much is at stake here for the defendants and for the People. I just ask you to remember that it is your sworn duty to rely solely on the evidence as you hear it from the witness stand, and from whatever exhibits are admitted into evidence. Please keep an open mind until you've heard all the evidence, as well as the summations from counsel, and then I will charge you with the law. We'll resume in about fifteen minutes."

19

Joey Barros closed the door of Vitteli's office at union headquarters across from the Hudson River docks and turned to face the other three men in the room. "Sorry I'm late, boss," he said, addressing Vitteli. "I was just talking to a couple of my boys, and they said that there's starting to be some grumbling with the membership about this stuff in court about somebody paying to have Vince killed. Some of Vince's guys, including T. J. Martindale, are watching the trial and reporting back to the others."

"The Malcheks are getting nervous, too," Syd Kowalski added. He was standing near the window looking out at the docks. "They got a lot of money invested in this project. They need docks where they can count on everybody looking the other way. That was the deal."

"Tell them to relax, we'll handle it, as long as they do their part," Vitteli growled.

"You tell them to relax," Kowalski countered. "The Russians aren't good at relaxing when there's money involved; in fact, they're fuckin' uptight. They ain't going to like it if this trial screws things up."

Vitteli sat back and studied the other three — Kowalski, Barros, and Jackie Corcione — as he pulled out a cigar and lit it. "What about our other problem children?"

"I wouldn't worry about Bebnev," Barros answered. "He's a few cards short of a full deck and that idiot Lvov should have never used him, but the Malcheks have reached out to him in the Tombs. They got him thinking that if he gets convicted, they'll get him out and then he'll be a big man with the organization. He's probably dreaming up his prison tattoos right now; they're the same thing as bragging rights with the Russian mob."

"Yeah, well, if he gets convicted and then realizes that he's going to be in the can for a long fucking time, his attitude could change," Vitteli pointed out.

"Syd and I already had this discussion with the Malcheks," Barros said. "They're willing to play the game for now and then take care of the problem later. Soon as he gets in general population, he's done."

"What about this DiMarzo punk?" Kowalski said. "My girl in the courtroom says he don't look so good, like he's falling apart or something. His mom made quite the scene today."

"Yeah, well, he's got his family to worry about," Barros said. "Apparently he got some mail from an unknown source awhile back with a photograph of his mom outside the house in Red Hook; I guess some real a-hole drew a black line across her. So he's kept his mouth shut and doesn't dare open it. The same thing happens to him when he gets in general population."

"But what if he talks first?" Vitteli asked. "Wouldn't be the first time some punk gave up his own mother to save his ass."

Barros shrugged. "He can't know much anyway," he said. "Me and Jackie only met Bebnev, and even he didn't know our last names or who we work for. He might have known that Lvov was involved, but that fat fuck ain't talking no more. And this kid, Gnat Miller, he knows even less than Di-Marzo. He's never even heard of you or Karp would have used it by now."

"You should have killed them before they got caught," Corcione, who'd been sitting in a chair in the corner, blurted out.

Barros looked at him and laughed. "See who's turned all blood-thirsty. The little faggot's suddenly a stone-cold killer. Tell you what, Jackie, you wet your pants when the going gets rough, that's why your old man sent you off to college. So leave the bloody stuff to real men."

Vitteli rapped his knuckles on the table. "Knock it off. The last thing we need is to be at each other's throats. Joey's got this under control, Jackie, just stay cool."

Barros said nothing and looked up at the ceiling. Corcione nodded and got out of his chair, holding out his hand to Barros. "I'm sorry, Joey," he apologized. "I'm just tired. I haven't been sleeping much."

Glancing at the proffered hand, Barros sneered. "No way you're touching me," he said. "I have no idea where that hand's been. Just remember to keep your mouth shut around your little boyfriends."

Corcione dropped his hand and turned to Vitteli. "We know Karp thinks we're guilty," he said. "Otherwise he would have called us as witnesses. He's not going to let it go."

"Fuck him," Vitteli said. "He don't have shit on us, as long as we stick together. I can trust you, right, Jackie?"

Corcione looked at Charlie Vitteli and saw the danger behind the suspicious look. "Yeah, yeah, of course," he said. "We're all in this, sink or swim."

"Yeah, that's right, sink or swim." Vitteli nodded and took another drag on his cigar. "You know I'm not real happy about testifying, not with Karp waiting to ask questions."

"You know the deal, it's no big deal," Kowalski assured them. "You guys get on the stand, say you don't recognize the defendants and that's that. Clooney's a high-priced shyster who wants to be a federal judge and it takes a lot of money to buy that seat on the bench. I've already had a chat with him on behalf of your new Russian partners and the union; of course, he's going to treat you with kid gloves. He knows enough to make it look good, but he's just looking for a little airtime and to make a few speeches. If by some miracle he gets an acquittal, we'll get these guys as soon as they're back on the streets. As far as Karp goes, he's limited on what he can do on cross-examination."

"I still don't like it."

"It'll be all right, Charlie," Corcione chimed in. "Syd's right. Karp can't do much." He looked at his watch. "Well, I've got to be going."

"What's the matter? All that tough talk got you all hot and bothered for your boyfriend?" Barros scoffed.

"You know what, Joey, my boyfriend could kick your ass," Corcione said.

"Give the faggot my address, and we'll see," Barros countered.

"You're a jerk," Corcione said. "I'm out of here."

After he was gone, Kowalski said, "I've got to go, too. You want to write me that check for my services?"

"Sure," Vitteli said, opening the drawer of his desk and removing a checkbook. "Five thousand, right?"

"Correct. Hey, I didn't know you were left-handed; so am I," Kowalski said. "We southpaws got to stick together. Just make sure you tie up any loose ends, or your business partners may do it for you."

When both men were gone, Barros turned to Vitteli. "He's right about loose ends, and you know who I'm talking about."

"You need to lay off Jackie," Vitteli replied tersely. "He's hanging in there; he's in too deep to do anything else."

"I can't stand queers," Barros said. "They're weak. He's the only one who could really fuck us."

Vitteli thought about it and then shook his head. "Let's see how things go with this trial and cleaning up the other issues, including Gnat Miller." He was quiet for a moment and then cleared his throat as if he had something difficult to talk about. "Those three bitches were in the courtroom when I went in this afternoon," he said.

"What three bitches?"

"The ones from the alley," Vitteli said.

Barros rolled his eyes. "You're starting to worry me, boss," he said. "I haven't seen those old hags since that night we saw them by the fire barrel. But you see them every-where — back at the alley after Vince got shot, now in the courtroom. I think your mind's just playing tricks on you. Relax."

Vitteli slammed his fist down on his desk, partly rising from his seat as he glared at his henchman. "Don't fuckin' tell me to relax, Joey," he said. "Those bitches are following me around, and I don't like it."

"Okay, okay, don't get your blood pressure going," Barros said. "I'll keep my eye out for them tomorrow, and if they're around, I'll deal with 'em."

Vitteli nodded and sat back in his chair. "Yeah, thanks," he said. "I admit I some-times wonder if maybe I'd imagined them. But they were sitting in the back of the courtroom today. The black one looked at me and whispered, 'It's time' again, what-ever the fuck that means."

"Don't worry, boss," Barros assured him.

"They can't hurt us. Even if they were outside of Marlon's, they're just three weird old women nobody will listen to."

"Yeah, you're right, Joey," Vitteli agreed, then shivered. "But Jesus H. Christ, they give me the creeps."

20

Karp looked up at the large black man on the witness stand as he handed him two envelopes. "Detective Fulton, I am handing you People's Exhibits Eighteen and Nineteen marked for identification. First of all, can you identify them?"

Always thorough and smart on and off the stand, Clay Fulton made a show of examining the outside of each envelope. "Yes, they are envelopes in which I placed evidence gathered at two sites in New Rochelle: the first approximately one block north of the Carlotta residence in close proximity to the Hudson Day School; the second, approximately twenty feet from the front door of the residence at 141 Fieldstone Way."

"Please tell us how you know these are the same envelopes?" Karp asked.

Fulton turned the envelopes around to show the jurors as he pointed to writing in the top left-hand corner of each. "I initialed and dated them," he said.

"Are there other initials and a date besides yours on the envelope?"

"Yes, the initials J.S. and also the date."

"Do you know the identity of the man with the initials J.S.?"

"His name is Jack Swanburg."

"Please tell us who Dr. Swanburg is and how he came into possession of these envelopes."

"Dr. Swanburg is a forensic pathologist, as well as an expert in a number of other forensic sciences. He runs a nonprofit agency that assists law enforcement with forensic expertise, including DNA testing. . . ."

Standing beside the jury box and directly in front of the witness stand while Fulton was testifying, Karp was studying the jurors' reaction to the testimony and noticed how even the most laid-back snapped to attention at the mention of DNA. Like it or not, television crime shows had made prosecutors' jobs that much more difficult by conditioning the public to believe that most murders were solved with DNA tests, when the truth was that most were solved the old-fashioned way, with a mix of nongenetic physical and circumstantial evidence. But if you had some DNA in the evidentiary arsenal, it helped satisfy jurors' expectations and kept them alert.

"... sent the items to the Baker Street Irregulars offices in Denver, Colorado."

"Is that common practice to use an outside agency for these tests?" Karp asked.

"Well, most of the forensic testing conducted for the New York Police Department and District Attorney's Office is conducted by in-house laboratories," Fulton said. "However, both will occasionally go outside for help."

"And what reasons would they have for doing so?"

Fulton shrugged. "It could be owing to a possible conflict of interest, or for a more specialized type of forensic testing, or, say, time is of the essence and the in-house labs are swamped with work, which is typical. In this case, we wanted the greater variety of forensic expertise offered by the Baker Street Irregulars and needed it done quickly."

"But couldn't the NYPD or my office have requested an expedited analysis?"

"Yes, but given the extensive caseload at the city lab we felt why disrupt their ongoing obligations when we had access to an expert and reliable outside agency? So you suggested the evidence be sent to Swanburg's lab in Colorado."

"Have we in fact used this group's expertise before?"

Fulton nodded his big head. "Yes, several times, as have district attorney's offices and police departments all over the country. They are very highly regarded."

"So that's the reason why the jurors will also find Jack Swanburg's initials on the envelope?"

Clooney, feeling he had to say something, stood. "Objection, Your Honor," he said in his sonorous voice. "If the initials belong to Swanburg, let him testify to it."

Shaking his head and smiling, Karp replied, "Your Honor, trials — like most everything in life — have an order to them. With all due respect, I've already listed Dr. Swanburg as a witness, and read the People's witness list to the jurors prior to jury selection. And the People, of course, will call Dr. Swanburg to the stand in the orderly process. Moreover, I've given the defense a copy of Dr. Swanburg's expert report."

"Mr. Clooney, you do recall the People's intention to call Dr. Swanburg as a witness. I will allow this testimony, subject to connection. If the prosecution doesn't call Dr. Swanburg I will strike this last statement.

So your objection is overruled; please proceed, Mr. Karp."

"Detective, can you identify the contents of the envelopes, starting with People's Exhibit Eighteen?"

"Yes, People's Exhibit Eighteen contains five partially smoked tobacco cigarettes."

"Any particular brand?"

"Yes, they are all Belomorkanal."

"Could you tell us a little bit about them?"

"They're a cheap Russian brand," Fulton replied, sticking with the theme of getting under Bebnev's skin.

"Are they widely available?"

"Objection!" Clooney shouted. "The witness has not been qualified as any sort of expert witness on the distribution of this particular brand of cigarette."

"Mr. Karp?" Judge See asked.

"Your Honor, if I may ask another question," Karp replied, "I believe I may be able to shed some light on this."

"Go ahead."

"Detective Fulton, during the course of your investigation did you at any time look into the availability of the Belomorkanal cigarette brand?"

"Yes," Fulton replied pleasantly. He and Karp had gone over this very scenario knowing that Clooney would walk right into it. "I assigned one of the detectives who works for the District Attorney's Office, Fran Verbeyst, to do just that. It was actually easier than I would have thought, because the cigarettes are imported and not widely distributed like an American cigarette, at least not in Verbeyst's canvassing of more than fifty New York tobacco product distributors."

"Thank you," Karp said and looked at the judge. "Your Honor, I'd suggest that for the general answer to my question, Detective Fulton, through one of his colleagues, has done his homework enough to render an informed opinion."

"Objection overruled, but unless he also wants to get into more detailed data, let's keep this short and general," Judge See said, looking at Karp from under his bushy eyebrows.

"We'll be brief, Your Honor," Karp replied and turned to Fulton. "Detective, you were about to answer my question as to the availability of Belomorkanal cigarettes in the greater New York City vicinity."

"Well, it is possible to order these cigarettes online," Fulton noted. "However, they are a cheap brand, even in Russia, so it would seem to defeat the purpose. As for over-the-counter sales, they are mostly confined to traditionally Russian immigrant communities."

"Such as the neighborhood known as Little Odessa in Brighton Beach over in Brooklyn?"

"That would be a good example. There are several shops in that area, as well as two vending machines we could locate, that carry that brand."

"Thank you," Karp said. "Now, let's move on to People's Exhibit Nineteen marked for identification. Please explain its contents."

Again, Fulton carefully picked up the envelope from the ledge of the witness stand and looked inside. "Sure, this exhibit found in front of the Carlotta residence contains a single cigarette butt, also Belomorkanal."

Karp retrieved the envelopes and brought them back to the prosecution table. "Detective, is there a reason the cigarette butts are in paper envelopes as opposed to, say, a plastic bag?"

"Yes, plastic bags retain moisture that can damage DNA evidence."

With another *CSI* moment locking in the jury, Karp turned back to the witness stand. "Detective, in a moment I'm going to ask you where the contents of each envelope were located, but could you first explain why you happened to be in New Rochelle on that particular evening?"

"I received a telephone call from the Carlotta residence indicating that some evidence pertaining to this case may have been located."

"Who placed the call?"

Here it comes, Karp thought, though his face gave no indication.

"Marlene Ciampi."

"And that is the same Marlene Ciampi who just happens to be my wife?"

"She sure is," Fulton shot back with a full-moon-sized grin that gave rise to titters throughout the courtroom.

Judge See interrupted the moment. "Sometimes in these matters of extreme importance, tension breakers do occur. Let's hope that they serve as an aid helping us refocus our undivided attention on the testimony we're about to hear." The courtroom was hushed as Judge See smiled and said, "Please proceed, Mr. Karp."

"Okay, Detective Fulton, do you know what she was doing at the Carlotta residence?"

"It's my understanding that she was working as the attorney for Nicoli Lopez, the girlfriend of William 'Gnat' Miller."

"Why would she have been at the Carlotta residence?"

"Apparently, her client had indicated that her boyfriend might have implicated himself in this crime, and she was attempting to interview the victim's wife, Antonia Carlotta, to help determine if that was true or not."

"Please explain the circumstances that caused you to go to New Rochelle after you received her call."

"She discovered what she felt was evidence related to the case," Fulton explained. "She immediately called me as the head of the district attorney's detective squad so that I could ensure the chain of custody and secure the evidence."

"And did you meet with Ms. Ciampi when you arrived on the scene?"

"Yes. She was standing in front of the Hudson Day School."

"What was she doing?"

"She had just located one of the cigarette butts contained in People's Exhibit Eighteen."

"Why was she at that particular location?"

"Mrs. Antonia Carlotta had indicated to Ms. Ciampi that one or more of the men was smoking when she and her family passed them on the night of December second. Marlene had asked the victim's wife to take her to where the men were parked."

Karp walked over to the prosecution desk

and picked up two photographs, which he then handed to Fulton. "Detective, I've handed you People's Exhibits Fourteen and Fifteen. Are you familiar with these photographs?"

"Yes, I am."

"Starting with People's Exhibit Fourteen in evidence, would you please tell the jury what each depicts?"

Fulton held up the first photograph and showed it to the jury. "This shows three small flags attached to wire stakes that have been stuck in the ground. Each flag represents the place where a cigarette butt was located." He put that photograph down and picked up the other. "People's Exhibit Fifteen in evidence shows two more stakes indicating where two more butts were located, a little closer to the curb."

"I see," Karp said, "and why would these cigarette butts interest you?"

"Several reasons," Fulton said. "One was to corroborate Mrs. Carlotta's account of what she saw in regard to the parked car and its occupants. We also knew from talking to Nicoli Lopez that William Miller's car had smelled like cigarette smoke after the nights of December second, the night the defendants drove to New Rochelle, and December fifth, the night of the murder.

But according to Miss Lopez, neither Miller nor the defendant Frank DiMarzo smoked. We were trying to establish the identity of a third man, a man with a Russian accent, who may have been with the other two. We hoped that there might be traces of DNA left on the butts to help identify him."

"Your Honor, with the court's permission, may Detective Fulton step down and help us view the diagram, People's Exhibit Two in evidence?" Karp asked.

"Yes, he may," Judge See replied.

Walking over to the easel with the detective, Karp said, "Detective Fulton, do you see on the diagram where the cigarette butts were located?"

"Yes."

"Please indicate."

"Right where the letter 'B' is already marked on the exhibit. That's the approximate area where I located the cigarette butts contained in People's Eighteen, and the location of the stakes in the photographs in People's Exhibits Fourteen and Fifteen."

Walking back to the prosecution table again, Karp held up a plastic bag and its contents. "Detective, can you identify People's Exhibit Twenty-Four for the jury, please?"

"Yes, it's a beer bottle."

"And did you collect this beer bottle?"

"I did."

"Please indicate on the diagram, People's Two in evidence, where you retrieved this beer bottle, People's Exhibit Twenty-Four?

"Right here in this area," Fulton said, pointing. "Right on the hedge area there."

"Would you please write the letters 'BB' for 'beer bottle' on the diagram?"

"Was there a reason for you to be looking for evidence by the hedge?" Karp asked.

"Mrs. Carlotta indicated that when she and her husband passed the parked car, one of the men was outside standing near the hedge."

"Was there anything else you noted at that spot?"

"Yes, there was an area beneath the hedge that contained snow left over from the previous week's snowfall in the area," Fulton replied. "And I noted a spot that was yellowish in color."

"Did you happen to collect a sample of the yellowish snow?"

"I did."

As Karp walked over to the prosecution table, Guma handed him three envelopes, which Karp took over to Fulton. "The record should reflect that I've given the witness People's Exhibit Nineteen marked for identification, can you identify it and its contents?"

Fulton opened the envelope matter-of-factly and looked up and nodded. "Yes, it is an envelope containing a single Belomorkanal cigarette butt I collected from the lawn of the Carlotta residence."

Karp held out his hand for the envelope and exchanged it for the other two. "Can you identify People's Exhibits Twenty-One and Twenty-Two?"

Fulton looked at the envelopes carefully, then glanced inside them and appeared to be counting.

"Would you please describe the contents?" Karp asked.

"The first, with my initials and date, contains three cigarette butts," Fulton replied. "The other contains nine cigarette butts."

"Where did you locate the cigarette butts, and describe the circumstances that led to your finding them?"

Fulton turned to look at the jury. "Following my trip to New Rochelle, where I took custody of the evidence from Marlene . . . Mrs. Ciampi . . . I returned to Hell's Kitchen. I was thinking about the witness statements that the robbers jumped out of the alley. I thought if one or more of them were heavy smokers, they might have left cigarette butts behind in or around the alley that could be matched to those found near the Carlotta residence."

"Tell us what, if anything, you found."

"Well, I located twelve cigarette butts near the entrance to the alley and collected all of them in that first envelope," Fulton said.

"Were you able to determine the brands?"

"Three were Belomorkanal, and the other nine were different brands," Fulton said.

Karp now walked quickly over to the prosecution table, where Guma had one last envelope waiting. "And do you recognize this envelope and its contents? People's Exhibit Twenty-Three?"

Fulton checked out the proffered envelope. "Yes. It contains a cigarette butt found on the floor behind the front seat of the car registered to William 'Gnat' Miller."

"What brand is it?"

"Belomorkanal."

"Have you seen the car?"

"Yes."

"Please describe it for us?"

"It's a Delta 88, four-door sedan, a little banged up. It appears to have been green, but the paint is pretty faded. . . . There's a lot of gray primer on it."

"Where was the primer located on the Delta 88 sedan?"

"On a large area of the trunk."

"Did you record the license plate number of that car?"

"I have it written down here on my note-pad," Fulton replied. "FPB eight-one-nine-six . . . registered to William Miller at a Brooklyn address."

"Thank you. Now, returning to the evidence you collected — the cigarette butts, beer bottle, and yellowish snow — what was done with these items?"

"I sent them to the Jack Swanburg's Baker Street Irregulars office for DNA testing."

"Your Honor, no more questions," Karp said.

"Detective Fulton, would you please return to the witness stand?" Judge See asked. "Would the defense like to question the witness?"

"Indeed, Your Honor," Conrad Clooney announced as he rose from his seat and walked over to the witness stand. "Detective," he began with a knowing smile, "if I understand your testimony, you got a call from Marlene Ciampi saying she'd located evidence at the Carlotta residence."

"That's correct."

"And this evidence pointed to three young men, two of whom are seated here as defendants."

"Eventually, yes," Fulton agreed.

"But this was the first the police had heard about three young men visiting the Carlotta residence?"

"Not exactly," Fulton said.

"What do you mean, not exactly?" Clooney said with a scowl.

"The day after the shooting, Mahlon Gorman, the attorney for the deceased, Vince Carlotta, paid a visit to the District Attorney's Office and —"

Clooney interrupted. "But suddenly Mrs. Carlotta remembered the visit?"

Karp jumped up. "Your Honor, Mr. Clooney just clipped Detective Fulton's answer. Mr. Clooney opened the door and needs to let Detective Fulton finish his answer."

Emotionally, Clooney argued, "This is a profound setup. A conspiracy of lies. It's entirely inadmissible."

Judge See frowned. "That's quite enough, Mr. Clooney. First of all, I've already advised you, you must be more careful about asking questions to which you may get surprise answers. And secondly, while I'm presiding, I will decide the admissibility of evidence. Is that clear, Mr. Clooney?"

Red-faced and humiliated, Clooney didn't answer and just stood looking down at his shoes. Judge See waited patiently before finally saying, "I will interpret your silence and failure to respond as acceptance of my ruling. The witness may finish his answer."

"As I said, the day after the shooting, Mr. Carlotta's attorney, Mahlon Gorman, came to the District Attorney's Office and told us about the three men who visited the Carlotta residence in New Rochelle."

"But suddenly Mrs. Carlotta remembered the visit, and Marlene Ciampi happened to find all these items that are now being used to convict the defendants?" Clooney demanded incredulously.

"No, not suddenly. She said she never forgot that visit, because it was unusual and she feared for her husband's safety."

"I ask that answer be stricken as not responsive," Clooney said.

"Mr. Clooney, there you go again, your objection is overruled," Judge See said.

Infuriated, Clooney snapped at Fulton. "And then you," he said, raising his voice as he paced over to stand in front of the jurors, "returned to the scene of the crime in Hell's Kitchen and, wouldn't you know it, found more cigarette butts of the same brand."

"Among others, yes."

"Don't you find that just a little coincidental?"

"No," the detective replied. "It actually makes sense if one of the defendants was a heavy smoker."

"Didn't you go to the scene of the crime on the night it happened?" Clooney asked.

"Yes."

"Then you'd know if the crime scene technicians, officers, and detectives at the scene did a thorough job of looking for evidence?"

"I would and they did," Fulton replied. "But they weren't looking for cigarette butts. New York City's alleys, sidewalks, and gutters are filled with cigarette butts."

"Or maybe these particular cigarette butts weren't there until later?" Clooney retorted. "Doesn't it seem just a little odd that the police miss the evidence at the Carlotta residence and then again in that alley until Marlene Ciampi, the wife of the district attorney, comes into the picture?"

"Sometimes it's the little things that initially slip through the cracks that are important later when someone asks the right questions," Fulton countered, obviously making an effort to keep his temper.

"And sometimes evidence gets manufactured," Clooney retorted.

"Maybe in grade B or C movies, but not

here on my watch," Fulton replied while
glaring at Clooney.

21

"The People call Jack Swanburg."

The door in the side of the courtroom leading to the witness waiting rooms opened and a man who looked like Santa Claus on vacation walked in. He was wearing green suspenders over a bright yellow shirt that barely covered his prodigious belly; his nose was red and poked out of a full white beard though the rest of his head was bald.

The former forensic pathologist from Denver, Colorado, was the founder of the Baker Street Irregulars, a group of scientists who volunteered their expertise to help solve crimes. They were particularly noted for using sciences such as geophysics, botany, and archeology for locating clandestine graves, but they also offered a wide range of forensic abilities, including a laboratory for chemical analysis and DNA testing. Taking their name from the home of fictional detective extraordinaire Sherlock

Holmes, of whom they were avid fans, they had worked with Karp in the past, and he had found them to be excellent scientific sleuths and wonderful expert witnesses on the stand.

Among them, Jack Swanburg was his favorite. A pathologist by profession, he was probably the most well-rounded of the group and could expertly comment on many areas of forensic sciences, including DNA testing.

After swearing to tell the truth, Swanburg sat down in the witness chair and smiled benignly at the jurors, most of whom could not help but smile back. But his face turned serious as Karp asked him to list his credentials, education, and courtroom experience, after which the defense had little choice but to accept him as an expert witness.

After discussing the details of how the prosecution evidence was transported and examined at the Baker Street lab in Colorado, Karp moved on to the findings. "Dr. Swanburg, I ask you to turn your attention to People's Exhibit Twenty-Four, which contains a beer bottle. I note that it has a gray stopper on it, please explain."

"It's a rubber stopper designed for wine bottles. There is a small slit in the top that allows a plunger to create a vacuum inside the bottle while preventing leaks as well as, in this case, preventing any changes to the contents that might occur with continued contact with the air."

"Did you have the opportunity to examine the contents of the bottle?" Karp asked.

"Yes," Swanburg said, pulling out a small pair of reading glasses to look at the papers he'd brought with him to the stand. "I understood that the contents were partly frozen when the bottle was collected, but they arrived in my office in liquid form."

"Could you identify the contents?"

"Of course," Swanburg replied. "As expected with a beer bottle, there was evidence of malt, hops, yeast, and, of course, alcohol. However, this material was greatly overshadowed by the residue of *Nicotiana tabacum,* or tobacco, as well as human saliva."

"As a result of your analysis, what conclusions were you able to reach?" Karp asked.

"Well, that someone was masticating tobacco and spitting the residue into the bottle," Swanburg said. "A rather nasty habit that can lead to gum, mouth, and throat cancers."

"And was it possible for you to determine whose saliva was contained in the bottle?"

"Indeed, through DNA testing," Swanburg answered, looking at the jurors.

"You can test saliva for DNA?" Karp asked, as if it was the first time he'd heard of it.

"Sure," Swanburg replied. "Any body fluid or secretion with nucleated cells — that is, any cell with a nucleus — contains DNA that can be analyzed. Even tears and ear wax have nucleated cells."

Like a kindly old professor lecturing his favorite students, Swanburg spoke earnestly but with a smile as he explained. "Forensic saliva DNA testing has been used since the early 1980s to match suspects to evidence left behind at a crime scene. It's now used more often than comparing DNA from blood samples, and in fact, seventy-four percent of DNA in saliva comes from white blood cells."

"And were you able to match the DNA in this bottle to a person?" Karp asked.

"Yes." Swanburg nodded. "We were given DNA samples taken from several people involved in this case, and the saliva matched one of those." He referred back to his papers. "A William Miller."

"To a reasonable degree of scientific certainty?" Karp asked.

"Mr. Miller matched to a very high degree of scientific certainty; only one in five billion people would have an identical DNA sequence."

Karp walked over to the prosecution table, where he put the beer bottle down and picked up a clear jar containing a liquid. He returned to the witness stand and handed the jar to Swanburg. "Have you seen this container before?"

"Yes, it's a container from my laboratory," Swanburg said, turning the jar around so that the jury could see markings on the side. "See, it's got our logo and it's date and time stamped."

"Were you able to determine the jar's contents?" Karp asked.

"Yes, indeed, I transferred it there after testing in order to preserve it for the defense laboratories," Swanburg said. "Basically, it's a combination of water, urea, creatinine, uric acid, and trace amounts of enzymes, carbohydrates, hormones, fatty acids, pigments, and mucins, as well as inorganic ions such as sodium, potassium, chloride, magnesium, calcium, ammonium, sulfates, and phosphates."

Karp smiled. "Please tell us how you would describe the contents in everyday terms."

"Human urine." Swanburg chuckled.

"Pee-pee."

"Thank you." Karp grinned. "Doctor, are you able to test urine for DNA?"

"Oh yes," Swanburg said. "DNA in urine comes from nucleated cells that line the bladder and ureters. A small number of cells are fluffed off every day, and with the techniques that are available today, DNA profiles can be obtained from a very small number of cells."

"Were you able to match this urine sample to a DNA profile?" Karp asked.

"Yes, as with the tobacco spit, it was a match for William Miller."

"Doctor," Karp said as he returned the jar of urine to the prosecution table and picked up the envelopes Fulton had used to collect cigarette butts, which he handed to Swanburg, "have you seen these envelopes before?"

Squinting through his reading glasses, Swanburg reached out for the first envelope that Karp handed up to him. "Yes. There are my initials in the top corner on the left, and the date I received it in my lab."

"Would you open the envelope marked People's Exhibit Eighteen, collected from the area in front of the Hudson Day School in close proximity to the Carlotta residence, and describe the contents," Karp directed.

Swanburg did as told, then looked back at the jurors. "There are five partially burned cigarettes, or cigarette butts, if you prefer."

"And do you recognize them?"

The scientist smiled. "Yes, we're old friends. I marked each with a small blue dot that is also visible in ultraviolet lighting."

"What can you tell the jurors about these five cigarette butts?"

"Well, they are all the same brand, Belomorkanal, which is somewhat unusual in the United States, though more prevalent in Russian immigrant communities," Swanburg said. "They are manufactured in St. Petersburg and are considered a poor man's cigarette even there."

"Anything more?"

"Um, yes, at least three of these butts contained tobacco from a similar batch and likely were from the same pack."

As Swanburg spoke, Karp glanced at the jury and was pleased to see how intently they were following the forensic testimony. "And were you able to determine who smoked the cigarettes?"

"Yes, again, to a high degree of scientific certainty," Swanburg said, then backtracked. "Actually, cigarette butts have a fascinating history in the annals of forensic criminal investigations. One of the very first uses of bloodtyping to solve a murder occurred in the late 1880s. A quick-thinking detective, who was aware of the brand-new science of blood typing, was following the suspect in a murder case when he saw the man smoke a cigarette and throw the butt on the ground. He picked up the butt and had it tested. The smoker's blood type matched that of the perpetrator of the crime and he was convicted. Of course, blood types are much more common among people. Advances in DNA testing have enabled us to go beyond that and compare saliva DNA, even dried saliva, on a cigarette to a suspect's DNA, which is a much more exact science for identifying people."

"And you were able to do that in this instance?"

"Yes, for four of the butts from this envelope," Swanburg said, this time looking over at the defense table. "They matched to a very high degree of scientific certainty the DNA of the defendant, Alexei Bebnev."

Karp retrieved the envelope from Swanburg and handed him another. "Do you recognize People's Exhibit Nineteen, which was collected from the lawn in front of the Carlotta house?"

"Yes. Same thing; there are my initials and the date," Swanburg said and opened the envelope. "It contains one butt with a blue mark on it."

"Were you able to determine who smoked the cigarette?"

"Yes, again, DNA testing indicated to a very high degree of scientific certainty that the smoker was Alexei Bebnev."

With his eyes on the defense table, where Bebnev nervously licked his lips and Di-Marzo hung his head, Karp walked back to the prosecution table and exchanged the two envelopes for two more.

"Doctor, I am handing you envelopes marked People's Exhibits Twenty-One and Twenty-Two, collected from an alley in Hell's Kitchen," Karp said. "Do you recognize them and their contents?"

Swanburg glanced at the envelopes and nodded. "Yes, one is an envelope I received that originally contained a dozen cigarette butts; it now contains three Belomorkanal butts, or what's left of them after testing," he said. "The other is an envelope from my office, and it now contains the other nine butts."

"Why did you separate them?"

"Because the three were all the same brand and tested positive for Mr. Bebnev's DNA," Swanburg said. "The other nine were a variety of brands and did not have

Mr. Bebnev's DNA, nor any other defendant's DNA on them."

After getting the envelopes back from Swanburg, Karp returned to the prosecution table one more time and picked up another envelope, People's Exhibit 23 marked for identification, "containing a cigarette butt collected from the floor of the vehicle registered to William Miller." He then went through the same process of identifying the envelope and asking if Swanburg had been able to determine who had smoked the cigarette.

This time, the portly scientist shook his head. "I'm afraid not," he said. "It's Belomorkanal, but it was quite crushed and I was not able to get a good enough DNA specimen to test."

"Thank you, Dr. Swanburg," Karp said and looked at Judge See. "No further questions."

Over at the defense table, Bebnev grabbed the arm of his attorney and said something. Clooney nodded and rose to his feet, though he remained behind the defense table.

"Dr. Swanburg, for all of your comprehensive tests and scientific knowledge, you do not have any evidence that Mr. Bebnev placed those cigarette butts either across the street from the Carlotta residence, next to the driveway, or in Mr. Miller's car, is that correct?"

Swanburg looked confused for a moment, then shrugged. "I guess logic would dictate otherwise, but you're correct. I can prove he placed those cigarettes in his mouth, but not that he left the butts in those areas."

"Then if someone was attempting to frame Mr. Bebnev, it might be a good idea to collect cigarette butts from his home or while in a bar and then plant them to be found by someone else, correct?"

"Objection, Your Honor," Karp said. "I ask for a good faith offer of proof to justify Mr. Clooney's suggestion of a frame."

"Your Honor, given all the reports we're now reading about people who are unjustly convicted of murder who are on death row, I believe I am permitted to delve into this area," Clooney said.

"Do you have anything more concrete, Mr. Clooney, other than reports in newspapers to suggest in this particular case that there may have been wrongdoing committed by the police or District Attorney's Office?" the judge asked.

"Not right now; that's why I want to get answers," Clooney retorted.

"Then I am going to sustain the objection, direct the jury to please disregard Mr.

Clooney's question, it will be stricken from the record, and I admonish you, Mr. Clooney, that you should not engage in this conduct again unless you have a good faith basis backed up by facts that relate directly to this case."

Embarrassed and not even bothering to look at the gallery anymore, Clooney sat down, and Frank DiMarzo's attorney, Irv Westin, stood. "Dr. Swanburg," he asked, "in all of that testing you did — of cigarettes and beer bottles and saliva — was there any evidence connected to my client, Frank DiMarzo?"

"I believe that there were some hair samples taken from the car that matched Mr. DiMarzo," Swanburg replied.

"Would you consider it unusual for Mr. DiMarzo's hair to be found in a vehicle owned by his best friend?"

Swanburg pursed his lips and shook his head. "No. That's pretty logical to assume."

Westin smiled as if he'd scored an important point. "Thank you. No further questions."

As Swanburg stepped down from the witness stand, Judge See looked at Karp. "I believe we have time for you to call another witness," he said.

"As a matter of fact, I have one who

should just about take us to the end of the day," Karp said. "The People call Randy McMahon."

Vince Carlotta's driver walked into the courtroom like a man carrying an enormous burden on his broad shoulders. His head and eyes were down as he took the stand and, after reciting his working relationship with Vince Carlotta, he soon broke down after Karp asked him to recount the events of the night his boss was shot and killed.

"I wasn't where I should have been," the former Golden Gloves heavyweight boxer wept. "I should have never gone to get the car and left him alone. But he told me to go with Sal Amaya."

"And Sal Amaya is Charlie Vitteli's bodyguard?"

"Yeah, that's him."

McMahon recounted how he'd arrived back at the scene in time to see two men wearing masks run across the street and jump into a car. "An old Delta 88 with gray primer on the trunk."

"Did you get a license number?"

Shaking his head, McMahon wiped at his eyes. "No, I messed up, but I didn't know what was going on," he said. "Not until I looked across where they'd been and saw several men around someone on the ground.

It wasn't until I got out of the car and ran over there that I knew it was . . . it was Vince."

On cross-examination, Clooney asked if the only witnesses to the actual shooting were Charlie Vitteli, Joey Barros, and Jackie Corcione. But the defense attorney was surprised by his answer.

"Yeah, well, no . . . maybe . . ." McMahon stumbled. "There were these three women . . . sort of street people, dressed in rags and old coats, who were hanging out down the sidewalk when I went to get the car. But I don't know if they saw anything. They were gone when I got to Vince."

During the last witness prep session the evening before McMahon testified, he had informed Karp of this recollection. Immediately, Karp dispatched Fulton to locate the women and learn what if anything they'd seen of value. However, the detective was unable to locate anyone who fit that description.

Wondering if the women had anything to do with Dirty Warren's assertion that street gossips claimed there were other witnesses to the murder, he watched McMahon step down from the witness stand. So far the little news vendor had been unable to confirm the rumors but had told him just that morning that they had not gone away.

"I think it's time for us to adjourn for the day," Judge See said. He dismissed the jury and the people in the gallery began to file out.

Facing Karp, the judge asked, "Mr. Karp, how many more witnesses will you have?"

"Just a couple more, Your Honor," Karp replied. "And I believe we should be done by noon tomorrow."

"Very well," the judge said. "Then, Mr. Clooney, please be prepared to begin at that time. Will you be giving an opening statement now?"

"Indeed, I will, Your Honor," Clooney announced loudly for the members of the media that lingered in the courtroom.

"We'll look forward to it, Mr. Clooney," Judge See said. "Court is adjourned."

Gathering his papers and notepads, Karp was just about to say something to Guma about the three women when he heard a voice behind him.

"Mr. Karp?"

Turning, Karp saw one of the tough-looking men who'd been attending every day of the trial. The group of men generally sat a few rows back on the prosecution side of the aisle, and he'd noticed that the others all seemed to defer to this man; a tall, thin but muscular-looking individual with a permanent five-o'clock shadow. He walked up the aisle to the wooden gate separating the well from the gallery.

"Can I help you?" Karp asked.

"My name's T. J. Martindale," the man said without offering his hand to shake, though his voice wasn't unfriendly. "I was wondering if I could talk to you for a minute. It's about Vince's murder and who's behind it."

"What do you have?" Karp said as he motioned to the approaching court security officer to back off.

Martindale looked him hard in the eyes, his brow furrowed. "I'd like to speak in private, if you don't mind."

"Were you friends with Vince?" Karp asked, surprised by his own question.

Martindale's face suddenly softened in sorrow. "More like his brother," he said.

The two men held each other's gaze a moment more and then Karp nodded. "Let's go to my office. We can talk there."

22

"The People call Antonia Carlotta."

The courtroom buzzed excitedly for a moment as all eyes followed Karp's to where the witness would appear. *All the world's a stage and we are but players in it,* Karp paraphrased in his mind as the young woman, only recently returned from four months in Italy, entered, her eyes shiny with tears and fear.

With her lustrous dark hair piled high atop her head, luminous eyes, full lips, and willowy figure, she was stunning, and moved as though playing a part in a drama. *Comes now the beautiful widow to confront the villains who murdered her husband.* But he noticed when he spoke to her earlier that morning the lines around her eyes and the sadness within them remained. It was no play, and he knew from talking to her that she was still just "going through the motions" of living.

"Are you going to win?" she asked him when he sat down in the witness waiting room to talk about what to expect.

Karp had hesitated. Thousands of cases into his career, he knew there were no guarantees. And there were no guarantees because the system relied on human beings, and human beings, jurors, were fallible; they didn't always listen to what common sense dictated or the law indicated.

There's a first time for everything, he thought. He told Antonia the same thing he told the attorneys who worked for his office: "I can't make any promises, but I know that the defendants are factually guilty, and I believe I have the legally admissible evidence to prove it beyond any doubt. I'm going to do my very best to make sure these men spend the rest of their lives in prison."

"And what about the others . . . the men who caused this?"

"Rest assured, everyone responsible for your husband's death will be held accountable," Karp replied.

Antonia had looked at him hard as if judging his words. Then her eyes filled with tears and she nodded. "I'm sorry, Mr. Karp," she said. "When Vince was murdered, the world became a very dark and frightening place to me. I have forgotten how to trust. I know

318

you're doing everything you can."

As Karp waited now for Antonia to pass in front of the gallery and step up to the witness chair, he glanced at the defense table. Bebnev looked like he was undressing her with his odd blue eyes, but DiMarzo kept his head down and stared straight at the table in front of him.

"Good morning, Mrs. Carlotta," Karp, who remained standing behind the prosecution table, began. "Please state your relationship to the deceased, Vince Carlotta."

"He is . . . will always be . . . my husband."

"Would you please tell the jury where you lived with your husband?"

"One forty-one Fieldstone Way in New Rochelle."

"And how long had you lived at that residence?"

"Approximately eighteen months."

"When was the last time you saw your husband?"

"The night he was murdered."

"And that would have been December fifth of last year?"

"Yes."

"Do you know where he was going that night?"

"He was going to Manhattan . . . to a restaurant in Hell's Kitchen called Marlon's."

"And what was the purpose of his trip?"

"He was going to meet with Charlie Vitteli."

"Would you please tell the jury who Charlie Vitteli is?"

Karp watched as Antonia grimly struggled to avoid saying what she really wanted to say. He nodded ever so slightly. "Did they work together?"

"Yes," Antonia said. "They both worked for the North American Brotherhood of Stevedores, a dockworkers' union. Mr. Vitteli had recently taken over the union. He and Vince both ran for union president. Charlie . . . won. . . . Vince lost."

"I see," Karp said inwardly breathing a sigh of relief that he and Antonia had navigated the waters of how much to say about Charlie Vitteli. "How did your husband get to the meeting at Marlon's Restaurant?"

"His driver, Randy McMahon, took him."

"What, if anything, did your husband do just before he left the house to go to this meeting?"

"He removed a note he'd written on a sticky pad and put it in his pocket."

"And what had he written down?"

"The license plate number of a car."

Karp turned toward the jurors. "Would you please explain to the jury the significance of this license plate number?"

"Yes," she said, but then faltered for a moment as she choked up. "I'm sorry. . . . Three days before my husband was murdered, a car stopped by our house in the evening."

"Who was in the car?"

"Three young men. Two came to the door and the other stayed in the car."

"Did you know these young men?"

Antonia looked over at the defense table and shook her head. "No. We did not know them."

Karp walked over to the prosecution table and picked up five photographs marked People's Exhibit Twenty-Five A–E inclusive. "Mrs. Carlotta, do you recall that last January I showed you photographs of different cars?" he asked, handing them to her.

"Yes, I remember that."

"Please tell the jury how you know these are the same photographs?"

"Because you asked me to put my initials and the date on the side of each photograph, which I did."

"And did you then identify one of these photographs?"

"Yes. This one right here, Exhibit Twenty-Five D."

"And what is the significance of Twenty-

Five D?"

"It's the same car the men who came to my house drove."

Turning to the judge, Karp said, "Your Honor, I ask that People's Exhibit Twenty-Five D be placed into evidence."

"Any objection, Mr. Clooney?"

"May I ask a few questions?" Clooney said, rising. "I have one important one."

"Please proceed, Mr. Clooney."

"Mrs. Carlotta, Exhibit Twenty-Five D shows a Delta 88 sedan car, correct?"

"Yes."

"And there are many Delta 88 sedan cars, right?"

"Yes, I believe there are."

"Tens of thousands?"

"Perhaps."

"So this car is just one of thousands of Delta 88 sedans, isn't it, Mrs. Carlotta?"

"Not exactly, Mr. Clooney."

"What?"

"Well, Mr. Clooney, while there may be thousands of Delta 88 sedans, I haven't seen one with a large gray spot on the trunk that sort of looks like a dragon on any other car." Antonia Carlotta picked up the photograph and showed it to Clooney.

Having walked into another trap, Clooney was speechless. Judge See again broke the silence and asked, "Mr. Clooney, do you have any more questions."

"No, Your Honor," the defense attorney mumbled and sat down.

Judge See nodded. "Having heard your voir dire of the witness on the admissibility of the People's Exhibit Twenty-Five D, I now receive it into evidence."

Karp smiled. The first time Antonia told him that the large splotch of gray primer on the trunk of Miller's car looked like a dragon, he'd seen it right away and knew the jurors would, too.

Retrieving the photograph, Karp remained in the well of the courtroom. "Did you see this car at some point prior to when these young men drove up to your house?"

"Yes. When we came home from the store that night, we passed that car. It was parked in front of the Hudson Day School up the street from our home."

"You're sure it was this car?"

"Well, yes, it was unusual to see a car like that — an older car — in that neighborhood. I noticed it and the big gray dragon spot."

"Was there anyone in the car when you passed it?"

"I couldn't see them clearly, but yes, I saw at least two heads in our lights," Antonia said. "When we passed, I looked over and saw someone standing next to the hedge, like he was trying to hide. But we passed quickly and it was dark."

"Were there any other indications that someone was in the car?"

"Yes. Someone was smoking I think; smoke was coming from a back window."

"Could you tell which window?"

"I believe the back right-hand side."

Karp walked over toward the easel. "Mrs. Carlotta, can you see this aerial photograph easily from your seat?"

"Yes."

"Have you seen the photograph before?"

"Yes. You showed it to me in January and again a few days ago in your office. It's an aerial photograph of our home . . . what was our home and neighborhood."

"That's correct," Karp said. He pointed to the photograph. "Mrs. Carlotta, there is a circle with the letter 'C' in the center. Does that accurately reflect where the car containing the unknown men was parked the night of December second?"

"Yes."

"And what direction would you have been coming from when you passed the car?"

"We came from the side and rear of the car. That's why I noticed the gray paint on the trunk."

Karp walked back over to the prosecution table, where he picked up a plastic bag containing the sticky-note pad before he returned to the well of the court. "Mrs. Carlotta, after your husband's murder did an attorney named Marlene Ciampi come to your house?"

"Yes."

"And what, if anything, did you discuss with her regarding the license plate number and a notepad?"

"I told her that Vince wrote the number down but that he took the note with him."

"Then what happened?"

"I showed her the notepad on Vince's desk on which he wrote the license plate number of the car the men were in."

"And what did Marlene do?"

"She used a pencil to shade the top page so she could see the imprint of what Vince wrote."

Karp walked over and handed her the bag containing the sticky note. "And would this be the page she shaded?"

"Yes."

After Karp returned it to the prosecution table, he asked, "And did you tell Marlene anything else about the young men?"

"Yes. I told her where they had been

parked near the school."

"And what did she do?"

"She asked to see where the car had been parked."

"And did you show her?"

"Yes. We both walked there."

"And did Ms. Ciampi do anything while you were there?"

"She found a cigarette butt," Antonia responded. "And then asked me if I would go get some envelopes from my house."

"And you did that."

"Yes."

"How long did it take you to go to your home, get the envelopes, and return?"

Antonia thought about it for a moment and then shrugged. "A few minutes. I tried to hurry."

"When you returned, was someone else with Marlene?"

"Yes, Detective Fulton was there," she said.

"And what did he do?"

"I guess he took over," Antonia said. "He and Marlene looked for cigarette butts and he found the beer bottle. Then some other officers arrived. . . . I believe they were there to help with the evidence."

Karp nodded and walked over toward the defense table. "Mrs. Carlotta, did you tell the police investigators who came to your house after your husband's murder about the three young men who came to your home?"

Antonia shrugged. "I'm not sure what I told them," she said. The young woman's head dropped and she covered her face with her hands. Walking quickly over to the witness stand, Karp picked up a box of tissues and offered it to her. "Take your time," he said gently. "I know this is tough."

Antonia took one of the tissues and dabbed at her eyes. "I'm sorry," she apologized. "It's still so raw." She dabbed at her eyes again, blew her nose lightly, then looked at Karp. "When they came and said that Vince was dead . . . murdered . . . I fell apart. I know someone, a paramedic I think, gave me some medication to calm me and help me sleep. I spoke to detectives again the next day, but I don't think I told them about the three young men. They asked me if Vince was worried about any threats and I told them —"

"Mrs. Carlotta," Karp interjected quickly, "let me interrupt you for a moment. I'm not asking what you told the police about anyone other than the three young men."

Antonia understood and bit her lip. "It never came up. And to be honest, I didn't think of it until Ms. Ciampi asked me."

Karp walked slowly over toward the defense table. "Mrs. Carlotta, you testified that neither you nor your husband had seen the three young men before that night. Did these young men say what they wanted?"

"Only one spoke. He said they were dockworkers from San Francisco and were looking for work."

"What did your husband tell them?"

"He told them to show up at the docks the next day and apply."

"And did your husband comment on their visit after they left?"

"Yes. He said that he didn't believe they were dockworkers."

"Why not?"

"He shook the one man's hand. It was soft, like he didn't work with his hands."

"After the men left, what did your husband do?"

"He wrote down the license plate number of the car with the gray paint on the trunk."

"Did he say why he did that?"

"He told me there had been some burglaries in the neighborhood and that maybe these men were involved. He said he was going to turn the note over to the police."

"Did you believe him?"

"No."

"Why not?"

Antonia paused for a moment before answering. "Because I knew he was lying," she said. "Although we were only married for two years, I knew him better than anyone. He was such an honest man that he was a very bad liar. I knew he was worried about the men but not because he thought they were burglars."

Karp was now standing directly in front of the defense table when he asked, "Mrs. Carlotta, was there anything distinguishable about the man who did most of the talking?"

"Yes, he had rather odd eyes, set wide apart . . . and bad teeth."

As he'd planned, Karp noticed the jurors turn to look at Bebnev, who blushed at the description and looked angry. "Was there anything else about this man?"

"Yes, he spoke with a Russian accent."

"How do you know it was Russian?"

"I worked in Russia when I was a model," Antonia replied. "I am very familiar with the accent."

"Mrs. Carlotta, in December of last year, you were asked to view three different police lineups each with about a half-dozen men through a one-way mirror, is that correct?"

"Yes."

"And were you able to identify any of the men in the first lineup?"

Antonia shook her head. "No, I did not recognize any of those men."

"If one of those men was the driver of the car, is it possible you would not have been able to identify him?"

"I did not see the driver," she replied. "He stayed in the car and I didn't look."

"Did your husband see him?"

"Not very well. But he said he had red hair."

"And were you able to identify any of the men in the second lineup?"

"I wasn't completely sure, but I thought one of the men looked like the second man — the one standing behind the Russian."

"And is that man in the courtroom now?"

Antonia nodded and looked over at the defense team. "Yes, he is the man sitting on the far right of that table," she said.

"You're sure? You weren't quite as positive at the lineup."

"He stood sort of back and to the side, but I did see his face briefly and I'm sure that's him now."

"Let the record show that the witness identified Frank DiMarzo," Karp said. "And Mrs. Carlotta, were you able to identify anyone in the third lineup?"

This time Antonia's eyes hardened as she looked at Bebnev, who glared back at her. "Yes," she said, her voice coming out as a hiss. She didn't waver when she raised her hand and pointed at Bebnev. "That's him sitting on the left-hand side."

His accuser's identification seemed to unnerve Bebnev for a moment. He licked his lips nervously and shook his head as Karp moved to stand directly in front of him. This time it was Karp who pointed, his finger just a couple of feet from the Russian's face. "This man here," Karp said.

"Yes, that's him."

Karp turned to the court reporter. "Let the record reflect that the witness identified Alexei Bebnev."

"So be it," Judge See agreed. "Any further questions, Mr. Karp?"

"Not at this time, Your Honor."

"Thank you. Mr. Clooney, you may question the witness."

The defense attorney rose from his seat but did not move from behind the table. "Mrs. Carlotta, were you present when your husband was murdered?"

Antonia frowned. "No, I wasn't."

"Did you see or hear the man or men who fired the shots that killed your husband?"

"No, of course not, I said I wasn't —"

"Then the only time you say you've seen my clients was the night that you claim that they came to your house looking for work?"

"Well, yes —"

"And this conversation lasted how long?"

"A few minutes, that's all."

"And was it dark outside?"

"Yes, but the porch light was on."

"But you saw these men for maybe a couple of minutes at the most?"

"Yes."

"And you weren't sure that Mr. DiMarzo was one of the men when you saw him in the lineup?"

"I wasn't sure. I am now."

"You are now, five months later."

"Yes."

"And you're absolutely sure that my client, Mr. Bebnev, was the man who spoke to your husband?"

"Absolutely."

Clooney pursed his lips. "And it's not because you saw him in the police lineup."

"No. I knew it was him as soon as I saw him in the lineup."

"Mrs. Carlotta, are you aware that Ms. Ciampi is the wife of District Attorney Karp?"

"She told me that, yes."

"And before she came to your house, did you go up the street to the school where you claim the defendants were parked on the night of December second?"

"No. I don't think so."

"So you really have no idea if those cigarette butts and beer bottle were there before Ms. Ciampi's arrival?"

Antonia looked confused. She shook her head. "No, I guess not."

"But you didn't mention these men to the police who came to your house after the murder of your husband?"

"No. I . . . I didn't make the connection."

"And in fact, you didn't make this connection until Marlene Ciampi showed up at your house."

"It came up during our conversation."

"Yes, how convenient," Clooney scoffed. "No further questions, Your Honor."

"Mr. Karp?"

Karp walked in front of his table. "Mrs. Carlotta, do you stand by your statements that three men, including the two defendants who you just identified, came to your house several nights before your husband's murder?" Karp asked, his voice starting to rise with the anger he felt.

"Yes."

"They parked across the street and waited

for you to arrive?"

"Yes."

"They walked up to your door and asked for work, claiming they were dockworkers from San Francisco?

"Yes, all of that is true."

Karp's expression suggested to the jurors that he shouldn't have even had to ask his last question. "Mrs. Carlotta, has anyone ever come to your house in New Rochelle in the dark of night, or any other time of the day for that matter, looking for a job with your husband's union?"

Antonia shook her head. "No. Never."

"Thank you, Mrs. Carlotta. No further questions."

23

"Mr. Vitteli, I know you've been through this with the police and the District Attorney's Office, but one last time for the record, would you describe the events leading up to Mr. Carlotta's murder?"

Looking up at Charlie Vitteli on the witness stand, Conrad Clooney leaned nonchalantly against the jury rail with his hands in the pockets of his expensive gray silk suit as if he was quietly discussing politics at a Madison Avenue cocktail party. The look on his face was one of polite concentration and studied confidence.

"Well, we'd just come out of Marlon's — me, Vince, Joey, and Jackie — where we'd been discussing union business over a couple of beers," Vitteli recalled. "We turned the corner and we're walking down the sidewalk towards where we'd parked — Vince had sent his driver ahead to get his car warmed up — when these two yahoos jumped out of the alley. One of 'em had a gun or I'd have —"

"Let me interrupt you for a moment," Clooney said, pushing away from the rail and slowly strolling over to stand in front of Viteli. "These — how did you describe them? — yahoos . . . how were they dressed?"

"Oh . . . all in black . . . with ski masks and gloves," Vitteli replied.

"I see. Go on. . . . One of them had a gun or you would have . . ."

"Yeah, well, I might have tried something . . . you know, took a swing. They were both pretty big guys, but maybe I could have got lucky," Vitteli said and looked down at his big hands resting on the witness box ledge as though he blamed them for his failure. "Now I wish I would have . . . and maybe Vince would be here today."

False face must hide what false heart doth know. Although he kept his face passive, Karp was nauseated watching Vitteli's performance on the first full day of the defense case. He'd rested the People's case the day before following Antonia Carlotta's gripping testimony that had left many of the jurors in tears and casting hard looks at the defendants. At noon, Judge See had sent the jury to lunch.

When the trial resumed, Clooney rambled through a one-hour opening statement that was short on substance but long on innuendo. Openings are normally a "road map" of the case for the "finders of fact" — the judge and jury — presented by the attorneys of both sides. Although often dramatic, they are supposed to be limited to the evidence the jurors can expect to see presented, and then usually end with the assertion that the attorney believes that when all the facts are presented, the jury will have no option but to find in favor of their case. Openings are not supposed to be arguments regarding what the evidence does or doesn't demonstrate — that's what summations are for — or opportunities to give long-winded speeches having nothing to do with the evidence and everything to do with trying to confuse jurors with smoke and mirrors. But Clooney had done both.

However, Karp had listened stoically as Clooney used the stage to refute the People's case while insinuating that the prosecution was trying to frame his clients but without citing what, if any, evidence he'd be providing to back up such theories. Without objection, he let Clooney go on and on about the "curious timing and effect" of Marlene's involvement in the investigation.

"Indeed, until the district attorney's wife serendipitously meets the girlfriend of Gnat Miller, who by outrageous coincidence happens to be involved in the Carlotta murder, there was no mention of any three young men coming to the residence on December second," the defense attorney noted as he walked slowly along the jury rail, looking at each juror.

"No license plate number indented into a sticky pad. No cigarette butts. No beer bottle. No convenient witness to turn on his buddies to help the district attorney solve a high-profile case. And for what, you have to ask yourselves, ladies and gentlemen? What does Gnat Miller get out of it? Well, he hasn't been sentenced. Nor charged with assault on his girlfriend. And note that in his story, he is only the driver, not a participant in the actual murder, and thus subject, perhaps, to a lesser sentence. And I think that when we're finished laying this out for you, you will see that there is doubt, serious doubt, with the People's case and you will acquit the defendants."

Nor was Clooney satisfied with one defense strategy. He then told the jurors that even if the three young men had gone to the Carlotta home as described in the People's case, "which is doubtful to say the least, where is the evidence that it was not an attempt to find work in these hard economic times?" He paused and looked over at DiMarzo and Bebnev before shaking his head. "I admit my clients are no angels, maybe they were there to case the Carlotta residence; after all, they have had brushes with the law for burglary and theft. But that doesn't make them murderers three nights later and thirty miles away."

Clooney's opening was truly a "tale told by an idiot, full of sound and fury, signifying nothing," but Karp's silence throughout wasn't due to the usual practice of not interrupting the opposition's opening statements even if they strayed over into objectionable territory. And it wasn't that his anger over Clooney's insinuations wasn't bubbling just beneath the surface of his calm demeanor.

Moreover, it did rankle that a pompous, overpaid white-shoe Fifth Avenue conceit with political juice and aspirations thought he could manipulate the process Karp believed in to the depths of his soul. And Karp could have objected, and been sustained, at numerous points. But like a chess grand master, he quietly let the defense attorney maneuver himself into a trap, knowing that by letting him blindly rush forward now in defense of the two pawns sitting at the defense table, there was a chance of someday putting Charlie Vitteli in checkmate.

After his opening, Clooney asked the judge if they could adjourn "a little early so that I can have my witnesses ready in the morning." Although exasperated with the defense attorney's delay, Judge See granted him his request.

The next morning, Clooney showed up at the Criminal Courts Building as if the setbacks he'd experienced during the prosecution's case were mere bumps in the road. He preened for the news cameras in front of the main entrance, though he declined comment "except to say that I am giving my all to prevent a travesty of justice though the allied forces of government are difficult for any one man to defeat."

Back in court, he began his case by calling two "expert" witnesses to the stand. The first, a handwriting analyst from NYU, essentially testified that the note bearing the license plate number "with a high degree of probability" had been written by a woman and that the indentations "appeared to have been caused deliberately, as though someone was trying to leave an impression in the sheet beneath the original by pressing hard and uniformly throughout."

Knowing this was coming because he had the expert report, Karp had Guma, Fulton, and Darla Milquetost write the line from *Macbeth* he'd been thinking about at the beginning of the defense case, *False face must hide what false heart doth know,* on separate sheets of paper. He then had them sign and date copies of the pages, which he placed into a sealed envelope. He kept the originals in his trial folder.

Now, during cross-examination, Karp stood and said, "Your Honor, for the purpose of this demonstration, may I hand you this sealed envelope to be opened at the appropriate moment during this cross-examination?"

"Yes, you may, let the drama proceed."

Karp smiled. "Thank you, Your Honor." Turning to the witness, he asked, "Is it your testimony you can tell the difference between a note written by a man or a woman?"

"Absolutely."

"What, if any, scientific justification is there for this ability?"

"Well, I'm one of the leading proponents of this particular methodology, but it is gaining stature in the graphologist community. As I noted, I've written several well-received articles on this subject for various graphology periodicals."

"I see. So if I were to hand you several examples of a line of poetry, you would be able to tell which were written by a man and which were written by a woman?"

"Absolutely."

"Okay, in that case with the court's permission, I'd like to hand the witness these three sheets, People's Exhibits Twenty-Six A, B, and C," Karp said.

"Yes, you may," Judge See said.

Karp handed the originals of the three sheets of paper to the witness, who pulled a magnifying glass from her purse and carefully examined the writing. She looked up. "I believe I have reached a conclusion."

"Would you tell us what that conclusion is, please?" Karp asked.

"Yes, two of these, A and C, were definitely written by women," the witness claimed. "The third, Example B, was written by a man."

"Thank you," Karp said and turned to the judge. "Your Honor, would you now open the envelope and read the signature on the back of Example A, please?"

Looking amused, Judge See opened the envelope and pulled out the three sheets of paper. He then studied one and raised an eyebrow. "Example A was signed by Detective Clay Fulton."

Karp smiled and turned to the gallery. "Detective Fulton, would you stand, please?"

Fulton, who was sitting in the first row behind the prosecution table, stood up. Karp turned back to the witness, who was blushing and looking again through her magnifying glass at the copies of the writing she had. "It would appear that Detective Fulton is a very large man," Karp said. "Can you explain the discrepancy between that fact and your assertion?"

"Well, I . . . there is a certain small percentage of people whose writing is transgender," she stammered.

"Are you saying that Detective Fulton writes like a girl?" Karp said with a smile. The courtroom burst into laughter as the detective scowled at those giggling around him.

"Um, well, yes," the woman replied to more laughter.

Smiling, Karp turned back to the judge. "And now, if you would, Your Honor, please read the signature on the back of Example B, identified as a male writer by the witness."

"Darla Milquetost."

The courtroom erupted into more laughter as the witness turned even more crimson. "I'd like to explain," the witness said. "I believe in my haste I may have missed several indicators."

"Apparently," Karp replied. "Darla Milquetost is my office manager. Darla, would you stand, please?"

Blushing herself, Milquetost stood as several people around her applauded. "Obviously, Darla is a lovely woman," Karp noted to more laughter. He looked over at the defense table where Clooney sat with his forehead in his hand, as Bebnev scowled up at the ceiling and DiMarzo looked at the floor, shaking his head.

"I would just like to —"

"Yes, but before you do," Karp said. "Your Honor, please read the signature on Example C."

"Ray Guma."

This time Judge See lightly tapped his gavel to cut short the laughter as ADA Guma stood and did a little curtsy. Laughing with the others, Karp said, "I believe that's strike three."

The witness didn't try speaking anymore but just sat with her head down as Karp spoke to her again. "I have just one more request. Would you please read the line of poetry written on any one of those pages you have?"

Without looking at her antagonist, the woman cleared her throat. " 'False face must hide what false heart doth know.' "

Karp looked over at the defense table. "Thank you, no further questions."

Clooney's last expert witness was a former NYPD detective and "ballistics expert" who testified that, based on the trajectory of the bullet that had struck Carlotta in the head, he'd concluded that the shooter was a much taller man than Bebnev.

However, Karp nullified him through a series of questions meant to demonstrate that the trajectory was subject to a variety of factors, including the level at which the shooter held the gun, and whether either of the men were standing straight or crouched. The most damaging question to the defense case, however, and one that actually played into the prosecution narrative, was his last. "What if the deceased had been grabbed by his right arm and pulled downward, would that have affected the trajectory?"

"Yes, that could have affected the height and body posture of the victim," the witness conceded.

The defense expert witnesses had done no damage to the prosecution case and, if anything, had worked against the defense. Karp was much more interested in Clooney's last three witnesses, starting after lunch with Jackie Corcione. *Here's another one who looks like he hasn't been getting much sleep,* Karp thought when the young man settled into the witness chair. *The weak link in the next match, perhaps?*

Corcione toed the company line when describing the murder. Two unknown masked men had stepped from the alley and demanded their wallets. "Vince had a gun," he testified, shaking his head sadly. "I didn't know he even owned one. But the guy shot him, first in the chest and then in the head. They grabbed our stuff and ran across the street to a car and took off."

"Do you recognize any one in this court as either of the men who robbed you and murdered Vince Carlotta?" Clooney asked.

Corcione looked over at the defense table and shook his head. "No. They were wearing ski masks."

"Did the man who demanded your wallets speak with a notable accent?"

Corcione shook his head. "I don't remember," he said, glancing nervously at Bebnev, who smiled. "Everything happened so fast, and to be honest, I've blocked some of it out."

Joey Barros, who followed Corcione to the stand, was no more forthcoming. Hardly expressing any emotion at all as he recounted what happened, he shrugged when he said he couldn't remember if the shooter had an accent.

"Have you ever seen either of those two men sitting on either end of the defense table?" Clooney asked.

Barros looked over at Bebnev and Di-Marzo. His face looked like he'd smelled something distasteful but he shook his head. "Nope. Don't know 'em."

Karp hadn't expected much from Corcione and particularly Barros. But he did watch with interest when Barros stepped down from the witness stand and stopped a few feet from the defense table. For just a moment, he fixed Bebnev and then Di-Marzo with a hard glare.

Everyone else may think that's just anger, Karp thought when he saw the look, *but I'm betting it's a warning.*

Clooney had then called Vitteli to the stand. This time when the union boss walked into the courtroom, wearing a gray silk suit with a purple handkerchief in the pocket, looked around and saw Karp, he didn't smirk. His eyes hardened and he quickly shifted his gaze elsewhere. But he found himself looking at T. J. Martindale and other members of the union who'd supported Vince Carlotta, as well as the attorney Mahlon Gorman.

If anything, the hatred that passed between Vitteli and the other men was even greater than the union boss reserved for Karp after they'd had a confrontation at the DAO a few weeks after Carlotta's murder. That's when Karp took another statement from the union boss about events with Kowalski present and then point-blank accused Vitteli to his face. Vitteli's face had turned crimson with rage as his lawyer announced that they were "through cooperating" and stormed out of the office.

If Charlie only knew about a little conversation I had with Martindale and Gorman the other day, Karp thought now, *the look would be even uglier.*

"Mr. Vitteli, if you'd come forward to be sworn in," Judge See said, pointing to the witness stand.

Vitteli broke off his stare-down with the union men and, avoiding Karp's eyes, swaggered up to the stand with his chest out and head up. He smiled at the jurors when he was sworn in and took his seat, at which point he focused on Clooney, who began by asking him to describe the events leading to the murder.

"So given the chance, you might have

tried to intervene," Clooney asked.

"Yeah, maybe, but it happened so quick, all any of us could do was go along with it," Vitteli said. "It was like, 'Hands up, this is a robbery!' "

"So you did what?"

"I put my hands in the air like this," Vitteli said, demonstrating.

"Did you say anything?"

"Hell no. I just wanted that gun out of my face."

"What did Vince Carlotta do?"

"He reached into his pocket. I guess he had a gun," Vitteli replied. "That's when the fucker, excuse my French, shot him. Then he shot him again."

"What happened after that?"

"The guy demanded our wallets and watches. We gave 'em up, and they took off across the street and jumped in the car."

"You see the car?"

"I don't remember it," Vitteli said. "Maybe a sedan, but I don't know. I was too busy trying to help Vince."

"How about the men who accosted you?" Clooney asked. "Did you get a good look at them?"

Vitteli shrugged. "Like I said, they was wearing masks. They were big guys, but all I could see was their eyes."

"Do you recognize the two defendants sitting on either end of the table over there?"

Looking over at the defense table, Vitteli studied each man, then shook his head. "No, I can't say that I do. But those two ain't the guys who killed Vince."

"Why not?"

"One thing is they ain't big enough," Vitteli said. "And I don't think either of the assholes had blue eyes like pumpkin-head over there."

"And the robber who demanded your wallets and then shot Mr. Carlotta, did he speak with an accent?" Clooney asked.

"Yeah," Vitteli said slowly, as if it was the first time he'd considered the question. "He sounded Puerto Rican or Mexican, something like that."

"But not Russian?"

Vitteli furrowed his brow and thought about the question before shaking his head again. "No. I'd say Puerto Rican. You know, singsongy bullshit."

"Uh, thank you, Mr. Vitteli, no further questions," Clooney said. He appeared pleased and confident as he walked back to his seat.

Judge See looked at the clock on the wall. "We have about thirty minutes, Mr. Karp," he said. "Will that be enough time for your cross-examination, or would you like to break and come back and start in the morning?"

"Oh, that should be more than enough time, Your Honor," Karp replied as he rose from his seat and walked over to stand alongside the jury as he faced the witness.

Eschewing all pleasantries, Karp moved quickly to take advantage of the opening his opponent had given him. "Mr. Vitteli, you and Vince Carlotta didn't like each other much, did you?"

Vitteli frowned. "Oh, I don't know," he said. "We butted heads over union business sometimes, if that's what you mean. But we sort of grew up together in the union, and we got along pretty good."

"You ran against each other for union president a little over a year ago, is that correct?"

"Yeah, there was an election," Vitteli said.

"A pretty heated election, right? Some pretty serious accusations thrown back and forth, am I correct?"

"It got a little down and dirty, like the last time you ran for DA, right? But no big deal, that's just politics."

"No big deal?" Karp asked, ignoring the dig. "Isn't it true that Mr. Carlotta and some of his followers accused you of cheating and tampering with the results?"

"Sure, like any sore losers," Vitteli said and winked at the jurors.

"Sore enough to take a complaint to the U.S. Department of Labor and ask for a federal investigation?"

"Objection!" Clooney shouted, jumping to his feet. "These questions are outside of the scope of direct examination."

"Your Honor, I'd ask you to take this subject to connection. But if you want, Your Honor, I could recall Mr. Vitteli during the People's rebuttal case," Karp said.

"NO WAY, KARP!" Vitteli shouted, standing up in the witness box and waving Clooney off. "I'm here now, ask me anything you want!"

"Objection withdrawn," Clooney replied meekly.

"Okay, I asked you if Mr. Carlotta was angry enough about the election to take his complaint to the United States Department of Labor in Washington, D.C., and ask for a federal investigation," Karp demanded.

"I wouldn't know nothin' about that," Vitteli said.

Karp raised his eyebrows as if surprised. "You wouldn't know nothin' about that?"

"No, I wouldn't."

"You never heard that Vince Carlotta and

Mahlon Gorman asked the Labor Department to investigate the election results and their accusations that you committed election fraud?"

"Oh, I thought you asked if the feds actually got involved," Vitteli shot back. " 'Cause they didn't. Vince and his boy went to Washington to complain about that nonsense and got told to take it to the union to settle."

"That's right," Karp said. "And was there a subsequent investigation by the union?"

"Yeah, and nothing came of the allegations," Vitteli said. "It was all a bunch of crap."

"Who conducted the investigation?"

"What do you mean who?"

"Who . . . which individuals?"

Again Vitteli hunched his massive shoulders and pursed his lips before answering. "I don't know . . . been a while, some of the regular members . . ."

"All of them appointed by you, right?"

"By myself and other members of management."

"Was Joey Barros part of the management and one of the individuals appointed to investigate the claims?"

Vitteli hesitated, then shrugged. "Yeah."

"Jackie Corcione?"

"No, Jackie's the chief financial officer for

the union and counsel to the president. He sort of sat in on it to give legal advice, but he didn't vote."

"How about you?"

"How about me what?" Vitteli played dumb.

"Were you part of the investigation?"

Vitteli tilted his head to the side. "I oversaw it, but I didn't interfere. That's the way the rules are set up," he said.

"So this investigation into Carlotta's accusations that you committed acts of wrongdoing were conducted by yourself, your closest 'associates,' and a few flunkies you appointed?"

"Like I said, I didn't make the rules."

"Sort of like asking the fox to investigate why the hens are disappearing, right?"

"If you got something to say, Karp, come out with it," Vitteli demanded.

"Everything in its time, Mr. Vitteli," Karp said. He crossed his arms as he walked over to stand in the center of the court well and faced Vitteli. The gallery was silent as the prosecutor and the union boss glared at one another; two big men, physically powerful, and openly hostile. "Isn't it true that you were seen arguing with Vince Carlotta at Marlon's on the night of the murder?"

"Actually, my associates Joey Barros and

Vince had some words," Vitteli corrected him.

"And you?"

"Some things was said, maybe, but we worked it out," Vitteli said. "Ask anybody who was there. We had a disagreement, we got over it, and the rest of the night we enjoyed a few beers, smoked some stogies, and talked about old times."

"Oh yeah, the good old days," Karp said, stepping even closer. "Speaking of the good old days, it can be pretty rough on the docks, can't it?"

Vitteli scowled at the sudden change of direction with Karp's question but then smiled and nodded. "Yeah, you learn to take care of yourself."

"It can be pretty dangerous, right?"

"I don't know. It ain't Afghanistan."

"I was thinking more along the lines of dangers from outsiders who might want to encroach on your turf. Like other unions, or even the mob."

Vitteli laughed. "You saw *On the Waterfront,* too, eh? It ain't like the movies, but yeah, you got to be vigilant."

Stepping forward until he stood only a few feet in front of the stand, Karp rocked back on his heels as he looked up. "Vigilant, that's a good word. And you're vigilant, aren't you, Mr. Vitteli?"

"I try to be."

"Somebody could have it in for you. Or maybe somebody had it in for Vince Carlotta?"

"You know," Vitteli said, sitting back in the chair, "I thought of that. What if the guys who did it had it in for Vince in particular?"

"Yeah, what if?" Karp retorted. "He was apparently worried enough to carry a gun, isn't that true?"

"Yes, I guess so."

"And along with being vigilant, you're a smart guy, right, Mr. Vitteli?"

"I ain't a Columbia grad or nothin'," Vitteli replied. "But I get by."

"Yes, you do," Karp said. "And wouldn't a smart, vigilant union boss who knows it's a dangerous world out there take steps to protect himself? Like Vince Carlotta tried to do?"

"Like I said, you learn to handle yourself pretty good on the docks."

"That's right, I remember now, if the Puerto Rican yahoo didn't have a gun you would have decked him, right? Like Joe Louis decked Max Schmeling?"

"Yeah, just like the Brown Bomber, I might have taken a swing, only I'm Eyetie, so maybe a better example would be Rocky Graziano."

"Good choice, tough as nails, ate punches and asked for more," Karp said as he turned back toward the jury. "Mr. Vitteli, aren't you forgetting someone else who was with you that night at the bar?"

Vitteli looked suddenly wary. "I don't know who you mean."

"Well, there's you, Vince, Joey, Jackie, Randy McMahon and . . ." Karp broke his sentence off. "And someone else wasn't there?"

Vitteli's eyes widened for a moment and shifted out toward the gallery. Karp turned to see who he was looking at and saw Kowalski raise his shoulders as the intern scowled and made notes.

"Yeah, of course, my driver, Sal Amaya, was there."

"Your driver? Isn't Mr. Amaya your bodyguard?" Karp asked.

"He's both."

Karp looked from one juror's face to another, holding their eyes for just a moment. "Why didn't you mention him when you told the jury who was with you at the bar?"

"I guess I forgot."

"Did you also forget that you sent Mr.

Amaya ahead with Randy McMahon that night?"

"I might have. Yeah, now that I think about it, me and Vince had a couple more things to talk about in private while we walked."

"Is that it? Or did you send him ahead so that there'd be one less witness to the murder of Vince Carlotta?"

"What? That's crap . . . !"

"Or maybe you were worried that Mr. Amaya might do his job and take on these so-called yahoos just like Rocky Graziano, right?"

Unable to help himself, Vitteli shot a hard look at Clooney, who seemed stunned at the turn of events and only then remembered to jump up and object.

"On precisely what grounds, Mr. Clooney, might I ask?" the judge asked.

Not sure of what to say, Clooney used the old standard. "Uh, he's badgering the witness."

"Sit down, Mr. Clooney, overruled."

Clooney slumped back into his seat. "So I ask you again, Mr. Vitteli," Karp persisted, "why on a dark night in Hell's Kitchen would a smart, vigilant man send his bodyguard away?"

"I can take care of myself. I wasn't worried about it."

"Then why a bodyguard at all?"

"Just in case. I ain't as young as I used to be."

"Isn't it true that you don't go anywhere without your bodyguard, Mr. Vitteli?"

"That's right. That's what I said."

"So let me ask you again: at night, in Hell's Kitchen, you sent your bodyguard away?"

"I told ya, I didn't need him!" Vitteli snarled, a vein starting to bulge on his forehead.

"No, you didn't," Karp shot back. "Because you knew who was going to be murdered that night. You knew you were safe and that the target was Vince Carlotta." His voice grew louder as he went on. "And Vince Carlotta is dead now because he was coming after you, and you were going to lose it all, weren't you? So you hired three nobodies to do your dirty work, isn't that right!"

"That's bullshit!" Vitteli shouted, the vein getting bigger as his face blushed darker.

Pointing at Vitteli, Karp fired back. "Oh no, Mr. Vitteli, you gave the order to kill Vince Carlotta because that's how you really take care of yourself."

"You son of a bitch!" Vitteli yelled, then

looked at Clooney with his eyes bugging out of his purple face. "OBJECT, YOU DUMB FUCK!"

"OBJECTION!" Clooney cried out as he shot to his feet like a puppet on strings. Then he stood there looking stunned and unsure of what to do next. The witness looked like he might climb down from the stand and attack him.

Judge See banged his gavel, something he rarely ever did. "Mr. Vitteli, be seated."

As Vitteli turned to the judge to speak, Judge See said, "Enough, Mr. Vitteli, you've already said a mouthful."

Karp said calmly and somewhat amused. "I'm done here, Your Honor, no further questions."

"Care to redirect, Mr. Clooney?" See asked.

Visibly shaken, Clooney shook his head violently. "No, absolutely no more questions."

"You may step down, Mr. Vitteli," Judge See said to the witness, who was mopping his face with his silk handkerchief.

Vitteli stormed down from the stand and without looking to either side passed between the defense and prosecution tables. As he passed the pews in the gallery where T. J. Martindale, Mahlon Gorman, and the other union members were sitting, they stood, their faces angry and their jaws set, but Vitteli didn't try to engage them or stare them down this time. He'd almost reached the doors at the back of the courtroom when he was frozen in his tracks by a voice behind him.

"Careful, my sisters, something wicked this way comes."

Vitteli turned to see who spoke and his face grew ashen as he saw the three women in the back of the courtroom. He slammed the doors of the courtroom open and stalked out.

24

Alexei Bebnev lowered his white prison T-shirt and scratched at his chest. He was proud of the large new tattoo created by burning a shoe sole and mixing the soot with urine, which was then injected into his skin with a piece of guitar string. But he was also worried that the redness and swelling he'd been told to expect by the inmate artist was more than usual and indicated an infection.

Still, he smiled as he thought about the somewhat blurry image of a cathedral with two spires. It indicated in Russian Mafia symbolism that he'd been in two prisons: the notorious Butyrka in central Moscow and now Sing Sing, the maximum security prison thirty miles north of Manhattan on the east side of the Hudson River in Ossining, New York. Of course that wasn't true about Butyrka. He'd been a small-time hoodlum in the working-class Kapotnya neighborhood of Moscow and had never set foot inside a Russian prison as an inmate or visitor. But he reasoned that he would have been sent to prison or worse if he'd been caught for killing the old Jew jeweler in Moscow, so he thought he deserved the second spire.

When he saved enough cigarettes, or perhaps made some money in the prison drug trade helping his new comrades in the Malchek *bratka,* he'd also get four small teardrops tattooed next to his right eye to represent the men he'd killed. *Maybe six,* he thought. *Who's to know?* Then the other inmates would show respect for Alexei Bebnev.

Perhaps his new friends would give him a prison nickname that he'd take back out on the streets when he was released. He thought he might suggest *"Vohlk,"* or the English translation, "Wolf." Wolf Bebnev. The chicks would dig that.

As he prepared to leave his cell and join his comrades in the exercise yard, Bebnev idly wondered how long he would be in prison. The sentence following the trial had been life with a mandatory minimum of twenty-five years, but the Malcheks had assured him that now that he'd shown his loyalty and value, they would pay for a good new attorney, work the system, in a manner of speaking, and get him out of prison one way or the other. There would be an appeal, and in the meantime, the rat Gnat Miller would be eliminated, and without Miller, the bastard Karp would not have a case.

Except for the tattoos, Bebnev would have preferred to avoid prison. But his idiot attorney Clooney had made a mess of the case, especially the testimony of Charlie Vitteli, who'd looked like he was going to strangle Clooney after Karp got done tearing him apart.

Stunned, Clooney had then lamely rested the defense case. His summation had basically been a repeat of what he'd said at the beginning of the trial, the lies about the District Attorney's Office and the cops trying to frame him and DiMarzo. He pointed to the bullshit defense "experts" testimony and the testimony of Corcione, Barros, and Vitteli as proof of reasonable doubt. "Those two ain't the guys who killed Vince," Clooney repeated the union boss's words, but Bebnev could see that the jury wasn't buying it. Not after what Karp had done to Vitteli.

Even as someone inexperienced with the American justice system, Bebnev wasn't surprised when Karp made short work of

Clooney's summation arguments, deriding them as "baseless, contemptuous, and without one scintilla of evidence to support his outrageous slanders." And when the prosecutor urged the jury to base their decision "by looking at the People's evidence as a whole, and using your common sense to differentiate between cheap, dime-store fantasy and the truth," Bebnev knew then that he and DiMarzo were going down. And, in fact, it had taken the jurors less than two hours to return a verdict of guilty.

It doesn't matter, Bebnev thought as he maintained what he thought was a cold, impenetrable expression as he made his way past other inmates and guards. *What's a little time in prison?* Sure, the nights could be pretty frightening, filled with screams, shouts, and curses. And though he tried not to show it, he was scared of the black, Asian, and Hispanic gangs. However, no one bothered him because of his fine new friends. And when he got out, he'd be a made man with plenty of money, admiring women, and the respect of the Russian mob.

As Bebnev wandered out into the exercise yard he looked over toward one of the weight-lifting areas that the *bratka* of the Russian Mafia had staked out as their own. Although there were several Russian gangs represented there, for the most part they maintained a truce and cooperated on dividing up their piece of the prison black market in drugs, sex, cell phones, and food.

Many of the men working out had their shirts off in the June sun, displaying a wide assortment of ornate tattoos that indicated gang affiliation and rank within their organization, separated killers from mere thieves, and, like Bebnev's, indicated the number of times they'd been incarcerated. Most had roses on their chests, the symbol for loyalty, and he wondered if perhaps he should have done that first. But he was more interested in displaying something that would indicate he was a hard-core criminal, and he'd only had enough cigarettes for the cathedral.

As he crossed over to the dozen or so men, Bebnev stripped off his T-shirt and tried not to smile, imagining how his comrades would react to his new art. He noted how muscular the other men were as they curled, pushed, and pulled the weights, and how the sweat made their bodies glisten and their dark tattoos darker.

He wanted muscles like that and became self-consciously aware of his pale, flaccid physique. It was enough to make him think about putting his shirt back on, especially when the other men saw him coming and began nudging each other and laughing. But then his friend Yuri looked up from the curling bench and waved him over.

The St. Petersburg native was the first inmate who'd befriended him at Sing Sing, a massive man with a face that resembled a gorilla's who was known to be one of the Malchek gang's chief enforcers. His chest, back, and arms were almost completely covered with tattoos, including a cathedral with five spires. No one disrespected Yuri, not even the blacks, which meant that no one had disrespected Bebnev in the week since he'd arrived at Sing Sing.

"Comrade Alexei," the big man shouted and grinned, exposing a mouthful of gold teeth with diamonds imbedded in the incisors top and bottom. He slapped the leg of another large man lying on his back on the bench press. "Get up," he growled, and when the man instantly complied, he gestured at the bench and said to Bebnev. "You're next, my friend."

Conscious of the snickering, grinning circle of men who had suddenly surrounded him and the bench press, Bebnev demurred. He rubbed a shoulder and shook his head. "I think I pulled something yesterday," he said. "I'm going to give it a rest today."

"Ha," one of the other men laughed. "The

only thing you've been pulling is your dick at night."

The other men laughed, including Yuri, who patted Bebnev on the shoulder. "Nonsense," he said. "It's just the muscle rebuilding itself. A killer like you will want to stay in shape. You never know when things could turn ugly in here, and you'll have to defend yourself."

Bebnev didn't like the sound of that, but he wasn't sure what to say to get out of lying down on the bench. He didn't have much of a chance, as Yuri grabbed him by the arm and propelled him toward the weights. "If you're going to run with the Malcheks, we'll want to know that you are a man who can take care of himself."

Run with the Malcheks. Bebnev liked that. "Don't worry, I can take care of myself, comrade," he said confidently. "I put the gun in that asshole's face and 'bang, bang,' asshole was dead." He laughed and looked around the thick circle of men, who were smiling, but he couldn't tell if they were impressed or just humoring him.

Deciding that he had no choice but to try to fit in, Bebnev lay down on the bench. As he went through the motions of warming up his arms, rubbing his "injured" shoulder, and taking deep breaths, one of the men on one side of him near the end of the bench press bar, a great bear-like man with a patch over one eye named Viktor, stepped forward to look at his tattoo.

"Two spires," Viktor grunted. "One for Sing Sing. What is the other?"

"Butyrka," Bebnev lied.

"Butyrka?" When was this?"

Bebnev shrugged. "About, uh, five or six years ago."

"About five or six years ago?" Viktor replied with an incredulous look. "How is it a man does not know exactly how much time he spent in hell? I was in Butyrka for fifteen long years, and I can tell you the day I arrived and the day I was released. I lost this in Butyrka." He lifted the eyepatch to expose an empty socket.

Another large, squat man on the other side of the bench leaned over and looked closely at Bebnev's face. "I was in Butyrka, too. But I don't remember you."

"It's a big place," Bebnev said, swallowing hard. "I was in solitary a lot."

"It is a big place," the second man conceded. "But I think I would remember you, with those crazy eyes and that round head."

"Ah, his mother was just a whore who drank too much bad vodka before she pumped out this frog-eyed bastard," Yuri explained to general laughter.

Bebnev sat up on the bench. This wasn't going well at all. "Well, maybe she was," he said meekly. "It wasn't my fault. But I think I'll go back to my cell now." He made a move to get up, but Yuri, who was standing at the head of the bench hovering over the weight bar, grabbed him by his shoulders and pushed him back down.

"Wait! Where are you going so fast?" Yuri asked with a smile. "We were just kidding you, right, brothers? If you're going to hang with the *bratka,* you're going to have to grow a thicker skin. Come, enough of this teasing, you're here to work out. Let's start with something light and build up."

Lying on his back, looking up at the upside-down face of Yuri grinning with his gold teeth shining in the sun, Bebnev managed a weak smile. *They're just kidding,* a voice inside his head assured him. Yuri was his friend, and he needed to have such a friend in a place like Sing Sing. At least until he won his appeal and was back on the streets of Little Odessa, where women would want him and men would envy and fear him.

Bebnev licked his lips nervously as his two antagonists from Butyrka put forty-five-pound weights on each end of the forty-pound bench press bar. *One hundred thirty pounds total, I should be able to do this,* he thought as he raised his hands to grip the bar. With Yuri's help and encouragement, he managed to press the bar five times before placing it back on the rack.

Proud of himself, Bebnev smiled and started to sit up but again Yuri pressed him back down. "Come on," the big man exclaimed. "That was too easy for a tough guy like you; you hardly even broke a sweat. Let's get a real workout in!"

Sighing, Bebnev lay back down as two more forty-five-pound weights were added to the bar. *Two hundred twenty pounds!* "I don't think I can —"

"Sure you can, Alexei," Yuri assured him. "I am here to spot for you. What could go wrong?" He laughed and looked around the circle of a dozen other large men, who also laughed.

Again, Alexei gripped the bar and with Yuri's help was able to lift it off the rack. The weights felt impossibly heavy, but he managed to lower it a few inches before trying to press it back up.

"No cheating! All the way down to your chest," Yuri insisted as he pushed the bar down.

Again with Yuri's assistance, he was able

to lower the bar and raise it twice. When he placed it back on the rack, Yuri led the other men in cheering. Bebnev soaked their praise in and was beginning to feel that with this sort of support, he might someday have the big chest, wide shoulders, and bulging muscles of his friends. However, his fantasy didn't last long.

"Okay, last set," Yuri said, nodding at his two assistants, who each picked up another forty-five-pound weight. *Three hundred ten pounds . . .* "I'll never be able to do so much."

"Nonsense," Yuri chided. "We'll do just one. Then you will feel like you really did something. And I'll be right here to make sure nothing happens."

"Okay, but this is it!"

Yuri grinned, a wolfish expression. "Yes, this will be the last one."

Bebnev gripped the bar and focused on Yuri's ugly face; the enforcer's hands hovered just under the bar, ready to assist him with the lift. Summoning all of his strength, Bebnev pushed.

"Come on, you can do it, man!" Yuri shouted while the others cheered and clapped.

The bar moved up and then slowly started to sink toward Bebnev's chest no matter how hard he pushed. "Help," he said.

Sweating profusely so that drops fell into Bebnev's eyes, Yuri sneered. "Come on, killer, you can do it!"

"I can't," Bebnev cried, panic starting to set in as the weight bar sank to his chest and began to move toward his throat.

"Oh, all right," Yuri said. "I will relieve you of your burden." But instead of helping the struggling man lift the weight, he leaned over, placed his hands on top of the bar, and pressed down.

Realizing the man's intent, Bebnev tried to roll to the side off the bench, but the men on either side of him pinned his legs and torso so that he was stuck. He struggled to keep the bar up but it was no use. "Help," he tried to shout, but it came out as a strangled yelp.

Then the bar was on his throat, the pressure increasing until he felt the moment that the bar crushed his windpipe and he could no longer breathe. The pain and fear were unbearable, and his body bucked, stronger in his death throes than he had ever been in life. He was still alive when the capillaries in his eyes burst and the world went dark. Then there was a terrible crunching as the bar broke the vertebrae in his neck.

Bebnev's body went limp and his hands

released their death grip on the bar as his bowels voided. With a last push to make sure his victim was dead, Yuri then stood up. With the others who'd gathered around the bench press to shield it from view, he walked away, leaving the carcass of Alexei Bebnev, would-be hit man for the Russian mob lying there with his weird, pale, and now bloodshot eyes staring sightlessly up at the sun.

25

Marlene and the young woman ignored the catcalls they heard from inmate trustees cleaning up the parking lot when they arrived at Sing Sing penitentiary. They were both dressed conservatively in loose clothes with their hair under scarves, but it didn't matter in proximity to two thousand incarcerated men and very few women.

"Is it always like this?" Liza Zito shuddered as an inmate shouted a request for a quick assignation in the bushes.

"Worse sometimes," Marlene answered. "Especially in the visiting room, except it's usually quieter because the guards don't put up with it if they hear it. We're lucky we'll be in an interview room usually reserved for attorneys and law enforcement to meet in private with inmates."

Actually, there was more than luck involved. It so happened that the assistant warden in charge of prisoner visitations was a former NYPD detective who'd been assigned to the DAO's sex crimes bureau when Marlene was in charge. They'd been friends for more than fifteen years, and Assistant Warden Dave Whitney, a confirmed bachelor, had often let her know that "if you should ever tire of you-know-who, I'm available." But it was all in good fun, and he'd listened like the old friend he was when she asked for a favor.

"I'm representing inmate Frank DiMarzo's sister Liza Zito. I think if we can get a few minutes alone with Frank, we can bust the Carlotta case wide open," Marlene said during her telephone call.

"I thought I read where the guys who did it were doing beaucoup time, two of 'em right here in our little country club?" Whitney asked.

"Those were the nobodies who did the hit," Marlene replied. "We want the guy who ordered it."

"Well, it's a little out of the ordinary," Whitney said. "But there's not much about Sing Sing that isn't. So yeah, we'll figure something out. I take it that it wouldn't be a good idea for the general population to know that DiMarzo's getting a visit from the wife of you-know-who."

"No, probably not. I'd appreciate it if we

can sign in as Liza Zito and attorney Jodi Vannoy," Marlene said. "Jodi's a friend, by the way, and we look close enough to be sisters."

"Not a problem, as long as this doesn't come back to bite me in the ass. Let me know when you're coming, and I'll make sure I'm at the visitors' desk and we'll slip you in."

"Thanks, Dave."

"No worries. Nothin' I wouldn't do for the girl of my dreams."

Marlene laughed. "You're incorrigible!"

"I think you've said that a few hundred times in the past."

Assistant Warden Dave Whitney was all business when they checked in. "I'll handle this," he said to the guard on duty when they arrived. He went through the formality of getting them to fill in the paperwork, and then personally escorted them to an interview room. "I'll get the prisoner," he said and left, but not without winking at Marlene when Liza wasn't looking.

As they took their seats at a table in the otherwise bare room, Marlene smiled at Liza, recalling the first time she'd talked to the young woman after the sentencing of her brother and Alexei Bebnev. The sentence of life had elicited screams and cries from DiMarzo's mother and sisters, except for Liza, whose face was covered with tears, but she'd otherwise remained calm, attending to her elderly parents.

Marlene had attended parts of the trial and been present after Gnat Miller's testimony when Frank DiMarzo broke down as his mother was led out of the courtroom. And she'd talked to her husband quite a bit about DiMarzo's deteriorating physical appearance and demeanor. Then, as he'd been taken away after sentencing, he'd wailed, "I'm sorry, Mom, Pops. Forget about me!" And that's when she'd decided to play her hunch.

Seeing an opportunity in the hallway outside the courtroom following the verdict when Liza was momentarily away from the others, Marlene had walked up to her. "Could I speak to you for a minute, please?"

Liza's eyes had widened when Marlene introduced herself. "What in the hell makes you think I want to talk to you?" she answered. "You've got some nerve!"

"Maybe," Marlene conceded. "And I know this is a difficult time for you, but I'm really not the enemy. You sat every day in that courtroom and you know what the truth is. Nobody made that stuff up and nobody planted evidence to frame your brother. But I do think that he and the other two are not the only ones who deserve to pay for Vince Carlotta's murder."

"Go on," the tough Brooklyn woman said.

"You do know that Bebnev intended to shoot Frank and Gnat Miller at that landfill," Marlene said. "Where do you think he got that idea?"

"You tell me."

"He got it from the same person, or persons, who wanted Vince Carlotta out of the way," Marlene said. "Frank made a mistake, and it's going to cost him dearly. But he wouldn't have been tempted into making that mistake if somebody hadn't dangled a bunch of money in front of him."

Tears had appeared in Liza's eyes as Marlene spoke and she wiped at them angrily. "Frank ain't a bad guy. He made bad choices, and now he's got to pay. But I know him, and I know that in his heart he's not a killer by nature. I didn't know what was eating at him, but I knew all last December before he got arrested that something was tearing him apart."

"So why didn't he follow his friend Miller's example? Was it the code-of-the-streets nonsense? Didn't want to be an informant?"

Liza nodded. "That's part of it. He's quite a bit younger than the rest of us, and Mom and Pops had their hands full looking out for us girls. So maybe he was allowed to run a little wild, and Red Hook is a tough place to grow up on the straight and narrow if nobody's kicking your ass every now and again to make sure you're on track. So he picked up that crap running with the wrong crowd. . . . But that's not all of it."

Pausing, Liza looked up and down the hallway. "A few days after Frankie's arrest, Pops got a photograph in the mail," she said. "It was a picture of Mom going to one of her doctor visits. There was a black line drawn across her. We're not stupid; we understood the message, and so did Frankie when one of my sisters told him about it."

"Now that makes sense," Marlene said. "We Italians are all about family, especially our mothers. But sometimes we have to do what's right, too. I don't give a damn about Alexei Bebnev; he was looking to make a name for himself, but your brother and his friend Gnat got used and then were cast aside by the men who used them. Unfortunately, Miller was low man on the totem pole and doesn't know much more than he talked about at the trial. But Frank was the conduit between Gnat and Bebnev, and it's possible he holds the keys to getting to the guys at the top."

Standing in the institution-green hallway of the Criminal Courts Building, tears streaming down her face as her devastated family stood twenty yards away wondering what she was doing talking to the wife of the district attorney, Liza looked up at the ceiling and then back to Marlene. "I'll talk to my family," she said. "I ain't promising anything. Mom still doesn't believe that Frankie was involved, or if he was that he knew what was going to happen. I'm not sure I do. But she's a very religious woman, and if Frankie was in on it, his soul is going to hell if he doesn't try to make it right."

A week passed with no word and Marlene was beginning to think her plea was going to be ignored when Liza called. "Is this person, this asshole who paid for this to happen, Charlie Vitteli?"

"I don't want to put words in anyone's mouth," Marlene replied.

Liza was quiet for a moment, then said, "You don't have to; it was pretty clear the way your husband went after him. Anyway, I need to see my brother face-to-face. And if you want to come with me, you can."

Marlene had then called her friend Dave Whitney and made arrangements for the visit. When she finished talking to him, she had another thought and placed a call to an unlisted number in Brighton Beach.

"Don't worry, no one will touch the Di-Marzo family," Ivgeny Karchovski assured her after she explained what was going on. "The Malchek gang is vicious and arrogant. But they are also good businessmen and aren't going to go to war over something like this. I don't guarantee they won't cause troubles for you in some other regard — word is they have something going with Charlie Vitteli over on the docks — but I'll make sure the word goes out that the Di-Marzo family is off-limits."

Marlene had picked Liza up in the Red Hook, Brooklyn, neighborhood not far from the Fairway Market for the drive to the city of Ossining, about fifty miles north on the east bank of the Hudson River and since 1826 the location of the third-oldest penitentiary in New York State.

As Marlene drove, her passenger told her a little about the family. "Mom and Pops are second generation. Their parents came over on a boat from small villages in Sicily after World War Two," she said. "They met standing in line at the Coney Island Ferris wheel and been together ever since. Dad got a job selling shoes and never stopped selling shoes until he retired at seventy years old when they made him. It was a good life.

Four girls and then long after they thought they were done, or was healthy, Frankie came along as a 'surprise.' I'm thirty-five and Mom had me when she was forty, so she's getting up there. Her pregnancy with Frankie was a tough one, the doctors wanted to abort him, but Mom's Catholic through and through and that was out of the question. Pops says she was never the same after she gave birth. 'Frail' he calls her. She's got a bad ticker and the prognosis ain't good."

After that Liza had looked out the window without speaking for ten minutes. Marlene thought she might be crying and so let her be. But then the young woman added, "Pops don't let on much but he's slowed down a lot, especially since Frankie's arrest, and I don't think he'll outlive her by much. He won't know what to do with himself without her. This whole thing has taken years off their lives."

There was a knock on the door of the interview room, which was then opened by a guard. He stepped back and Frank Di-Marzo walked in.

Marlene was shocked at the change that had come over him even since the trial. He'd already looked like death warmed over, a man who'd given up hope, but now he was even more gaunt, his eyes sunken and lacking any spark.

"What the fuck is she doing here?" he said when he saw Marlene. "Jesus, I can't trust my own sister?"

"I'll let her explain what she's here for in a minute," Liza said. "But shut up and listen to me, Frankie. Mom's dying. . . ."

In an instant, Frank's demeanor changed from that of hostile inmate to that of worried son. "What? Can't they do something? Maybe a transplant or something?"

Liza shook her head. "She's just failing, Frankie. The doctors say she wouldn't survive a transplant."

Frank's head fell forward and his shoulders sagged. "It's my fault," he said. "I put her in an early grave."

"I'm not going to sugarcoat it, Frankie, this didn't help," Liza said. "You made some bad choices that hurt your family and destroyed your life, but you can choose to do the right thing now. Mom wants to believe you're innocent, but if you're not, and you don't make it right, she won't see you in heaven someday and that's tearing her up inside. So I want you to hear Ms. Ciampi out."

"It's not as simple as coming clean, Liza," Frank said.

"What do you mean, Frankie? You talking about the photograph of Mom?"

"Yeah, that. These guys are mixed up with the Russian mob and those fuckers don't mess around."

Marlene decided to interrupt. "I know someone in the Russian community who is willing to guarantee your family's safety," she said.

"Bullshit," DiMarzo spat. "Who's got that kind of muscle?"

"I'm not naming names here," Marlene said, then lowered her voice as she looked in his eyes. "You remember who stopped Bebnev from killing you in the landfill? That's who's got that kind of muscle."

A look of comprehension came over DiMarzo as he carefully regarded Marlene, but then he smiled. "So I got to make some sort of deal or my family could pay for it."

Marlene shook her head. "No. The people who hired you to kill Vince Carlotta are like that, but I'm not holding your family hostage. My friend will look out after your family whether you decide to do the right thing or not. This is about your conscience and your soul, not playing with innocent people's lives."

Frank's brown eyes filled with tears and his head dropped. "Please, Frankie," his sister pleaded as she reached across the table and grabbed his hand. "These people don't deserve your protection. You made a bad choice, but they're the ones who put it in front of you. They flushed your life down the toilet, and they're threatening your family. We want you to do the right thing, all of us, no matter what."

"You can protect my family?" Frank asked Marlene.

"We'll move them into a safe house," she replied. "Around-the-clock security and medical care for your mom, just to be sure. Then, when this is all over, my friend will make sure that they can go home in peace."

Reaching out for his sister's other hand, Frank said to Marlene, "Tell your husband I'll talk to him. And sis, next time you visit, bring the Bible from my room."

Liza smiled. "I'm glad you're doing this," she said. "And reading your Bible will help."

Frank smiled slightly. "Yeah, I think it will take a load off. But be careful; there's some loose pages in it that I don't want to fall out."

Suddenly there was a knock on the door and Dave Whitney walked in. "Sorry, Marlene. We're going on lockdown. I need to get the prisoner back to his cell immediately!"

"What happened?" Marlene asked.

"Goddamned Russians killed somebody out in the yard," Whitney replied.

A warning bell went off in Marlene's head. A bell she'd heard many times before and knew better than to ignore. "Do you know who was killed?"

"Marlene, I don't have time —"

"Please, Dave, ask."

Whitney frowned but spoke into a hand-held radio he was carrying. "This is Assistant Warden Whitney. Do we have an ID on the victim yet?"

There was a long pause before the radio crackled and a voice said, "Inmate Alexei Bebnev. Prisoner Number 80346-A."

"Oh, my God," Liza Zito cried out, her hand going to her mouth.

Marlene grabbed her friend Whitney's arm. "You can't take DiMarzo to his cell," she implored him. "They'll kill him."

Whitney thought about it and nodded. "I'll put him in AdSeg until we get this sorted out."

"Even trying to get there could be risky if all the inmates aren't accounted for," Marlene said.

"Got ya," Whitney replied and picked up the radio again. "I want a SWAT team to Interview Room B, ASAP, full gear, and there better not be a Russian within a cell block of here when I move out."

"Roger that," the voice on the radio said. "SWAT on the way."

"Thanks, Dave," Marlene said. She turned to Frank. "You still ready to go through with this?"

The young man looked at his sister, who nodded. "Yeah. It's time."

Marlene took out her cell phone and punched in a number. "Hi, Butch," she said. "Yes, me too . . . Hey, I think you and Guma might want to take a drive with Clay to Sing Sing. What? Yeah, right now." She looked over to where Frank was hugging his tearful trembling sister in the corner of the room and turned away. "I thought I'd be the first to tell you that Alexei Bebnev just completed his life sentence. But more important, Frank DiMarzo is ready to sing."

26

Charlie Vitteli puffed furiously on a cigar as he paced in front of the window of his office in the dock warehouse, waiting for Joey Barros to arrive. He could have told Barros to call with the news he wanted to hear, but he didn't trust the telephone lines, and cell phone calls were too easy to intercept. As it was, he regularly had his office, home, and cars swept by a high-priced security company, and still he didn't feel safe.

Everybody seemed to be looking at him. Talking behind his back. People on the streets and in restaurants — the waiters at Marlon's acted as if they were reluctant to serve him. *Or is it all in your mind, like Joey says? Screw that! I seen their eyes, the way they whisper to each other.* His wife and kids had left to visit her mother in Illinois without saying when, or if, she was coming back, and even his mistress's ardor had cooled.

More significantly, the union was split between the old guard, whose loyalty he'd bought or coerced, and T. J. Martindale and his crew, who grumbled openly and were demanding a new election. So far he had enough support to hold off the calls, but every day the demands for his resignation grew. Or so it seemed.

And it all started when Karp publicly humiliated him in the courtroom. The media had wasted no time jumping all over it, running up and shouting at him as he emerged from the Criminal Courts Building that afternoon.

"Vitteli, is it true you paid to have Vince Carlotta killed!"

"How does it feel to be accused of murder by the district attorney?"

"Did you do it?"

Vitteli had snarled and pushed his way through the jostling throng as Barros waited for him in a car at the curb. "Get the fuck out of my way! Move, damn you, or I'll shove that camera up your . . ."

The pack of journalists just laughed like hyenas as they tore into him. Then his scowling face and curses, bleeped for the profanity, appeared on the evening newscasts, and again on the front page of the morning newspapers. Nor had they let up much after Bebnev and DiMarzo were convicted and sentenced to life; in fact, the story had gone national and he'd been besieged with calls from everywhere from Washington, D.C., to San Francisco. His contact with the U.S. Department of Labor had called to say that Mahlon Gorman was demanding an audience with the higher-ups and might get it. He'd told the man that if he went down, he was taking him down, too. "So you better stay on board, or your ass will fry with mine!"

It didn't matter to him that Karp was right, that he *was* guilty. He was outraged that the district attorney had convicted him in the court of public opinion, and life had been hell ever since. Just about every night in the weeks since, he'd woken up in a cold sweat from a dream of Karp shouting up at him on the witness stand. "There are three men in this courtroom who should be standing trial for the murder of Vince Carlotta! The two defendants sitting right there, and you, right, Mr. Vitteli?!"

Later, over a beer at Marlon's, Syd Kowalski had tried to brush off the nightmare on the witness stand. "Karp did that because he ain't got a real case," the attorney said. "He was baiting you."

"Can't we sue the bastard?" Vitteli complained. "How can he get away with that crap?"

"You really don't want to go there, Charlie," Kowalski replied. "And look at it this way, Karp making you look bad put the nail in the coffins, so to speak, of Bebnev and DiMarzo. They're going to Sing Sing, which is right where we want them. Those two rats would have run for whatever hole they could find if they got off. Now I suggest you forget about it and let the Malchek gang take care of those two little problems."

Looking down at the road that ran past the docks, Vitteli saw Barros's car turn the corner. "About fucking time," he swore and wondered why it had taken so long. Even Joey wasn't the loyal dog he'd always been. He'd caught him watching him with an apprising look on his face and he'd begun questioning his decisions. *Well, the dog can either come to heel, or I'll get a new mutt.*

Vitteli pasted a smile on his face when Barros knocked and walked in. "So, is our little problem taken care of? I . . ." The words died in his mouth when he saw his man's face.

"One isn't an issue anymore," Barros said quietly, aware of Vitteli's concerns about the office being bugged. "But the second . . ."

"Let's take a walk," Vitteli interrupted.

When they were outside, Vitteli headed for one of the docks. "Okay, what gives?"

"Bebnev is dead," Barros said. "But DiMarzo got a visitor and wasn't in his cell."

"Visitor? What visitor?"

"Not sure. Family maybe, but Kowalski said there were two and it wasn't in the visiting room."

Vitteli furrowed his brow. "I don't like it. This was supposed to be taken care of," he complained angrily.

"Shit happens," Barros replied. "Kowalski's on his way and . . . Speak of the devil."

Vitteli turned to look in the direction that Barros indicated and saw a sedan headed for them. It stopped and the stocky attorney pried himself out of the backseat and waddled toward them.

"Joey give you the news?" he asked Vitteli.

"So far only that Bebnev is dead but DiMarzo's still alive?"

"Yeah, it was all set up," Kowalski said. "The right people were paid to look the other way, but last minute, DiMarzo got a visitor and wasn't in his cell. According to my sources, he didn't go to the visiting room; they took him to an interview room."

"Who'd he see?"

"One of his sisters and some attorney

named Jodi Vannoy. Then when it went down with Bebnev, the SWAT team whisked him off to administrative segregation and our friends can't get to him."

"Fuck!" Vitteli exclaimed. "Now what?"

"Don't work yourself up," Kowalski cautioned him. "DiMarzo's family is probably just working with this lawyer to appeal his conviction."

"Which means he may talk to get a deal."

"I really don't think that's going to happen," Kowalski said. "For one thing, Karp doesn't make deals. And even if he did, how much of a threat is DiMarzo anyway? He didn't meet Joey or Jackie. Anything he says he heard from Bebnev is hearsay and now it can't be corroborated. I talked to Clooney after the trial — that transfer into his account is a done deal, by the way — and he said that DiMarzo knows shit."

Just then, Kowalski's cell phone rang. He pulled it out of his pocket and frowned as he looked at the caller ID. "Excuse me, I need to take this," he said and then spoke into the phone. "Yeah?"

As he listened, the attorney's frown grew deeper. He stepped away from Vitteli and Barros and when he turned back to them a minute later, he didn't look any happier as he hung up.

"What is it?" Vitteli demanded.

"Let's not panic," Kowalski began ominously, "but that was our friends the Malcheks. Apparently, Karp, some guy from his office, and that black detective who's always around him showed up at Sing Sing a few minutes ago to talk to DiMarzo. I still don't think it's a problem."

"What in the hell do you mean it's not a problem?" Vitteli cursed. "It means Karp's asking questions and DiMarzo's ratting!"

"So what?" Kowalski shot back. "What could DiMarzo say that changes the situation?"

"How the fuck do I know? I want him gone!" Vitteli complained. "Maybe our friend or Joey needs to pay a visit to the punk's family?"

Kowalski shook his head. "That was another part of the conversation," he said. "This DiMarzo apparently has friends in low places. The family is off-limits; the Malcheks say they won't go near them and to think real seriously before we do. Essentially, until this gets cleared up, you're on your own."

"On my own . . ." Vitteli's voice was right on the edge of hysteria. "What about Karp? He's got it in for me, if he's gone . . ."

"Are you insane?" Kowalski asked. "Hit

the District Attorney of New York and you'll bring down a firestorm of shit that will destroy you and anybody else who has anything to do with it. If the Malcheks knew you were even thinking of such a thing — with all the heat it would bring to their business interests, including the project at the docks — they'd kill you themselves."

Vitteli swallowed hard. His chest felt suddenly tight and he wondered if he was having a heart attack. The whole thing was driving him crazy. Just the night before, his mistress had found him in the bathroom sleepwalking. She said he was washing his hands, complaining that the spots wouldn't come off. Then he'd woken up. He wondered if he was losing his mind.

Kowalski patted him on the shoulder. "Look, this is all part of Karp's plan to rattle you and make you do something stupid," he said. "Bebnev was the only connection to Barros and Jackie. Karp still doesn't have a case, so stay cool and ride this one out —"

"Bebnev wasn't the only connection," Barros interjected. "Jackie Corcione can fuck us all. He needs to have an accident and it needs to be soon."

Sweat dripping from his brow, Vitteli looked from Barros to Kowalski. "I don't know. . . ." he said.

"Damn it! We got no choice, Charlie," Barros snarled. "If Karp gets to the little faggot, we're all going down!"

Vitteli's shoulders sagged. "You're right. But how do we get the bank accounts and passwords? You can't be slicing him up and have it look like an accident."

Smiling, Barros reached inside his coat and pulled out what appeared to be a flashlight. "My little toy here will get it out of him," he said. "A few million volts will light him up and he'll talk. After that, he goes over the balcony . . . just another queer who couldn't handle the shame."

"When?"

"Tonight, now," Barros answered. "Before Karp gets to him. Give him a call, make sure he's alone. Tell him I'm coming over to deliver some legal papers that he needs to sign and I don't want to see none of his fag friends."

Vitteli swallowed hard and nodded. "Okay, do it."

"Stick him good and we'll be okay," Kowalski added.

Barros grinned like a skeleton. "Don't worry about that; I've been looking forward to this for a long time."

27

Jackie Corcione stood alone at the rail of the balcony of his Hell's Kitchen rooftop loft gazing west. The setting sun cast a warm orange glow on the Hudson River and South Jersey shore. Near and far, boat traffic of all sorts — barges, cargo vessels, sailboats, tourist cruises — moved in and out of his vision like actors going on- and offstage in a never-ending play.

A warm breeze stirred the air and the pigeons on the eaves cooed and strutted in their mating rituals, a sure sign that spring had sprung in Manhattan. In the parks, the crabapple and cherry trees were blossoming and others were newly sheathed in lime-green leaves; daffodils, tulips, and forsythia competed for Best in Show. On the sidewalks below, the florists and rug merchants were bringing their merchandise in for the night, and the first of the Friday dinner crowd were carrying on without a care in the world as they waltzed along to their destinations.

Corcione sighed. It seemed incongruous to him that the world went obliviously about its business while he suffered so much. Physically and emotionally exhausted, he couldn't remember the last time he'd had a good night's sleep, but it most certainly was sometime before the murder of Vince Carlotta, when he was still living the high life, the quintessential New Yorker and feeling the first harbingers of love. It all seemed surreal now, as if it had been an art movie he watched in another lifetime at some trendy Manhattan scene, like the cinema in the Tribeca Grand Hotel.

A tear trickled down a cheek just as he heard the sliding glass door open behind him. He didn't turn around; he didn't want Greg to see him crying. However, his resolve evaporated when his boyfriend walked up and put his arms around his waist.

"God, it's beautiful up here," Corcione whispered just before the tears began to flow in earnest, and he shook as he struggled to maintain control.

"Hey, hey, what's the matter, handsome?" Greg asked.

Corcione shook his head as he looked down at one of Greg's muscular forearms and the green-black tattoo of a trident. After college and the end of his football aspirations, Greg had joined the Navy to become a SEAL commando. He'd passed the rigorous testing, then served in the first Gulf War and then reupped for Afghanistan after 9/11. He'd been wounded once and awarded the Silver Star for gallantry in combat.

Yet he was the kindest, gentlest person Corcione had ever known, as well as the steadiest. "It's nothing, just stress," Jackie replied with a sniff.

Greg released his hold around Jackie's waist and placed his hands on his shoulders and gently turned him around. Jackie tried to keep his head down, but Greg put a finger under his chin and lifted, forcing him to look into his eyes.

"Jackie, you've been stressed since December," Greg said. "I know you were upset by the death of Mr. Carlotta, but you're not getting past it. You don't sleep; you're losing weight; you're distracted, an emotional wreck most of the time, and — sorry, I love you but — lazy as hell. Maybe you should see someone, a professional; better living through pharmaceuticals and all that. There's nothing wrong with asking for help when you're going through a rough patch."

Corcione tried to smile but only half managed. *Rough patch,* he thought. *I have murdered sleep,* as the Bard once wrote. "I'm okay," he replied. "It's really not something a shrink can do anything about."

"Then what is it? Let me help you," Greg insisted. "If you can't trust someone who loves you, then who can you trust?"

Corcione's lip began to quiver, and then his hands flew to his face as he let go and broke down. "I want to die," he sobbed.

"And I want you to live. But tell me why you'd feel that way."

"You're going to hate me."

"Try me," Greg replied, his steel-gray eyes unwavering.

A long moment passed before Corcione nodded. "Let's go sit down," he said, indicating the living room. "This is going to take a while." Thirty minutes later he reached the end of his story and sat quietly with his head down.

Greg, his own eyes wet with tears, let out a deep breath. "Jesus, Jackie, I didn't expect that," he said. "An affair maybe, or you were having second thoughts about us. But murder?" He shook his head. "I guess I knew that the docks have a reputation as a tough place, but I thought the murder-for-hire and mob shit was crap they made up for the

401

movies."

"Sorry to say, but wherever you have ports of entry into this country, you have somebody who wants to control what goes in and what goes out," Corcione explained. "It's worth an awful lot of money, and some people will do anything to get a piece of it." He looked down at his feet and sighed. "Even people you wouldn't expect. Every once in a while some reform-minded guy like Vince comes along and tries to clean it up. Somewhere he got the crazy idea that a union's purpose isn't to make its bosses rich or powerful, but to look out for the little guy, the members. But that runs contrary to the bosses and the criminals."

"But why, Jackie?" Greg asked. "I know you — probably as well as anybody ever has — and you're not a killer or without a conscience."

Corcione shrugged. "First it was greed, then it was fear. Fear of getting caught. Fear of going to prison. Then I was so far in it, I didn't know how to turn back. Or, more accurately, I was too much of a coward to do anything about it."

Both men sat in the silence of their own thoughts for a minute until, without looking up, Corcione asked, "So do you want me to take a hike while you pack?"

"I didn't say I was leaving," Greg replied as he stood up and stretched. "But I'm going for a run; I need some time alone to think."

Corcione nodded and wiped at his eyes. "What do you think I should do?"

Greg didn't answer at first as he zipped up the front of his gray U.S. Navy sweatshirt. Then he shook his head. "That's something you need to answer for yourself, Jackie, and not just for your freedom, but for your sanity and your soul. All I know is that this has been pulling you apart at the seams and that can't go on forever."

"Will you be back?"

"This evening, yes. I'm not going to leave you alone with this hanging over your head," Greg replied. "But after tonight, I don't know, Jackie. You helped kill a good man, or at least you did nothing to stop it. And if that wasn't bad enough, by doing that you betrayed us and any chance we had at a future together."

Corcione reached out and grabbed Greg's hand. "Please . . . we could go away," he pleaded desperately. "Costa Rica . . . or, or Venezuela; they don't have an extradition agreement with the U.S. I have plenty of money. We could live . . ." His voice trailed off as his boyfriend withdrew his hand.

"Even if I was willing to leave my work and my country," Greg said, "do you really think I could live off blood money? Don't you know me better than that? But more than that, this isn't something you can run away from, sweetheart — it will follow you wherever you go. You have to decide if you can live with that."

Corcione hung his head and nodded. Greg furrowed his brow. "You won't do anything stupid while I'm gone?"

Realizing the reason for Greg's concern, Corcione smiled. "Don't worry, I don't think I have the courage for that either," he said. "I'm more the run-away-and-hope-they-don't-find-me kind of guy."

Greg reached down and stroked Corcione's hair. "You're a good man, Jackie; you did a terrible thing, but it's never too late to do the right thing. I'll be back in a half hour." With that, he turned and left the apartment.

A few minutes later, Corcione was still sitting on the couch contemplating his next step when his cell phone went off. He looked at the caller ID and ignored it. But when the cell went off again with the same caller ID, he angrily picked it up.

"What do you want, Charlie?" he demanded and listened before replying, "Not now. I just don't feel like seeing Joey Barros, or dealing with any union business at the moment." He scowled and then swore. "Goddamn it, all right, the asshole can drop off the fucking papers, and I'll look them over and get back to you tomorrow. . . . What? Why? . . . Joey doesn't want to meet any of my friends? Fuck him, but you can let him know I'm alone so there's only one fag he has to be near. . . . Yeah, good; the sooner he gets here, the sooner he can leave."

Hanging up, Corcione went into the bathroom to wash his face. He didn't want Barros to know he'd been crying; he wasn't going to give the bastard any more ammunition for his homophobic bullshit.

He'd just returned to the living room when the door intercom buzzed. "Yeah?" he answered, his gut clenching at the thought of the ghoulish Joey Barros standing in the doorway of his building fifteen floors below.

"You alone?" Barros asked.

"Yeah, Barros," Corcione replied. "Don't worry, you're not going to get gang-raped by a pack of wild homos."

There was a pause and Corcione imagined that he could feel the man's cold hatred for him radiating up to the loft. "Let me in," Barros replied tersely.

Corcione shivered as he pressed the button and waited impatiently at the door for his visitor. At the soft knock, he turned the deadbolt and opened the door to see his antagonist dressed in a black raincoat and fedora. *Looks like a funeral director,* he thought. He expected the look of disgust in the man's dark eyes, but he didn't expect the expression to morph into a grin as Barros extended his right hand, in which he held what looked like a flashlight.

"Night-night, fairy," Barros sneered as he pressed the stun gun just below Corcione's rib cage and pushed the button.

The electroshock weapon immediately sent a bolt of intense pain shooting through Corcione's body as well as caused his muscles to contract and spasm, knocking him backward off his feet. He was twitching and completely disoriented as Barros calmly shut the door and threw the deadbolt.

Barros then walked around and, grabbing him by the back of his sweatshirt, dragged him into the living room, where he left him before disappearing from sight. Corcione could hear him moving through the apartment, calling out, "Hello? Is there anybody here?" When there were no answers, he returned.

Barros walked over to the dining room

table and picked up a chair that he placed in the middle of the living room. He grabbed the still-dazed Corcione by the hair and yanked him up and into the chair. Binding his victim's wrists to the arms of the chair with a roll of duct tape, he grabbed Corcione's sweatpants and yanked them down, exposing his genitals, before taping his ankles to the chair's front legs. Barros stood up, panting lightly.

As he came increasingly to his senses, Corcione struggled against his bonds, which seemed to please Barros, who smiled and reached into his raincoat pocket. He pulled out a notepad and pen, which he showed to Corcione and placed on the coffee table. "We're going to have a little conversation and I'm going to take notes," he explained. His hand disappeared back inside the pocket and emerged with the stun gun.

Holding the weapon in front of the terrified man's face, Barros pressed the button again; the electrodes arced wickedly with a crackling flash of blue light and the smell of burned ozone. He then lowered the device until it was hovering just above Corcione's groin.

"I want the location and number of all your bank accounts and the passwords," Barros demanded. "I have an associate standing by who will let me know if the information you give me is accurate." He leaned over to speak quietly into Corcione's ear. "And if you even think of lying to me, I'm going to fry your balls into jelly, you little cocksucker, and then I'm going to do the same thing to your boyfriend."

At the mention of Greg, his boyfriend's face flashed in Corcione's mind. Suddenly, love overwhelmed his fear and in that moment he found his courage. "You know what I think, Joey?"

Arching an eyebrow at the sudden resolve in Corcione's voice, Barros smirked and shook his head. "No, Jackie. What *do* you think?"

"I think you're queer and still in the closet — that's why you wanted a look at my junk."

Corcione only had a moment to enjoy the look of shock and rage that came over Barros's face before the most intense pain he'd never even tried to imagine shot from one point of his body and into every molecule of his being. It hurt so much that he couldn't even scream before he blacked out.

The next thing he knew, somebody was slapping him. "Wake up, funny boy," Barros snarled as he struck him again with the flat of his hand. "I want the information now, or I'm going to light you up like a fucking

Christmas tree. I had my electric friend here set on low; now it's on high and you are not going to like what it does one little bit."

A part of Corcione's mind screamed at him to tell Barros anything he wanted to know. *Sooner or later you're going to cave, so why not save yourself the pain. He's going to kill you anyway. Do you want to suffer first?*

However, as the coward in Jackie Corcione pleaded for him to get it over with, something else in him was fighting back. *What does it matter? You've lost Greg. And why? Because you wanted to live like a prince, sure, but that was theft; the point of no return was when Charlie Vitteli decided that Vince Carlotta had to die. Up yours, Charlie, your dog Barros can kill me but I'm not giving you two a goddamned thing!*

Corcione was about to say just that and geared up to resist the next bout of pain when he noticed movement behind Barros, who had his back to the front door. Greg was creeping up and getting ready to pounce.

"Fuck you, Barros!" Corcione shouted and spit at his attacker to distract him.

Enraged, Barros almost missed the warning sign when his victim's eyes suddenly focused on something over his shoulder. But quick as thought, he spun around, jabbing with the stun gun.

A well-built younger man in a gray sweat suit leaped back just in time to avoid being electrocuted. But Barros attacked without hesitation, thrusting the weapon like a fencer. He was fast, vicious, experienced, and normally would have overwhelmed his opponent. But the former Navy SEAL in front of him, blocking and twisting away from the weapon, was better trained, in better shape, fearless, and mad as hell.

Greg was also patient, and though at first surprised by the assassin's speed and skill, he focused on frustrating his opponent's attack, letting him wear himself down in the flurry of initial attacks, and then methodically countering while watching for his opportunities. He saw an opening and chop-blocked a thrust with his right hand, slightly turning his opponent, exposing his back; he stepped in and delivered a short, powerful, roundhouse punch to the man's kidney area.

Barros grunted in pain and swung wildly, but the younger man had already retreated outside of his reach. The blow to his lower back made it difficult to catch his breath. Many years had passed, and a lot of blood had been shed since he'd last doubted the outcome of a fight, but he now recognized the chill of possible defeat in his bones. It made him more desperate as he slashed with a backhand motion.

Rather than retreat, this time Greg stepped inside the arc of Barros's swing and delivered such a hard two-handed block into the other man's arm that it stopped the motion as surely as if Barros had struck a wall. Then, before Barros could recover from the shock, Greg's right hand slid down to his opponent's right wrist, extending it out, locking the elbow. He then stepped forward with his left leg, twisting into the blow he delivered with his left forearm into the back of his opponent's locked elbow.

There was an audible snap as the joint dislocated, followed by an even louder scream. The stun gun went clattering across the floor as Greg followed up with a side kick to the back of Barros's knee, driving him to the ground, where momentum carried his face into the coffee table. The killer groaned as he pushed himself up from the table and knelt on his knees, swaying slightly.

Greg stood directly behind him, every bit of his training telling him to finish the job now. But he'd finished too many jobs in the not-so-distant past, and he'd sworn when they put him on a medical evacuation plane out of Kabul that he was done killing. So he hesitated. "Get on the ground, asshole," he demanded. "Or I'll break your fucking neck."

Barros didn't turn around. "Please, no more," he begged. "I got a family . . . daughters, they have queer friends. You can turn me in to the cops."

"Don't trust him!" Corcione yelled.

Corcione's shout distracted Greg just long enough for Barros to spin on one knee, slashing at his legs with his razor. This time when Greg tried to leap out of the way, he wasn't quite fast enough. He felt a sharp, burning pain halfway up his thigh and when he glanced down, the leg of his sweatpants was cut clean and already red with blood. He knew he needed to end the fight quickly or risk passing out from blood loss.

However, Barros had other plans. Bleeding profusely from his mangled nose, he jumped to his feet and came at Greg scything his blade back and forth so rapidly that the polished steel looked like a silver blur. Suddenly the assassin's hand shot forward and Greg turned his face just fast enough to avoid losing an eye, though the razor laid open a cheek.

Sensing a change in the momentum, Barros pressed his attack as he forced Greg to retreat past where Corcione sat strapped in his chair. Greg planted his wounded leg and appeared to stumble slightly, which caused Barros to shout triumphantly as he leaped forward to deliver a fatal cut. However, his progress was suddenly diverted when Corcione threw himself and the chair he sat in sideways into him.

The move gave Greg just enough time to regain his footing. He stepped inside of Barros's next forehand slash and pinned his opponent's arm and weapon against the side of his body. Using his free hand, he chopped into the dislocated elbow, causing Barros to scream in pain and rage.

The scream was cut short when Greg drove the web of his left hand into the man's exposed throat. He then grabbed Barros's larynx, squeezing like an iron vise as he shoved up and back, propelling the two of them through the screen door to the balcony. He drove Barros into the railing so hard that it knocked the wind out of the killer.

Barros gasped and the straight razor fell at his feet. But Greg continued to bend him backward over the rail toward the street fifteen floors below.

"Mercy!" Barros cried in a strangled voice.

Greg stopped pushing for a moment, but it was only to look in the defeated man's eyes and say, "Burn me once, shame on you. Burn me twice . . ." He smiled. "I don't get burned twice." He gave a little shove and Barros was gone with a shriek that ended abruptly with a crash that sounded like a bomb had gone off fifteen stories below. A woman screamed as a car alarm started bleating, and then several more people screamed and shouted.

Greg looked over the railing. Approximately 180 feet from the balcony railing, what had once been Joey Barros was sticking half in and half out of a Mercedes windshield. He'd gone in headfirst so only the lower half of his body was visible, but that was enough to show the man was beyond dead.

Suddenly faint, Greg stumbled back from the railing. He hobbled over to an area on the roof where he liked to work out. He picked up a piece of exercise tubing that he swiftly tied around his leg above the wound as a tourniquet. But he knew he was still losing blood and needed help fast.

Returning to the doorway, Greg picked up the razor and stumbled over to where Corcione still lay on his side, struggling to get free. "Hold on a second, Jackie," he gasped and then sliced through the tape binding his boyfriend's wrists and ankles.

He then slumped back against the couch, his legs splayed in front of him as he pulled on the tubing to slow the flow of blood.

Corcione crawled over to him on his hands and knees. "God, you're hurt!"

Greg smiled weakly. "I've seen worse."

"Barros?"

"He left by the back door."

"Back door? . . . Oh . . . You came back . . . I thought maybe you'd just keep running."

"I told you back when this all started that I wasn't going anywhere unless you told me to leave," Greg replied. "I don't give up on people I love."

"I don't deserve you."

"I don't know what you deserve, Jackie, but it's for a higher power than me to decide," Greg said. He winced. "Now, if you wouldn't mind calling 911 and asking for a medic, I'd appreciate it, or I may be answering for my sins a long time before you do."

28

The dog days of August slapped Karp in the face like a warm, wet sponge as he emerged from the Criminal Courts Building during the noon recess in *The People of the State of New York vs. Charles E. Vitteli.* The heat and humidity were overwhelming. Everyone standing or walking on the sidewalk along Centre Street — tourists, cops, lawyers, businessmen, and street people alike — looked damp, drained, and in a foul, sweaty mood.

As he stood at the door trying to decide whether to proceed, the three tattered women who'd been watching parts of the trial approached. They stopped when they saw him and appeared about ready to flee. He opened the door for them. "Afternoon, ladies," he said. "Care to get out of the heat?"

The women looked at each other and then nodded. "Thank you," they said and hurried past him just as he heard his name, followed by an epithet, shouted from the newsstand next to the curb.

Dirty Warren, who appeared to have been watching for him, waved and called out again as he scurried over toward Karp holding out a newspaper. "There you . . . oh boy oh boy whoop . . . are. You forgot to pick up your copy of the *Times* this morning."

"That's right, and thank you, the trial has me running," Karp said as he walked forward to meet his friend. Then he paused and looked suspiciously at the news vendor. "What gives with the restraint? Why aren't you challenging me with *On the Waterfront* trivia questions now that we're into the trial?"

Dirty Warren grinned as he peered up at Karp, his light blue eyes magnified like a cartoon character's by the Coke-bottle lenses of his glasses. "Thought you'd never ask, but since you insist . . ." he said as he assumed a role. "Who am I? 'You want to know what's' . . . fucking-a whoop . . . 'wrong with our watefront? It's the love of a lousy buck. It's' . . . oh boy ohhhhh boy . . . 'making love of a buck — the cushy job — more important than the love of man!' Whoop oh boy."

"Actually, that's not too bad a rendition of Karl Malden as Father Barry," Karp admitted. "At least compared to your usual lame attempts and, I have to say, rather on point for this trial."

Dirty Warren beamed at the backhanded compliment as he hopped from one foot to the next. "I been practicing," he boasted, continuing to hop. "It's about time you recognized real . . . ah fuck shit . . . talent." He stopped hopping and looked around to make sure none of the passersby were listening before sidling closer and speaking in a low voice. "Actually, I was about to . . . whoooop . . . come find you. I think I got something for you . . . balls vagina whoop whoop . . . regarding the trial."

Karp's mind switched from movie trivia to paying attention to whatever his little friend was trying to tell him between profanities. He never knew what the vendor, with all of his contacts among the city's street people, whose grapevine of information often astounded him, might have heard.

As sure as New York garbage workers always choose to strike during the hottest week of the summer, he knew that Vitteli was guilty of murder and believed that he had the evidence and witnesses to prove it beyond any doubt. But Vitteli's lawyer, Syd

Kowalski, was several cuts above Clooney when it came to trying a criminal case and, lacking any compunction regarding using whatever means he could to get his client off, a dangerous adversary.

Clooney was a joke who didn't belong in a courtroom. Looking for major ink and airtime to further his ambitions, he'd taken on a high-profile case in which he believed he could out-finesse the prosecution.

When Jackie Corcione confessed to his role in the murder of Vince Carlotta, he also told Karp that Vitteli had paid Clooney's legal bills for Bebnev, as well as the two lawyers assigned to DiMarzo. "Vitteli wanted to make sure he was in control of everything that happened from the defense standpoint and know everything the defendants were telling their lawyers," Corcione said. That Clooney had been so incompetent and turned into such a laughingstock by Karp was not part of the white-shoe lawyer's plan. He'd slunk away after the trial and, at least according to press accounts Karp had read, wasn't returning telephone calls.

Karp would deal with Clooney and the other two lawyers later. However, Kowalski was no paper-pushing white-shoe attorney who didn't know habeas corpus from a hole in the ground. Much like Guma, he was a courtroom brawler who reminded Karp of Edward G. Robinson in the film *Illegal*. He had a lot of experience and success defending union members, as well as organized-crime figures; and while he and Karp had never butted heads in court, he'd won acquittals against some of the five boroughs' best prosecutors, as well as his share of dog-fights in federal court.

Built like a bulldog, with a toughness to match, Kowalski was one of those savvy, articulate lawyers who, through the sheer force of his will, a compelling courtroom persona, and a con man's understanding of human nature, was capable of manipulating the average, trusting juror. As such, he occasionally blew up so-called motion picture, can't-lose cases — the ones that have confessions, eyewitnesses, and corroboration to choke a rhino — by persuading at least one juror that the prosecution's motives and/or conclusions were suspect, potentially leading to at least a hung jury. But no case is a slam-dunk, airtight sure thing; it's generally tempestuous drama dealing with real people, real fears, real misgivings, and at times compounded by faulty recollections, angst, and nervousness. And *The People vs. Vitteli* was no exception, especially with an amoral "win at all cost" defense attorney in the other corner.

In Part 30 Supreme Court New York County, the courtroom where the presiding judge arraigns defendants and entertains bail hearings on returned indictments handed up by the grand jury, Karp demanded Vitteli be held without bail. Laying out the case, he contended that Vitteli with "premeditation and malice ordered the execution of the deceased, Vince Carlotta, his rival in the union. The People are ready to try this case immediately."

As a matter of principle, Karp believed in moving forward with trials as quickly as possible, and didn't believe in pretrial detention per se. Generally, he had always been low-bail oriented; however, certain murder cases warranted that the defendant be held without bail. And although he intended to see Vitteli convicted and sentenced to the maximum, he believed that any man's freedom was precious and shouldn't be denied without due process, especially if the defendant was incarcerated in a hellhole like the Tombs. In fact, it was usually the defense attorneys who stalled and asked for continuances so that they could ostensibly conduct their own investigations and prepare for trial while, not coincidentally, increasing their billable hours.

Going in, Kowalski knew that he'd met his match in Karp. Infuriated after the bail hearing, he'd immediately gone on the attack, holding a press conference outside of the Criminal Courts Building after Vitteli's bail hearing conducted at the time of his arraignment on the indictment — *a fiction based on the word of thieves and murderers, as well as politically motivated.* Then he dropped his bombshell.

In front of the media, who were delighted by the dramatics, Kowalski began:

"My client recently uncovered evidence that the government's star witness, Jackie Corcione, the estranged son of our founder and the union's chief financial officer, has over the course of several years siphoned millions of dollars out of the North American Brotherhood of Stevedores pension accounts.

"It is our belief that Vince Carlotta may have also discovered the theft by Mr. Corcione, who then arranged Vince's murder to cover his tracks. When confronted by Mr. Vitteli approximately two weeks ago, Mr. Corcione decided that the jig was up and that he'd better make a preemptive move to downplay his role while serving up a prize he knew the district attorney coveted. So he ran to the DAO with his wild, self-serving tale. It is obvious to us that Corcione wants a deal and thinks he can get one from the DA by pointing a finger at Charles Vitteli and saying the murder of Vince Carlotta was all my client's doing."

When one member of the press pointed out that, according to the indictment, Corcione had implicated himself in the murder to the grand jury, Kowalski shrugged. "So what? He knew it was coming. Mr. Vitteli was preparing to go to the authorities himself regarding Corcione, but considering his past treatment by District Attorney Karp, he first contacted the U.S. Department of Labor with his concerns."

When asked to explain the connection, Kowalski described the well-publicized death of Joey Barros as resulting from "a falling-out among confederates in that we believe Barros was also involved with Mr. Corcione in the murder of Vince Carlotta, and some of the testimony of the State's own witnesses will bear that out." He called it a "convenient fiction" that the police determined that Barros had been the aggressor and that his death at the hands of Greg Lusk, a former Navy SEAL and "Corcione's homosexual lover," had been self-defense. He hinted that homosexuality was connected to the "personal reason" that

Corcione wanted Carlotta and Vitteli to be "eliminated."

Kowalski had gone on to paint Karp as an anti-union conservative "who sees this tragedy as an opportunity to drive a wedge between the members of the North American Brotherhood of Stevedores, as well as cast doubt among our friends in the labor movement." Then, having provided ample sound bites for the evening news and in the morning papers, the attorney had declined to comment further, saying that he didn't want to "try this case in the media.

"Suffice it to say that my client looks forward to the opportunity to clear his name and restore his reputation that the District Attorney of New York County has unfairly and unconscionably besmirched since attacking him on the witness stand during the trial of the men who actually participated with Mr. Corcione and Mr. Barros in the murder of Vince Carlotta."

Of course, Karp did not respond when the media came calling for return fire other than the usual bland statement issued by his office that there would be no comment outside of the courtroom. He recognized Kowalski's attempt to influence the jury pool through the media, but there wasn't much he could do about it other than prepare for all eventualities.

Nor did he let Vitteli bait him into answering when the union boss granted an interview at the Tombs to a local television muckraker who'd promised him carte blanche to say whatever he wanted. "I'm ready; let's go, Mr. District Attorney," Vitteli had snarled for the camera. "You put me in this stinkin' hole without bail to make yourself look good while destroying the hard work of honest, hardworking union men like Leo Corcione, Vince Carlotta, myself, and thousands of members of the North American Brotherhood of Stevedores. The sooner we go to trial, the sooner I get out of here and return to serving the men and women who honored me with their votes in the past election."

Sitting on the couch with Marlene at home in the loft when he saw the newscast, Karp looked at his wife and rolled his eyes. "I guess I've been personally called out," he said.

"It would seem that the gauntlet has been thrown down," she responded. "Hasn't he heard the expression 'Let sleeping dogs lie'?"

"Wouldn't matter," Karp growled. "This dog is already wide awake. As the man said, let's get it on; the sooner, the better."

Karp could tell by Kowalski's demeanor at the hearing to set the trial date that while the defense attorney was playing the good soldier and going along with his client's demands to speed things up, he wasn't too happy about it. Delay, particularly in Vitteli's case, usually worked in favor of the defense: witnesses "disappeared" or "grew forgetful." But Vitteli's ego and carefully disguised lack of self-confidence that Gorman had told Karp about forced Kowalski to go along with demanding a speedy trial.

While taking note of Vitteli's weaknesses, Karp didn't count on Kowalski allowing his client to make too many other strategic mistakes in the lead-up to the trial. Nor did Karp believe that the defense attorney would make missteps at trial the same way Clooney had with his miserable failure at trying to claim a government frame job without any evidence. For all his bluster when in front of the cameras, Kowalski was too subtle for such amateurism but could still be expected to insinuate what he wouldn't dare say and leave himself open to being shot down by Karp and the judge.

Because of the high-profile nature of the case, the talking-head TV experts and intense media coverage, jury selection took two and a half weeks. But at last they had a jury of twelve men and women, plus four alternates, and that morning they'd been sworn in by New York State Supreme Court Justice Robert See, who'd also taken this trial so that a new judge wouldn't have to be brought up to speed or wade through repetitive motions from the first trial.

As always, Karp in his opening statement carefully laid out the road map of the People's case. Then it was Kowalski's turn to go to work.

With an accent straight out of his native Newark, the pugnacious defense attorney fired off a passionate opening statement, sticking with the theme he'd thrown out four months earlier to the press that Corcione was the guilty party trying to place the blame on Vitteli after being confronted by his boss, "who testimony will show contacted the U.S. Department of Labor with his concerns prior to Corcione's confession." The evidence would also demonstrate, he said, that Corcione set up the slush fund accounts and that only he and Joey Barros had ever signed paperwork transferring funds among those accounts.

Kowalski cautioned the jury that after the prosecution had presented its case, "and you've seen what passes for evidence and heard the testimony of the government's witnesses, as they are led down the primrose path by the prosecution, you will be ready to convict my client." However, he urged, if they would keep an open mind until hearing the defense case, "which will include plausible alternate explanations for the State's so-called evidence, I'm sure you will agree that there is more than reasonable doubt and will vote to acquit Mr. Vitteli and end this witch hunt."

The opening statements had taken them right up to the lunch hour. When court resumed, Karp planned to call the civil engineer Jack Farrell and the NYPD crime scene photographer who had testified at the trial of Bebnev and DiMarzo. This time, however, they would only lay out the crime scene in Hell's Kitchen, which would probably take up to the afternoon break. Then he'd call Jackie Corcione.

A knish and a celery soda had sounded like just the ticket before battle, until he stepped outside the 100 Centre Street courthouse into an oven and was met by Dirty Warren. Playing along with the news vendor's furtive glances, Karp looked around and then asked quietly, "So, my friend, what do you have?"

Squinting through his smudged glasses, Dirty Warren wiped a droplet of sweat off the end of his long, pointed nose. "I talked to David Grale last night. He said to tell you . . . oh boy fuck me . . . that those rumors about there being another witness were correct. Apparently . . . whoop whoop . . . three women were in the alley when it all went down."

Karp's ears pricked up. Randy McMahon had testified about seeing three bag women near the alley, and Jackie Corcione said that Vitteli had seen three women, though he and Barros didn't.

"Anyway, these women have been getting out of the cold in one of David's enclaves beneath the . . . piss shit balls whoop . . . city. The one you want to talk to is named Anne and . . . hey . . . whoop whoop . . . where are you going? I've got another trivia question."

Karp didn't wait to hear Warren's complaint. He was already back in the building, heading for the eleventh-floor courtroom. He turned the corner into the hallway and was disappointed not to see anyone standing outside of the locked courtroom. Or at least he thought it was locked.

Then he heard the sound of several voices coming from behind the doors. Listening for a moment, he then pulled open the doors and was surprised to see the three shabby women he'd spoken to briefly at the previous trial; one of them stood near the defense table and the other two were at the railing between her and the gallery. He had not noticed them at the morning session, but he'd been preoccupied with his opening statement.

"Excuse me?" he said.

The three women jumped and turned at the sound of his voice. The black one made some sort of sign in his direction. "Oh, we were just leaving," the one standing near the defense table said.

"Not so fast," Karp said, walking slowly toward them. "How did you get in here? I know the door was locked."

The women looked at one another; then the pale-skinned woman who'd been standing with the black one spoke up. "It was me, sir."

"You?" Karp asked.

"She can pick any lock, quick as magic," the woman next to the defense table said.

"Are you going to arrest me?" the lock picker asked in a frightened voice.

"Depends," Karp replied. "What are you doing here? Why did you pick the lock?"

The two women standing in the gallery glanced at their third compatriot next to the defense table, who looked down at the floor.

That's when Karp noticed a bag containing some object lying on the table. "That wasn't there," he said. "I think you better explain."

"I don't want to get involved," the woman cried. "I'm scared!"

Realizing the woman truly was frightened, Karp softened his tone. "I think you already are involved. And I think maybe you know something that I need to hear. It has to do with what's right and just."

"He's right, Anne," said the other white woman.

"It's time," added the black woman.

The one they called Anne wiped a grungy sleeve across her face, then nodded. She reached over to the defense table and picked up the plastic bag. He could now see that it contained a piece of cloth with a dark stain on part of it.

"My name is Anne Devulder and I want to give you this and tell you how I got it," she said, her voice trembling. "It contains the blood of a martyr."

Karp nodded. "Let's go to the prosecution witness room, where we can talk privately," he said, indicating they should go out the side door of the courtroom. As they walked, he dialed Guma on his cell phone. "Hey, I need you and Clay and a stenographer up to the witness waiting room as soon

431

as you can get there."

As they entered the waiting room, Karp asked the women to sit down. "It was very brave of you to come here," he said. "But why were you going to place the bag on the defense table and leave?"

"I wanted that evil man to know that even if he got off for killing Vince Carlotta, the blood of that good man would follow him the rest of his life," she said. "I didn't think you needed me . . . or would believe me. I'm sorry it took so long, but I didn't think anybody would care about what I had to say . . . but Mr. Carlotta cared, and I've been watching you, and I know you care, too."

Just then, there was a knock, followed by the appearance of Guma, Fulton, and a stenographer. "Ladies, I'd like you to meet Special Assistant District Attorney Ray Guma, Detective Clay Fulton, and stenographer Bob Johnson," he said. "And gentlemen, I'm pleased to introduce Anne Devulder, and her two friends. . . ."

"I'm Rosie LaMontagne, and she's Cindy Lange," the black woman volunteered.

Karp continued. "Ray, Mrs. Devulder has come forward to give a statement regarding the murder of Vince Carlotta. After which, Clay, would you arrange for their protection and safekeeping as material witnesses? Oh, and maybe talk to Mrs. Milquetost about getting them some, um, clean clothes so that they can change if they'd like. I'll see you all in about an hour and a half when we take our afternoon break." He turned to the women. "Is that agreeable with you, ladies?"

"Will we be getting room service?" Rosie LaMontagne asked, eyeing him as if putting the final touches on a delicate deal.

"We'll make sure you're well fed," Karp replied with a laugh. "And if you're hungry now, let Detective Fulton know and he'll be happy to order in."

"Good! Pizza with the works, boy, and make it hot and snappy," Rosie ordered, looking happily at Guma. " 'Tis time . . . for lunch."

29

Anne Devulder's revelations and how to use them were still swirling about in Karp's mind as court resumed after the lunch hour. As an officer of the court, he had a duty to be able to vouch for the credibility of any witness he put on the stand. He believed Devulder's story — it corroborated with those of his other witnesses — but he needed to be able to put her at the scene, which was why he'd told Fulton to get the handkerchief she'd brought to the courtroom tested as soon as possible.

However, for the moment, he needed to put her out of his mind and focus on his strategy to use Vitteli's phony bravado that he'd noticed in the first trial to goad him into testifying. Such a plan had a far-from-certain outcome and was usually strategically inadvisable from the defense point of view. Hopefully, all that would follow in logical sequence. Now the demands of the trial order beckoned his complete attention as he prepared to question his key witness.

"The People call Jackie Corcione," Karp said, standing behind the prosecution table.

Looking frightened and like a man on the verge of changing his mind, the witness entered the courtroom from the side door and hesitated as he glanced at the defense table, where Vitteli and his attorney sat with their backs to him. Neither looked around, as if dismissing him and the danger he represented.

Karp watched as the witness scanned the gallery, searching for that one face in the crowd that he needed to see. Spotting Greg Lusk, who sat several rows behind the prosecution table smiling slightly and nodding encouragement, Corcione visibly straightened and strode forward until he reached the gate and entered the well of the court. Having then sworn to tell the truth, he stepped up into the witness box and took a seat, focusing on Karp.

Despite Corcione's initial reaction upon walking into the courtroom, Karp thought he recovered nicely and overall seemed like a different person than the guilt-ridden, tired man with haunted eyes and shaky hands he'd met four months earlier.

He'd been driving back from Sing Sing

with Fulton when he got the call from Guma that Jackie Corcione wanted to talk to him. The young man was at Bellevue Hospital, where he'd been transported with Lusk following the fight with Joey Barros. "A detective was asking him about the assault when apparently Corcione stopped the interview and said he would only talk to you," Guma told him. "The detective called the night desk, and I happened to be kicking back in your office when the ADA on call came looking for you."

"Guma, kicking back in my office? Oh no! Please tell me that Mrs. Milquetost had already gone home for the day?" Karp pleaded only half-jokingly as he tried to banish the image of "the Italian Stallion," as Guma liked to refer to himself, and his widowed receptionist "kicking back" in the inner sanctum.

Guma had laughed, though it was hard to interpret what that meant, as was how he replied. "I do believe she was still around here someplace. But what are you getting at?"

Karp wisely dropped the subject and instead asked, "What about Barros?"

"Apparently he did a swan dive into a windshield from Corcione's loft," Guma replied. "Official cause of death was VERY blunt force trauma. Seems that he went to Corcione's place to kill him but ran into the wrong friend. I have to say, it couldn't have happened to a nicer ghoul. The friend, a guy named Greg Lusk, nearly bled out after Barros slashed his thigh, but I talked to the ER doc, and it looks like he'll pull through."

Karp had already been planning his next move following his talk with Frank DiMarzo, and to have this dropped in his lap was serendipitous. Karp had asked Guma to arrange for Corcione to be brought to the Criminal Courts Building. He and Fulton had arrived an hour later and found Guma and the young man waiting in his office conference room.

Wondering how this conversation would go, Karp barely had time to take a seat when Corcione blurted out, "I was part of a conspiracy with Charlie Vitteli and Joey Barros to murder Vince Carlotta." He stopped the young man long enough to give him the Miranda warnings, which Corcione waived, and then mostly listened as the shaken but determined co-conspirator laid it all out. After that, Karp spent two more hours taking a Q&A statement to fill in the details and cross-reference to what he'd just learned from DiMarzo, as well as his encyclopedic knowledge of all the facts of the case. The next day, Corcione and Frank Di-Marzo had appeared with Karp before a grand jury, which had then not hesitated to indict Vitteli for murder.

Afterward, while Kowalski and Vitteli were doing damage control and trying to manipulate the jury pool through the media, Karp moved quickly to separate the wheat from the chaff with his case. He passed on the potential case against Vitteli for the murder of the Russian gangster Marat Lvov to the Brooklyn district attorney, who'd since decided to wait on the outcome of the New York trial before determining whether to go forward. Karp had also dismissed the idea of adding the attempted murder of Corcione by Barros to the charges against Vitteli. He would have had to prove the linkage between the now-deceased Barros acting in concert with his boss, while the defense was already spinning the assault as a falling-out between the killer and Corcione. Karp wasn't a believer in adding a bunch of lesser charges to a murder indictment; it showed a lack of confidence in the murder case. It cluttered up a straightforward trial, and gave a potentially deadlocked jury an easy way out if some juror held out against the murder charge. Simply, Karp was no believer in getting compromised verdicts.

Now, with a last glance at his yellow legal pad, Karp walked out from behind the prosecution table to stand alongside the jury rail. After asking Corcione to describe briefly to the jury his educational and professional background, Karp moved in for the kill. "Mr. Corcione, would you please explain to the jury why you're here today?"

Corcione glanced down for a moment and cleared his throat before looking back up at the jurors. "I was one of the men who plotted the murder of Vince Carlotta, and I'm here because I couldn't live with the guilt anymore."

"And who were the other men?"

"Joey Barros was one," Corcione said before looking over at the defense table where the two men seated there now glared at him. He pointed. "And that man, Charles Vitteli."

Karp turned to face Vitteli, who, seated only a few feet away, had no choice but to look up at him. "You've identified the defendant as the man who in concert with you and Joey Barros planned the cold-blooded execution of Vince Carlotta."

Corcione swallowed hard and nodded. "Yes."

"What was the defendant's role amongst the three of you?"

"He was calling the shots."

"And Joey Barros?"

"He was Vitteli's right-hand man. They kind of came up on the docks together. Joey was his attack dog."

"What do you mean by 'attack dog'?"

"Joey Barros is . . . was . . . a violent man."

"You said 'was' because Joey Barros is now deceased?"

"Yes."

"You just testified that Barros would essentially do whatever Vitteli told him to do, is that correct?"

"Yes."

"Please give us an example."

"Commit murder."

"Objection!" Kowalski growled as he rose from his seat. "Your Honor, what is the point of this questioning? I mean, who is on trial here? The ghost of Joey Barros or my client?"

"No, no, Your Honor, counsel doesn't quite understand. It's not that Barros was a killer," Karp retorted, "it's that he killed at the direction of the defendant."

"Overruled," Judge See remarked. "Be careful, Mr. Kowalski, which doors you open, because they can swing back at you. Please proceed, Mr. Karp."

Karp turned back to Corcione. "So it's

your testimony that the defendant Vitteli was the puppet master and that you and Barros were on his strings."

"I guess you'd call me the moneyman," Corcione replied. "I was the union's chief financial officer and counsel to Vitteli, the union boss, who directed me to siphon money from union accounts, especially the pension fund, into offshore banks and eventually our pockets."

Karp leaned against the jury box rail. "Can you tell us how the plot to murder Vince Carlotta began?"

"Yes," Corcione replied, but it took him a moment to gather his thoughts before letting out a deep breath and continuing. "I suppose it really began when I started stealing money from the union . . . a few thousand a month . . . then one day Charlie Vitteli walked into my office and said he knew what I was doing."

"What, if anything, did the defendant do or say?"

"He threatened me. He said he would tell my father, the union members, and the police. He said I would go to prison if my father and the membership didn't kill me first."

"Did he demand something in return for keeping your secret?"

"Yes. He wanted me to keep stealing, only now he wanted me to steal much more than I had been, and the three of us, the defendant," he said now staring at Vitteli, "Barros, and me would get wealthy. He called it his 'retirement account.' "

"How much did he want you to steal?"

"Instead of a few thousand a month, he wanted me to figure out how to steal millions every year."

"This money rightfully belonged to union members and their families?"

Looking out to where T. J. Martindale and his men sat scowling, Corcione nodded sadly. "Yes, I took their money."

"In addition to threatening to expose your illegal activities, did the defendant make any other sort of threat in order to get you to cooperate with his demands?"

"Yes, he said he would tell my father, Leo Corcione, that I was gay."

"Are you gay?"

"Yes."

"And do you have a companion who was living with you at the time you came to my office to confess this crime?"

"I did," Corcione said, his voice cracking slightly as he smiled wistfully at Lusk. "We're just friends now."

"Did you consider Vitteli's statement that

he would tell your father you were gay a serious threat?"

"Yes. I know my father loved me, but he was pretty old-school and I thought it would have been difficult for him to accept my life-style choice. I already believed that he was disappointed in me — for not being more like him — and I thought being told I was gay would be the last straw. That he might stop . . . that he might stop loving me."

"Do you still believe he would have re-acted negatively?"

Pausing for a moment to consider the question, Corcione then shook his head. "No. I've thought about this a lot, and while he may not have liked it, I know he loved me and would have done his best to sup-port me . . . if that had been all there was to it. But stealing the money from union people he'd fought for all of his life would have been a much bigger disappointment; I don't know that he would have forgiven me for that."

"So between the threat to expose your criminal activities and tell your father about your lifestyle, you agreed to participate in Vitteli's schemes?"

"Yes."

"Could you have said no?"

Corcione looked at Vitteli, whose brow

443

knitted above his look of hatred. "At the time, I didn't think I had a choice. But in hindsight, yes, I could have refused to go along with the plan and suffered the consequences. But I was a coward."

"Mr. Corcione, would you please explain how the scheme to siphon millions of dollars from union accounts was accomplished without being detected?" Karp asked.

"Yes," Corcione replied.

As simply as he could, so that the jurors could follow, Karp then had Corcione explain the formation of offshore accounts "not subject to U.S. reporting laws," and how phony corporations and "pass-through" bank accounts covered up the theft of "approximately forty-seven million dollars" from pension funds, as well as dividends paid for investments of those funds.

"There were fifteen main accounts in the Cayman Islands that the money went to first," Corcione said. "Some of the money would remain there to keep those banks happy and uncooperative if investigators from the U.S. came calling. The rest of the money would be transferred into other accounts held by several layers of dummy corporations, each passing the money further down the chain, and gradually into three accounts I set up for each of us — under fictitious names of course."

"Who created the fifteen main accounts?"

"I did."

"Who had access to them?"

"Two signatures were required from the corporation's executive committee members. ExCom was comprised of Vitteli, Barros, and me. To insulate himself, Vitteli never signed money transfers; he directed Barros and me to execute all the fraudulent documents."

Karp acted surprised, though he was far from it. "But if Charles Vitteli was 'calling the shots,' like you said, why would he not be the one who controlled the accounts?"

"Because if someone got suspicious and looked into it, Barros and I would be the only ones with signatures on anything and the only ones to take the fall," Corcione said. "He controlled the accounts by controlling us."

"Who had access to the three personal accounts into which the stolen money was deposited?"

"We each only had access to our own account."

"How did you figure out who got how much money?"

"Charlie got fifty percent. Barros got thirty. And I got twenty."

"Who decided who received these shares?"

"Vitteli."

"Do you know what happened to the money once it reached these three personal accounts?"

"Only mine," Corcione replied. "In my case, I reported the income from my investments to the IRS to keep Uncle Sam from getting suspicious. After taxes everything else was gravy."

"A lot of gravy?"

"Millions of dollars' worth of gravy."

"Was there just one way, or were there many different ways, you went about stealing these funds?" Karp asked.

"Quite a number," Corcione replied. "I found new ways, or we changed things around sometimes to avoid raising suspicions."

"Could you give the jury an example of one way?"

"Yes. Part of my job was to invest union funds, including the pension accounts, into stocks, or mutual funds, or hard assets like gold," Corcione explained. "And as with any investments, there were risks involved; even some legitimate investments turn sour, though you try to offset those by making more good choices than bad. However, sometimes I'd invest in dummy corporations that we'd set up under fictitious names; then when these companies 'went out of business,' or filed for bankruptcy, we'd just declare it the cost of doing business and write it off as a loss. Of course, the money wasn't actually gone; it just passed through to our other accounts."

"Was there another source of income for the three of you besides stealing union money?"

"Yes," Corcione answered. "Vitteli had worked out an agreement with a Russian organized crime syndicate called the Malcheks to use our docks for shipping in exchange for monthly cash payments based on their activities, which to my understanding was mostly going to involve drugs and gunrunning."

Corcione's answer brought an angry murmur from the union men seated in the gallery. Someone seated in the row alongside Martindale muttered just loud enough to be heard, "Vitteli, you son of a bitch," before Judge See gaveled him into silence. "Members of the gallery will refrain from responding to what the witness says or be removed from the courtroom, am I clear?" the judge growled. When he was satisfied that his point had been made, he looked back at Karp. "Continue, please."

Karp left the rail and moved in front of the prosecution table. "Mr. Corcione, after confessing to this crime, did you reveal the location, accounts, and passwords of the fifteen main accounts, as well as identify the dummy corporations and pass-through accounts to one of my assistant district attorneys, V. T. Newbury, the chief of the Frauds Bureau in the District Attorney's Office, so that he could attempt to trace and recover the stolen money?"

"Yes."

"And did you also include your personal accounts, as well as investment portfolio and assets?"

"Yes, I did."

"And of the approximately forty-seven million dollars you estimate was stolen, do you know how much of that was recovered?"

"I worked with ADA Newbury on some of this and the last time I talked to him, a few days ago, about seventeen million had been recovered."

"Where's the other thirty million?"

"Some of it's been spent. The rest would be wherever Vitteli and Barros sent it after it reached the personal accounts I set up for them."

"How long could this scheme have lasted?"

Corcione looked up at the ceiling and exhaled through his pursed lips. "As long as no one really looked at the books or tried to account for all the money that was coming in and going out, it could have lasted indefinitely," he said.

"In fact, how long did it last?"

"For several years while my father was alive, right up until I told you about it in May."

"Did your father suspect?"

Corcione hung his head. "I don't think so. He trusted me."

"Am I correct then to state that so long as you, Vitteli, and Barros controlled the union and its accounting, the three of you were safe from discovery?" Karp asked.

"Yes. However, if someone had any suspicions and a qualified independent auditor with real access to the books, it would have fallen apart like a house of cards."

"Did there come a time when the three of you became concerned that this house of cards might be in jeopardy?"

"Yes. Just before my father, Leo, died, Vitteli was worried that he was getting ready to name Vince Carlotta to succeed him as president," Corcione said. "That would have been a disaster for us, because we knew Vince would have insisted on an audit when he took over, if for no other reason than to follow the money in and out of the union."

"What happened?"

The question seemed to strike Corcione hard. He started to speak but choked up and wiped at his eyes. Finally, he said quietly, "My father died. So there was an election for union president between Mr. Carlotta and Vitteli."

"Who won?"

"Vitteli."

"Was it a fair election?"

"No. Vitteli and Barros, along with some of the old guard who were paid off or owed favors, rigged the results. Otherwise Vince would have won, and we would have been caught."

For the next twenty minutes, Karp led Corcione through the history of Carlotta's attempt to demand that the allegations of fraud be investigated, including by the U.S. Department of Labor. "Where Vitteli had a spy who made sure he intercepted the complaint and let us know what was going on," Corcione testified.

"Do you know the name of this spy?"

"No," Corcione replied. "Vitteli likes to keep those sorts of things to himself; he doesn't want anybody besides himself to know everything about his business."

Karp glanced at the clock. Corcione's testimony about siphoning funds and election fraud was important for the jury to understand. Motive, although not required to be proven, was certainly extraordinary to explain to the jurors to have them understand the underlying reasons for the defendant to commit the crime.

"Your Honor," he said to the judge. "Mr. Corcione will be on the stand for the remainder of the day, but I've reached a place where it might be good to recess for the afternoon break."

Judge See nodded. "Yes, as a matter of fact, I have some scheduling issues on several unrelated cases that will extend our regular afternoon break for about forty-five minutes, so we will reconvene in about an hour."

30

The sound of Judge See's gavel had barely echoed around the courtroom before Karp was striding down the aisle and out the doors, headed for his office. He hoped for two things: that Guma was still questioning Anne Devulder and that no one had made off with his copy of the *New York Times.*

He reached his office's reception area just as the three women in the company of Fulton and Guma were about to leave. Asking the women to wait with the detective, he pulled Guma back into his inner office. "How'd it go?" he asked quietly.

"Great," Guma replied. "Pretty damning when put in context with the rest of our case."

"Where are they going now?" Karp asked.

"We were just arranging an escort to the East Village Women's Shelter. Marlene set it up and got it okayed by the director, at least until we figure out something better."

Karp nodded and then poked his head out of the door. "Anne, could I speak to you alone for a minute, please?"

The woman looked apprehensively at her friends, but they smiled and nodded in his direction so she relaxed and entered the office. "I told Mr. Guma everything I know," she said, like a child who thought she was in trouble.

"I'm sure you did," Karp replied. "And again, I can't thank you enough for your cooperation. I don't know for sure, but I may need you to testify in this trial."

A wave of fear passed over Devulder's face, but then she said, "I understand. I should have come in sooner."

"What matters is that you're here now," Karp replied, "but I want to go over two points you made when you and I first talked. I just want to be clear about something before court resumes again."

A few minutes later, Devulder left his office accompanied by plainclothes detectives from Fulton's squad. She headed off with her friends to the women's shelter. Sitting at his desk, Karp looked down at the front page of the *Times* that Dirty Warren had given him. Under the headline UNION BOSS TRIAL was a stock photograph of Vitteli from the night of the Carlotta murder and some general observations of the current state of the stevedores' union and the outrage and betrayal felt by a large segment of its membership. He opened his desk drawer and took out a pair of scissors.

Soon he was back in court, where he asked Corcione to describe the meeting with Vitteli at which the union boss said his spy in the Labor Department had told him that Carlotta was not giving up his quest to overturn the election results.

"That's when Vitteli said that Vince had to go."

"Go? What do you mean by 'go'?"

"That Vince Carlotta had to die."

"Did you agree to the plan to murder Vince Carlotta?"

"I didn't want to at first . . ." Corcione started to explain, but then stopped and shook his head. "Yes, I went along with the plan."

"Why? Did Vince Carlotta ever do anything to you personally for you to want to cause his death?"

The question seemed to take Corcione aback. "No, not at all. Vince Carlotta was a good man. He always treated me well."

"Then why go along with a plan to kill him?"

"I was afraid."

"Afraid of what?"

"Prison. Or that I'd be next if I tried to stop them. Most of all . . ." Corcione tried to finish his statement but couldn't; his words just came out in gasps as tears poured down his face.

As the young man struggled, Karp stepped up to the witness stand and poured water from a pitcher that was on the stand into a paper cup. He handed the cup to Corcione, who gratefully accepted it and took a few sips before placing the cup beside the pitcher.

The witness sat still on the stand for a few more moments, looking down at his hands, which were now clasped in his lap. At long last he let out a deep sigh. "Most of all, I was afraid I'd lose the person I loved more than anyone, and who loved me, my life partner, Greg."

Corcione looked as if one more question in that vein would send him over the edge, and mercifully, Karp moved on. "Did you know a man named Marat Lvov?"

"I knew who he was," Corcione replied.

"Could you explain to the jury what you knew about him?"

"He was a small-time gangster who lived in the Russian section of Brighton Beach. He was the contact between Charlie Vitteli and the Malchek gang in Brooklyn."

"Objection," Kowalski said. "Russian gangs have nothing to do with this case and such a reference is highly prejudicial. I ask that it be stricken from the record and a mistrial declared."

"Your Honor, all of the People's evidence is *per force* prejudicial to the defendant," Karp said. "It's necessary for the jury and this court to hear and understand all the planning and scheming by the defendant and his intermediaries and conduits that resulted in the execution of the deceased, Vince Carlotta. Simply, Your Honor, all of these overt acts in furtherance of the conspiracy to murder are relevant and admissible."

"Objection overruled. Please proceed."

Karp continued: "Was there a time when you met with Marat Lvov in regard to the plan to murder Vince Carlotta?"

"Yes, Barros and I met with Lvov and a man named Alexei Bebnev at Marlon's Restaurant in Hell's Kitchen."

"Who asked you to attend this meeting?"

"Charles Vitteli sent us."

"Why didn't he attend?"

"Vitteli wanted to keep his hands clean by putting layers between himself and whatever might come back to haunt him. He doesn't trust anybody, except maybe Barros, and I don't think he even told Joey everything."

"And what was the purpose of this meeting?"

"To arrange the murder of Vince Carlotta. Bebnev was introduced to us by Lvov as a man who would be willing to kill Vince Carlotta."

"Was there an agreement to pay Alexei Bebnev to murder Vince Carlotta?"

"Yes. We said we would pay thirty thousand dollars."

"How would Bebnev get paid?"

"We paid Lvov and he paid Bebnev."

"Then why meet with Bebnev at all?"

"Vitteli wanted us to check him out," Corcione replied. "But more than that, he wanted to make sure Bebnev knew who to kill and how he wanted it done."

As Corcione answered the question, Karp again moved toward the defense table, bringing frowns to the faces of Kowalski and Vitteli, who flushed deep red as his six-foot-five nemesis approached. "Prior to Bebnev arriving, do you recall any conversations between you, Barros, and Lvov regarding Vitteli's instructions for when the murder was to take place?"

"When we were waiting for Bebnev to arrive, Lvov asked how soon it was supposed to happen. Barros told him that Vitteli wanted it done as soon as possible. Or words to that effect."

Karp turned to face Vitteli. "Words to the effect that Charlie Vitteli wanted Vince Carlotta to die as soon as possible, correct?"

"Yes."

"You indicated that you were waiting for Alexei Bebnev to arrive," Karp said, looking back at the witness stand. "Was there any chance that Bebnev would have overheard the conversation?"

"Quite possibly. I remember that at the time I was a little surprised when he came around the corner . . . just sort of appeared at our booth right as Barros said Charlie wanted it done as soon as possible. Like I said, Vitteli's paranoid and he wouldn't have wanted Bebnev to know his first name. Even Barros and I weren't too happy when Lvov introduced us by our first names to Bebnev."

"Did Bebnev know Vince Carlotta before this?"

"Not to my knowledge," Corcione replied.

"Then how was he supposed to know if he was targeting the right man?"

"He was given a photograph by Barros from the *Dock,* the in-house magazine of

458

the North American Brotherhood of Stevedores. Vince was in the photograph."

"Was anyone else in the photograph?"

"Yes, Vitteli, Barros, and me."

"Was there anything else to help Bebnev identify which of the four men in the photograph he was supposed to kill?"

"Yes, Vitteli drew a circle around Vince's face and wrote 'Vince Carlotta.' "

"How do you know that the defendant drew the circle and wrote that name on the photograph?"

"I was in his office with Barros when he did it. It was right before we were supposed to meet Lvov and Bebnev," Corcione replied. "After he wrote on the photo, he cut the page out of the magazine and gave it to Barros."

Walking over to the prosecution table, Karp picked up a magazine and a clear plastic envelope and then returned to the witness stand. He first handed the magazine to Corcione.

"Would you please identify People's Exhibit Twenty-Seven for identification, the magazine I just handed you, along with the date of the publication?" Karp asked.

"Yes. This is last year's winter edition of the *Dock*."

"How often is the magazine published?"

"Quarterly."

"And to whom is it distributed?"

"It's sent to the 250,000 union members and it's also available in union offices across North America," Corcione replied.

"And who has final say regarding the magazine's content?"

"The president of the union . . . Charlie Vitteli."

"Would you please open the magazine to page fifteen — there is a marker, I believe, taped to the page — and describe what you see?"

"It's a copy of the photograph I was describing."

"Is it the same photograph?"

"Oh no, it's the same photograph that appeared in all editions of this magazine, but it's not the one given to Bebnev that Vitteli wrote on."

"When and where was the photograph taken?"

"It was taken in August of last year at the annual union management convention in Atlantic City."

"In the photograph, there are four men standing on what appears to be the Atlantic City boardwalk. Who are they?"

"Left to right that's Barros, Vitteli, me, and standing a little apart from us with his arms crossed is Vince Carlotta."

Karp next handed the plastic envelope to Corcione. "Can you identify the contents of People's Exhibit Twenty-Eight for identification, this envelope?"

"Yes, now this is the same photograph that Vitteli wrote on and that Barros gave to Bebnev."

Karp reached up and retrieved the photograph. However, he did not yet offer it into evidence.

"Were you aware that Bebnev was going to hire other accomplices to help him murder Vince Carlotta?"

"Not at this meeting," Corcione said. "We only heard there were two more men with him after the first attempt failed."

"First attempt?"

"Yes," Corcione explained. "Originally the plan was that Bebnev would shoot Vince at his home in New Rochelle on December second. That way the police would think it was a home invasion or even a mob hit — Vince was pretty adamant about keeping organized crime off the docks and made enemies of some pretty dangerous people."

"Were you told why the first attempt failed?"

"Just that Vince's wife showed up with their kid, and Bebnev decided not to go through with it."

"What happened next?"

"Charlie was upset," Corcione recalled. "But then he came up with another plan to lure Vince to Hell's Kitchen. Bebnev and his guys were supposed to make it look like a botched robbery. Vitteli thought it would give us all a good alibi to be there."

Under Karp's guidance, Corcione described the meeting at the restaurant, from the initial confrontation in which Carlotta threw the note with the license plate number of the car at Vitteli, to his nearly coming to blows with Barros, to Vitteli's offer to step down from the union presidency. "It ended with everybody acting like old friends," Corcione said. "And I played along with the whole thing, even though I knew Bebnev was waiting outside to kill Vince."

"Besides the four you have mentioned, were there two other men in the bar who were part of the group?" As he asked his question, Karp turned to look at Vitteli as if to say, "Now do you understand why I came after you at the first trial?" hoping the defendant would rise to the bait.

"Yes, Carlotta's driver, Randy McMahon, and Vitteli's bodyguard, Sal Amaya," Corcione said.

"Did they leave the bar with you?"

"Yes, but Carlotta told McMahon to go get the car, and Vitteli sent Sal with him."

"In the ordinary course, how would you describe Sal Amaya's role in respect to his boss, Vitteli?"

"Whenever Vitteli left the office, Amaya stuck to him like glue."

"Yet you just testified that the defendant sent Sal Amaya away with Vince Carlotta's driver, Randy McMahon, and it was after midnight, when the defendant would be following down a dark alley? Can you explain the discrepancy?"

"Objection," Kowalski stated. "He's not a psychiatrist and he can't give testimony to the state of mind of Mr. Vitteli as to the reasons he may have had for directing his bodyguard to accompany Mr. Carlotta's driver."

"Your Honor, permit me to have the witness be more precise as to why he is able to describe the defendant's state of mind during their relationship," Karp said. "That way I can lay the predicate with respect to this issue."

The judge narrowed his eyes and thought about it. "Okay, but be very brief, Mr. Karp, we're in some tenuous territory. Let's hear it and see how we can proceed."

Karp turned back to the witness stand.

"Mr. Corcione, based upon your long-standing relationship with the defendant, what were the reasons for Mr. Vitteli to have a bodyguard?"

"I've known the defendant since I was a kid hanging out at my dad's office and around the docks," Corcione recalled, now staring at Vitteli. "He's always played the role of the big shot. He talks real tough and likes to call names, but he's a scared man, paranoid about people coming after him. Basically, he's a bully and a coward."

"You mean Charlie Vitteli is, in the vernacular, a chicken?"

"Exactly," Corcione retorted.

With a guttural shout, Vitteli shot to his feet and pointed a thick finger at Corcione. "We'll see who's chicken, you faggot!" he screamed as the vein in his forehead pulsed and his face turned purple with rage.

Judge See banged the gavel. "That will be quite enough, gentlemen," he said calmly but firmly, without raising his voice. He kept his eyes on Vitteli, who continued to glare at Corcione as he straightened his suit jacket, but he sat back down. "Good. Now, Mr. Karp, return to what happened in the alley. Please ask your question again so we can get back on track."

Pointing at Vitteli, Karp asked Corcione,

"So, again, why would that man over there, send his bodyguard — a man who shadows him even during daylight hours when he's out in public — away on a dark night in Hell's Kitchen."

"Because Charlie knew what was going to happen and that he was safe," Corcione replied. "But also he couldn't take a chance that Amaya might see or hear something; like I said, Vitteli doesn't trust anybody. And unless he told Amaya what was going to happen, which he didn't do for the same reason, Sal might have tried to intervene and messed everything up."

As it was, Corcione went on, the plan was nearly foiled by Vince Carlotta when the two "robbers" jumped out of the alley. "Vince had a gun in his coat pocket and pulled it out. The other guy, Bebnev, was kind of slow, and Vince probably would have got him, but Vitteli saw what was happening and grabbed Vince's arm and sort of pulled down on him so he couldn't aim."

"You said the other guy was Bebnev; how did you know that?" Karp asked. "I thought the killers were wearing ski masks?"

"They were," Corcione said. "But Bebnev had these really odd, pale blue eyes and a round head, like a pumpkin sitting on his neck, and he was easy to pick out. He also

465

spoke with an accent."

"Do you know what sort of an accent?"

Corcione shrugged. "I would assume Russian. He was from that community in Brighton Beach and was an associate of Lvov who said he was from Russia. I guess he could have been something else, but that makes the most sense."

"So Vitteli has his hands up in the air like this?" Karp said as he demonstrated. "Then you're saying he saw Carlotta pull a gun, so Vitteli reached and grabbed Carlotta's arm to stop him?"

"Yes," Corcione said, raising his own hands. "I was standing on Vitteli's right and Vince was on his left. Vitteli is left-handed, so he reached down like this." The young man simulated dropping his left hand and grabbing someone's arm.

"What, if anything, did Vince do when Vitteli grabbed his arm?"

"He called Vitteli a 'son of a bitch!' Those were his words."

"What happened then?"

"Vitteli shouted at Bebnev, 'Do it!' "

"Did the defendant say anything to Bebnev after he shot the deceased twice?" Karp asked.

"Yeah, I remember Vitteli told him to take our wallets and watches so that it would

466

look like a robbery," Corcione replied. "We handed our stuff over and then Bebnev and the other guy ran across the street, got into a car, and raced off."

"What did Vitteli do after the killers left?"

"He made a big show of pretending to help Vince, like trying to give him CPR, though it was pretty clear that Vince was beyond help," Corcione recalled. "Vitteli's hands were covered with blood."

As Corcione spoke, Karp walked over to the prosecution table and picked up the front page of that day's *Times* he'd cut out in his office with the photograph from the night of the murder. "Mr. Corcione, I am handing you the front page of today's *New York Times,* marked People's Exhibit Twenty-Nine for identification," he said as he walked back up to the witness stand. "Please describe it and tell us if it fairly and accurately depicts the scene as you observed it?"

"Yes, it does," Corcione answered after glancing at the page. "It shows Vitteli leaning against a wall of a building next to an alley; Barros and I are on either side of him. Charlie's got blood on his shirt, and you can see it on his hands and sleeves."

"What, if anything, is the defendant holding in his hands?"

Corcione looked back at the photograph. "I believe that's a handkerchief he used to try to wipe the blood off his hands."

"Have you ever known the defendant to carry a handkerchief?"

"Pretty much anytime he's in a suit. He even gets them monogrammed with his initials."

"Thank you, Mr. Corcione," Karp said, holding up his hand to retrieve the front page of the newspaper. "Your Honor, I'm offering People's Exhibit Twenty-Nine for identification in evidence."

As Judge See accepted the new evidence, Karp turned to gauge what was going on over at the defense table. Kowalski looked confused and worried. Vitteli's eyes registered doubt, fear, and anger. The two of them looked like cornered vermin thinking about fighting their way out of impending disaster, which was just what Karp wanted.

"Mr. Corcione, do you recall the defendant indicating that he thought he saw other individuals besides the four of you and the two robbers at the scene when Vince Carlotta was shot?"

"Charlie said he saw some old bag ladies hanging out in the alley. He kind of freaked out. Apparently, he'd had some kind of run-in with them before that night."

"Did you see them yourself?"

"No, Barros and I both looked but we didn't see anybody. We thought Charlie imagined them."

Karp moved closer to Corcione until he was at the front of the jury rail nearest to the witness box so that the jurors would get a good look at his face when he asked the next question. "What if I were to accuse you of working with Joey Barros, but not Charles Vitteli, to steal union money and then murder Vince Carlotta?"

"That's not true," Corcione said angrily. "Vitteli called the shots; we worked for him."

"Were you in fact afraid of Joey Barros?"

"Very."

"Did Joey Barros ever threaten you prior to the day you called my office to confess?"

"Frequently," Corcione said. "He was very homophobic and liked tormenting me with the crap he'd say. But it was more than just words. I knew that if Vitteli let him, he would have killed me just for the fun of it."

"Objection, Your Honor," Kowalski said. "This is highly speculative."

Judge See held up his hand to stop Karp from responding. "Gentlemen, please approach the bench and let's have a sidebar on this."

When the attorneys were assembled to the side of his dais away from the jury box, he continued. "Mr. Kowalski, we've already had an evidentiary hearing on your pretrial motion regarding the events that happened inside the Corcione apartment that led to the death of Joey Barros and the injuries to Greg Lusk and Jackie Corcione. I granted your motion *in limine* to prohibit Mr. Karp from bringing up those violent details as matters collateral and highly prejudicial since they were not charged in the indictment. But if you persist in your objection and thereby attempt to mislead this jury, you may very well be opening the door and permit this information to come into evidence and be heard before this jury. Do you really want to do that, Mr. Kowalski?"

"No, Your Honor, I withdraw my objection."

"Very well, return to your places and let's proceed."

31

The following morning Syd Kowalski rose from his chair to cross-examine Jackie Corcione with the expression on his face of a man who'd been given an unpleasant task to perform with someone who couldn't be trusted to do his part. He stuck his hands into the pockets of his silk suit as he walked out from behind the defense table and shook his head.

"There's been a lot of dramatics, alligator tears, and pointing the finger at everyone else here, Mr. Corcione," he growled, "but I'd like to cut to the chase and get some of this straight in my mind, as well as the minds of these good people on the jury. Let's start by clarifying exactly who has admitted to stealing money that belonged to the members, and their families, of the North American Brotherhood of Stevedores."

"I did."

"At the time you started stealing, were you being paid a salary by the union as its chief financial officer and as legal adviser to union chief Charles Vitteli?"

"I was."

"Was it a decent salary?"

"Yes, it was."

"But apparently not enough for your life-style?"

"I wanted more than what I could afford, that's true."

"What did this stolen money go toward?"

Corcione shrugged. "My loft. Clothes. A car. Entertainment."

"Entertainment? Theater tickets and extravagant vacations with your homosexual friends?"

At his seat, Karp noted the disdain in Kowalski's voice when he said "homosexual." Such undisguised virulence might not sit well with most of the jurors, but he knew that the defense attorney was fishing for that one juror who didn't like gays. He'd tried to guard against homophobia during voir dire in jury selection, but it was the sort of aversion a potential juror might not be willing to admit to in a public forum but secretly harbored.

"Yes, all of those things."

"Partying?"

"Yes."

"Illegal drugs?"

Corcione took a deep breath before letting it out and answering. "In the past, I've used cocaine and smoked pot," he said. "But it's been a long time."

"A long time as in?"

"More than a year."

"A whole year?"

"Ever since I met Greg."

"Greg, your lover."

"Yes."

Kowalski glanced over at the jury to see how his opening gambit was going. "So you started stealing — what was it you testified, thousands a month? — to support your extravagant lifestyle?"

"Yes."

"Then, out of the blue, Charlie Vitteli and Joey Barros showed up at your office and said they knew what you'd been up to and now they wanted a piece of the pie . . . only they wanted a much bigger pie?"

"That's one way to put it."

"And you decided to go along because you were afraid they'd turn you in and tell your father that you were queer, right?"

"Yes."

"So you set up this complicated scheme to steal millions of dollars?"

"Yes."

"Did Charlie Vitteli help you set it up?"

"No," Corcione answered. "He wouldn't have known how."

"Right, he's no financial mastermind, is he?"

"He's smart, but no, he didn't know how offshore banking, dummy corporations, and pass-through accounts worked."

"That's right; according to you he 'called the shots,' but only you knew how to actually steal the money and get away with it, correct?"

"Yes."

"And I believe that your testimony is that two board members of this dummy corporation management — supposedly comprised of you, Joey Barros, and the defendant — had to sign in order for this money to be transferred?"

"That's correct."

"But only you and Joey Barros ever signed."

"Yes, because —"

"We've heard your explanation — my client was trying to insulate himself — but if he's being so careful, why have his name on it at all?"

Corcione shook his head and half smiled as if trying to explain something fairly simple to the village idiot. "If something happened to me or Barros, he'd want to be able to access the accounts."

"Or, Mr. Corcione, is it possible that you and Jackie Barros set up these accounts and told my client, Charlie Vitteli, that they were simply union accounts set up for the legitimate investment of union pension funds?"

Karp's eyes narrowed. He'd expected the defense to make an attempt to distract the jurors from the facts of the case. So trying to suggest that Vitteli wasn't involved in the theft of union funds by Corcione and Barros — and therefore had no motive to murder Carlotta — was par for the course.

Following Corcione's testimony for the People, Karp had submitted into evidence the paper trail uncovered by ADA V. T. Newbury, the Frauds Bureau chief, under Corcione's guidance from the Cayman Island banks, to the multiple layers of dummy corporations and investments, right down to the three personal accounts. However, the one missing piece in the trail was that there was no record of Vitteli making any withdrawals on his account; apparently it really was his "retirement account," waiting for the day he decided he had enough.

The smoke-and-mirrors ploy was a desperate gamble on the part of the defense.

As with the gay-baiting, it was intended to find that one juror more inclined to believe conspiracy theories than facts. But Karp was fine with it; he would expose the ploy for what it was in summations. But for now it played into his goal of backing Vitteli into a corner so that he had no choice but to testify on his own behalf.

"What? No!" Corcione replied, scowling at the defense attorney's accusations. "Like I said, Mr. Kowalski, Charlie Vitteli called the shots."

"Did Charlie Vitteli make any withdrawals from this supposedly 'personal' account?"

"You know he didn't," Corcione countered. "Mr. Karp went over that when he submitted the statements into evidence."

Kowalski walked back over to the defense table, where he placed a hand on Vitteli's shoulder. "Mr. Corcione, you testified that you were VERY afraid of Joey Barros, a man you claim was capable of murder. Were you also VERY afraid of Charlie Vitteli?"

"I was afraid he might turn me in, or tell my dad I was gay."

"I'm not talking about him exposing you as a thief or your homosexuality," Kowalski sneered. "I mean, were you VERY afraid of Charlie Vitteli in the same way you were VERY afraid of Joey Barros?"

Corcione looked at Vitteli and shook his head. "No. I thought he probably had enough loyalty to my father that he wouldn't have wanted to hurt me."

Kowalski smiled as if he'd made an important point. "Mr. Corcione, wouldn't you agree that it makes more sense that the only man you feared in all of this was Joey Barros?"

"In a physical sense," Corcione answered. "But Barros only did what Charlie told him to do."

"Just a vicious dog doing his master's bidding, right?"

"That's an accurate description, yes."

Kowalski patted Vitteli on the shoulder and moved toward the jury with his eyes on their faces. "Mr. Corcione, who met with the triggerman Alexei Bebnev and this alleged Russian gangster, Marat Lvov?"

"Joey Barros and me."

"But not Charlie Vitteli?"

"No."

"Who gave the money to Lvov to pay Bebnev and his cronies?"

"Barros."

"But not Charlie Vitteli."

"Charlie told me to give Barros the money."

"That's your story, but there's no proof of

that, is there, Mr. Corcione?"

"Mr. Kowalski, the proof is what I've already told the jurors," Corcione retorted. "This was no robbery; it was a setup orchestrated by Vitteli. Barros and I worked for him. Why would I have turned myself in and pleaded guilty to manslaughter if this was just a robbery?"

Kowalski smiled. "Oh, I don't know, Mr. Corcione, maybe because you heard that Frank DiMarzo was talking and you wanted to get a deal by giving the DA a bigger fish to fry than little ol' Jackie Corcione."

"I didn't know anything about what Mr. DiMarzo was saying."

"No? So it's just a coincidence that on the same afternoon the district attorney was at Sing Sing penitentiary taking a statement from Frank DiMarzo, you decided to confess as well?"

"I don't know if it's a coincidence," Corcione said. "I was having trouble dealing with the guilt, and told my boyfriend what I'd done."

"Would it surprise you if later, when the defense puts on its case, it's revealed that a call was placed from Sing Sing to a cell phone registered to Joey Barros while Mr. Karp was at the penitentiary?"

"No. That makes sense if Charlie had a

spy at the penitentiary."

Kowalski scoffed. "Wow, Vitteli had more spies than the CIA according to your testimony. The Department of Labor. Sing Sing penitentiary. Is there anywhere the long arm of spymaster Charlie Vitteli didn't reach?"

"Apparently not," Corcione agreed.

"Then why wouldn't this spy just call Vitteli? Why only Barros?"

"Like I said, Charlie likes to insulate himself from any possible repercussions."

"Yes, of course. That's why the *only* reference to anyone named Charlie in *all* of the testimony, which you conveniently remembered when the district attorney was questioning your original statement, was some remark this Bebnev supposedly heard as he approached your booth?"

"I hadn't remembered that when I gave my statement," Corcione explained.

"No, you didn't," Kowalski said. "You only 'remembered' that — if that's what you call it — when the district attorney asked you if there was some mention of Charlie Vitteli, and lo and behold, 'Yeah, Mr. District Attorney, something was said and Bebnev might have heard it.' "

Kowalski angrily pointed his finger at Corcione and said, "The fact of the matter is that when you confessed to the district attorney, more than three hours after Mr. Karp spoke to Frank DiMarzo at Sing Sing, you didn't say anything about any conversation regarding Charlie Vitteli's name coming up when you hired Alexei Bebnev to murder Vince Carlotta, isn't that right?"

"I didn't remember it at first," Corcione replied quietly.

"Indeed you didn't," Kowalski sneered as he stalked over to the defense table and picked up several pieces of paper, which he held up as he walked back to the witness stand. "I'm referring here to the question-and-answer statement you gave to Mr. Karp AFTER your original confession. This is pages thirty-five through thirty-six, which the jurors will have with them during their deliberations. Question from Mr. Karp: 'Prior to Mr. Bebnev arriving, did you, Joey Barros, and Marat Lvov have a conversation in which Charlie Vitteli's name was mentioned?' Answer: 'I don't recall.' "

The defense attorney glared at the witness, who blinked and swallowed hard. "Wasn't that your answer, Mr. Corcione?"

"If that's what it says there," Corcione replied.

"That IS what it says here," Kowalski shot back as he held up the papers. "But then with a little prodding, you suddenly answer:

'Oh yeah, Lvov asked when the murder was to take place and Joey Barros said something about Mr. Vitteli wanting it done as soon as possible.' "

"But that's the truth," Corcione insisted.

"Is it, Mr. Corcione? Or is it a convenient fabrication by someone hoping to give the district attorney what he wants, the life of Charlie Vitteli?"

"Objection!" Karp said as he rose to his feet. "Your Honor, if counsel has proof, any evidence at all" — he gestured with his arms akimbo — "that this was a personal vendetta between the defendant and me, let him put it on the record now!"

"Maybe we should go into your spurious attack at the trial of Alexei Bebnev!" Kowalski shouted back.

"GENTLEMEN! Not another word!" Judge See demanded. He turned to the stenographer. "Strike that last comment by defense counsel." Then he scowled at Kowalski. "If the defense has any legitimate, legally admissible evidence regarding these accusations, I'll allow it. But I will not permit, or tolerate, questionable tactics by either party to be practiced in this courtroom. The jury will disregard the last comment."

Kowalski remained standing, glaring at the judge, but said nothing. Judge See in-

terrupted the pregnant silence, "Mr. Kowalski, once again, I take your silence as an acceptance and understanding of my
admonition. Please proceed."

Returning the Q&A statement to the defense table as Corcione filled his paper cup
and took a drink of water, Kowalski then
faced the witness and asked, "First, according to your testimony, after a brief confrontation at Marlon's Restaurant, the issues
between my client and Vince Carlotta were
essentially settled and the rest of the evening
was spent recalling the 'old days' and drinking, is that correct?"

"Only because Vitteli knew what was going to happen," Corcione pointed out. "It
was a sham so that Vince wouldn't suspect."

Kowalski looked to the side and shook his
head as if dealing with a not-so-bright child.
"I asked you a simple question. You testified
that after this supposed confrontation and
agreement to work out their differences, the
evening ended on a positive note, right?"

"Yes . . . but —"

"No 'but,' please, Mr. Corcione," Kowalski interrupted, "just 'yes' or 'no,' please."

"Yes."

"Thank you. You further testified, and the
district attorney made much of the fact, that
my client told his bodyguard, Sal Amaya, to

go on ahead and accompany Randy Mc-Mahon to get Mr. Carlotta's car."

"Yes."

"And during Mr. Karp's examination he got you to state categorically that except for this one instance, Sal Amaya never left Mr. Vitteli's side."

"I didn't say never, but it would have been very unusual."

"Well, let's look at that whole scenario in another way," Kowalski said as he again stuck his hands in his pockets and strolled over in front of the witness stand. "Isn't it possible that Mr. Vitteli sent his bodyguard with Randy McMahon, Vince's driver, so that he could spot any potential danger before his employer walked that same route?"

"Anything may be possible. . . ."

"Just answer my question yes or no, please," Kowalski interjected.

"Yes, that's a possibility."

"And haven't you testified that Joey Barros was a thoroughly dangerous man himself?"

"Yes, Joey Barros was a dangerous man."

"And wasn't Vince Carlotta a tough guy who came up on the docks the same way Charlie Vitteli and Joey Barros did and wasn't afraid of a physical confrontation?"

"That's true."

"And in fact, according to your testimony, Vince Carlotta wasn't afraid to take on the dangerous Mr. Barros, right?"

"He wasn't afraid."

Kowalski turned toward the defense table. "And if you look at my client, he's not exactly a delicate wallflower, now, is he?" he asked as Vitteli smiled slightly at the description.

"No, Charlie at least looks like a big tough guy, too."

"So by sending Sal Amaya ahead to scout for danger, and in the company of two other tough guys, maybe my client didn't feel he needed a bodyguard to babysit him, especially if he wanted to talk privately with Vince Carlotta as they walked? Isn't that a possibility?"

"It's a possibility, but I never saw Amaya leave him under similar circumstance before."

"Never? I believe Sal Amaya has worked for Mr. Vitteli for five years and in all that time, you can state that he never left his employer's side?"

"I can't say that and I haven't testified to that."

"Of course you can't, because it's not true," Kowalski said.

"Objection," Karp said. "The witness testified as to his experience in this matter, not what may or may not have occurred outside of his knowledge."

"Sustained," Judge See replied. "The jury will disregard Mr. Kowalski's comment."

"Let's continue, Mr. Corcione," Kowalski said. "It's my recollection that when your party was accosted by two of the men you hired to kill Vince Carlotta, their intended victim began to draw his weapon and at that point you claim my client reached down and grabbed his arm. Is that right?"

"Yes."

"Well, I know how the district attorney has framed this, but aren't there other explanations?"

"What do you mean?"

"Well, is it possible that my client saw that the man you hired already had his gun ready to fire and was trying to stop Mr. Carlotta from endangering them all by engaging in a shootout?"

"Like I previously stated, anything may be possible."

"And in regard to your testimony in which you claim Mr. Carlotta said, 'You son of a bitch,' as he was drawing his gun, isn't it a possibility that he was speaking to the robber?"

"No. He was looking at Charlie."

Kowalski's eyebrows shot up. "Really? You're sure about that? Let me ask you something, Mr. Corcione, were you looking at the gunman or at Vince Carlotta when he allegedly said, 'You son of a bitch!' "

"I was looking at the robber. But I saw Vince turn to Vitteli when he said that."

Kowalski walked along the jury rail, looking at each juror as he then asked, "The truth is, this all happened quickly didn't it? The killers you hired jumped out of the alley pretending this was a robbery, Vince tried to pull a gun while saying 'You son of a bitch,' and then Bebnev shot him. Isn't that correct?"

"Yes, it happened quickly."

"And you didn't have time to look from these hired killers to Vince to see who he was calling a son of a bitch. Nor did you know what was going through Charlie Vitteli's mind, IF — and that's a big if — he indeed tried to stop Vince from getting in a shootout, or who he was talking to IF he shouted, 'Shoot him.' "

"That's not true," Corcione replied. "Charlie Vitteli wanted Vince Carlotta to die, and that's what was going through his mind."

And the challenger comes off the ropes to land a counterpunch, Karp thought without

486

showing the smile he felt. Although he'd expected this attack from Kowalski, and had warned Corcione during trial prep it would come, taken by itself, the defense attorney was landing some shots but hadn't expected Corcione's response this time.

Kowalski's face revealed that he knew he'd stepped into the blow, but he quickly recovered. "Mr. Corcione, you were asked some questions regarding the union magazine, the *Dock,* as well as about a page from an edition of the magazine with a photograph depicting Joey Barros, my client, Vince Carlotta, and you. Is this magazine available in the main office of the North American Brotherhood of Stevedores by the Hudson River docks?"

"Yes."

"And is it likely that, as the editor in chief, Charles Vitteli would come into contact with one or more copies of each edition?"

"Yes."

"You also testified that you were in my client's office when he wrote on a photograph from the magazine. Did anyone else see this?"

"Joey Barros."

"And Joey Barros is dead."

"Yes."

"Mr. Corcione, the jury has now heard

that there may be other explanations or possibilities in regard to this tragedy," Kowalski said and paused as he now looked at the jurors. "Isn't another possibility that the reason you and Joey Barros met with a Russian gangster and hired Alexei Bebnev to murder Vince Carlotta was because he had discovered your theft of union money and confronted you about it?"

Corcione's jaw dropped. "No! That's not true!"

"Isn't that the real reason Mr. Carlotta approached the Department of Labor?"

"Absolutely not," Corcione cried out. "He complained to the Department of Labor about the election results!"

"Do you know if he brought his concerns about the theft of union money by you and Joey Barros to Charlie Vitteli?"

"That's a lie!" Corcione retorted.

"What's the lie, Mr. Corcione?" Kowalski shouted back and as quickly as he could followed up. "Maybe it was that Vince found out about your thievery and you had him murdered? Or that when Charlie Vitteli became suspicious four months ago and went to the Department of Labor himself, you decided that your only way out was to point the finger at my client, knowing about the bad blood between him and the district attorney?"

"OBJECTION!" Karp thundered. "Once again, defense counsel with absolutely no evidence is falsely accusing the prosecution of misconduct. I demand that if he has any evidence of his alleged theories that he put it on the record now!"

"You're the one who put an admitted thief, liar, and murderer on the stand, Mr. Karp!" Kowalski shouted back. "Is that how you get at the truth?"

Judge See banged his gavel. "Mr. Kowalski, to quote a memorable moment in presidential debate history, and much to my bewilderment, 'There you go again.' How many times must I admonish you about making bold assertions regarding defense theories of the case for which you offer no evidence. If you have any facts to support your hypotheses, I want to hear an offer of proof now! If you're not able to satisfy an offer of proof, then save your possibilities for summation and do not make reference to them again. Is that clear, counselor?"

"Very well, Your Honor, I'll save it for the defense case," Kowalski replied. He then approached the witness stand again, appearing ill at ease. "Mr. Corcione, you testified that you went to the district attorney with your story of your own free will."

"That's correct."

"And though it's kind of nebulous, this has something to do with your conscience bothering you?"

"Yes. I couldn't live with it anymore."

"But you managed to live with it up until the very day that Frank DiMarzo also decided he couldn't live with his conscience anymore and confessed."

"I didn't know he was going to do that."

"I know, Mr. Corcione, it was all just a big coincidence that both of you had an attack of conscience at the same time, miles apart, one of you in prison and the other living in the lap of luxury with his boyfriend," Kowalski said, every word dripping with sarcasm. "But it's a hell of a coincidence, isn't it, Mr. Corcione?"

"That," Corcione agreed, "or karma."

32

As Kowalski turned on his heel and stalked back to the defense table, Karp sat tapping a pencil on his yellow legal pad, contemplating the notes he'd just taken. In his long career as a prosecutor, Karp could not remember a case that hinged more on the consciences of the perpetrators bringing them to the witness stand rather than self-serving attempts to get deals or mitigate their own guilt by blaming others. In a world in which words like "conscience" and "values" were tossed around like footballs whenever politically expedient or financially advantageous, he knew jurors might view such motives with suspicion.

Syd Kowalski had done his best to play on those suspicions. The irony was that even with DiMarzo's confession, Karp wouldn't have had the evidence he felt necessary to charge Vitteli with Carlotta's murder. If not for Corcione's conscience — and his testimony tying all the pieces together, including DiMarzo's upcoming testimony — they would not have been in court that day.

However, Karp had planned for such a ploy by the defense and devised a strategy to counter it. During his direct examination, he'd purposely avoided going much into the reasons Corcione had come forward so that it would have greater impact now when he rose from his seat for redirect. With that in mind, he wasn't going to address Kowalski's ludicrous suggestions about a conspiracy to "get" Charlie Vitteli. To do so would have only given them more credence than they deserved; by ignoring them, he dismissed their impact.

Instead, he would clear up any potential questions raised by Kowalski during summations at the end of the trial when he and the defense counsel would present their arguments as to what the evidence demonstrated and why the defendant was or wasn't guilty as charged. But now, he would concentrate on why Corcione, a young man who might well have gotten away with murder and the theft of millions of dollars, was willing to go to prison for his crimes.

Walking over to stand near one end of the jury box and looking past the jurors at the witness stand on the other end, he began.

"Mr. Corcione, you've testified as to why you began stealing money from the union, and then why you agreed to help Charlie Vitteli when he demanded that you include him in the scheme to steal millions more. You've told us that you were afraid of going to prison, concerned that Charlie Vitteli would tell your father that you were gay and you'd lose his love and respect, and also that it would destroy your relationship with your boyfriend. You also testified that when it appeared that Vince Carlotta might topple this house of cards you'd built with Vitteli and Barros, you agreed with the defendant's plan to silence him forever. Is that a fair and accurate representation of what you've testified to so far?"

"Yes," Corcione responded with his head down, still feeling the effects of Kowalski's attack.

"So we know why you covered up your crimes," Karp said as he moved along the jury rail, "but defense counsel has called into question your motives for taking the stand. So what we haven't heard much about from you is why, in your own words, you decided to confess. You said you couldn't live with the guilt; would you now tell us what you meant by that?"

Slowly, Corcione raised his head to look

at Karp, then set his jaw and turned slightly to face the jurors. "I no longer enjoyed being alive," he said. "The material things I wanted and stole other people's money to get . . . and then helped kill Vince Carlotta to protect . . . none of them seemed important or worthwhile anymore. I was never hungry; nothing tasted good; great wines were just bitter. I would walk on some tropical beach and it was as if I couldn't feel the sun's warmth. Or enjoy the company of my friends. Or appreciate good music. I would lose my temper over the smallest things. . . . I was losing myself."

Corcione paused to wipe away tears that had begun rolling down his face. But his voice was strong and clear as he looked back at Karp. "I don't know if I ever told you this, but before I got my MBA, I was an English Lit major," he said. "I loved it and wish now, as I did then, that I could have just been a professor or even high school teacher. Anyway, there's a line from *Macbeth* after he's killed the king in which he says, 'I have murdered sleep.' I can't tell you the number of nights after Vince's death when that line ran through my head as I lay awake. But I murdered more than sleep. I murdered everything that makes life worth living." He looked out at the gallery. "Most of all I murdered love. . . . If it wasn't for Greg, the one bright spot that remained in my life . . . I would have ended it all. But even that may be a lie, because I'm probably too much of a coward to take my own life."

Glancing at the jurors, many of whom were also teary-eyed, Karp hammered home his last few points. "Are you guilty of acting in concert to murder Vince Carlotta in order to cover up the theft of about forty-seven million dollars belonging to the North American Brotherhood of Stevedores?"

"Yes, I am."

"Have you already pled guilty to manslaughter in the first degree?"

Corcione nodded, then remembered that he had to speak. "Yes. I did plead guilty."

"And what do you expect will happen after you plead guilty to manslaughter."

"I will be sentenced to prison," Corcione replied, "for a very long time."

"So those things you feared would happen if Vince Carlotta had exposed your crimes while scheming with Joey Barros and the defendant will come to pass anyway?"

"Yes."

"You'll lose your freedom and be imprisoned."

"Yes."

"You'll lose all the things you've gained through theft . . . the loft apartment, the car, the vacations, the theater tickets and expensive dinners?"

"Yes."

Karp looked out into the gallery, where Greg Lusk sat with his face in his hands and shoulders shaking. "And any hope at a normal relationship with the man you love?"

"Yes, oh God, yes," Corcione sobbed and also buried his face in his hands.

Karp waited for Corcione to regain his composure. "Mr. Corcione, you've now told us what you will lose," he said at last. "What, if anything, do you hope to gain?"

Corcione sat quietly for a moment longer. Then, with the slightest smile coming to his lips as he looked past the jurors to his boyfriend, he answered. "My self-respect . . . maybe my soul."

Karp nodded and turned to Judge See. "No further questions."

The judge cleared his throat and asked Kowalski if he had any follow-up questions for recross, but the defense attorney just scowled and shook his head. "Very well," the judge said. "I believe we'll take our lunch break now. We'll resume at one." He looked at Corcione and, not unkindly, said, "You are dismissed."

The courtroom was silent as Jackie Corcione stepped down from the witness stand. As he approached the space between the defense and prosecution tables, he slowed and looked at Vitteli. Their eyes locked for a moment before Vitteli broke off and stared straight ahead. Corcione shrugged and walked on.

After lunch, Karp followed up on Corcione's appearance with less dramatic but nevertheless important testimony, filling in the puzzle with other pieces necessary to form the big picture. But Kowalski fought him every step of the way, the two attorneys exchanging shots like heavyweight prize-fighters.

It started again when Gnat Miller was called to the stand to recount an abridged version of his testimony from the trial of Bebnev and DiMarzo. This time the emphasis wasn't on proving that the three killers had been in New Rochelle and Hell's Kitchen but to lay the groundwork for Di-Marzo's upcoming testimony, especially Miller's recollection of the magazine photograph he'd briefly seen his friend looking at when the Carlotta family arrived at their home in New Rochelle.

Kowalski had, of course, attacked Miller's credibility. Taking a page from Clooney's cross-examination in the previous trial, he'd noted Miller's criminal history. He'd also noted that Miller would be up for parole in eight years, four months, and questioned if his testimony now was part of an effort to manipulate a parole board later.

Anticipating the defense attack on Miller's motivations, Karp had focused the jury's attention on what his confession and testimony had cost him. And with that he'd been helped by something Miller had told him that morning before the trial.

After a brief discussion during witness preparation about his upcoming testimony, Karp had asked Miller about his relationship with Nicoli Lopez and their son now that he'd been sent to prison. "She moved to the town where the prison is located and visits pretty often, but she's working and trying to take care of Billy on her own, so sometimes she's too tired," the young man had told him. "Billy's growing like a weed. If she can't bring him to visit for a week or two, the next time I see him, it's like he's a whole new kid."

Miller shook his head sadly. "I know that someday Nicoli will move on; then they'll visit once a month, then every few months and finally, maybe, once a year. After that, if I'm lucky, I'll get photographs. I'll tell ya, it's a tough way to watch your son grow up, Mr. Karp, and a visiting room is no place for a kid to get to know his dad."

Karp had known then how he would respond to Kowalski's expected attack. In the courtroom, he'd asked Miller to repeat what he'd told him that evening after Judge See had adjourned for the day.

After Miller's tearful testimony, Karp called an NYPD graphologist to the stand to testify about the writing on the photograph. Following Vitteli's indictment, he'd sought a court order to obtain "exemplars" — samples of Vitteli's handwriting — to compare. Initially there was some difficulty because most of what was located was the defendant's cursive signature, but he'd written on the photograph in block letters. Meeting with Karp and Guma in the office, she'd said that while she could to a reasonable degree of scientific certainty testify that both were written by a left-handed person, to link it to Vitteli she'd need an example of Vitteli's printing. Again, it was V. T. Newbury who obtained a court-ordered search warrant for union records, including everything in Vitteli's office and home, and located printed notes that the defendant, ironically, made at the union meeting when Carlotta filed his formal complaint about the election.

On the witness stand, the handwriting expert testified that whoever wrote on the photograph was left-handed, pointing out several factors that led her to that conclusion. One was that the circle drawn around Carlotta's face had been drawn with a clockwise motion. "And in almost all cases, left-handed people prefer to draw circles clockwise and most right-handed people prefer to draw circles counterclockwise. This is probably attributable to brain hemispheres."

Other indicators had to do with the different way that left-handed writers have to tilt the page to get the forward slant to their letters; left-handed writers also tended to make vertical pen strokes from left to right going up, while right-handers did the opposite. "Also, you'll notice the slight smudging of the letters, which is caused when a left-handed person writes left to right and drags his hand across the ink."

On cross-examination, Kowalski asked if it was possible that whoever wrote on the photograph could have been a right-handed person "trying to emulate" a left-handed writer.

"It's possible," the graphologist conceded, "with a lot of practice. But normally it would appear more forced. I would also expect to see evidence of forgery; there are small nuances to writing, unconscious habits, if you will, that anyone who's not a professional forger or a trained handwriting analyst probably wouldn't know, such as left-handed and right-handed people tilt the page differently. The circle is a good example; a right-handed person trying to pretend to be left-handed would need to remember to draw the circle counterclockwise. There was no evidence of forgery in this case, the writer was left-handed and a match to the defendant's handwriting to a high degree of scientific certainty."

After the handwriting analyst, Karp called a fingerprint expert. There wasn't much to discuss, just a partial thumbprint on the top right-hand corner of the page — only enough to note "several points of similarity and no discrepancies" to the defendant's. As a demonstration, Karp asked the witness to place his thumb at the same spot on the same page in another copy of the *Dock* to demonstrate how that was a logical place for someone tearing the page from the magazine.

During cross, Kowalski countered by getting the expert to show that the placement of the thumbprint could have also been from someone "thumbing" through the magazine. Apparently content to concede that the print was Vitteli's, Kowalski did not challenge the identification.

Throwing jabs and roundhouses, the attorneys continued to spar, especially after Karp put Mahlon Gorman on the stand.

Karp began by questioning Gorman about the union election and Carlotta's efforts to overturn the results. Gorman described the first meeting with a Labor Department attorney named Martin Bryant who told them that federal law required that the complainant exhaust union procedures according to the Landrum-Griffin Act before federal officials could get involved. When the union investigation headed by Charles Vitteli determined that the charges were unwarranted, "as expected," Gorman had gone to Washington, D.C., to "go up the ladder" and over the head of Bryant about their complaint, and that even the alleged union investigation was rigged.

Karp's questions had then turned to the meeting in Gorman's office after the three men had showed up at Carlotta's home. The young attorney testified that when he expressed concern for Carlotta's safety, his friend had shown him the .380 handgun he was carrying in his coat.

"Had you known Mr. Carlotta to carry a handgun on other occasions?" Karp asked.

"I didn't even know he owned one," Gorman responded.

"Just to clarify, did he say he had the gun to protect himself because he was going to be walking down the street at night in a rough neighborhood?" Karp asked.

"No, he was carrying it because of the three guys who came to his house the night before. He was pissed off because he thought Vitteli sent them as a threat."

"Do you know the names of the three men who went to Mr. Carlotta's home?"

"Yes, Alexei Bebnev, William Miller, and Frank DiMarzo."

"And how do you know those names?"

"Bebnev and DiMarzo were convicted of Vince's murder," Gorman said. "Miller pleaded guilty and testified against the other two."

Gorman wrapped up his testimony recalling the telephone call he received from Carlotta the night of the murder. "He said Vitteli had agreed to step down if Vince would drop his complaint with the Labor Department and pay him to 'retire.' I could tell he'd been drinking and was pretty happy with the way things had gone."

Rising swiftly to his feet to cross, Kowalski asked, "Was this meeting with the Labor Department attorney informational, or did you file a formal complaint?"

"We attempted to file a formal complaint, but Bryant said we had to go through the union first."

"Well, did you see Bryant create any sort of record of this meeting?" Kowalski asked.

"He took notes, but there was no recording that I'm aware of," Gorman replied.

Karp frowned and picked up his pencil. Fulton had interviewed Bryant, who seemed to have only a vague recollection of the meeting with Gorman and Carlotta. He'd struck the detective as a lazy bureaucrat who had been only too happy to pass the problem back to the union. "He probably thought it would go away," Fulton had said at the time. Now Karp wondered what Kowalski was up to with his line of questioning and made a note on his legal pad to consider later.

"If I understand your testimony, Mr. Gorman," Kowalski said, "the reason you went to the Labor Department was to complain about the election."

"That's correct."

"It didn't have anything to do with concerns that someone in management might be stealing union funds?"

"We weren't aware of the thefts at the time."

"So there was no reason to kill Vince Carlotta over union funds," Kowalski pointed out.

"Not yet," Gorman said. "But if they were worried that Vince would get in and then find out what they'd done —"

"If, if, if, Mr. Gorman. We don't convict citizens based on if," Kowalski retorted, then moved onto the meeting the night of the murder.

"Mr. Gorman, did Mr. Carlotta tell you that he had a confrontation with Jackie Corcione and Barros at Marlon's Restaurant in Hell's Kitchen that night?"

"No," Gorman replied. "It started with Barros, and then Vitteli got involved. Jackie's about the last person to confront someone else, much less Vince, who'd known him all of his life and treated him like a kid brother."

"A kid brother willing to kill him to cover up the theft of union money," Kowalski interjected.

Gorman hesitated then nodded. "Apparently so. But Vince didn't say anything about Jackie being involved in the stuff at the beginning of the meeting."

"Tell me, Mr. Gorman, was Vince Carlotta carrying his gun to protect himself from Charlie Vitteli?"

"Not directly from Vitteli, if that's what you mean. Charlie wouldn't have had the balls to take on Vince man-to-man," Gorman said, looking directly at Vitteli. "Charlie's a coward who has other guys to do his dirty work for him."

"Why you little . . ." Vitteli snarled as he started to stand.

Judge See's gavel banged down hard. "The defendant will sit down and be quiet," the judge ordered. "Counsel, please control your client."

"Your Honor, the witness's response went beyond answering the question and was intended to bait my client," Kowalski complained. "He got the response he was hoping for."

"I believe the 'baiting' goes both ways," Judge See said. "And I want it to stop. I'd like to see direct questions from counsel, and succinct answers from the witness. It that clear?"

"Yes, Your Honor," Kowalski and Gorman answered.

"Good. Mr. Kowalski, please continue."

"Mr. Gorman, you just said that my client would not have physically challenged Mr.

Carlotta," Kowalski said. "So wouldn't it be more accurate to say that Mr. Carlotta was carrying a gun because of Joey Barros?"

"As far as a direct threat, yes. But Barros didn't sneeze unless Vitteli told him to."

"That's a cute metaphor, Mr. Gorman, but how well did you know Joey Barros?"

"Mostly by reputation, but —"

"The reality is, you didn't know Joey Barros except by reputation, so if he was involved in some sort of scheme with Jackie Corcione, or was acting on his own accord without the knowledge or approval of Charlie Vitteli, you wouldn't really have known, would you?"

"No," Gorman replied tersely. "I would not have necessarily known."

"You would not have known," Kowalski corrected him. "I have no more questions."

"Mr. Karp?"

"No more questions."

"Very well. The hour is late. We'll adjourn until tomorrow morning. Are we near the end of the People's case, Mr. Karp?"

"We are, Your Honor, possibly by noon," Karp responded.

"Very well, Mr. Karp. Mr. Kowalski, have your first witness ready to go as soon as the People rest."

33

The prisoner who looked down at Karp from the witness stand appeared pale and haggard. Yet, the District Attorney of New York County knew that Frank DiMarzo was more at peace than at any time since the murder of Vince Carlotta. It was the sort of change that, had the jury been able to compare DiMarzo as Karp had seen him four months earlier and now, there would have been no question that an enormous burden had been lifted from his shoulders.

Over the intervening months, Marlene had kept tabs on the prisoner through Assistant Warden Dave Whitney. Whitney reported that the young man had been attending Catholic Mass daily and reading the Bible his sister had delivered to him from home, the same Bible in which he'd kept the photograph from the *Dock* used to identify Carlotta. The young prisoner had also asked to be involved in prison ministries, though that would not occur until he'd been removed from administrative segregation, where he was currently housed for his own protection.

When DiMarzo appeared at the side door leading into the courtroom, his eyes sought out his family, who this time were sitting on the prosecution side of the courtroom. He'd teared up at the sight of his parents and sisters, but he smiled slightly and gave a small wave. From the sad, proud looks on his family's faces, especially that of his mother, someone who didn't know the circumstances would have thought he was the hero of this tale, not a convicted murderer.

As DiMarzo made his way to the witness stand, Karp's gaze had switched to the beautiful woman in black sitting two rows in front of the DiMarzo family and just behind the prosecution table. Antonia Carlotta was watching the young man who'd participated in her husband's murder with a frown, her dark eyes hard and unforgiving.

After Vitteli's indictment, Karp had spoken to her about the trial and the possibility of calling her as a witness. She begged him not to, because she wanted to watch the proceedings. "I want to see Vitteli squirm when he is exposed for the coward he is," she'd pleaded.

Karp considered her request and whether he would need her to testify. There was no question that Miller and DiMarzo had come to her house; Miller already had admitted it on the stand, and soon DiMarzo would follow suit. So she wasn't needed for that. She could have testified about what her husband had said about the election and his distrust of Charlie Vitteli, as well as his comments about Joey Barros and Jackie Corcione. But Mahlon Gorman was sufficient in that regard, and he'd seen the gun and knew why Vince Carlotta was carrying it.

In fact, probably to keep his wife from worrying, Vince Carlotta had downplayed any danger to his person in his conversations with her, though he was clearly angry about the three men who came to their house. She didn't buy his excuse about burglars in the neighborhood, and believed that it had something to do with Vitteli, but that wasn't what he told her.

So Karp acceded to her request, and she'd been there every day from jury selection to Frank DiMarzo taking the stand as the People's final witness. And with each witness, he'd caught glimpses as her face mirrored what she was going through. Angry and bitter when Jackie Corcione took the stand, Karp then saw her crying as he wept over lost love. She'd stared with hatred at Vitteli as Gorman testified about her husband's telephone call saying Vitteli was stepping down and everything would be all right, and shaken her head sadly as Gnat Miller described what it was like watching his son grow older from a prison visiting room.

Earlier that morning, Antonia came to his office to thank him for his efforts. Her words had humbled him. Reminded of her reactions to other witnesses, he'd then asked her how she felt about the upcoming testimony of Frank DiMarzo. "I feel sorry for his family," she'd said. "I've watched them during jury selection. They seem very close and remind me of my family back in Italy. I'm sure this has been devastating for them. But I don't know how to feel about him. I'm glad he's testifying now, but he could have stopped the whole plot by going to the police. Or at least he could have confessed instead of pretending he was innocent during that first trial. He was a coward when he helped kill my husband, and he was a coward after he got caught. I guess I'll see how I feel when today is over."

Antonia saw him looking at her and nodded. He nodded back and then turned to begin his questioning by asking DiMarzo to describe his friendship with Gnat Miller and then how he'd become acquainted with Alexei Bebnev. He'd then moved on to "the job" Bebnev recruited him for and the promised payment of fourteen thousand dollars to be split between him and his friend.

"You agreed to help murder a man you didn't know for money?" Karp asked.

"Yes," DiMarzo replied. "That's all it was, just a lousy seven grand."

"Did you know the name of the man Bebnev intended to murder?"

"No. Just that two guys he met in Hell's Kitchen named Joey and Jackie paid him to kill a union big shot who lived in New Rochelle."

"Who introduced Bebnev to Joey and Jackie?"

"A Russian gangster named Lvov."

"Did Alexei Bebnev tell you that he overheard one of these men say who wanted Vince Carlotta murdered and when it was to happen?"

DiMarzo's ability to answer that question represented a prime example of how carefully every detail in a trial needed to be considered, prepared for, and laid out in the proper order. If Jackie Corcione had not come forward and already testified that Barros told Lvov that "Charlie wants this to happen as soon as possible," and that Bebnev was in a position to overhear the statement, DiMarzo could not have answered him, as it would have been hearsay and inadmissible.

In fact, Kowalski had fought tooth and nail at a pretrial hearing to keep it out on those grounds. But Corcione's testimony established the predicate upon which DiMarzo's testimony could be admitted into evidence. It was deemed part of the overt acts of the conspiracy — the defendants acting in concert — to kill Vincent Carlotta.

So now when Kowalski objected for the record and was quickly overruled by Judge See, DiMarzo was allowed to answer, "Yeah. He said he walked up on those guys at the restaurant and heard one of them tell Lvov that 'Charlie wants it done as soon as possible.' "

Watching the jurors as DiMarzo answered, Karp saw the piece of the puzzle linking Corcione's testimony and DiMarzo's click together in their heads. "Why did you ask your friend William Miller to help?"

"We needed a car," DiMarzo explained. "And I knew he needed money so that he and his girlfriend could move out of her parents' basement."

The answer, of course, mirrored Gnat

Miller's own testimony about his reasons for committing the crime, and again Karp saw pieces fall into place and noted this in the eyes of the jury. The comment about living in the basement of Nicoli Lopez's parents wasn't a big deal on its face, just a small detail that could have gone unnoticed if DiMarzo hadn't repeated it. But sometimes the connectivity — the linkage — of small details remembered by multiple witnesses carried more weight than any one "significant" item on its own.

Karp walked over to the prosecution table and picked up the plastic envelope containing the magazine photograph from the *Dock*. "Mr. DiMarzo, you testified that you didn't know Vince Carlotta, correct?"

"That's right."

"Did you know what he looked like before the night you went to New Rochelle with Alexei Bebnev and William 'Gnat' Miller to murder him?"

"I'd never seen him before."

"Were you given some way to identify him so that you'd know you were killing the right man?"

"Yeah. Bebnev gave me a photograph from a magazine."

"Where'd he get the photograph?"

"From one of those guys, Joey, I think,

that night he went to Hell's Kitchen and met those guys."

"Could you describe the photograph?"

"Yeah, there was four guys in it," Di-Marzo said. "They were standing on a boardwalk."

Karp handed the photograph and envelope to DiMarzo. "Can you identify the contents of this envelope?"

DiMarzo looked at it and immediately nodded his head. "Yes, this is the photograph from the magazine that Bebnev gave me."

"How do you know that?"

"I recognize the picture, and it's got the same writing on it. My initials and the date I handed it over to you are also on the back."

"What did you do with the photograph after Mr. Carlotta was murdered?"

"I put it in my Bible."

"Why? Why not get rid of it?"

"I don't know, really," DiMarzo replied, and then thought about it for a moment longer before adding, "Maybe for this reason."

"Which is?"

"To help prove that what I'm saying is the truth."

"Do you recognize anyone in the photograph now?"

"Yeah, Mr. Carlotta," he said before nodding at Vitteli, "and that guy over there, Vitteli."

Walking over to the defense table and staring down at the defendant, Karp pointed. "This man right here?"

"Yeah."

Breaking off his eye contact with Vitteli, Karp turned toward the court reporter and judge's dais. "Let the record reflect that the witness identified the defendant as one of the men pictured in People's Exhibit Twenty-Eight, which I now ask the court to receive into evidence."

"Without objection so accepted," Judge See ordered.

Looking back at the witness, Karp asked, "Why did Bebnev give you the photograph? If he was going to do the shooting, why didn't he use it to identify the victim himself?"

"One thing was, Bebnev's eyesight wasn't so good," DiMarzo replied. "He needed glasses, but he thought they made him look weak. But it was probably so that I would be more involved in the whole thing, too."

"Did you use the photograph?"

"Yes, the night we went to his house in New Rochelle," DiMarzo said. "They weren't home when we drove by, so we waited up the block. After they drove past us and Mr. Carlotta got out of the car, I knew it was him from the photograph. He was a good-looking guy, pretty distinctive. As a matter of fact, Bebnev asked me if he was the guy. He kept saying, 'Check the photograph.' "

"Did you use the photograph again?"

"No. We didn't need it. Lvov called Bebnev and told him —"

"Objection," Kowalski said, rising to his feet. "Whatever, if anything, this Lvov character said to Bebnev would be hearsay."

"Sustained," Judge See said.

Karp rephrased. "Did Bebnev tell you about a new plan to murder Vince Carlotta?"

"Yeah. He said that Carlotta was going to the restaurant where Bebnev had met Lvov and the two other guys, Joey and Jackie, and that Carlotta would be coming out of the restaurant with three other guys," DiMarzo said. "We were supposed to wait in the alley and then pretend it was a robbery, only Bebnev was going to shoot Carlotta."

"But you didn't need the photograph, because you'd already met Mr. Carlotta when he came to the door of his home in New Rochelle?"

"That's right."

517

Retrieving the photograph and returning it to the prosecution table, Karp moved on to the night of Carlotta's murder by asking DiMarzo to recall what happened after he and Miller picked Bebnev up in Little Odessa and drove to Hell's Kitchen. DiMarzo described how they'd waited for an hour in the alley, with Bebnev nervously smoking Belomorkanal cigarettes while DiMarzo kept his eye on Miller sitting in the car across the street watching for their victim to appear. They'd slipped farther into the shadows when sometime after midnight two men, one of them very large, walked past. A few minutes later, they got the signal from Miller, who waved and pointed, that their quarry was approaching.

"We waited until their voices were close; then we jumped out," DiMarzo said. "Bebnev pointed his gun at Mr. Carlotta and demanded their wallets. He was supposed to pull the trigger right away, but he hesitated, and that's when Mr. Carlotta went for his gun."

"What were you supposed to be doing at this time?"

DiMarzo shrugged. "I guess looking out for cops. But I think mostly Bebnev didn't have the nerve to do it on his own."

"Did the defendant do anything at that

time?" Karp asked.

"Yeah, he had his hands up in the air," DiMarzo said, demonstrating, "then reached down and grabbed Mr. Carlotta's arm."

"Did Mr. Carlotta say anything then to the defendant?"

"He said something but I didn't hear what it was," DiMarzo replied. "I had the ski mask pulled down over my ears that kind of muffled the sound, and to be honest, I think I was just sort of freaking out myself. I couldn't believe it was all happening."

"Did the defendant say anything to Bebnev?"

"He yelled, 'Shoot!' Something like that. He told Bebnev to shoot."

"What happened then?"

DiMarzo sighed. "Bebnev shot him in the chest. It knocked Mr. Carlotta down. He was trying to get up, but Bebnev shot him in the head."

"Did the defendant say anything then?"

"Yeah, Bebnev and I were just kind of standing there, so Vitteli," DiMarzo said, again nodding toward the defense table, "told us to take their wallets and watches so it would look like a robbery. Then we took off across the street and peeled out of there."

Karp walked back to the prosecution table

and glanced briefly at his notepad before turning back to the witness. "When did you get paid?"

"I got some of it from Bebnev the next day," DiMarzo said. "Seven thousand bucks for the two of us. But I had to bug him for the rest. That's when he told me to meet him at a bar in Little Odessa and he'd give me the rest. Lvov showed up —"

"How did you know it was Marat Lvov?" Karp interrupted.

"Bebnev called him by his name when he walked into the bar," DiMarzo said. "Lvov came over to our table. He wasn't too happy to see me and told me to get lost. I was like 'no problem' and went across the street to wait for my money."

"Did you get your money?"

"Not all of it. Lvov or one of his goons hit Bebnev in the bar, so he said he was keeping some of our share because he had to do the tough stuff," DiMarzo said. "At that point, I just wanted nothing more to do with Bebnev, so I took it and left."

Crossing his arms, Karp walked slowly over to stand in front of DiMarzo. "How did you feel after the murder and you got your money?"

DiMarzo's mouth twisted as he considered his answer. "You know, at first it felt good to have a roll of dough in my pockets," he said. "I don't know. I kept telling myself that these guys — Mr. Carlotta and Vitteli and Joey and Jackie — were caught up in mob stuff and who cared if they wanted to kill each other. Then I read a couple of newspaper articles and people were saying all these good things about Mr. Carlotta, about how he cared for his union guys and was a . . . what was the word they used . . . a reformer. Then I watched the funeral services for him on television and I saw his wife and his baby and . . ."

For the first time since he'd taken the stand, DiMarzo's voice faltered. "I saw her face and how much she loved him and what pain she was in. I started thinking about Mom and how she'd feel if Dad got killed. . . ."

In the gallery, someone in DiMarzo's family cried out, but the judge ignored them as DiMarzo continued. "And I felt like shit. I hardly slept, and when I did all I did was dream about her face, and I kept hearing Mr. Carlotta's voice saying, 'You son of a bitch.' Only he wasn't saying it to Vitteli, he was saying it to me, and I knew he was right, I was a son of a bitch."

"So why didn't you turn yourself in?" Karp asked.

DiMarzo considered the question and shook his head. "I was scared. I didn't want to go to prison for murder. But mostly I didn't want my family to know I'd done this terrible thing. I just kept hoping it would all go away."

"But after you were arrested and indicted, you pleaded not guilty and decided to go to trial with Alexei Bebnev," Karp noted. "If you felt so bad about all of this, why not plead guilty then and take responsibility for what you'd done?"

"The same reasons — I was scared and didn't want my family to know — and also after I got arrested, my family got a photograph in the mail," DiMarzo said. He scowled and looked at Vitteli. "It was a picture of my mom getting in our car and somebody drew a black mark across it. Some piece-of-shit coward was threatening my mom."

"Were you convicted of acting in concert to murder Vince Carlotta?"

"Yes."

"Were you indeed guilty of acting in concert to murder Vince Carlotta?"

"Yes."

"Was that conviction later vacated by my office?"

"Yes."

"Would you please explain to the jury why?" Karp asked.

"Evidently you found out there were some shenanigans with my court-assigned lawyers," DiMarzo replied.

Karp left it at that without explaining that during the Q&A statement he'd taken from him, Jackie Corcione had mentioned that Vitteli had paid the freight on Clooney's legal fees but also for DiMarzo's court-appointed private counsel. Vitteli basically called the shots on the defense and paid off DiMarzo's counsel to let Conrad Clooney, ostensibly Bebnev's lawyer, run the whole show. In effect, DiMarzo was denied effective assistance of counsel, compromising his Sixth Amendent rights.

Prior to Vitteli's trial, Karp had disclosed all of this on the record, *in camera,* with Kowalski present, indicating that DiMarzo would give the jury a very abbreviated, precise answer with respect to the vacating of his first conviction. Pointedly, he was directed to leave out any of Vitteli's misconduct. Both parties agreed and the court so ordered.

A less ethical prosecutor might have let the whole issue pass; after all, the defendants were guilty, as Miller and, later, DiMarzo had admitted. But not Karp. He'd immediately filed to vacate the verdicts and then explained to DiMarzo what it meant. "You are entitled to another trial with a competent attorney to truly represent you," he said.

But DiMarzo shook his head. "Don't bother, I'm going to plead guilty," he said. "I've lived with this long enough." Karp insisted that he confer with his newly assigned counsel before proceeding to a final disposition of his case.

Thereafter, Karp agreed to let DiMarzo plead guilty to manslaughter in the first degree, carrying a maximum of twenty-five years with a mandatory minimum of eight years, four months. The deal was in part due to DiMarzo's willingness to accept responsibility and testify. But Karp also believed that justice required it; there was a difference between Miller as a wheelman, DiMarzo as the lookout, and the shooter Bebnev. The only other person in the whole tragedy whose debt equaled that of the triggerman — besides Barros, who'd already paid his bill — was the man who caused it all to happen, Charlie Vitteli.

"So you could have gone to trial again with a different attorney?" Karp asked.

"Yes, I could have had another trial," Di-Marzo answered.

"Then why not take your chances that another jury might not convict you?"

DiMarzo looked out into the gallery at his family as he answered. "Because I was guilty, and I needed to come clean."

"But aren't you still afraid of prison?"

"I was, but I'm not anymore."

"Why not?"

"Because I walk with Jesus now, and I'm not afraid," DiMarzo replied. "I've asked God for forgiveness, and I know that if something happens to me in prison, I'll go to heaven and wait for my family."

"But how about your family? Weren't you worried about disappointing them and how your admitting the truth might affect your mother's health?"

"Of course," DiMarzo said. "But it was harder on her — knowing I was guilty, even if she didn't want to admit it, and terrified that I couldn't go to heaven to be with her someday if I didn't confess and ask for forgiveness."

"But what about the photograph with the black mark across your mom; aren't you afraid for her and the rest of your family?"

"No," DiMarzo said. "I think they're going to be okay. But either way, they're not afraid; they're all stronger than I ever was because of their faith."

Karp nodded. Marlene had told him about Ivgeny's promise to shield the Di-Marzos from any repercussions, particularly from the Malchek gang. *Sometimes it truly is good to have relatives in low places,* he thought. "But it's one thing to confess to your own crime," he said. "Why agree to testify against Charlie Vitteli?"

DiMarzo looked to the side for a moment to gather his thoughts. "Well, just like I believe it wouldn't be enough to ask God for forgiveness — that I also had to confess to you and pay the price, if I was going to deserve to be forgiven — I knew I needed to do whatever I could to make this . . ." He stopped talking for a moment then: "Well, 'right' isn't the word, I can't make this right, but I can try to do the right thing. Mrs. Carlotta and her baby deserve justice."

Slowly, DiMarzo turned in his seat until he faced Vitteli, whose lip curled like a junkyard dog's as he was confronted. "But it's not just that. Me and Gnat and even Bebnev, we're guilty as sin, but we got used, and the guy that used us is the same guy who wrecked Mrs. Carlotta's life, and he needs to pay the price, too."

"And for the record, Mr. DiMarzo, who was this 'guy' you just referred to?" Karp asked.

"Sitting right over there, Vitteli," DiMarzo said, pointing at him.

As the witness and defendant continued to glare at each other in the hushed courtroom, Karp turned to the judge. "No more questions, Your Honor."

Judge See looked over at Kowalski. "Will you be cross-examining the witness, Mr. Kowalski?"

The defense attorney rose to his feet. "By all means, Your Honor," he said. "But I'd like to wait until after lunch. I know it's a little early, but I'd rather not get started before we break and then have to come back."

Judge See looked at the clock on the wall. He and Karp both knew that following such emotionally powerful testimony, Kowalski wanted its impact on the jury to dissipate before he attacked the witness. But it was not an unreasonable request.

"Very well," the judge said. "We'll break now and resume at twelve thirty sharp." When the jury had left, he said, "The witness may step down."

As DiMarzo rose from his seat, the witness's sister Liza Zito yelled, "We're proud of you, Frankie. Jesus loves you." Her brother smiled and replied, "I love you, too."

Karp looked at the judge to see if he'd reprimand the sister or the witness. Judge

See seemed about to say something but then turned without a word and left the courtroom.

Looking back, Karp watched as DiMarzo hesitated briefly at the gate leading from the well of the courtroom. The young man's eyes were on Antonia Carlotta, whose face was hard and impassive. "I'm sorry," DiMarzo said.

Antonia's expression softened. "Me, too," she said quietly and began to cry.

After lunch, Kowalski's cross-examination of Frank DiMarzo followed his pattern of questioning the witness's motives, and what he derisively called DiMarzo's "jailhouse conversion." However, he concentrated the bulk of his attack on what in his opening statement he called "the lack of anything beyond the word of admitted murderers and liars, and manufactured evidence" tying Charlie Vitteli to the murder of Vince Carlotta.

In particular, he questioned DiMarzo regarding the statement Bebnev overheard and "supposedly" told him about "Charlie wanting this done," then moved on to his recollection of the murder. "Did you hear what Vince Carlotta allegedly said to my client?"

"No. I know he said something."

"But it could have been anything?"

"I didn't hear what he said."

"But you did hear my client say, 'Shoot him'?"

"Yes, because he yelled it."

"If that's what he said, are you sure whether he was talking to Carlotta or Bebnev?"

"He was looking at Bebnev."

"Wasn't everybody looking at Bebnev — Carlotta, my client, Joey Barros — I mean, after all, he's the one holding the gun?"

"Yes, except when Carlotta looked at Vitteli."

"So you don't know who my client was actually speaking to?"

"You're not listening," DiMarzo shot back. "Vitteli was ordering Bebnev to shoot Carlotta. He was holding Mr. Carlotta's arm down."

"Could my client have been trying to get Mr. Carlotta to shoot, or desperately trying to get the gun so he could shoot?"

"That's not what it looked like to me."

"Was it dark outside?"

"Yeah, pretty dark . . . just a streetlight down on the corner."

"And it all happened fast, right?"

"Yes, very fast."

"So is it possible that, along with being

afraid, maybe even having second thoughts, the dark, and the speed with which this went down, you could be mistaken about my client's intentions and what you saw?"

"I don't think so."

"But you don't know for sure, do you?"

"I believe what I said is true."

"Fortunately," Kowalski scoffed, "determining what is true won't be up to you."

"Fortunately," DiMarzo replied, "it's not up to you, either."

For a moment, the defense attorney's face contorted in anger at DiMarzo's quick response. But then he moved on.

However, Karp was surprised that Kowalski spent so little time on the magazine photograph other than to ask DiMarzo when he'd received it from Bebnev. Guma whispered that he thought it was because Kowalski knew how damning the photo was and wanted to deemphasize it, but Karp wasn't so sure. "I think he's up to something," he whispered back, and made another note on his legal pad.

As expected, Kowalski tried to beat DiMarzo up on the sentencing "deal" he'd received. "And won't it be nice to have a letter in your parole file from the District Attorney of New York County stating what a help you were in putting away Charlie Vitteli?" the attorney sneered.

There was a lull. The defense attorney was obviously waiting for DiMarzo to protest. But instead, he nodded. "I know I deserve to be punished. But yes, I don't want to spend twenty-five years of my life in prison, and every year that goes by will be tougher than the one before it. The sooner I can return to my home and family and make them proud of me again, the better. So if I can get out in eight and four, I'm praying that God will be merciful."

Kowalski seemed confused for a moment, but then scowled. "In other words, you're hoping that your testimony here today will buy you that letter?"

Karp felt Guma tense in his seat. He knew that his combative colleague was champing at the bit to object at defense counsel's insinuations. But that was Guma, all-out bull rush. Karp was more subtle; he knew this witness and believed he would rise to this occasion, which would impress the jury more than the prosecutor "rescuing" the witness by objecting.

"I'm not trying to 'buy' anything, but I am trying to earn some things," DiMarzo replied softly. "My self-respect. My family's love and support . . . forgiveness." He looked out at Antonia Carlotta and then at the jurors. "But only God knows when I deserve to walk out of prison, and I'm willing to leave it in His hands. Mr. Karp has promised me nothing but what you've already been told."

Karp hid it well but inside he was smiling. He noted that Guma had relaxed, too. *Sometimes in a trial you just have to trust your instincts,* he thought.

Then it was over. Kowalski said he had no more questions, and Karp didn't feel he could improve on DiMarzo's last statement by asking more himself. Instead, he rested the People's case. Now it was time to see if Vitteli was going to take the bait.

34

As it was nearly time for the afternoon break, Judge See sent the jury off so that Kowalski could make the perfunctory argument that the prosecution had not proved its case beyond a reasonable doubt and demand that it be dismissed. The judge denied his motion and told him to be ready to begin the defense case as soon as they returned from break.

When everyone else was gone, Karp left the courtroom through the side door and made his way to the prosecution witness waiting room. Knocking, he entered. Inside were Marlene and Frank DiMarzo's family. "You'll have twenty minutes," he said gently to the old woman, who sat at a table surrounded by her husband and daughters.

"Thank you, you are kind," the old woman replied.

There was a knock on the door, which opened to allow a court security officer to enter, followed by Frank DiMarzo, who'd changed from the civilian clothes he'd worn into the courtroom back into a gray prison jumpsuit.

The young man wouldn't let his parents visit him in prison. "I don't want them to see or hear what goes on there," he told Marlene during one of her visits with his sister Liza. "I don't want them picturing me in this place." But there hadn't been the opportunity for him to hug his parents one last time after his trial, and that was the one thing he'd asked.

DiMarzo was engulfed by his family, who wept at the same time they patted him on the back and told him how proud they were of him. Karp looked at the security officer and pointed toward the door. "Think it would be okay if you and I waited outside, Lyle?" he asked. "Marlene will keep an eye on things here."

The officer glanced at the grieving family and nodded. "Yeah," he said. "He's not going anywhere, and they've all been through security."

Twenty minutes passed. With court convening soon, Karp knocked on the door and poked his head inside. Frank DiMarzo was sitting next to his mother with his head on her shoulder while she patted his cheek.

"I'm sorry, but it's time," he said.

Tears streamed down her cheeks, but the old woman smiled as she looked up at him and nodded. "My boy's ready, Mr. Karp," she said. "And so am I." She lifted her son's face and looked down into his eyes before kissing his forehead. "*Vai con Dio, mio figlio.* Good-bye for now, my little Frankie. Don't worry, we'll all be together someday in the arms of Jesus. I'm proud of you."

Frank DiMarzo sobbed as he kissed her cheek and stood. But he pulled himself together to shake his father's hand and hug each of his sisters. "I love you all," he said, then turned to Karp. "Thank you." He then walked up to Marlene and held out his hand. "I'm glad we met," he said with a smile. "I owe you more than you know."

Tears in her own eyes, Marlene grasped his hand. "I do know; I've been there myself. As your mother just said, go with God and stay safe, Frank."

This sidebar in the tragedy of Vince Carlotta's murder was still playing in Karp's mind when court reconvened and Judge See asked the court clerk to bring the jury in. Karp had little sympathy for Alexei Bebnev, who he believed was a conscienceless sociopath, especially after Ivgeny told Marlene that Bebnev likely killed two old men for

535

Lvov prior to the Carlotta murder. Nor was Karp in the least bit troubled by the death of Joey Barros, another murderous sociopath, though he did feel sorry for the wife and two daughters Barros had left behind. They'd apparently known nothing of his dark side until his death; the man was pure evil, but his family were also victims.

It was all a reminder to Karp that evil came in shades of gray. Jackie Corcione had been lured by greed and then paralyzed by fear until unable to live with the guilt. He'd done an evil thing, but he wasn't by nature an evil man, like Barros. Nor were Miller and DiMarzo, despite their petty crimes as youths and their willing participation in exchange for money. It didn't mean they weren't guilty of murder or deserving of their fates; with all DiMarzo's talk of God, Karp believed that God allowed men to make their own choices, good or evil, and they'd made theirs and had to suffer the consequences. But the ruined lives of three young men — Corcione, Miller, and DiMarzo, all with good people who loved them and mourned their loss — was nothing to celebrate or even take satisfaction in. Nor was the waste limited to the perpetrators and the man they killed.

Like a stone cast into a still pond, Vince

Carlotta's murder had had a ripple effect, one that devastated many lives. Antonia Carlotta and her son, who would grow up without ever knowing his father, were closest to where the stone had gone in. But also caught in the widening circle were Nicoli Lopez and Billy Jr., Frank DiMarzo's family, and Greg Lusk. Farther out from the center, but still impacted, was the North American Brotherhood of Stevedores, some of whose members, like T. J. Martindale, had attended every day of the trial. They counted on leaders with integrity, like Vince Carlotta, to protect their interests, not rob them and put their safety below the lust for power and money.

Karp looked over at Vitteli. He wondered where the defendant fell along the spectrum of evil. Was his conscience at all troubled by what he'd done? Could he get the blood off his hands? *Closer to Barros than Corcione,* he thought, *and it was his evil that spread to the others. He threw the stone.*

As Kowalski rose to call his first witness, Karp added to the notes on his legal pad. *Shades of gray. Free will. Conscience. Blood on hands. The stone.* The foundational substance, the persuasive power, of his summation had been laid out before the trial even began. But he considered the final arguments afforded attorneys in a case to be subject to an organic process allowing for adjustments depending on from his point of view the defense strategy, as well as thoughts that occurred to him during the course of testimony.

Kowalski's first witness was Al Rubio, a foreman on the docks and a union steward with the North American Brotherhood of Stevedores. He claimed that shortly before his death, Vince Carlotta told him that he suspected Jackie Corcione and Joey Barros of stealing union funds.

"Vince was suspicious because Jackie's little gay-boy lifestyle didn't fit with his salary," Rubio, a big man with a hound dog's jowly face, said. "But he didn't think Corcione would have the balls to do it on his own, and he'd kind of been watching how Corcione and Barros seemed to always have their heads together when Charlie wasn't around."

"What did you think when Vince Carlotta told you he suspected Joey Barros and Jackie Corcione?"

"Ah, I thought it was bullshit," Rubio said with a wave of his hand. "I didn't believe it. I mean, Joey, yeah okay; he was pretty rough, and I never did like the guy. But Leo Corcione's own kid? Stealing the pension funds would be like robbing his old man's grave, and I didn't think Jackie would do that. At least I didn't back then."

"Did he mention Charlie Vitteli as another possible suspect in the thefts?" Kowalski asked.

"Nah, nothin' about Charlie," the man claimed. "I know there was some bad blood about the election, so I think if he thought something like that he would have said so. But Charlie and Vince was like brothers; they grew up on the docks together. Sure, they had their beefs, but after they had it out, they'd sit down over a couple of beers and things was cool again."

Karp noted the obvious attempt to remind the jurors of how the evening at Marlon's had begun and ended. Of course, it was all a lie, and it didn't take him long to tear into it during cross-examination. "Mr. Rubio," he began, "did you ever tell anybody else about this alleged conversation with Mr. Carlotta prior to his death?"

Rubio shook his head. "No, like I said, I didn't want to believe that Leo's kid would do such a thing. I thought Vince was just bitter about the election."

"If he was just bitter about the election, why wouldn't his accusations include Charlie Vitteli, the man who beat him out for union president?"

"Beats me," Rubio replied with a shrug. "Maybe he knew better already and had something on Jackie."

"But he didn't tell you what this 'something' he had was?"

"No, he didn't."

"Did you take any notes or record in any way this alleged conversation?"

"No."

"You just had a hard time believing it so you dismissed it?"

"That's right."

"Did you tell anybody about this alleged conversation with Vince Carlotta after he was murdered and police were looking for suspects?"

Rubio's eyes flicked over to Kowalski and Vitteli before returning to Karp. "No, I heard they caught the guys," he said. "So I figured that was it."

"But the suspects weren't arrested for several weeks," Karp noted. "I guess during that time the idea didn't pop into your head that maybe the murder had something to do with Carlotta's alleged accusations about Corcione and Barros?"

Rubio sat back in his chair and studied Karp. "Yeah, I thought about it," he said. "But those are pretty heavy things to say about somebody if you don't have any evidence."

"Did you make any efforts to gather evidence? Or share yours with the police, who were collecting their own?"

"I might have asked around a little down at the docks," Rubio replied. "But I didn't hear nothin'."

"Can you give us the name of someone you talked to?"

Rubio squirmed a little on the chair. "Uh, you know, my mind's a little discombobulated being up here and all," he said, making an effort to smile at the jurors. "Give me a minute, and I'll try to recall who I talked to."

"While you're trying to recall who you talked to," Karp said as he walked over to the prosecution table where Guma handed him a notebook, "do you remember giving a statement to Detective Fulton and my colleague Mr. Guma a month ago when you first came forward with this information?"

With his eyes fastened on the notebook as Karp walked back to stand in front of him, Rubio nodded. "Uh, yeah, I remember that . . . the guy sitting over there and a big black cop, right?"

"Yes, the man sitting at the prosecution table and a big black cop," Karp repeated drily. He opened the notebook to a tabbed page and then held it up to the witness. "I'm handing you a copy of the transcript of that conversation you had with ADA Guma and Detective Fulton as it was recorded by a stenographer from the District Attorney's Office. I've opened it to page forty-three, where you can see a portion highlighted in yellow. Do you see that?"

"Yes."

"I'd like you to read it to the jury, please."

Rubio frowned and turned to Judge See. "Do I hafta?" he asked.

The judge raised an eyebrow and nodded. "Yes, you hafta."

Looking back down at the page, Rubio let out a deep breath and said, "Okay, here goes. Question: 'Who did you tell about this conversation with Mr. Carlotta?' Answer: 'No one. I didn't think it was important.' "

Rubio stopped and glanced up at Karp, who said, "Go on, all of what's highlighted in yellow."

"Question: 'Did you tell anybody about this conversation after Mr. Carlotta's murder?' Answer: 'No, the papers said it was a robbery and that's what I figured it was.' Question: 'Did you ever talk to anybody at any time about this conversation with Mr. Carlotta?' Answer: 'Not until today with you.' Question: 'No one?' Answer: 'Nope. Nada. Zip.' " Rubio reached the end of the highlighted portion and extended the notebook toward Karp like it was uncomfortably hot in his hands.

As Karp accepted the transcript back, he asked, "So which is it, Mr. Rubio? 'Nope. Nada. Zip'? Or you asked around and can provide us with a name so that we can get that person in here to corroborate your story?"

"Objection," Kowalski said. "The witness already said he's nervous and having a problem remembering who he talked to."

"No," Karp corrected him, "he said that he asked around but he needed a minute to think about who he spoke to. In the meantime, he just testified about a statement he gave to Mr. Guma and Detective Fulton a month ago in which he stated categorically that he didn't tell anybody. 'Nope. Nada. Zip.' I'm trying to ascertain which version is the truth."

"Overruled," Judge See said.

"So which version is it, Mr. Rubio?" Karp demanded.

"I . . . I . . . like I said, I didn't really talk to anybody," Rubio stammered. "It was more listening around, you know, seeing if there was any scuttlebutt down on the docks."

"So you didn't really 'ask around' regarding your alleged conversation with Mr. Carlotta?"

"Uh . . . no," Rubio replied.

"Why not?"

Rubio stared at Karp like a rat looking at a terrier that just wouldn't give him a break. "Like I said, I didn't think it was important," he growled.

"Not important that Vince Carlotta told you he suspected that Jackie Corcione and Joey Barros were stealing union funds, and then a short time later he's gunned down in the presence of both of them? That wasn't important?"

"I didn't put two and two together," Rubio replied.

"Let's turn to your comment that there was bad blood between the defendant and Mr. Carlotta from the election."

"Yeah, a little, but they patched it up. No big deal."

"Are you aware that Mr. Carlotta complained to the U.S. Department of Labor regarding the election?"

"I don't know nothin' about that."

"No? But you are aware that he filed a complaint with union management regarding the election and that his complaint was investigated?"

"Yeah, I know."

"You know because you were part of the investigation that determined his complaint was without merit, right?"

"Yeah. We looked into it and it was bogus, just sour grapes."

"Who appointed you to that investigation?"

Rubio looked over at the defense table. "Mr. Vitteli."

"Mr. Vitteli appointed you to help investigate Mr. Carlotta's allegations that Mr. Vitteli stole the election," Karp said.

"It was a good investigation," Rubio mumbled looking down at his hands.

"Mr. Rubio, who was in charge of Charlie Vitteli's election campaign for the Manhattan office of the North American Brotherhood of Stevedores?"

Rubio licked his lips nervously. "Uh, that would be me."

"And who appointed you union steward, which, if I understand correctly, is a paid position?"

"Vitteli."

"And weren't you recently promoted to foreman, also by Charlie Vitteli?" Karp asked.

"I been with him thirty years, the union, I mean," Rubio said angrily. "I deserved it."

Karp smiled grimly. "I bet you did. No further questions."

Judge See looked at the defense table. "Redirect, Mr. Kowalski?"

"No," Kowalski said rudely as he stood. He caught the glare from See and corrected himself. "No, thank you, Your Honor. We call Sal Amaya."

As the big man squeezed himself into the witness chair, he clearly gave the impression that he didn't want to be there. If he'd had his preference, he would have done whatever he could to avoid testifying. Gone into hiding. Left the country. Even taken the stand and immediately pleaded the Fifth Amendment against self-incrimination. However, the defense needed him to refute Corcione's testimony.

"Mr. Amaya, are you just a bodyguard?" Kowalski asked shortly after questioning began.

"I do a lot of things for Mr. Vitteli," Amaya claimed. "I drive and, uh, sometimes go get the car warmed up. Or sometimes he wants me to deliver something."

"Were you concerned when he told you to go with Randy McMahon on the night of Vince Carlotta's murder?"

"Nah, I wasn't real worried," he said. "He was with two other pretty big dudes, all of 'em tough as nails, plus Jackie, who's a fairy but at least he's another guy."

"Would it be unusual for Mr. Vitteli to send you on ahead?"

"Nah, sometimes I go first to make sure the coast is clear."

"No further questions."

Writing a note on a different pad, Karp rose from his seat but remained at the table. "Mr. Amaya, is that what you were doing when you left Mr. Vitteli? Making sure the coast was clear?"

Amaya considered the question suspiciously. "Yeah, sure I did."

"So did you look in the alley you passed on the way to get Mr. Carlotta's car?"

"Uh, what?

"I asked if you bothered to look in the dark alley that your boss would be walking past after you?"

Amaya nodded. "Uh, yeah, I looked in but didn't see nothin'. I guess those guys must have been hiding behind something. Or maybe they were in the car across the street still."

"That's a good point," Karp said. "Did you notice the car parked across the street from the alley with a man sitting at the steering wheel?"

Amaya frowned. "Uh, yeah, I noticed him."

"But you weren't worried about him," Karp pointed out, "even though he was the getaway driver for the two killers waiting in the alley who you also didn't see?"

"He looked harmless."

"But he was the wheelman for the murderers, so I guess he wasn't harmless?"

Squinting at Karp, Amaya shrugged. "Guess not."

"I guess you're just not very good at your job are you?"

The big man's face contorted into a scowl. "I do my job," he growled.

"Well, you didn't check an alley where two killers were hiding, or wonder if the wheelman parked across a dark street was up to no good," Karp pointed out. "And you were nowhere to be seen when your boss and the others were jumped. Do you think that's doing your job?"

Amaya crossed his arms and glared at Karp. "I'm done talkin'."

Karp turned to the judge. "Your Honor?"

Judge See leaned across his desk toward the witness. "You need to answer Mr. Karp's questions, or I'll hold you in contempt of court."

"Do what you gotta do, Judge," Amaya replied. "I ain't sayin' no more."

"Your Honor, if I may," Karp interjected, holding up the papers he had in his hand.

"Go ahead, Mr. Karp."

"Mr. Amaya, are you refusing to answer any more of my questions?" Karp asked.

Amaya didn't say a word.

"Okay," Karp said. "In lieu of that, let me just read from the Q and A transcript you gave to Assistant DA Ray Guma, who is sitting right here in the courtroom. This is from page nine of that transcript. Question: 'Was it your usual practice to leave Mr. Vitteli when working as his security guard?' Answer: 'No, I stick to him like white on rice.' Question: 'Then why did you leave him on the night of December fifth?' Answer: 'The boss told me to get lost and that's what I did.' Question: 'Was that unusual?' Answer: 'Yeah, and I didn't like it.' Do you recall being asked those questions and giving those answers, Mr. Amaya?"

Silence.

Karp, holding the transcript, asked, "Any of this ringing a bell, Mr. Amaya?" The big man stayed silent with his arms crossed. "No? Then let me continue. Question: 'Did you look in the alley as you went past?' Answer: 'No.' Question: 'Did you notice a car parked across the street with a man sitting in the dark at the steering wheel?' Answer: 'I don't remember.' Do you recall being asked those questions and giving those answers to Assistant DA Ray Guma, who questioned you for this Q and A?"

Returning the transcript to the prosecution table, Karp looked at Vitteli as he asked, "Your story seems to have changed, Mr. Amaya. Have you anything to say about that?"

Amaya glared once more at Karp and then looked up at the ceiling like a petulant child.

Judge See crooked a finger to summon two security officers. "Mr. Amaya, I'm holding you in contempt of court. You'll be escorted from this courtroom and held in the Tombs until I've had a chance to deal with you." Turning to the jury, he said, "I'm directing you to disregard this witness's entire testimony." He then looked to where Kowalski and Vitteli sat tight-lipped. "Mr. Kowalski, call your next witness."

"We call Martin Bryant," Kowalski said, ignoring the scene of Amaya being escorted from the courtroom by the security officers. The defense attorney looked over at Karp and furrowed his brow as the prosecutor began leafing through some papers before leaning over to whisper to Guma, who got up and left the courtroom.

"Mr. Bryant is an attorney with the complaints division of the U.S. Department of Labor in Washington, D.C., and, although unnamed, has been referenced by Mr. Karp during this trial, as well as interviewed by Detective Fulton. The People are well aware of his relationship to this case," Kowalski argued.

Judge See sighed. It was normal, particularly in a murder case, to grant the defense more leeway than the prosecution, and this was one of those times. "I'm going to allow it," he said.

A minute later, a balding, mousy-looking man with round, wire-rim glasses entered the courtroom and froze until instructed by the judge to come forward and be sworn in. He then climbed up on the witness stand and sat there blinking rapidly and adjusting his glasses as Kowalski approached the stand. "Mr. Bryant, do you recall meeting with Vince Carlotta and Mahlon Gorman in the late fall of last year?" the defense attorney asked.

"I have a vague recollection of a very short meeting with them," Bryant replied.

"Can you give the jury a synopsis of what the meeting entailed?"

Bryant swallowed and nodded. "As I recall, it was mostly informational," he said. "They had some concerns about a recent election of the North American Brotherhood of Stevedores union and wanted to know what their options were as far as the federal government's possible involvement."

"Did they mention anyone with the union in particular whose actions concerned them?"

"I recall one," Bryant replied, blinking even more rapidly. "They apparently had some concerns about the union's chief financial officer, Jackie Corcione."

At the mention of Corcione's name, the gallery of the courtroom buzzed. But Karp sat impassively as Kowalski asked his next question. "Did they say how their concerns about Corcione and the election were related?"

"Well, they didn't have any evidence, at least nothing they showed me," Bryant said, "but my recollection was that there was some concern that Corcione might have been stealing from the union pension fund and that he was worried about an audit if Mr. Carlotta became president."

"But Corcione wasn't worried about an audit with Mr. Vitteli as president?"

Bryant nodded. "I asked them that, but

apparently they felt that Mr. Corcione had pulled the wool over Mr. Vitteli's eyes. If I understand the dynamics right, Mr. Vitteli was very loyal to the union founder, Leo Corcione, and perhaps blind in that regard as far as the senior Corcione's son."

"So were you able to answer their questions?"

"As far as I know," Bryant said with a shrug. "I told them that due to the Landrum-Griffin Act, the federal government — i.e., the Labor Department — couldn't legally get involved until they'd exhausted all their remedies through the union's own processes."

"Did they seem satisfied with your answer?"

"I don't know if they were happy," Bryant replied. "But it's the law and I think they understood that."

"Did you hear from Mr. Carlotta or his attorney, Mahlon Gorman, again?"

"No. The next thing I heard was that Mr. Carlotta had been killed during the course of a robbery."

"Were you aware that in the meantime, Mr. Carlotta filed a formal complaint with the union and that an investigation was conducted?" Kowalski asked.

"Not until well after the fact," Bryant replied.

"When did you learn about the investigation conducted by the union?"

"I was told about it by Mr. Vitteli," Bryant said.

"When was this?"

"In June, after the trial."

"The trial of Alexei Bebnev and Frank Di-Marzo, who were convicted of Mr. Carlotta's murder?"

"I don't know the names, but yes."

"And what was the purpose of your contact with Mr. Vitteli?"

"He contacted me," Bryant said. "He said he had some concerns that Mr. Carlotta might have been correct about irregularities in the union election."

"Was there anyone in particular he mentioned?"

"Yes. Jackie Corcione."

"Did Mr. Vitteli tell you what he felt was amiss?"

Bryant adjusted his glasses again and nodded. "It was similar to what I was told by Mr. Carlotta. He believed there were some indications that Mr. Corcione was trying to prevent an audit by Mr. Carlotta."

"Who was in charge of the union investigation?"

"It's my understanding that Mr. Corcione was in charge."

The murmurs that had swept back and forth across the gallery increased in volume. "What did you tell him?"

"Again, the law requires that any such grievances be handled by the union's own bylaws and practices before the Labor Department would get involved," Bryant said. "I discussed the law with Mr. Vitteli and he agreed to reopen the union investigation into the alleged election irregularities, as well as an audit of the union accounts."

"Do you know if either of these occurred?"

"I don't know," Bryant said. "Mr. Vitteli was arrested a short time later, and there was no further contact with my office until I received a subpoena from you."

Kowalski walked over to the defense table and picked up three sets of papers, one of which he deposited on the prosecution table before returning to the witness stand. "Mr. Bryant, did you take any notes or recordings of your first meeting with Mr. Carlotta and Mr. Gorman?"

Bryant shook his head. "No. As I said, it was mostly informational."

"What about the subsequent meeting with Mr. Vitteli? Did you take notes of that meeting?"

"I did," Bryant agreed. "Not many but some."

"Why did you take notes of this second meeting but not the first with Mr. Gorman and Mr. Carlotta?"

"Well, several reasons," Bryant said. "Obviously, the murder of Mr. Carlotta got my attention, especially after hearing from Mr. Vitteli. And this was the second time I'd heard similar allegations."

Kowalski handed a set of the papers to Bryant. "Do you recognize these papers?"

"Um, yes," Bryant said as he leafed through his set. "This appears to be a copy of the originals of my notes from my discussion with Mr. Vitteli."

"I noticed that these notes are mostly a word or two, sometimes three," Kowalski said, looking at his copy. "For instance, I see 'Corcione,' followed by a fairly large space and then 'voting irregularities.' And then there are the words 'pension funds' and 'Cayman Islands.' A little farther down I see, 'Joey Barros' with a question mark. And finally a statement, 'Vince was right,' with an exclamation point."

"Yes. Those are my notes and they fit with my recollection of my discussion with Mr. Vitteli."

Kowalski turned to Karp. "No more questions, your witness."

Sitting for a moment, studying the witness, Karp furrowed his brow. He then rose from his seat and made his way to the jury rail. "So my understanding is that Mr. Carlotta and Mr. Gorman traveled to Washington, D.C., for a short informational meeting with you?"

Licking his lips nervously, Bryant nodded. "Yes, that's correct."

"And they mentioned issues with the election and some concerns about Jackie Corcione?"

"Yes."

"And you told them that because of the Landrum-Griffin Act, they had to first go through the union grievance process?"

"Yes."

"And to your knowledge, that's what happened?"

"Yes."

"Do you remember the date of that meeting."

"Not precisely. Sometime in the latter part of November."

"Would November eighteenth sound about right?"

"Yes. That's about what I was thinking."

"Then in June, following the trial of Alexei Bebnev and Frank DiMarzo, you testified that the defendant also contacted you with similar concerns regarding the election and Jackie Corcione, and something to do with Joey Barros?"

Bryant shoved his glasses back up his nose. "That's correct."

"Was that the first time the defendant contacted you or you him?"

"Yes. I believe so."

"You don't know?"

"No, I do. That was the first time."

"Did you file a report regarding the defendant's concerns regarding the election, Jackie Corcione, or Joey Barros?"

"Um, no."

"Why not? You said there were several reasons, including the murder of Vince Carlotta, that you took notes of this meeting. But it didn't warrant filing any sort of official report?"

Bryant pulled a handkerchief from his back pocket and dabbed at his forehead. "I was waiting to see what would become of Mr. Vitteli's efforts to reopen the union investigation."

"I see," Karp said as he returned to the prosecution table, where he picked up a thick brown manual. "Mr. Bryant, does the U.S. Department of Labor have any sort of rules and procedures about what to do in a case like this?"

Seeing what Karp had in his hand caused Bryant to swallow hard several times. "Um, yes, and I see that you have a copy of our department manual."

"Yes, this book," Karp said, holding it up, "is the U.S. Department of Labor manual dealing with, among other things, the protocol to be followed by your office in regard to complaints. You're familiar with it?"

"Yes."

"Then are you aware of Section Twenty-Four B that states that such complaints, whether they're verbal or formal written complaints, be noted and a report filed with a supervisor?"

Bryant tried to smile but it looked more like a nervous grin. "Actually, that's more of a guideline than strict protocol."

Placing the manual on the jury rail, Karp opened it. "I'm reading here from page 241 that, and I quote, 'any contact with union representatives or union members regarding potential malfeasance and/ or criminal conduct involving union management be reported by the grievance officer to his direct supervisor.' Does that sound familiar?"

"I'm aware of that section," Bryant replied. "But like I said, we are given a lot of latitude on what constitutes an issue rising to the level of filing a formal report."

"Is there anything in this manual that you are aware of that says anything about this purported latitude?" Karp asked.

"Um, no, it's more of an understanding that reporting every contact would be a paperwork nightmare. We get dozens if not hundreds of complaints every year."

"Did you file a report after meeting with the defendant?"

"Uh, not yet."

"Not yet?"

"Well, I'm running a bit behind with my paperwork."

"A bit behind reporting contact with union representatives involved in a murder case?"

Bryant took off his glasses and wiped them with a shirtsleeve before putting them back on. "I know it seems odd," he said. "But I find I need to do things in the order in which —"

"Mr. Bryant, who is your direct supervisor?" Karp interrupted.

"Uh, that would be Bill Clark."

"Did you ever say or write anything to Bill Clark regarding any of these contacts or the allegations?"

"Well, uh, now that you mention it, I think I did say something to him at one of our meetings."

"And what was his reaction?"

"That I should continue to monitor the situation."

"Really?" Karp said and turned to the back of courtroom, where Guma had reappeared. He nodded and Guma opened the door to let another man enter.

Bryant, as well as everyone else in the courtroom, turned to look and his eyes grew suddenly wide. "Mr. Bryant, do you recognize the man standing in the aisle at the back of this room?"

The witness's hands were shaking as he reached for a cup of water and knocked it over. "I'm sorry, I —"

As the witness tried to recover, Karp turned to face the defense table as he demanded, "Answer the question, Mr. Bryant. Do you recognize the man standing in the back of the courtroom?"

As if afraid to look, Bryant kept his eyes on his cup of water as he nodded.

"I'm afraid a nod won't do, Mr. Bryant," Karp said.

"Yes, he's my supervisor, Mr. Clark," Bryant squeaked.

"I'm going to ask you again, Mr. Bryant, if anything was said to Mr. Clark regarding your contact with Mr. Carlotta or Mr. Vitteli?"

"I . . . uh . . . I don't remember. I might have meant to but —"

"And is it true that you are given a 'lot of latitude' on reporting this sort of contact?"

"I may have misspoken about that."

"Is it true that the first time you had any contact with the defendant was when he contacted you in June after the trial of Alexei Bebnev and Frank DiMarzo?"

Mopping now at this forehead, Bryant looked up at the ceiling, then at the defense table, and finally back to Karp. He shrugged his shoulders but still didn't say anything.

"Mr. Bryant, answer my question."

"I can't," Bryant replied.

"Why not?"

"Because I'm going to . . . uh . . . plead the Fifth and . . . uh . . . that's about what I can say about that," Bryant replied. His head dropped and he sat staring at his feet, shaking his head back and forth.

With a wry smile on his face, Karp continued to look at Vitteli as he said to the judge, "I ask that the witness's entire testimony be stricken and that he be remanded pending further official action." *One last act before the final curtain,* he thought. *Vitteli has no choice but to take the stand.*

35

Glancing over his shoulder at where Kowalski and Vitteli argued quietly but vehe-
mently, Karp knew that the curtain was rising and the last act was about to begin. The
scorned, beleaguered villain, backed into a
corner of his own making, believed his only
option was to try to fight his way out by
taking the stand in his own defense.

Most defendants chose not to testify. If
they did, though, it would allow the defendant, again through his attorney's questions,
to explain his actions or attempt to discredit
other witnesses or evidence, it also opened
them to grilling by the prosecution and the
admission of evidence that otherwise would
not have been heard or seen by the jury.
However, that wasn't always enough to stop
a defendant who believed that he had to
take the stand to win.

Human nature comes into play, especially
if the prosecution's case is so strong that

defendants feel their only chance is to persuade the jury that they are innocent, or at least attempt to cast some doubt. And perhaps in this case, the defense hoped to find that one homophobic juror, or one whose distrust of government was so strong that they'd cling to whatever conspiracy theory the defense threw out, no matter how lacking in evidence.

There's probably some of all of that going on here, Karp thought. The People's case was strong. The witnesses had been credible, bolstered by convincing corroborating evidence. That and the defense witnesses had been worthless . . . or worse. Kowalski knew that after the defense rested, Karp would be bringing Bill Clark, the supervisor of Martin Bryant at the Department of Labor, as a rebuttal witness to impeach his employee's testimony. And because Clark was a rebuttal witness, and therefore what he had to say had not been turned over to the defense, Kowalski didn't know everything he would testify to: such as the half-dozen telephone calls between Bryant and Vitteli's office, or the fact that Bryant had been suspended without pay and was currently under investigation.

However, conventional defense wisdom went out the door with some defendants who simply let their egos — knocked about during the trial by the prosecution — override their attorneys' trial strategy. Karp knew that Vitteli was seething at the depictions of him as a coward to the public and especially the members of his union, a dozen of whom, including T. J. Martindale, were in the courtroom.

So as the two men argued on the other side of the aisle, Karp sat impassively like a chess grand master who had patiently laid his trap starting with his first move and now waited for his adversary to make one last mistake that would spell checkmate. But Kowalski was putting up a fight.

Karp knew the defense attorney's reasons went beyond protecting his client. If Vitteli took the stand and Kowalski asked him questions that he knew would elicit lies, he was suborning perjury, a felony that could get him disbarred and thrown in jail. Kowalski was already walking on thin ice by putting Bryant, who for whatever reason was willing to lie, on the stand. He had to know that Vitteli's only chance was to lie, too. All of which could put Kowalski on the hot seat after the trial.

"Mr. Kowalski, has the defendant decided whether to testify?" Judge See asked.

With a sigh, Kowalski stood up, glared one

more time at Vitteli, and then nodded. "Yes, Your Honor, the defendant will take the stand."

"All right then," See said, pointing at the witness chair, "let the defendant come forward to be sworn in."

Vitteli got up from the defense table and stalked over to the witness stand, where he placed his hand on the Bible and swore to tell the truth. He then stepped up into the witness box, straightened his suit with a jerk, adjusted his tie and handkerchief, and settled into the chair, looking like he wanted to hit somebody. But his attorney calmed him down by starting off with a series of softball questions about how he got started with the union, his relationship with Leo Corcione, and his role through the years leading up to the presidency.

"And how long have you known Jackie Corcione?" Kowalski asked.

"Since the day he was born," Vitteli answered. "I was already a union steward reporting directly to Leo. The kid was practically my little brother."

"Did you know he was a homosexual?"

Vitteli chuckled. "Of course I did. Knew it before he probably knew it himself."

"Did you ever tell his dad, Leo?"

"Nah," Vitteli said. "I figured it was his

566

business, you know? It would have broke his old man's heart; I know he wanted grandkids and all that." He paused as if having to control his emotions. "I loved that old man and didn't want to see him hurt or disappointed in his kid."

Kowalski switched his questioning to Joey Barros. "Did you ever have cause to suspect Barros of stealing union funds?"

"You see, that's what doesn't make sense," Vitteli said. "I mean, I knew Jackie lived pretty high on the hog, but I figured it was because he was getting an allowance from his old man above and beyond his salary; then when Leo died, Jackie was blowing through his inheritance. But Joey was a family guy. He turned his check over to his wife, for God's sake. He had two girls in college and was always complaining about how much he was paying in tuition and books and stuff like that."

"So did you see any indication that Barros was involved in these thefts?" Kowalski asked.

"Well, you know, like I said, at least not while the old man was alive," Vitteli answered. "But after Vince's death and I started nosing around, I noticed he wasn't complaining about his bills no more. Joey was a pretty dour guy, but he seemed happy all the time. I even wonder if he had some little chickie stashed away on the side and was just waiting for his kids to graduate and then he was going to be off to someplace sunny with this bimbo and his share of the money him and Jackie was stealing."

"Did you personally trust Joey Barros?"

"Like a brother," Vitteli said. "Him, me, and Vince grew up on the docks together. We always had each other's backs whenever any rough stuff went down — like when the mob tried to move in or the Longshoremen tried recruiting around our docks. Joey was a tough son of a bitch, but you'd have had to see him with his wife and kids to know that underneath the tough-guy persona he had a heart of gold. That's why I'm having such a hard time believing he was involved."

Walking over to the prosecution table, Kowalski picked up the photograph from the union magazine, the *Dock,* and held it up. "Mr. Vitteli, much has been made of People's Exhibit Twenty-Eight. Do you recognize this photograph?"

"Yeah, sure," Vitteli replied. "It's from the convention last year in Atlantic City."

"But do you recognize this particular copy of that page from the magazine?"

Vitteli nodded. "I brought it to the meeting at Marlon's," he explained. "I wanted to sort of remind Vince that we were all a team and about the good times we've had."

"And did you circle Mr. Carlotta's face and write his name on the photograph?"

"I did," Vitteli agreed. "It's sort of hard to explain out of context, but I did that there at the table. He was pissed off — some guys, like Mahlon Gorman — had been feeding him a bunch of crap, or at least I thought it was at the time, about the election. I was trying to say, this guy here — the one I was circling, Vince Carlotta — was one of us . . . me, Joey, and Jackie. That's sort of what finally broke the ice. After that, we was good and mostly tied one on talking about old times."

Kowalski returned the photograph to the prosecution table, raising an eyebrow as he looked at Karp. "Can you explain how this photograph came to be in the possession of Frank DiMarzo?"

Vitteli turned to the jurors. "Sure," he told them, "that's easy. It was in my wallet those guys took after they shot Vince. I don't know why that DiMarzo guy kept it. Pretty stupid to tie himself to a murder like that."

And you, Karp thought as he glanced at the jurors to see how they were taking the explanation. He noticed that a couple of jurors were taking notes and knew it was something he would need to address. Looking down at the photograph, he suddenly knew just how he'd do it.

After returning the photograph, Kowalski moved on to several questions regarding the slush fund accounts. "Were you aware of the accounts created by Jackie Corcione?"

"Yes," Vitteli admitted. "I received a report from Jackie every month."

"What was your understanding regarding the purpose of these accounts?"

"I was told that they were created to account for union investments using the pension funds," Vitteli said. "I asked about them once and Jackie explained that income and losses from the investments had to be kept separate from the pension accounts for tax purposes."

"Did this make sense to you?"

Vitteli shrugged. "Let me put it this way, I'm not much of a numbers guy with respect to this intricate accounting. I relied on Jackie, as our chief financial officer, to handle that part of union business and just keep me in the loop as far as general numbers regarding the big picture. Like, I needed to know how much we had in the bank and whether we were able to pay our bills on time."

"So Jackie Corcione's description that

these investments and outright theft of monies ended up in a slush fund, or, as he put it, 'retirement account,' for you, him, and Barros is a lie?"

"I can't say for the other two," Vitteli answered. "I mean, it looks bad, like they was involved in some nefarious stuff. But I never touched a dime of union money outside of my salary."

"But your name is on the accounts, and your signature on file as one of two needed to access the accounts?"

"I signed a lot of stuff," Vitteli said. "Maybe I should have been more careful, but whatever Jackie shoved in front of me, I put my John Hancock on it. But I know I never signed nothing that shows I took a cent. Like I said, Jackie handled the money side; I was up to my eyeballs trying to do what was right by my guys on the docks."

"Like steal our money," T. J. Martindale yelled from the gallery.

Judge See banged his gavel, staring at Martindale. He said quietly but firmly, "I'll tolerate no more outbursts. Everyone here will act like an adult. Failure to respect these proceedings will result in removal from this courtroom." He turned to the jury. "Please disregard that statement. I'm sure you are aware that it does not in any way constitute evidence for you to consider in your future deliberations. You may proceed, Mr. Kowalski."

Kowalski turned back to the witness. "Mr. Vitteli, are there some members of the North American Brotherhood of Stevedores who don't like you and would like to see you convicted?"

Vitteli's head dropped, as if the question troubled him. "Yeah, afraid so," he said.

"What are their motives?"

"Hard to say for all of them," Vitteli answered slowly. "But I know some of the young turks have been agitated thinking they'd get a better deal if we merged with the International Association. And . . ." He stopped talking for a moment.

"And?"

"I hate to say this, but some of 'em hear stuff about the mob wanting to buy in and get dollar signs in their eyes."

A low grumble began in the gallery, but Judge See stopped it with a look.

"Have you ever heard of an organized crime gang called the Malcheks?" Kowalski asked.

"I never heard of those guys until this trial," Vitteli said. "To be honest, it sounds like a bad B movie. But I do know that some Russian gangs have made it pretty clear that they'd like access to our docks. But we've also made it pretty clear that the North American Brotherhood of Stevedores will not let that happen."

"I know this has been said before, but let's make it clear. Were you at the meeting at Marlon's in which Jackie Corcione and Joey Barros met with Marat Lvov, an associate of the Malchek gang, and Alexei Bebnev, a convicted murderer?"

"No, I wasn't. I never even heard of this meeting until I read about it in the newspapers during Bebnev's trial."

Kowalski moved on to the election and Carlotta's attempts to have it overturned, before turning to Vitteli's role in the union investigation into the allegations. "I, of course, accepted the grievance as the representative of the union management board," the defendant explained.

"Were you in charge of the investigation?"

Vitteli scrunched up his face. "I guess as union president I am responsible for everything that goes on," he said. "But because of the conflict of interest, I put Jackie in charge of the investigation. Like I said, some of the guys unfortunately don't like me, but they knew that Vince and Jackie got along swell . . . or so I thought . . . so I thought they'd accept that he'd be fair. I wasn't worried; I figured that Vince was just having sour grapes or he was getting bad advice."

"Did something change your mind about these allegations about election improprieties?"

"Yeah, after Vince got killed, guys like Al Rubio were telling me that they were hearing rumors that maybe what Vince said wasn't all wrong . . . that maybe there'd been a cover-up by Jackie and Barros. I started asking questions myself and thought Vince was maybe onto something — not just the election, but maybe whatever those two were up to with the pension funds."

"What did you do from there?"

"That's when I contacted the Labor Department. I knew Vince had talked to somebody there, who sent him back to the union with his grievance. So I asked to speak to that guy."

"Martin Bryant?"

"Yeah."

"Did you know Mr. Bryant before this?"

"Never met him."

Kowalski half smiled when he asked, "Mr. Vitteli, are you an expert in how the Labor Department conducts its business?"

"No," Vitteli replied with a shake of his head. "A lot of it is Greek to me."

"Do you have any knowledge of whether

Mr. Bryant filed a report regarding Mr. Carlotta's alleged complaint with his superior?"

"No idea."

"Do you have any knowledge of whether Mr. Bryant filed a report with his superior regarding your concerns?"

"I saw him taking notes, but I don't know what he did with any of it. The only thing I got from him was that because of the federal law, I had to take my concerns up with the union grievance policy first."

"Would you have any idea why he would or wouldn't follow his department's rules?"

"Just another lazy bureaucrat, I guess," Vitteli said with a shrug. "Or maybe somebody paid him off."

"Were you that someone, Mr. Vitteli?"

"Absolutely not."

"And were you able to bring up your concerns to the union?"

Vitteli shook his head and stared hard at Karp. "No, the district attorney saw fit to charge me with a crime I didn't commit before I could."

"Are you aware of any reasons why the district attorney would do that?"

"Objection," Karp said, rising to his feet. "Your Honor, defense counsel has throughout these proceedings attempted to insinuate that I had some sort of personal vendetta against the defendant, and that my office and the NYPD somehow concocted this plot to unfairly convict him of murder. I have repeatedly requested that if counsel has any evidence to substantiate these outrageous statements to present it forthwith, and Your Honor has concurred. But defense counsel has given the jury nothing but a lot of hot air and continued efforts to obfuscate the facts. The reasons why Mr. Vitteli was indicted and sits here today on trial for murder are the facts, not some personal vendetta."

With equanimity, Judge See sighed. "Mr. Kowalski, we've been through this a few times already, haven't we? Yet you keep persisting by making these charges while offering no evidentiary support. Please think about my admonitions so that you won't repeat this conduct. The objection is sustained."

Red-faced and angry, Kowalski turned again to the witness. "All right, let's turn to the night Vince Carlotta was murdered by the man who met with Jackie Corcione and Joey Barros at Marlon's," he snarled. "First, would you please explain to the jurors about Sal Amaya."

"Sure, what do you want to know?" Vitteli said.

"Well, what about the testimony that he 'never' left your side if you were out in public?"

Vitteli snorted. "That's a laugh," he said. "To be honest, Sal's a big dumb guy who's more of an errands runner and driver than he is a bodyguard. I mean, it don't hurt to have a big body around sometimes; there's plenty of guys who don't like me and it's smart to have someone watching my back. But that night, I didn't need him watching nothin'."

"And why is that? As the district attorney pointed out, it was after midnight in Hell's Kitchen when you left Marlon's."

Vitteli shook his head and laughed. "With all due respect," he sneered, "the DA's been watching too many movies. Hell's Kitchen ain't the rough, tough place it used to be. Like every other neighborhood in Manhattan with buildings that can be turned into lofts, art galleries, and restaurants, it's been gentrified."

"Were there any other reasons you felt safe sending Mr. Amaya to get your car?"

"You bet. I was with Joey Barros and Vince Carlotta, neither one of them a shrinking violet, and then there's me. Forget Jackie, but there's not a lot of street punks who were going to look at the three of us other guys and want to fuck with us — pardon my French. In fact, the first thing I thought when the two guys jumped out of the alley was, *Now, here's a couple of idiots looking to get the shit kicked out of them.* But then I saw the gun."

"What was your reaction to seeing the gun?"

"Hell, I stuck my hands up in the air, like this," Vitteli said, demonstrating. "I ain't a fool to mess with a gun; for all I knew, the guy was some hyped-up junkie with an itchy finger and hair trigger."

"Is that why you grabbed Mr. Carlotta's arm?"

Vitteli nodded. "Yeah. I knew Vince was a hothead, and he'd had a bit much to drink. So I was kind of looking at him sideways to make sure he didn't do nothing stupid and cause this yahoo to pull the trigger. But sure enough, Vince has to go for a gun. I didn't even know he had one."

"So you grabbed his arm?"

"I did. I thought he was going to get us all shot, and our wallets weren't worth it," Vitteli said.

"What about the testimony that he called you a son of a bitch?"

"He wasn't talking to me," Vitteli said. "You sort of had to be there to understand, but he's saying it to the guy with the mask at the same time he's pulling his own gun."

"But the witnesses thought he was addressing you?"

"I guess it might have looked that way," Vitteli conceded. He turned toward the jurors. "You have to understand that all this stuff was happening at once. Vince goes for his gun and starts to call the guy a son of a bitch just when I grabbed his arm, so sure he's going to look at me, wondering what in the hell I'm doing."

"But all you were trying to do was prevent a shootout?"

"That's right," Vitteli agreed. "I was just trying to keep the situation from getting worse." He hung his head. "I've thought about that a lot. I wish now I'd just let Vince go for it. He might have got the guy. But I was honestly just doing what I thought was the smart thing. And, I don't know, maybe I sort of panicked."

"What about the testimony that you shouted, 'Do it!' "

"I don't know where they got that from," Vitteli complained. "I know what I said, and what I said was 'Don't do it!' "

"Who were you talking to, the gunman or Mr. Carlotta?"

"You know, this may sound funny, but I

can't tell you," Vitteli said. "I mean, two guys jump out of an alley, one of 'em's got a gun pointed at us. Vince goes for his gun, I try to grab him to prevent a bloodbath at the same time he calls the gunman a son of a bitch, and that's when I yelled, 'Don't do it,' but 'BOOM,' Vince goes down. In the heat of all that, I couldn't tell you whether I was yelling at Vince to stop or pleading with the gunman not to shoot."

"Mr. Vitteli, after Mr. Carlotta was shot, did you attempt to render aid?"

"Yeah, I was trying to give him CPR to keep his heart going," Vitteli said. Then his eyes narrowed. "And you know something that's only dawned on me now. Barros and Jackie kept telling me he was gone and that I needed to stop. I never thought about it before, but it's like they didn't want me to help him."

Nodding as if it was now clear to him, too, Kowalski walked over to the prosecution table and picked up the front page of the *Times* with the photograph from the murder scene. "I know you saw this photograph," he said, showing it to the jurors and the witness. "How would you describe what you were experiencing in this photograph?"

"I was in shock," Vitteli said. "Distraught. I mean, Vince and I sometimes fought, like brothers in any family will, and some of it wasn't too pretty. I know he wasn't happy about the election, and I know now he might have had a legitimate beef, but at the end of the day, we respected each other and were friends."

As Kowalski returned the front page to the prosecution table, he asked, "Oh, and Mr. Vitteli, do you recall saying anything about seeing any women near the alley entrance?"

"I didn't say nothin' about seeing no women," Vitteli scoffed. "That's really out of left field."

"Could you explain then why Mr. Carlotta's driver, Randy McMahon, said he saw three women on the way to pick up the car, and then Jackie Corcione claimed you made that statement?"

"You tell me," Vitteli replied, scowling at Karp. "It seems to me that maybe *somebody* got those two together so they could get their stories straight."

Kowalski and Vitteli both turned toward Karp as if expecting him to object again. But this time Karp simply looked at them like a predator sizing up his prey. *Welcome to my web, said the spider to the fly,* he thought.

The defense attorney furrowed his brow

581

and looked back at Vitteli, who shrugged. "No further questions."

36

As Karp stood at the end of the jury box closest to the witness stand, he and Vitteli locked eyes. Everyone present knew they were witnessing the last rounds of a fight between two men who loathed each other and in which no quarter would be offered.

"Mr. Vitteli, why is this the first time anybody, outside of your lawyer, has heard of your version of the events leading up to and including the night Vince Carlotta was murdered?" Karp asked.

"What do you mean?"

"Well, did you tell the police detective who took your statement that night what you just told the jury?"

"Maybe he didn't ask me the right questions," Vitteli countered. "And like I said, I was in shock."

"Were you in shock when you gave a statement two days later to Assistant District Attorney Ray Guma?"

"I might have been. That whole time is sort of fuzzy to me."

"Did you tell the detective or Mr. Guma anything about grabbing Vince's arm to prevent a shootout?"

"No."

"Did you say anything about Vince calling the gunman a son of a bitch?"

"No."

"Or that you yelled, 'Don't do it!' "

"Like I said, I wasn't thinking clearly."

"Yet you were thinking clearly enough," Karp said as he held up a transcript he'd been holding in his hand, "and I'm reading from the Q and A statement you gave to Mr. Guma, 'Two guys jumped out of the alley and demanded our wallets and watches'. . . . And, 'I didn't get a good look at them, they were dressed in black with ski masks'. . . . And, 'Vince went for his gun, but the guy shot him.' You recall telling that to Assistant DA Ray Guma?"

"That sounds about right," Vitteli replied.

"Well, you were thinking clearly enough to recount those items, isn't that right?"

"Yeah, so? I remembered some of it," Vitteli replied.

"And were you still in shock," Karp said, walking over to the prosecution table, where he put the transcript down and picked up another, "when you testified at the trial of Alexei Bebnev and Frank DiMarzo four months later?"

"No. I might have been a little nervous, but I wasn't in shock."

"Not so nervous that you didn't joke about the gunman, Alexei Bebnev, a Russian immigrant, having a singsongy Puerto Rican or Mexican accent, isn't that right?" Karp said, holding up the transcript.

"Yeah, sure," Vitteli responded. "Like I said, I was nervous and trying to break the ice a little. You were kind of in my face."

"Well, let's look at some of your other testimony from the trial," Karp said, ignoring the last comment. "Do you recall saying, 'He reached into his pocket; I guess he had a gun. That's when the fucker, excuse my French, shot him. Then shot him again.' Does that ring a bell?"

"I guess."

"You guess? Seems pretty definitive to me," Karp replied. "Again no mention of grabbing Mr. Carlotta's arm or any verbal exchanges, correct?"

"That's right. Maybe I wasn't asked the right question."

"Well, you were asked plenty of other questions," Karp shot back. "Here's your response when you were asked if you recognized either of the two defendants. You said no, and then followed up by adding, 'Those two ain't the guys who killed Vince.' Then you were asked a question on page twenty-three: 'Why not?' Answer: 'One thing is they ain't big enough. And I don't think either of the assholes had blue eyes like pumpkin-head over there.' You were pretty clear about that, but those men — Alexei Bebnev and Frank DiMarzo were both convicted, and Mr. DiMarzo testified at this trial that he was indeed one of the assailants. So those two guys were the two assailants who murdered Vince Carlotta?"

Vitteli pulled out his handkerchief and mopped at his brow. "It was dark. I was mistaken."

"Yes, you were," Karp replied. "But again, there was no mention of any of this story you just told the jury, was there?"

"It's been a while," Vitteli explained. "Some things came to me after that trial jogged my memory."

"So then you were also mistaken at the other trial when you testified that Jackie Corcione had no role in the union investigation into Vince Carlotta's complaint about the elections except, and I'm quoting from the trial transcript page 3015, 'He sort of sat in on it to give legal advice, but he didn't vote.' Am I correct?"

"I might have misspoke there," Vitteli said now reaching for a cup of water and taking a sip. "He was . . . uh . . . in charge of the investigation. He wasn't supposed to vote though . . . but I'm not sure what happened. I stayed out of it."

"Because it would have been a conflict of interest, right?"

"Yeah, right."

"I have one more question related to your testimony at the other trial," Karp said. "You were asked about the confrontation at Marlon's Restaurant and you said, 'My associate Joey Barros and Vince had some words,' but there's no mention of Jackie Corcione being involved in any confrontation with Mr. Carlotta. But yet that's what you told this jury. Why is that?"

"I forgot that Jackie kind of started it, and Joey came to his defense."

"Kind of hard to keep your stories straight when they're made up out of thin air, isn't it, Mr. Vitteli?"

"I'm telling the truth now, that's all I know," Vitteli replied.

Karp walked out in front of the witness box and stared up at Vitteli, who had no choice but to meet his look. "I just wanted to clear something up," Karp said. "Is it your testimony that you only had the one contact with Mr. Bryant at the Labor Department and that he informed you that you had to exhaust your remedies through the union, is that correct?"

"Uh, yeah," Vitteli said.

"But before you could initiate any such complaint, you were indicted on the charge for which you are now standing trial. Is that your testimony?"

"Yeah."

"So there wasn't time to go back to Mr. Bryant, or for him to assist you any further?"

"That's right," Vitteli nodded. "You decided you needed a scapegoat, so you came after me."

Karp ignored Vitteli's response. Instead, he walked over to the prosecution table and picked up the magazine photograph and held it up so that Vitteli could see it.

"Mr. Vitteli, is it your testimony that this photograph was in your wallet that was taken by the killers the night of Mr. Carlotta's murder?"

Vitteli's eyes narrowed and he licked his lips nervously, but he nodded. "Yeah, that's right."

Karp handed the photograph to the jury foreman to look at and pass around to the other jurors. He then picked up the complete copy of the *Dock* and turned to the page containing the same photograph as he walked up toward the witness stand.

"Mr. Vitteli, do you have a wallet with you today?"

"Yeah, sure I do."

"Would you pull it out, please?"

Vitteli looked at Kowalski, who shrugged and nodded. The witness reached into his back pocket and pulled out his wallet, which he held up.

"Is that similar to the one taken from you the night of the murder?"

"It's close."

"Close in size and design?"

"Yeah. Like I told you, it's close."

Karp nodded and then tore out the page with the photograph from the magazine. "Your Honor, I'd like to hand the witness this page from the *Dock* magazine with a copy of the photograph in question for demonstration purposes."

"You may, please proceed."

Turning back to the witness stand, Karp handed the page to Vitteli. "Would you demonstrate how this photograph was folded in order to fit into your wallet?"

"I don't see the point of this crap," Vitteli complained.

The more agitated Vitteli became, the more restrained Karp appeared. "Just show us, please, how you folded the photograph so that it fit into your wallet, which was stolen by the killers, one of whom — according to your testimony — Frank DiMarzo, then removed and kept it in his Bible," Karp insisted.

Vitteli glanced over at the jurors, the last of whom finished looking at the photograph in evidence and handed it back to the jury foreman. They were all looking at him intently. "I don't remember how it was folded," he said.

Walking over to the jury foreman, Karp retrieved the exhibit photograph. "Well, let's start by folding it once and then tell us if that is what you did?"

Looking at the page he held in his hand like it was a poisonous snake, Vitteli folded it in half. He shook his head. "No. It had to be smaller."

"Then go ahead and fold it in half again," Karp replied. "And tell us if it fits."

Again, Vitteli did as he was told. He started to place it in his wallet, but it was obviously still too large. "No. Maybe one more time."

"Go ahead," Karp encouraged. "A third time, please."

Vitteli folded the page again. This time he opened the wallet and stuck it in. "Like this," he said.

"Okay. The jury can see that there's quite a bit of the photograph sticking out of the wallet," Karp said. "But that's how you contend you stuck it in your back pants pocket until you took it out and handed it to Mr. Carlotta's killers, is that what you're saying?"

"Yeah," Vitteli said. "I wasn't real careful. It was just a photo to break the ice with Vince."

Karp glanced down at the photograph in his hand. "I'm looking at People's Exhibit Twenty-Eight, the photograph in evidence, and it doesn't appear that any of the edges of the page are folded or torn as might be expected if it was inserted into your wallet and pants pocket as you contend. Can you explain that?"

Vitteli shrugged. "I don't know. Maybe I folded it again," he said. "I don't remember."

"Well, why don't you fold the demonstration photograph one more time and see how that fits?"

Vitteli glowered for a moment at Karp but then did what he was told. He held up the wallet. "Yeah, I must have folded it again," he said.

"Four times?" Karp asked.

"Three or four times."

Stepping forward, Karp handed the evidentiary photograph up to Vitteli. "Would you look at it, please, and then tell the jury how many times it's been folded?"

Vitteli reached forward and grabbed the plastic sleeve containing the photograph from Karp, his eyes boring into his antagonist until finally looking down at what he held. His hands began to shake as his face turned red. He reached for the cup of water but gave up as his hands weren't steady enough to hold it.

"Mr. Vitteli? Your answer please," Karp asked mildly.

The courtroom was absolutely still, waiting for an answer that Vitteli refused to give. "You tricked me," he snarled instead, "you son of a bitch."

Unmoved, Karp turned to the judge. "Your Honor, I'd request that the witness answer my question."

Judge See leaned across his desk toward Vitteli. "Just answer the question, please."

Vitteli's eyes, filled with hate, flicked from Karp to the judge to Karp again. "Once, it's been folded once," he said venomously and tossed the photograph in the direction of Karp, who calmly leaned over and picked it up.

"So you were lying when you told this jury that the photograph was in your wallet that was taken by the killers?" Karp said.

"Maybe it wasn't in my wallet," Vitteli retorted. "Maybe it was just in my coat pocket. I don't remember. I'd been drinking."

"Well, do you remember reaching into your coat pocket and handing the gunman this photograph, Mr. Vitteli?"

Vitteli crossed his arms. "I told you what happened, and that's all I'm going to say about that."

"That's okay, Mr. Vitteli," Karp shot back. "You've said plenty."

Karp turned toward the prosecution table, and it appeared he was through questioning Vitteli, but then he pulled up as if he remembered one last thing. "Oh, by the way, whatever happened to that handkerchief you're holding in your hand in that newspaper photograph?"

Vitteli furrowed his brow. "It was ruined, covered with blood. Joey threw it away for me."

"Do you know where he threw it?"

"Yeah, in a barrel by the alley that the

bums use for fires."

"Do you know what happened to it from there?"

Vitteli's sneer disappeared, replaced by confusion. "I assume it got burned up."

Karp regarded his quarry for a moment, then smiled. "No further questions."

37

The final scene in the last act of the *People of the State of New York vs. Charles E. Vitteli* began with Judge See turning to Karp, who sat at the prosecution table having just listened to Kowalski's closing arguments. "Mr. Karp, would you care to deliver your summation at this time?" the judge asked.

"Yes, thank you, Your Honor," Karp replied as he rose and walked out in front of the jury. "As the district attorney in charge of presenting the evidence in this case on behalf of the People, the law gives me the opportunity to deliver a summation. At the outset, I'd first like to thank all of you for the patient and courteous attention you showed throughout this trial."

Looking from one juror to the next, he continued. "When all is said and done, what you have just witnessed from the People was a solemn and sacred search for the truth. And during my summation, I ask you to permit me to be your guide in this search. Given the drama and the passion you've observed over the course of this trial, after you've rendered your verdict of guilty and leave this courtroom to resume your everyday activities, you'll be asked by family, loved ones, friends, and business associates what caused you to vote guilty. And so to answer that question with precision and righteousness, let us count the ways we know that the defendant in this case is guilty not beyond a reasonable doubt but beyond any and all doubt."

Karp then launched into an hour and a half of unrelenting evidentiary analysis, devoid of any speculation or unfounded inferences, which he noted had characterized the defense summation, before looking over at Vitteli. The defendant sat with his head down, staring at the table in front of him, reminding Karp of his adversary's expressions of diminishing hopes when, after the defense rested its case, he'd announced that he would be calling three rebuttal witnesses. With each witness, Vitteli increasingly had taken on the look of a hunted man with nowhere to turn.

The first witness was Bill Clark, the supervisor of Martin Bryant at the U.S. Department of Labor, who testified about the department's protocol for dealing with complaints. "Which apparently were ignored in regard to Mr. Carlotta, and — if it ever occurred — Mr. Vitteli," Clark said. "Nor was I ever verbally informed about the alleged complaints, as is required." He wrapped up his testimony by stating that Bryant was under investigation for engaging in corrupt practices and had been suspended from the department. He then turned over department telephone logs that indicated nearly a dozen telephone calls were made between Bryant's office and Vitteli's beginning a month prior to Carlotta's murder and continuing up to Vitteli's arrest. The best Kowalski could do on cross was get Clark to concede that it was possible that Bryant had simply not followed department rules.

The second rebuttal witness was Jack Swanburg, who took the stand to testify regarding DNA and blood-testing conducted on a silk handkerchief sent to him by Detective Clay Fulton. He told the jury that the blood on the handkerchief "to an absolute scientific certainty" belonged to the deceased, Vince Carlotta, and that DNA testing also revealed the presence of skin cells and several hairs belonging to Charles Vitteli and even a few skin cells belonging to Joey Barros.

"There was also a minor amount of soot, as would be explained by the circumstances in which it's my understanding the item was found — that is, a fifty-gallon barrel used to contain fires," Swanburg testified. "However, the soot was only on one side and only on a few contact points, which indicates to me that it was only in the barrel for a short time and had not been disturbed prior to its being retrieved."

As if there was any doubt about who the handkerchief had belonged to, Karp asked the scientist if it was monogrammed. "Yes." The old man nodded. "With the letters 'C.E.V.'"

With each rebuttal witness, Vitteli seemed to sink farther into his seat. But Karp had saved the best for last and was pleased to watch the defendant's face when he called Anne Devulder to the stand. It had taken Vitteli a moment to recognize the name and put it together, seeing the nicely dressed woman standing in the doorway leading to the prosecution witness room. Then the color drained from his face as he leaned over and spoke urgently to his attorney.

"Your Honor, we object to this woman's testimony," Kowalski complained. "We have no idea what she's going to say, and it's obvious the prosecution has been sandbagging so that we'd have no opportunity to question her, or review her possible testimony, in order to prepare."

Karp listened to Kowalski and then turned to the judge. "Your Honor, may we approach the bench?"

"By all means, Mr. Karp," Judge See had said, looking somewhat bemused.

When they'd assembled at the sidebar, Karp explained the circumstances and chronology of Devulder's appearance as a witness. "She did not come forward until the last witness for the People's case was on the stand. However, we needed to await testing to be conducted on the handkerchief, in order to corroborate her potential testimony. If we had tried to 'spring' her on the defense during the People's case in chief, they might have an argument to at least delay the proceedings until they could examine her statements to Mr. Guma. However, her testimony now is completely appropriate in rebuttal."

"I agree that the witness's appearance is proper rebuttal, particularly given the defendant's testimony, and I'll allow it," Judge See determined. "Your objection is overruled."

When Kowalski returned to his seat, he broke the news to Vitteli, who slammed his fist on the table and glared at Anne Devulder as she approached the gate between the gallery and the well of the court. However, instead of cowing her, his obvious displeasure seemed to galvanize Devulder. She met his glare with her own as she picked up her head and straightened her shoulders as she walked between the defense and prosecution tables toward the witness stand.

Karp smiled as she was sworn in. He'd seen an amazing transformation from a street person in tattered rags and weeks' worth of filth on her weary face to an attractive middle-aged woman with short, bobbed hair and wearing a dress. The transformation wasn't just external — Marlene informed him that Devulder had quit drinking after the Carlotta murder and was attending AA meetings at the East Village Women's Shelter — nor was she alone in her quest to change her life. As she stepped up into the witness stand and settled in a chair, Devulder glanced out to the gallery where her two friends, Rosie and Cindy, cleaned up and smiling encouragement, were seated.

"How do you know Charlie Vitteli?" Karp asked early in the questioning.

"My husband, Sean, belonged to the

North American Brotherhood of Stevedores."

"And was Sean killed in an accident on the docks?"

Devulder looked at Vitteli when she replied. "It wasn't no accident," she said. "But yes, he was killed when the crane he was operating collapsed."

"Is it fair to say that you blame Charlie Vitteli for Sean's death?"

"My Sean told him that the new cranes weren't safe in high winds. Charlie was the president. It was his job to keep the men safe."

"Do you feel differently toward Vince Carlotta?"

"Yes, everybody did — except maybe some of the old crowd who keep their jobs by kowtowing to Vitteli. But we knew, the men that is, that Vince worked for them. If he'd been president, he would have looked into the crane operators' complaints and shut those cranes down if there was a problem. In fact, I think he blamed himself for not being more forceful about investigating the complaints before the accident."

"So we've established that you blame Charlie Vitteli for your husband's death but you and your husband liked Vince Carlotta

601

and felt he worked for the union membership?"

"Yes, that's fair to say."

"However, you've sworn to tell the truth
here today, regardless of your feelings for
either man, correct?"

Devulder's eyes narrowed. "I've been
called many things, Mr. Karp, but a liar isn't
one of them."

Having taken one of the defense's possible points of attack away, Karp had moved
on to the essence of Devulder's testimony.
"Did you see Charlie Vitteli in Hell's
Kitchen near Marlon's Restaurant prior to
the night when Vince Carlotta was murdered?"

"Yes," Devulder said. "Me and my two
friends, Rosie and Cindy, were hanging out
near the alley, trying to stay warm with a
barrel fire."

"Did you recognize him?"

"Oh yes."

"And did he know you?"

"Not at first. I had to remind him that I
was Sean's wife. Then he knew who I was."

"Did the two of you exchange words?"

"Yeah, things got a little heated," Devulder recalled. "I called him King Vitteli. He
didn't like that and told me to get the hell
out of his way. When I told him I was Sean's

widow, he said he was sorry for my loss and tried to give me twenty bucks. I wouldn't take it. I said I didn't want his blood money, but my friend Cindy grabbed it from him."

"And did you know Vince Carlotta by sight?"

"Yes, he came to Sean's funeral, but Charlie didn't," Devulder said, then choked up. "I saw him again going toward Marlon's the night he was murdered. He gave me and my friends all the money he had in his pockets — thirty bucks, I think — and told me to come down to the union offices the next day and he'd see if he could do more for me. I was a little on the down and out, you see."

Devulder shook her head sadly. "I told him not to go to that meeting with Charlie Vitteli. I told him to go home to his wife and child. I had a bad feeling in my bones. But Vince said he had to go; that it was for Sean and the other guys."

Recalling her warning, Devulder began to cry lightly. Karp stepped forward and handed her the box of tissues that was on the witness-box ledge. He waited patiently for her until she'd calmed and sat dabbing at her eyes and nose with the tissue. Then, gently, he led her through a series of questions, beginning with getting her to describe the events of the night of the murder.

"My friends and me were Dumpster diving in the back of the alley when two guys jumped out of an older car and walked into the entrance of the alley," she recalled. "They were dressed in black, and it was obvious they was up to no good. We were afraid they'd find us, so we hid real good, way back in the shadows, and we were ready to slip out our secret way between the buildings if we had to."

However, the men had remained at the mouth of the alley, one of them smoking cigarette after cigarette, until they apparently received some signal from the car across the street. "They pulled stocking masks over their faces. It was pretty dark, but there was a little bit of light from a streetlamp and I could see that one of them had a gun. I don't know why I did it — I was scared to death — but for some reason, I crept toward them. And when they jumped out, and I heard voices, I went all the way to the front and looked out."

"What did you see?"

"I saw four men sort of facing toward me — Mr. Carlotta, Vitteli, that creepy guy Joey Barros who's always with him, and some younger guy I didn't recognize. The two guys in the ski masks had their backs to me.

One was behind the other, and the guy in front had a gun pointed at Mr. Carlotta."

"Then what happened?"

"Mr. Carlotta put his hand in his pocket and pulled out a gun," Devulder said, then nodded at the defense table, "but he grabbed Vince's arm and pulled it down."

"What, if anything, did anybody say?"

"Mr. Carlotta called Vitteli a son of a bitch."

"You sure he wasn't speaking to the gunman?"

"I'm positive," Devulder said. "He looked down at his arm and then right at Vitteli and said it."

"How far from these men were you?" Karp asked.

The woman thought about it for a moment, then nodded toward the courtroom doors. "About from here to the back of this room," she said.

"And how's your eyesight?"

Devulder chuckled. "Not so good close up," she said. "But eyes like an eagle for anything over ten feet. I can see that guy in the back row has an American flag pin on his lapel." She pointed and all eyes turned to look in that direction at an older man whose hand now self-consciously went to the pin she'd described.

"Now, returning to the confrontation," Karp continued, "what, if anything, did the defendant, Charlie Vitteli, say?"

"He looked at the guy with the gun and yelled, 'Do it!'"

"He yelled, 'Do it'? You're sure?"

"Yes."

"You sure he didn't say, 'Don't do it'?"

"Yes, I'm sure. Plain as day I heard him yell, 'Do it!' And that's when the guy shot Vince." Devulder sniffled and wiped at her nose with the tissue. "Then he shot him again."

"What, if anything, did Charlie Vitteli say after that?"

"He told the two guys in the ski masks to take their wallets and watches. That's what they did. Then he told 'em 'get the fuck out of here,' pardon my language but that's what he said, and then they ran back across the street to the car."

"What happened after that?"

"People were starting to come out of Marlon's. So Charlie ran over to Vince and started acting like he was trying to save him. He yelled for help. That younger guy was yelling for help, too."

Karp walked over to the prosecution table and picked up the plastic bag containing the bloodstained handkerchief. Returning